A Death Divided

CLARE FRANCIS

A Death Divided

MACMILLAN

First published 2001 by Macmillan
an imprint of Pan Macmillan Ltd
Pan Macmillan, 20 New Wharf Road, London N1 9RR
Basingstoke and Oxford
Associated companies throughout the world
www.panmacmillan.com

ISBN 0 333 68304 8

A CIP catalogue record for this book is available from
the British Library.

Typeset by SetSystems Ltd, Saffron Walden, Essex
Printed and bound in Great Britain by
Mackays of Chatham plc, Chatham, Kent

For Rozzie

Chapter One

———

JOE MET the malign gaze of Mr Al Ritch from six thousand miles away, and wished the technology undone. The conference link had been installed at a time when the firm was in thrall to the power of eye contact and body language, but it seemed to Joe that, more often than not, one side came to see through a glass darkly, and for the last hour the only language his client's jutting head and lowering frown had conveyed was gathering mistrust.

Joe was stuck in a conference room with two members of his team, a fiery Scot called Anna, and Ed, a quiet junior with big ambition, both of them grim-faced after more than two hours at the coalface and no hope of an early reprieve. It was a Friday evening in the run-up to Christmas. The rest of the Merrow office had emptied for the weekend and the only sound was the muted hiss of traffic from a rain-soaked Gracechurch Street five floors below.

In front of them, the TV monitor relayed golden strips of sunlight, a pale wood table with water glasses and, seated centre-stage between four of his team, the bulbous figure of Mr Al Ritch, wearing short-sleeved shirt, gold Rolex and a thatch of compressed sandy hair which Anna swore he took off and put on a stand at night.

His heavy features were showing puzzlement. 'Now, how's that agin, Joe?'

For what had to be the third time Joe explained the importance of obtaining detailed witness statements from those who could support their case.

'Right down to the *project* managers?'

'Definitely. Yes.' With Al Ritch, Joe had long since taken to expressing himself in absolutes.

'But let's jus' get this straight, Joe – you're proposin' to go *see* these guys yourselves? Hell, they're spread all around the globe. Five o' them – nah, what is it, Larry?' He turned to his right-hand man. '*Six.*'

Anna gave a snort of exasperation and cleared her throat to hide it.

Joe said, 'This case is going to be decided on the facts, Mr — er, *Al*. It could turn on the smallest details. We need to obtain the most comprehensive witness statements possible. We—'

'Joe, perhaps you'd be kind enough to explain this one thing fer me,' Ritch interrupted in his slow drawl. 'Jus' exactly what is it you think *they* can tell you that I myself have not already told you? Is my word not good enough?'

Joe knew it would be a mistake to take Al Ritch for a fool – the man had built up a mineral exploration business worth hundreds of millions of dollars. He also knew that Ritch had never been involved in litigation before and must be allowed a degree of uncertainty, yet if Ritch was trying to screw up his chances of success he was going about it precisely the right way. He said carefully, 'Your word is good, Al, of course it is, but one person's word is never going to be enough in an English court of law, I'm afraid. They like corroborative evidence, the more the better.'

Ritch tipped his head towards one of his colleagues and said in a whisper that couldn't fail to be picked up by the microphones, 'Yer think these guys jus' tryin' ter jack up their fees, Larry?'

Joe saw Anna's hands splay out in silent fury, while Ed hissed softly between his teeth. For the moment Joe could think of nothing useful to say. Until then he'd always taken the view that the easy clients more than made up for the demanding ones, but in that instant, as he stared at the unlovely image of Mr Al Ritch, he longed to be free of them all. This realisation had an unnerving clarity to it, like a jog of recognition: subconsciously or otherwise, he had been here before.

He said, 'Perhaps I could put it this way, Al – if we obtain this corroborative evidence, we have a reasonable chance of winning. If we don't, our chances are going to be severely reduced.'

'But jus' how many o' these statements we talkin' about here, Joe? How many round-the-world air tickets for you and your guys, huh? Two? Four? *Six?*'

'You'll have to trust to our judgement on that, Al.'

But Ritch had not made his fortune by leaving too much to trust. 'Okay, Joe,' he conceded suspiciously. 'But, listen here—' He stabbed a warning finger at the camera. 'Let's start with *the* minimum, like you go and talk to jus' *two* o' these guys, and we take it on from there. You hear?'

'Sure, Al. We can start from there.'

Ritch leant back in his chair with the satisfaction of an old hand who has trounced an ill-advised attempt to hoodwink him, until his attention was taken by a fast-food carton which appeared camera-left and was pushed across the table towards him. Dipping into it, he pulled out a multi-tiered hamburger and, swivelling his chair away to face his colleagues, began to eat. The microphone was still on, the transmission faultless, and in London they were treated to the glutinous churnings of the hamburger as it progressed around Ritch's mouth.

For a second no one stirred, then Ed murmured, 'Well, thank you for sharing this with us.'

Anna growled, 'I think I'm going to be sick.'

Joe made a small quieting gesture and leant into the microphone. 'Al? Perhaps this might be a good time for us to take a break?'

But Ritch was too busy agreeing on the excellence of the fried onions to hear.

Joe lowered his forehead slowly onto his fingertips.

Anna touched his arm. 'Joe – for God's sake, we've been at this for *ever*. Let's call it a day.'

Joe pushed the microphone slowly out of range. 'Not an option.'

Watching her face fall, he asked, 'Did you have something special lined up for tonight?'

She gave an ironic laugh. 'Only my life, Joe. Only my life.'

Anna had been in the firm for less than a year, but already she had the slightly haunted look that Joe recognised from his own reflection in the mirror each morning. He saw in her, as he saw in Ed, the kind of lawyer he had been not so long ago, exultant at landing a job with Merrow, confident in his abilities, but worn down by the long hours which ate so regularly into his free time.

'And you, Ed?'

Ed's expression suggested he had plenty of things to do that night but would stay and man the barricades as necessary.

Coming to an abrupt decision, Joe said, 'Off you go, both of you. Go on – scoot.'

The two of them went through the motions of arguing, but he waved them rapidly away.

Anna hovered loyally. 'But what about you, Joe? What are you meant to be doing tonight?'

Joe put on a fierce look. 'None of your damned business. Salsa dancing, lying down with a large drink – I don't know. Quick, before I change my mind.'

'Not the new girlfriend?'

'Huh?'

'Someone called Sarah?'

His answering frown didn't entirely hide his surprise; he hadn't thought anyone knew. 'Your wild imagination again,' he protested too weakly and too late. 'Completely out of control.'

Anna made a face of mock contrition. 'Okay, but give yourself a break, Joe. You can't go on like this.'

'You're sounding like a stress therapist. Go on – bugger off.'

Anna touched his shoulder. 'Thanks for this, Joe. You're a total star.'

'What I am,' he grunted, 'is a total idiot.'

After they'd gone, Joe tried to work out how Anna had got to hear about Sarah and decided it must have come from the ex-Merrow lawyer who'd introduced them. It certainly hadn't come from his own mouth. Life at the firm was quite hard enough without providing fodder for the office gossips. There was a price to pay for non-participation of course – he'd got a reputation as a dark horse – but better that than the jokes and the need to explain the bewildering fact that, until Sarah, there had been no one special in his life for some time.

Fishing out his mobile, he went to the window to call her. It was half-past eight; he tried to guess where she'd be. Not at the office anyway. She worked for the West London division of the Crown Prosecution Service, and, frantic though the job was, they all knocked off at five. Shopping then, though peering out between the slats of the blind at the streaming rain he thought not. He decided she was most likely to be at home in a hot bath. He hadn't seen her flat yet – they always went to his place – but he imagined it to be neatly kept and cleverly furnished, because that was Sarah's style. He pictured her now in a white bath, pale hair tied up on top of her head, long legs stretched out in scented water, breasts just breaking the surface. Purely from wishful thinking, he liked to imagine she was thinking of him.

Her mobile didn't answer, nor, it seemed, would her house line. Then, just as he was leaving a message, she picked up.

The quiet solemnity of her voice still took him by surprise.

'I've got caught up,' he said, and explained about the video conference. 'Dinner could be late.'

But she never minded waiting, just as she never complained when he had to cancel at the last minute. 'That's okay,' she said. 'Whenever.'

'I'll call when I'm on my way. Nine thirty, with a bit of luck.'

'Shall I warn the restaurant?' It was typical of her to cover such practicalities.

'That'd be great.' Before ringing off, he had to ask, 'What are you doing?'

'Now? Oh, just Friday night stuff. You know. Sorting myself out. Talking to Fiona.' Her flatmate was also in the CPS, at another branch.

'Not in the bath?'

'Half an hour ago. Why?'

He didn't admit to his vision of her. They hadn't reached the stage of trading body talk, and with Sarah he wasn't sure they ever would; but then her reserve had been one of the attractions.

'Just jealous,' he replied, which was true.

When he rang off, his phone was showing voicemail, but he didn't retrieve it until he'd dropped back into his seat and checked on Al Ritch, now in side view. Watching Ritch root around his mouth for stray morsels, poking first his tongue then his finger deep into every crevice, Joe felt something like envy. Not to give a damn for other people's opinions, not to know the meaning of embarrassment, was surely to travel through life unscathed.

Joe dialled up his messages: a friend asking him to lunch; a sometime girlfriend organising a party. The automated voice was just timing the next message at 7.52 p.m. when Al Ritch dragged a paper napkin across his mouth and swivelled round to face the camera again. Joe met his gaze as the message began to run.

'Joe? It's Alan here.' At the sound of the familiar voice, Joe's chest tightened, he felt a sharp beat of alarm, and in an instinctive move twisted round in his chair and turned his back to Ritch.

The message was brief; Alan wanted Joe to phone when he had a moment. There was no hint of urgency in his voice, yet

Joe's mind raced all the same. Alan hardly ever used the phone for social reasons; he spent too much of his life chasing up unobtainable hospital appointments for his patients. Joe could only think that his father must be ill. Or forgetting to pay his bills again – Alan had alerted Joe before. Or – his first thought, if he was entirely honest, always his first thought where Alan was concerned – that there was news of Jenna.

Ritch's voice sounded from the monitor. 'You with us, Mr McGrath?'

'Won't be a moment, Mr Ritch.' Joe flung a brief placatory smile over his shoulder as he switched off the microphone.

He dialled Alan's home number and heard Helena answer in her distinctive throaty voice. 'He's not here, Joe. He's on a home visit.'

'He left a message, Helena. Do you know what it's about?'

'Best to ask him, Joe.'

'It's not Dad?'

'No. Your father's all right, Joe. You know.'

He knew. 'Nothing urgent then?'

'Not urgent, no.'

But there was something in her tone, a hesitation, a note of disapproval, that made Joe ask, 'It's not Jenna?'

The mention of her daughter produced a heavy pause. Finally she said, 'Speak to Alan, Joe. He'll be back around ten.'

'But Helena —'

'Better make it ten thirty to be on the safe side.'

'If it's about Jenna, tell me now,' he pleaded gently.

Helena was silent for so long that Joe thought he'd lost the connection. He was calling 'Hello?' for the second time when she replied in a flat voice, 'He wants you to find Jenna. That's what he wants.'

Joe felt a mixture of surprise, confusion and disappointment, but mainly confusion. 'Any particular reason, Helena? Has something happened?'

'Not happened exactly.'

'There's no news of Jenna?'

'No. Alan got excited about something the other day, but no, there's no news.'

'But something's happened?'

'It's a legal thing, Joe. A property. That's all I know.'

He tried to remember all the things he'd been planning to do over the weekend, and to work out whether he could put them off. 'I'd better come down, Helena. Is tomorrow morning okay?'

'For heaven's sake don't come specially, Joe.'

'I was going to see Dad anyway,' he lied.

'Well, surgery finishes at ten.' She added under her breath, 'In theory.'

Ringing off, Joe kept his back to the camera a little longer. To find Jenna: if only. How many times had he imagined it? How many times had he looked for ways of tracking her down? Helena spoke as if it was a matter of decision, almost of will, but it was four years since there'd been any sign of her and barely a week that Joe hadn't imagined the worst, the best, and almost everything in between. Why Alan should think he'd be able to do something after all this time, he had no idea. There was no magic wand, and there never would be. For Joe, there was only the certainty of his own guilt, like a shadow at his shoulder.

A full belly seemed to have done little for Al Ritch's mood. His sandy eyes had taken on a beady look. When Joe explained that Anna and Ed had been called away to another meeting, he put on his favourite expression of exaggerated puzzlement. 'Mr McGrath, I was given to understand there were to be *four* of your people working full-time on my case, and all I see is *one*. I am not – repeat *not* – gettin' a message of total one hundred per cent commitment here.'

'We are committed to winning, Al. Absolutely committed to winning.' The words rang mockingly in Joe's ears.

'Yeah? Well, where in hell's your senior guy then? Where's Galbraith? Glad enough to show his face when he wanted the business, but where's he now, that's what I'd like to know—'

'He's fully briefed—'

'—'Cos the way I see it, I'm not convinced of just how much weight you bring to my case, Mr Joe McGrath.' He jabbed a belligerent finger at the camera. 'Are you *the* man? That's what I'd like to know. I need to be one hundred per cent sure I'm talking to *the* man.'

Joe wasn't sure what went through his head just then, whether the tangle of anxiety that always attached itself to thoughts of Jenna tipped his judgement, whether he had simply reached his limits at the end of a long week, but he felt a sudden heat, a leap of impatience.

'I assure you that *this* man here has been doing his best for you, Mr Ritch, but since you're obviously having a problem about that I suggest we call it a day.'

Ritch cocked an ear. 'How's that?'

'You will not be charged for this meeting, Mr Ritch.'

'Now, hang on there—'

'We will contact you on Monday morning with four entire people in place. In the meantime—'

'You end this meetin', Mr McGrath, and that's the end—'

'I wish you a good evening, Mr Ritch. And a fine weekend.'

Moving rapidly, Joe went to the monitor and threw the switch.

The relief was transitory, the nasty feeling in the pit of his stomach longer lasting. He needed no reminding that, only a couple of months before, a colleague in Litigation had been fired for losing an important client, nor that the guy had been senior to Joe by three years, with the dubious protection of a partnership. Someone with a stronger sense of self-preservation might have called Ritch back right away, but, in the absence of a gun to his head, Joe was damned if he was going to grovel.

This didn't stop the cold jittery feeling from flitting around his stomach as he set off in the pouring rain for the restaurant. It wasn't until he came out of the Underground that he remembered he'd forgotten to tell Sarah he was on his way. She would still be at her flat, waiting for his call. He would have phoned there and then from the shelter of a doorway, but the restaurant was less than fifty yards away. It was one of those places with floor-length windows along the whole of one side which provides an unrestricted view of the diners, like something on reality TV. Crossing the road towards it, Joe almost bumped into the traffic island as he spotted a familiar head of ash-blonde hair, a half profile, a pair of long slim legs, and realised Sarah was already there, sitting at the bar. He felt confused again, pleasantly this time. Perhaps he'd got the arrangements wrong, perhaps they'd fixed a time after all; perhaps – and remembering her scrupulous practicality it seemed likely – she'd decided to come on ahead to be sure of arriving in good time. If so, he was touched and a little flattered, and a flattery never did anyone any harm at the end of a long week.

By some sixth sense – or a mirror he couldn't see – she lifted her head from her newspaper and looked round as he came up behind her.

'I forgot to phone,' he confessed as he kissed her. 'But you're here anyway.'

'You got away all right then?'

'I got away. Though I could be minus a job.'

She examined his face. 'What happened?'

'I think I told the client where to get off.'

'But not in so many words.'

'Oh, I suspect it was plain enough.'

She regarded him solemnly. 'He must have given you good reason then. Have a drink. You must need one.'

Despite everything, he began to feel calmer. Sarah had that effect on him. When his drink arrived she passed it over to him and closed his hand around the glass as if to imbue it with special restorative powers.

'So,' she said, 'tell me what happened.'

While he described the meeting, she listened closely, her grey-green eyes fixed on him with grave attention, and he had the sense that she was weighing the evidence, missing nothing, but fully intending to find for his side.

'Don't forget he's on strange ground,' she said when he'd finished. 'He's new to litigation. He's feeling insecure. There's a lot of money at stake. Though having said all that, he sounds like an up-front sort of person to me. He might respect you for speaking your mind.'

'What? When he's paying my fees?'

'I think you underestimate yourself, Joe. I think you carry more weight than you realise.'

He was glad she should think so; he would have liked to believe her. 'But not enough to save my skin.'

Sarah considered this idea gravely. 'I really can't believe it'll come to that, Joe. No, I can't believe the situation isn't salvageable. Especially if you get a letter to Ritch first thing on Monday morning. By fax, rather than e-mail. Strike a forceful note, restate your strategy in the most glowing terms, butter him up a little, talk about the big picture. Don't on any account apologise, of course. Just make him feel it would be unreasonable to dwell on such a minor difficulty when everything else is set fair—' She broke off with a small flush of embarrassment. 'But what am I saying? You'll know how best to play it, Joe. Once you start drafting it – you'll know.'

He wasn't sure he shared her faith in his judgement, but he was glad of her optimism all the same; he liked to think it was rubbing off on him. The champagne was beginning to do its magic too, but he resisted the temptation to drown his sorrows. Sarah didn't drink very much, and he didn't like to get too far out of step.

He asked brightly, 'And how was your day?'

She tried to shrug the question off – she rarely volunteered information about her work – but he pressed her.

'Oh, like always,' she said at last. 'The usual progression of no-show witnesses, hold-overs, failures to answer bail. Much work and no convictions.'

When they'd first met, Joe had wondered how she stuck
the Crown Prosecution Service, which was going through one
of its periodic spells of low staffing and poor morale. Sarah
was clever and in her understated way extremely determined;
she could easily have carved out a successful career as a defence
lawyer at twice the salary. But as he'd got to know her better
he'd come to see another side of her. She might bemoan the
inadequacies of the justice system, she might grumble at the
bureaucracy of the CPS, yet she got enormous fulfilment from
her work. Behind her offhand attitude lay a strong morality
and a dogged belief in the pursuit of justice which made her
perfectly suited to this branch of the law.

He said, 'What, nobody put away at all?'

She pretended to scour her memory. 'One mugging, one
breaking and entering.'

'Don't they count?'

'Not when I failed to get the one I really wanted.'

'And what was that?'

'A crack-head who enjoys burgling and terrorising old
ladies.'

'What went wrong?'

'Principal witness failed to show. And who can blame her?
A sixty-five-year-old widow living alone, terrified out of her
wits.'

'Can't the police protect her?'

Sarah gazed at him with a blend of pity and wonder. '*Joe*,
when did you last visit a sink estate in Stoke Newington?'

He conceded rapidly. 'Perhaps you'll get him next time
round.'

'Sure.' Draining her drink, she attempted a smile. 'Sorry.
By this stage in the week I've rather lost my sense of humour.'

'You're not alone. Want to risk dinner?'

'You bet – I've been looking forward to it all week.'

Instantly, her eyes shaded and she glanced away, as if this
show of enthusiasm had been in danger of saying too much.
They had met in a bar, introduced by a former Merrow lawyer

who knew Sarah from law school. Joe's first impression had been of a Valkyrie: slim and tall, with grey-green eyes, long legs, and ash-coloured hair worn straight and long. The next thing he noticed was her gaze, which fixed on him with quiet curiosity, and her mouth, which was extraordinarily full and expressive. A boisterous party was going on around them – someone's birthday, he wasn't sure whose – and they soon gravitated towards a corner where they talked for the rest of the evening. She was a good listener, those thoughtful eyes missed nothing, and she had a way of giving all her attention to the conversation, as though it was the most important thing in the world. If in the weeks since then she'd revealed an emotional caution that bordered on self-sufficiency then he could go along with that; he too had become wary of relation-ships that went too far, too fast. This caution did not, anyway, reach into the bedroom, where she showed a tender enthusiasm.

Now, taking their seats at the restaurant table, they drew their chairs closer, the better to talk.

Joe wasn't sure how long he stared at the wine list before Sarah said, 'What about that Chablis we had last time?' Leaning over, her head almost touching his, she pointed rapidly at the card with a long index finger, which she just as rapidly curled back into her palm. She bit her nails badly and she didn't like anyone to see.

He took the opportunity to kiss her. She gave a flicker of a smile, but in the fraction of a second before her gaze swung away Joe saw the familiar wariness drop over her eyes like a shutter, and wondered not for the first time what made her retreat from even the smallest gesture of affection. On their second date she'd told him she'd been married but it hadn't worked out. They'd been too young, it hadn't lasted long, they'd parted on reasonable terms, she hadn't seen him since. Her tone had been matter-of-fact, yet he couldn't help thinking that the damage had gone a lot deeper than she pretended.

The restaurant was a barn of a place with notorious acoustics. Their table was hard against the window but the noise seemed to come at them from all sides. Stupefied by the roar or the day, or both, Joe took an age to decide what to eat, only to realise too late that he'd ordered something he didn't terribly like.

Sarah eyed him speculatively. 'Mr Ritch still on your mind?'

'And whether I want to stay in Litigation.' Now he'd voiced it, the idea quickly gathered momentum in his mind. 'Whether I want to stay in the law, come to that.'

Sarah winced. 'Help, Joe. What else would you do?'

'Exactly. Fit for nothing.'

'What brought this on?'

'Oh, the usual. Working my socks off, feeding the inflated egos of overpaid executives who can't bring themselves to settle their disputes out of court. Knowing that none of it's that important at the end of the day.'

'Major thoughts, Joe.' Her eyes were fierce and bright. He had the feeling she was proud of him. 'So what *is* important at the end of the day?'

'God only knows. I think I came to a few idealistic conclusions when I was a student.'

'Which were?'

'Oh, you know.'

'Yes?' She really wanted to hear.

'Getting fulfilment from one's work. Friends. Family.'

She nodded, urging him on.

'That's about it,' he said.

'What – no changing the world?' Her quick smile did little to conceal the seriousness beneath.

'I wasn't that brave. Or that certain.' Immediately, Joe thought of Chetwood, who had taken on the world wholesale. And from Chetwood it was of course just a tiny step to Jenna.

'Something else came up today.'

If Sarah was disappointed by the change of subject, she hid it well. 'Oh?'

He hesitated, not because he didn't want to tell her, but because even after all this time he wasn't sure where to start. 'It's some old friends from home – Alan and Helena Laskey. Alan was our doctor. Still looks after my father, God bless him, for which he deserves a peace prize. But then Alan's a bit of a saint, old-style. Helena too. They sort of took me in when I was a kid. Fed me, helped me with my homework, generally kept me out of trouble after my mother died. Like family. Anyway . . .' He slowed up, he hesitated a little over the words. 'They've a daughter called Jenna. And she . . . disappeared four years ago. And this evening, out of the blue, they've asked me to try and find her. Why, I don't know. Why now, I mean. And maybe, why me.'

'They've looked before presumably?'

'Yes. Salvation Army. Missing Persons Helpline. Not a sign.'

'How old was she?'

'Twenty-six? No, twenty-seven.'

Sarah's eyebrows lifted slightly. 'Ah. I'd imagined a teenage runaway. That's the usual scenario, statistically speaking. A lost soul of sixteen or so, homeless, alienated, desperate. Looking for anyone who'll take them in.'

He barely nodded, and she moved swiftly on.

'So this daughter would be – what? – thirty-one by now. In fact . . . your exact contemporary.'

After a while, she dipped her head a little to catch his eye.

'We're the same age, yes.'

'And you were friends, the two of you?'

'Yes. The Laskeys lived in the next street. We spent a lot of time together as kids.'

'So what happened? Did she just vanish overnight? Could she have been abducted?'

'No. She didn't vanish so much as' – he searched for a way to explain the inexplicable – 'fail to stay in contact.'

'Ah. *Her* choice then?'

'That's the thing – she was extremely close to her family. They can't believe she would have chosen to stay out of touch for so long.'

'Well, if not her choice, then . . .?'

Joe had recycled the alternatives so often, he knew them by heart. She was abroad. Ill. Suffering a breakdown. She was living in fear of someone from her old life or – painful to imagine – someone in her present existence. At night, when he was half asleep and immune to logic, he added the bizarre and fantastical. She had lost her mind. She had become a dropout. She was lying in some faraway hospital in a vegetative state. Around dawn, when nothing seems impossible, he'd imagined her getting religion, and one particular morning, when his dreams had got hopelessly entangled with memories of Chetwood's spiritual quests, he'd even pictured her among buddhas, gurus and saffron-robed priests.

'Could she be dead?' Sarah asked.

'We don't think so.'

'Because?'

'We would have heard, one way or the other. She's not alone, you see. There's a husband.'

'And they've *both* disappeared?'

'Yes.'

'Ahhh.' Sarah managed to imbue the sound with a wealth of meaning. 'So . . . *his* choice then?'

'Possibly.'

'And the reason?'

Joe had to struggle for an answer. 'We don't know. He was . . . *unusual*.' He pulled the word out of the air, yet even as he said it he realised it was probably the only adjective that began to describe Chetwood with any accuracy.

'Unusual *mad*, or unusual *bad*?'

A barrage of laughter assaulted them from an adjacent table, and Joe raised his voice. 'I would say he was born out of his time.'

'Ah. Someone *difficult*. Isn't that what people usually mean when they say that?'

'Not difficult so much as – complicated.'

She considered this idea doubtfully, with a small frown. 'But he's probably responsible for this vanishing act?'

The fusillade of shrieks showed no sign of abating, and they were watching each other's lips with the concentration of lip-readers. 'That's what the family think.'

'What about you, Joe? What do you think?'

'I don't know. I only know that Jenna changed after they married. I only saw them twice, but Jenna had lost her spark, her energy.'

'She was unhappy, then. Depressed.'

'But she loved him. There's no doubt of that.' His words emerged in a shout as the noise from the next-door table subsided abruptly.

'Heavens, Joe, you can love someone and still be unhappy. In fact, some people would say that it's love and all the things that people do in the name of love that's the greatest single cause of unhappiness.'

'It's just that I can't believe—' But he hadn't managed to work out what he believed, either then or now. He could only repeat, 'She'd just changed, that's all.'

'Do people change that much?' Sarah argued mildly. 'Don't they just show an unfamiliar side of themselves? Frustration, or suppressed anger, or guilt, or whatever?' She let this thought pass with a small lift of one shoulder. 'But what's your theory, Joe? You must have a theory.'

'I have no theory.'

'You knew him, though, this husband – what was his name?'

'Chetwood. Yes, we were at university together. For a while anyway. He only stayed a year.'

'And was he *unusual* even then?'

For some reason the image of Chetwood that came into

Joe's mind was the one most likely to cause him pain. He saw Chetwood in the scruffy overgrown garden of a student house during a post-finals barbecue. Chetwood had been on one of his sporadic trips back to Bristol, dipping briefly into student life again. He had parked his tall frame in a rickety chair, his feet propped on a low wall. He was silent, looking up when spoken to, smiling vaguely, but answering no one, not under the influence of course – he never touched anything in those days – but deeply preoccupied, remote, distracted. Joe had congratulated himself on recognising the signs: such periods of intense soul-searching generally heralded a full-blown philosophical crisis, one of the regular intellectual upheavals that in the space of two years had taken Chetwood to India to attend the Kumbh Mela, to Bosnia to work in an orphanage, and to the Peaks to climb alone without ropes. Even after Joe twice caught Chetwood watching him surreptitiously and twice drop his eyes with a frown, he hadn't doubted the nature of Chetwood's self-absorption. It simply never occurred to him that Chetwood could have done anything so utterly prosaic, so utterly unimaginative as to have stolen Jenna from him.

Joe answered, 'He found ordinary life difficult.'

'A nonconformist.'

'A seeker.'

'A drifter, you mean.'

Not for the first time, Joe found himself defending Chetwood. 'Someone who couldn't let the brutality of the world go unchallenged.'

Sarah gave up then, as perhaps Joe had hoped she would. 'Well, I'll be glad to help, if you'd like me to,' she announced briskly. 'I can get a few checks run.'

She had taken him by surprise. 'You could? What sort of things?'

'A witness trace. We're always asking the police to find people for us.'

'It wouldn't be too much trouble?'

'God, no. It's a five-minute job. No big deal. I'll just pop her name into the hat with a whole lot of others. But don't get your hopes too high, Joe. If people make an active decision to lose themselves they can do it very effectively, believe me.'

'Even from the police?'

'Sure. Once someone decides to opt out of the nanny state, once they refuse to play the bureaucratic game – national insurance, electoral roll, driving licence, all that sort of stuff – then they effectively become a non-person. There's no way of tracing them through the data bases.'

'Then what happens?'

'With witnesses? If it's an important case, the police go and question their associates – relatives, lovers, enemies, creditors, drug dealers. Someone nearly always knows. Whether they talk, of course, is an entirely different matter.'

'And then?'

'Oh, there are still a couple of things one can try.'

Something in her tone should have warned him against asking, 'What kind of things?'

She frowned at him. 'I don't know because I don't ask.'

'Look, Sarah, I'm very grateful, but don't do anything that might be *difficult* for you.'

'It won't get me into trouble, if that's what you mean,' she replied crisply. She rummaged in her bag for a pen. 'Just give me her full name, Joe. And date of birth, and last known address. The national insurance number would help too, if you can get it, but it's not essential.'

She extracted a sheet of paper from her planner and passed it over. Joe wrote down Jenna's full name, birth date, married name, and the address of the rented flat in Brondesbury.

Watching him, Sarah murmured, 'My goodness – off by heart.'

Something in her tone made Joe glance up. In the moment before she dropped her eyes he caught a sharp quizzical expression and for a wild moment he wondered if she was jealous.

'And the husband,' Sarah added. 'His details as well, if you've got them.'

'His birthday's in March. I can't remember the exact date. But he's a year older than me, so . . .'

She wrote it down. 'And his full name?'

'Jamie – James – Chetwood. Middle name, not sure. I'll have to check.'

'Originally from?'

'Weston Farm, somewhere near Swindon, I think it was. Wiltshire anyway. But the village . . . No, can't remember.'

She added these fragments to the slip of paper. 'Occupation?'

'Ah, now there's a question. It's more a case of where you'd like to start. Aid worker – a lot of that in the early days – Somalia, Bosnia. Then waiter, travel guide, translator, importer of ethnic rugs. But the last time I saw him it was definitely rugs. Oh, and art dealer. Though, knowing Chetwood, that should probably be taken with a large pinch of salt. He had a soft spot for tat, the louder the better. Once, he caught me out, good and proper. Made this huge fuss about his latest find, went through all this rubbish about how lucky he was to have stumbled on it, and of course when he unveiled the bloody thing it was this cheap plastic madonna from Manila with an illuminated halo that flashed pink and blue to the sound of "Ave Maria". He loved it. Couldn't get enough of it.'

It was a moment before Sarah reacted. 'Oh, I see, yes. *Yes.*' She gave a belated nod. 'Shall we say rug importer then, with "art" as a question mark?'

Joe nodded.

'Anything else?'

'He used to go and work in an orphanage in Jakarta twice a year. Raised money in this country, shipped out equipment, books, that sort of thing.'

'And Jenna? Anything more there?'

'I don't think so. I'll get her national insurance number when I see Alan and Helena tomorrow.'

'Tomorrow?'

'I'm going down first thing.'

'Does that mean we're not going to the Gilbert Exhibition?'

Joe's face must have been a picture because she said quickly, 'It was a joke, Joe. A bad joke. Of *course* you must go and see your friends. Exhibitions can wait. I owe my family a visit anyway.'

Impulsively, Joe reached out and gripped her hand. 'Thanks.'

The food arrived just then. She had the perfect excuse to extract her hand and look away.

Joe's starter was good, but he lost his appetite with the next course, which was altogether too rich. Outside, it was still raining heavily and, when he put his face to the window, fingers of condensation wafted out across the glass. In the reflection of the street-lamps the raindrops seemed to hang on the glass like strings of amber, and in a shift of memory he was reminded of a day last winter, a steamy cab window streaked with rain, and a blurred figure half glimpsed on the far side of the street.

'I thought I saw her once – Jenna.'

Sarah looked up from her fish. 'Oh? Where?'

'In Oxford Street.'

'And was it really her?'

'I thought so at the time. In fact, I chased after her. But now . . . well, I'm not so certain. She always hated London.'

'You didn't manage to catch her then?'

'I was in a taxi, I had to pay it off, the streets were very crowded.'

'Did she see you?'

He hesitated unhappily. 'I'm not sure. She was a long way off. Maybe. But by the time I got to her she'd disappeared.'

'If it was Oxford Street she'd probably gone into a shop.'

'Oh no. I looked everywhere, I searched for ages, I searched every shop. No—' Reliving the frustration, he gave a ragged sigh.

In the pause that followed, he became aware that Sarah was looking at him with the same intense look as before. 'Why, Joe . . .' she breathed at last, so softly he almost missed it. 'You really cared for her.'

'*What?*' He made a face. 'No, I told you! I explained – we were just kids together.'

He had spoken more sharply than he'd meant to. She dropped her eyes, her mouth twitched in what looked like disappointment, as though it pained her to catch him out in such a needless untruth.

He couldn't believe she didn't get it. 'I feel responsible, Sarah. That's the problem.'

'But why?'

'Because I introduced them of course. Because everything was fine till she met him.'

'It's hardly your fault—'

'It *is* my fault. Okay?'

She stared at him before looking away across the restaurant. Beneath her expressionless gaze he thought he detected an undercurrent of anger. But he had misjudged her. Turning back, she said in a tone of commiseration, 'Heavens, what a week it's been for you, Joe!' She gave a sudden half-formed smile, and awkwardly, in a public gesture that obviously came to her with difficulty, leant across and kissed him quickly on the lips.

Joe's flat was on the sixth floor of a mansion block a street away from Battersea Park. It was two rooms with a shoe-box for a kitchen, and a bathroom only marginally larger. It was the first place he'd ever owned, and he still wasn't entirely used to the idea. It was dark and cold when they got in, an impression accentuated by the tall black rectangles of the windows, which had been without curtains since Joe had moved in eighteen months ago. He traced the source of the freezing air to the bathroom window, which he'd thrown open that morning and forgotten to close.

While Sarah made herself a cup of tea he rooted around

for some wine which Sarah wouldn't want and he almost certainly didn't need. Eventually he found a bottle of cheap Chianti left over from a party.

'Joe?' Sarah was leaning back against the counter, hunched in her coat. 'I was thinking – have you a photograph of your friend?'

'What, for the police?' He had a vision of a computerised image being flashed around the country.

She declined the wine with a small shake of her head. 'No, I was thinking that if the computer turned something up, you might want to hire a private investigator, to go and check.'

The wine tasted cold and sharp, and he almost abandoned it. 'Wouldn't it be easier just to go and knock on her door?'

'And if it's not her? If it's someone with the same name who inhabits the far north of Scotland?'

He saw immediately that she was always going to know more about this business than he ever would. 'I'll ask Alan and Helena tomorrow.'

'You haven't got a picture yourself?'

'If I do, I don't know where.' This wasn't quite true; he had several photographs of Jenna sitting in the top drawer of his desk among a batch he'd been meaning to sort and arrange in albums for some time. One showed him standing beside Jenna on a beach in Cornwall when they were both about seventeen, during one of the three or four summer holidays he'd spent with the Laskeys. Another, which he could picture in the clearest detail, showed Jenna standing on Glastonbury Tor, during a June weekend at the end of his first year at Bristol. It had been a blazing hot day, without cloud or wind, and she had a hand angled to shade her eyes from the sun, like a sailor executing a rather jaunty salute. With her broad infectious smile, she gave the impression of a girl in an old-fashioned musical, about to launch into 'Ship Ahoy'.

He said, 'They were from so long ago. They wouldn't be any good.'

Sarah nodded. She looked so pale and chill, with her coat

lapels clutched close under her chin, that he went over and gave her arms a brisk rub in one of those gestures that promises far more than it delivers. 'Sorry about the Arctic.'

She gave a pantomime shiver. 'I'll survive.'

He looked into her eyes – such a misty shade of grey-green – and it seemed to him that a spark of understanding passed between them. He thought: We're two of a kind, and she knows it. Both a little wary, both anxious not to ask for more than the other is ready to give, both wanting to avoid hurt: to each other, but also to ourselves. There must be hope for us.

It seemed to him that it was a terrible mistake to want it all – passion, love, commitment – and that only the most demanding of men would be dissatisfied with this: a quick mind, a beautiful mouth, and eyes that promised no harm.

'It would be warmer in bed,' he said.

Her eyes glittered. 'I would hope so. But I'd love a bath first, if that's all right.'

He checked the hot water and, leaving her in the bathroom, emptied his wine down the sink. In the darkened bedroom, he went to switch on the bedside lamp only to glance up at the rain-specked window and pause, caught once again by the image of the cab-ride down Oxford Street. Still in darkness, he went to the window and stared out over the street. While nothing he'd told Sarah about that day had been untrue, he hadn't quite told her everything either. In the weeks immediately after the sighting he'd re-run the scene obsessively, trying to decide what he'd seen, yet the more he'd tried to fix the images in his mind the more frayed and indistinct they'd become, like a flimsy map which with constant use threatens to fall apart in your hands. Now, driven to pick through the memory one more time, he cautioned himself: Take it slowly, go from one sure thing to the next. No agonising allowed. No what-ifs. Just firm ground.

*

January, eleven months ago. He'd been to see his dentist in Devonshire Place. With no early-morning appointments available, he'd settled for the first afternoon slot in the hope that his dentist would come back from lunch on time. In the event the guy was twenty minutes late – some sort of emergency, he said – and by the time Joe hit the street he was already fretting about getting to his three o'clock meeting late. It was raining steadily and he had to walk almost the full length of Wimpole Street before he found a taxi. The traffic was appalling; the cab took an age to nudge and inch its way into Oxford Street, and Joe began to wonder if he wouldn't do better to sprint for the Tube and take his chances there, though his meeting was miles from any station. The fretting was significant; it made him restless. Otherwise he would almost certainly have had his head down, going through the papers for the meeting. As it was, he kept rubbing the condensation from the window and staring in frustration at the traffic, wondering if it was ever going to free up.

The cab was fifty yards from Oxford Circus when he saw her in the crowd on the opposite pavement. At first she was just another woman in a pale coat, walking in the rain. He had no idea what made him look at her a second time. It might have been the absence of an umbrella or the way she held her head high despite the rain, or the long dark hair hanging in rats' tails around her shoulders. In the downpour the taxi window was like bottle-glass, it made her image distort and shimmy and blur. Yet even as he wiped the fog impatiently from the glass, something in the woman's half-profile, in the line of her jaw, in the way she walked, made him sit up and press his nose to the window. The red wall of a slow-moving bus blocked his vision at the critical moment, but he knew.

It was Jenna.

He must have yelled aloud because he remembered the cabbie twisting round and saying something. He didn't hear what it was though, he was too busy clawing at the narrow metal lug on the top of the window, trying to get enough purchase to haul it down. He forgot all about the window-lock set into the door, the lever that in a more rational moment he would have remembered to flick across before swinging his weight on the lug. He had the impression of almost losing his fingertips before he finally managed to overcome the resistance of the lock and drag the window half-way down.

He thrust his face against the opening. She was still there, walking parallel and just ahead of the cab. Now everything about her seemed totally familiar to him: the set of her shoulders, the fluidity of her stride, the shape of her head with its plastering of wet hair. He lost any remaining uncertainty: *it was her*. His heart gave a violent lurch of excitement and joy, rapidly followed by a surge of panic, the sort that comes from being trapped in a confined space, a sensation exacerbated by the sudden acceleration of the cab. He shouted for the cabbie to stop, he rattled and wrenched at the door handle. But if the battle with the window had been hard, the door was impossible – the red eye of the central-locking system wasn't glittering its warning for nothing – and it wasn't until the cabbie had stamped on the brakes and driven Joe hard against the jump-seat, not until the two of them had exchanged feverish insults through the partition, not until the cabbie had allowed himself to be bought off with a twenty-quid note, that the electronic click of the door-release finally set him free.

Joe burst out of the cab and stood in the middle of the road, scanning the opposite pavement. The crowd seemed to have thickened, the umbrellas to have formed an unbroken canopy of black, then at last, further ahead than he'd expected, he glimpsed the pale coat, the proud wet head. He stepped forward and, in the moment before the cyclist cannoned into him, he bellowed Jenna's name, he yelled so hard that his throat seemed to seize from the effort.

Suddenly, the man and bicycle were a fast-approaching blur on the periphery of Joe's vision. In the split second before impact, the cyclist tried to swerve and Joe tried to jump out of his way, but they both chose the same direction. As Joe flung up a protective arm, he held in his mind's eye the last fleeting image of Jenna as she looked round for the source of the shout, the dark wet head of hair giving way to the pale oval of her face.

It was all he needed. Even as the combined weight of man and bicycle slammed into him, even as he felt the breath driven out of his lungs, he was working out how to roll clear, how to scramble to his feet and get running. It was years since he'd paid scant attention to the rugby instructor's exhortations on how to fall harmlessly, but he succeeded in hitting the ground at a roll, shoulder first, and to feel nothing worse than a slight crack on the head before he managed to pick himself up and weave a path through the traffic to the opposite side of the road, where he ran parallel to the pavement, searching the crowd.

His lungs rebelled. Forced to halt and suck in great gulps of air, he looked ahead helplessly, only to see her – and this was where it all became indistinct – *maybe* to see her running away. His memory – or his imagination – had her running so fast that her hair was flying out behind her. It was the run of someone who had taken fright, or was desperate to escape, which was perhaps the same thing.

When his lungs allowed, he loped on, half in the road, half on the pavement. At one point he thought he glimpsed the top of her head, but after that, nothing. If she had gone into a shop, she had hidden herself well; he ducked into them all, he sprinted round each floor, he knocked into people who shouted and stared. Down at the gates of the Underground, facing three different escalators, he finally gave up. He looked down and saw blood. His cheek was dripping; by the time he found a handkerchief it had stained the front of his coat.

That night, the doubts began. Was the running woman Jenna or someone else with dark hair? Surely Jenna's hair had been too wet to fly out behind her? And he had no memory of the running woman wearing a pale coat – had he missed it, or had there been no pale coat to see? Even the desperation of her escape took on an innocent quality when he recast the woman as a fitness enthusiast trying to catch a bus.

It might have been the effect of hitting his head – going to bed, he discovered a large bump high on his temple – but it was only a short step to doubting he has seen Jenna at all. What had he really seen, after all, but a half-profile and a head of long bedraggled hair? And in the adrenalin-charged micro-second before the bicycle hit him, when he saw her stop and begin to turn, she'd been further away than before, her face no more than a pale smudge in a mass of jostling figures.

By morning, he was left with only one incontestable fact: that he had left his briefcase, stuffed with important papers, in the back of the taxi, never to be seen again.

Chapter Two

—◆—

JOE LEFT early the next morning before the Christmas shoppers clogged the streets. His car was a small runabout that he used rarely. Often forced to park three or more streets away, he was always rather surprised to find it intact and functional. Soon he was over the river and through the centre of town, heading north. The rain had gone, leaving a grey sheen on the roads, while in the east the first light lay in cold ribbons against the sky.

Somewhere near Stevenage he tried calling Sarah. She had got up with him before seven and, wrapped in his kimono, disappeared into the kitchen. When he emerged from the bathroom at a rush, she'd handed him a mug of filter coffee, diluted with cold water to bring it down to drinking temperature. Once again he was struck by her thoughtfulness; once again he wasn't quite sure what to make of her. Last night, in the aftermath of love, he'd broached the subject of his holiday entitlement, which he must use before March, and suggested she come with him to Morocco.

'I'm not sure I'll be able to get away.'

'What, at three months' notice?'

A pause. 'I'm not good at planning ahead.'

'In general, do you mean? Or for holidays with men?'

'It's work. We're short-staffed.'

'There's life outside work, Sarah. Or if there isn't, then we're all mad.'

Another silence, which seemed to stretch out into the darkness.

'I'll see if I can work something out.'

Stung, he made a bad joke of it. 'It's not compulsory.'

'No, I'd like to go to Morocco.'

'But do you want to go with me? That's rather more to the point, isn't it?'

'Yes. Yes, of course I do.' She was very still in his arms.

He said, 'That's fine then,' though it seemed to Joe that it was far from fine.

To break the silence, he said, 'It might actually be fun, you know.'

'Of course. Really – I'd love to come.'

She squeezed his hand. In confirmation? Secret regret? With the intention of keeping her options open? Perhaps she was terrified of committing herself even three months ahead. Perhaps she didn't think their relationship would last that long. Perhaps she made a habit of moving on before things got too serious.

They rolled apart to sleep. In the five minutes before Joe dropped off he was aware of Sarah lying tensely, as though she were reliving some secret sadness.

Her troubles seemed to vanish with the night, however, and as he rattled off instructions for locking up she kissed him firmly and told him to take care driving. As he ran down the stairs, she came out onto the landing and waved to him over the banisters. Like a proper lover, he thought; like someone who wants to come to Morocco.

Now, her mobile didn't respond. It was still early; she wouldn't have bothered to switch it on.

The town where Joe had grown up lay near the junction of three counties and was characterised by none. It wasn't quite the Midlands and it wasn't quite the North; to the stranger's eye it was flat country, but compared to the Fens twenty miles to the east it was positively undulating.

For decades the town had resisted the machinations of the housing lobby and maintained the boundaries shaped by the thirties planners who'd laid out the unoffensive tree-lined suburb where Joe had grown up. But government edict and the agricultural slump had finally defeated the conservationists, and now, within view of his old home on the pasture where he had so often walked as a child, a new road lay like a white gash across a sea of mud. Fanning out from the road a web of roped posts and fluttering ribbons extended across the ancient rabbit warrens, delineating the routes of drains or foundations, while the wooden frame of a show house stood like a sentry box beside the road.

He had known the developers were coming, but he was unprepared for the changes closer to home. Approaching the turn for Shirley Road, he saw that two of the six shops in the small arcade that served the neighbourhood had closed down since his last visit a month ago. The loss of the chemist's had a certain irony – his father banned even the mildest cough syrup from the house – but the sight of the shuttered and padlocked grocer's made his heart sink. Now, the only shops selling food within walking distance of home were a newsagent's, stocked with crisps, chocolate and fizzy drinks, and a gaudy Chinese takeaway, an unrepentant champion of monosodium gluta-mate.

Accelerating past Shirley Road, he drove on to the super-market which had undoubtedly brought about the grocer's demise. He filled a trolley with the nursery food his father liked – tins of steak and kidney pudding, mince, baked beans, stewed apple, custard – along with some fresh fruit and vegetables which the old man would leave to rot before throwing them out amid complaints of waste.

It wasn't difficult to spot his old home in the row of almost identical red-brick semis that made up Shirley Road; it stood out as a model of neglect in a world of conspicuous con-sumption. While the neighbours had acquired replacement windows and ruched curtains and gardens with water features, Woodside remained untouched by all but the most basic main-tenance. On his last visit, Joe had swept the rotting leaves from the path and hacked back the denser shrubs, but it had been

no more than a gesture. Parking now, he noticed new dilapi-
dations: the front fence was sagging out over the pavement,
while one of the bay windows had been covered with a sheet
of badly fitting chipboard. He carried the shopping to the side
gate, which swung on rotting hinges, and stepped around the
split and bulging wheely-bin. The kitchen door was locked. He
put his face to the window and saw gloom. He rapped loudly
on the door and called his father's name, then stepped back
onto the sodden ankle-high grass and aimed his calls at the
upper floor. Nothing moved in the dripping garden, and no
sound came from the silent windows. He went to the shed and
looked for the spare key on the nail above the door frame
where it used to hang in his mother's day, but there was no
key there now. In the end he tried phoning and heard a soft
warble deep in the house before the answering machine picked
up and relayed his father's rather querulous tones. *You have
reached the Campaign for Victims of Medical Negligence . . .*

Joe rang off before the beep sounded, and went back to the
lawn, where he stood, hands in pockets, in a stance of bound-
less patience, and repeatedly called his father's name in a
studiously neutral tone. The two of them had played this game
before; it was a matter of time.

Finally, Joe saw a movement behind the frosted glass of the
bathroom. A moment later a shadow darkened the small upper
window, which was latched open, and he caught what might
have been the glint of an eye.

Pretending not to have noticed, Joe made no move towards
the kitchen door until he heard the bolt turn. The door opened
a short way and his father's face loomed warily into the
opening.

'Hello, Dad.'

'Oh, it's *you*.'

As Joe pushed the door open, the old man turned and
walked away across the kitchen. Joe followed him into the hall.
'How are you, Dad?'

The old man halted in the doorway of the front room and

said over his shoulder in a fretful voice, 'You should have told me you were coming.'

'I left a message on the machine.'

'Oh, the *machine*.' He lived in a state of permanent irritation with the phone, which he regarded as an instrument of time-wasters and fools who failed to share his views on medical negligence. 'I was just about to start work.' He gestured hopelessly.

'I won't stay long then.'

'Well, I suppose I could . . .' He looked at his watch, he gazed longingly into the front room, he said on a note of painful compromise, 'A cup of tea then?'

'I'll go and make it.'

The old man peered at Joe as if for the first time and, blinking furiously, jerked his mouth into an approximation of a smile. 'It's the e-mails, you see. There are always hundreds on the weekends. It's just non-stop.'

For a moment Joe saw his father as others must see him: a string-bean of a man, too thin by far, with a stern expression and restless eyes, who looked older than his sixty-five years.

While the kettle was heating, Joe made a quick inventory of the kitchen. The fridge had a few scraps in it – milk, butter and a couple of sausages – while the cupboards contained a collection of tins and jars whose contents had seen better days. A half-consumed Dundee cake sat alone in the bread-bin.

He unpacked the shopping and arranged it on the shelves in food groups. Each surface was cold and greasy to the touch, every corner and crevice grouted with a thread of grime, while under his feet the lino was by turns uneven or slightly tacky from some ancient spillage. The last cleaning lady had stayed four weeks, which was long service where his father was concerned. Joe had tried offering above the going rate, but it seemed that money could not compensate for his father's obstructive tactics and childish resentments. It wasn't that the old man was opposed to a clean house, it was simply that he loved being alone infinitely more.

Joe added two slices of Dundee cake to the tea tray before carrying it in.

'They cheat on the almonds,' his father commented, his eyes already back on the computer screen. 'Halves instead of wholes. *And* thirty per cent fewer.' Joe didn't doubt he had counted them. 'And of course they whittled the weight down years ago. From two pounds to 800 grams.' He scoffed, 'That's what metrication did to us.'

He had set up his office in what had once been the front room. A few pictures still hung disconsolately on the walls, but the table and four remaining chairs had long since vanished under stacks of legal bundles, newspapers and boxes. The computer took pride of place, a beacon of brilliance in a sea of disorder.

The old man had a puritanical disdain for heating, but even by his Spartan standards the house was freezing. Joe asked about the broken window.

'Mmm? Oh, kids.'

'How did they do it?'

The old man was at the computer, scrolling down a list. 'What? Oh . . . a football.'

'Why were they playing so close to the house? They weren't bothering you, were they?'

'No, no.'

Something in his tone made Joe ask, 'Who were they, Dad? Have you reported them?'

The old man was stabbing impatiently at the keyboard. 'For heaven's sake! Where's it gone?' He rotated the mouse impatiently. 'Here! Here!' A bright screen began to download.

'Have they bothered you before, Dad?'

'Look! Just look at this! Someone's finally going to give it a go under the Human Rights Act. *Just* as I said they should.'

'They weren't trying to break in, were they?'

'See! This chap here – Turney – he's going for Article 2. I *always* said it was the way to go! I *always* told that fool Bartlett.'

Joe gave it one more try. 'You should call the police, you know, if—'

His father's temper had always been volatile, but nothing prepared Joe for the ferocity with which the old man turned on him. His hands flew into claws, the veins on his temple stood out, and he trembled so violently he might have been connected to a socket. '*You're not listening, Joe!* You're not listening! I'm trying to tell you something *important* and you're not listening! Why don't you listen?'

'Sorry.'

'*You come here and you simply don't listen!*' He gave a last shudder and seized up, eyes glaring, face rigid, completely immobile, before the rage dropped away almost as rapidly as it had come. He lowered his eyes and frowned.

'Sorry,' Joe said again in a low voice. 'I interrupted you.'

The old man blinked rapidly and shook his head, as if to clear it of some mysterious obstruction, and turned back to the computer.

'You were saying – you've found something important,' Joe prompted.

It was a job to get the old man to open up again. For a while he maintained a stiff silence and when he finally answered it was grudgingly, in monosyllables. Gradually, however, Joe managed to gather that through a new chat forum dedicated to medical negligence he had made contact with a bereaved husband whose case, like his own, had foundered in a morass of legal argument and time limitations.

'They tried to fob him off with the *Act*, of course,' the old man declared with a scathing snort, and Joe relaxed a little because the Limitation Act was always guaranteed to get his adrenalin flowing. Watching the old man grow increasingly animated, Joe wondered not for the first time at the strength of his purpose, at the unwavering sense of injustice that burned so fiercely in him even after so many years. Joe's memories of the months after his mother's death had been overshadowed by the disastrous term he'd spent at a weekly boarding school in Rutland, yet one picture had burned itself into his mind's eye, it must have been during the summer holidays, of his father sitting at the dining table hunched over a letter. It might have been a trick of memory, a replaying of a single scene, but Joe saw him returning to this letter time and again, day after day, picking over the words with increasing agitation. It was this letter, of course, that had given rise to his father's suspicion that 'something wasn't quite right' with his mother's death, that the family was being denied information that would reveal incompetence on the part of the surgeon or inadequacies in the hospital's standards of post-operative care, or both. The letter signalled the start of the lawyers, the outpouring of money, the reams of paper that spread across the dining table like so much volcanic dust. There had been friends in those early days, a sympathetic audience for the stream of anti-establishment grievances that spilled from his father's lips, but few friendships can survive the fervour of righteous outrage for long, and in time even the most loyal supporters had drifted away. But it was after the old man fell out with the national support organisation, after he brought a doomed and ruinously expensive action against his own lawyers, that his real isolation began. The cyber forums were his salvation. His fellow victims provided the one audience that would never desert him.

The old man's analysis of the Internet case was detailed and for all Joe knew legally impeccable. When at last he fell silent, Joe asked a question to show he'd been paying attention and saw his father become aware of him with an expression of faint surprise.

The old man shifted a little in his seat and peered at him sideways. 'Well . . .' His mouth lifted into an abrupt smile. 'And how are things with you, Joe? All right?'

'Oh, pretty busy, Dad. As always.'

'Good. Good.' He nodded vaguely. 'And they're looking after you all right, are they? Since the partnership.'

'It was senior associate, Dad. The partnership won't be for another couple of years yet. If I'm lucky.'

'Ah.' The old man would have turned back to the computer then, but feeling something more was expected of him he took a stab at another question. 'But interesting stuff?'

'It's all right, yes. Though sometimes – well, it's like two bullies slugging it out to see who's the tougher. There doesn't seem much point.'

This produced a look of mystification. 'Bullies?'

'Large corporations. You know – counter-claiming.'

The old man cast Joe a sharp glance, as if the nature of his work had come as a sudden and unpleasant revelation to him. 'But what are they claiming *for?*'

'Oh, breach of contract. Losses. That sort of thing.'

'Money.' The old man winced censoriously. '*Money.*' And then, in a tone of lingering disappointment, 'I suppose it has to be done.'

They had been here before; Joe knew better than to argue.

'Atkins now . . .' Atkins was the old man's latest hero, the latest in a long line of pioneering lawyers who were pushing at the boundaries of medical negligence law. 'He gave a fantastic interview in *The Times* – did you see it? How he nailed that Leeds gynaecologist who removed ovaries without consent. *Without consent!* I ask you. There's no limit, absolutely no limit.'

Joe put the tea mugs back on the tray. 'Sorry, Dad, I'm going to have to leave you to it. I need to catch Alan before he starts on his rounds.' No sooner were the words out of his mouth than Joe regretted them.

'*Alan?*'

'He's asked me to drop by.'

'Why?'

'To help with something.'

'What sort of thing?'

'He wants me to try and find Jenna.'

'*Alan* does?'

'Yes.'

'But why *you*? What on earth does he think *you* can do?'

'I can start things off, I suppose.'

His father shook his head slowly, with exaggerated wonder. 'Quite extraordinary. Asking *you*.'

'I'll send someone to fix the window, Dad, and the fence. And I'll try and find a cleaning lady. You'll have to have one, you know.'

The old man was still muttering his astonishment as Joe carried the tray out of the room.

Joe was washing up when he heard the steps coming across the hall. 'I suppose they blame you – is that it?' his father said. 'For Jenna going off. For introducing her to that awful chap.'

Joe stared out at the ragged garden. 'I don't think it's that.'

'I always knew he was bad news. That was obvious from the start. A complete waster. Never understood how you were taken in by him, Joe. How you never saw him for what he was.'

'I've left a bit of food for you, Dad.' Joe threw open the cupboard doors and stood to one side, like a salesman exhibiting his wares.

But the old man was still staring at him. 'You came down specially then?'

'I've come a week early, that's all, Dad. I was coming down next weekend anyway, if you remember. And then it'll be Christmas.'

'A week *early*.'

Joe caught the unspoken accusation: *because Alan asked you to*. In the old days, his father had been only too glad of the time Joe spent at Alan and Helena's. He'd been trying to keep the show on the road then, holding down a day job as a financial controller while devoting every spare moment to the 'case'. Something had to give, and it was the garden that went first, followed by the house and the cooking. Then, for no apparent reason, the old man's attitude to the Laskeys changed almost overnight. His gratitude soured, he became openly hostile, and Joe was forced to live two lives: the one at home, functional, solitary, secretive, the other at the Laskeys, open, uncritical, and all the more intense for being clandestine.

'It was my own idea to come down, Dad. Alan didn't ask me to.'

The old man's glare didn't falter.

'I'm not sure he even knows I'm coming.'

'In that case you're not going to catch him, are you? He spends all morning on his rounds.'

'Well, if I miss him, I miss him.'

'You *will* miss him. You'll miss him by hours. *I* could have told you that.' With a triumphant sniff, the old man turned his gaze on the cupboard. 'Good God, Joe, you've bought the shops out! Far too much. Everyone eats far too much nowadays. It's just greed, you know, nothing but greed. One meal a day's plenty, *plenty*.' He peered at the labels. '*Beans* . . . Get me going, I suppose. And custard . . . yes, yes . . . it'll make a change.' He said abruptly, 'Thanks, Joe. Thanks for—' His eye fell on the fruit bowl. 'What on earth d'you want to buy all this for? Good God. It'll only go and rot. It'll only have to be thrown away.'

At the door they embraced with the usual awkwardness. Joe had introduced the practice some years ago, but for his father it remained an ordeal of modern manners.

'Joe?' The old man shuffled awkwardly, as if he might offer belated reparations.

'Yes, Dad.'

'It may be she's just cut herself off, you know – Jennifer. Got herself a better life. She always had her sights set high.'

Joe sucked in his breath wearily.

'Oh, you may scoff, but she was always a very determined young lady. Always liked having things her own way. Most people saw no further than that pretty face of hers, that angelic look she used to get when she was singing. But there was another side to her, believe me. She enjoyed being the centre of attention. Alan's fault, of course. Spoilt her rotten.'

Joe could only shake his head and turn away.

'All I'm saying is she might have turned her nose up at the past. It's happened before.'

'Don't forget to lock up,' Joe called back.

The old man tutted irritably, but as Joe walked away down the mossy path he heard the sound of the bolt sliding across.

Joe found Alan outside his house, standing beside the open bonnet of his car, gazing at the engine with a kind of wistful bafflement. When he saw Joe he broke into a grin and spread his hands in a gesture of delighted retreat, as if to acknowledge the absurdity of placing himself so close to anything mechanical. 'Trouble?' Joe asked.

'Mysterious noises.'

'Can I do something?'

He laughed, 'No, Joe. It's just trying to provoke me, the blasted thing. It does it from time to time, just to add to my grey hairs.' It didn't occur to Joe until later that Alan had used the car as an excuse to catch him on his own, away from the house.

Alan held Joe at arm's length and examined his face for a moment before embracing him in a rapid bear-hug. 'Joe! Joe!' he sang affectionately. 'Good of you to come.'

'I meant to drop in last time —'

'But we're never here, are we? No, no, of course you couldn't find us. No, don't even think about it, Joe. We're impossible!' He chuckled happily. He had a lively round face, a quick smile, and small dancing eyes, but in the winter light it seemed to Joe that his plump cheeks had developed an unhealthy tinge and the skin around his eyes a dark and puffy look, while his wispy hair floated across his balding pate like down. For as long as Joe had known him he had talked about dieting and for just as long had failed to get round to it, but now for the first time the weight seemed to rest heavily on his frame. There was a bow to his shoulders, a sag to his belly. He was wearing the uniform of the English country doctor he'd always longed to be: old tweeds, a brushed cotton shirt with a worn collar, its points skew-whiff, and sturdy leather shoes. Only the lilt in his voice and the precision of his enunciation gave a hint of his parents' Polish ancestry.

'You've seen your old man?' he asked.

'When I could persuade him to answer the door. I thought he was just avoiding the tradesmen, but I think the local kids have been giving him trouble.'

'Do you want me to look into it? Of course I'll look into it!'

'No, you've got quite enough on your plate. I couldn't ask you—'

'But it's no trouble, Joe. For your father? No trouble at all! If it's the local kids, I'll be able to sort it out in five minutes. A word with the parents,' he whispered conspiratorially, 'still works wonders.'

'Well, if you're sure.'

Alan blocked any further discussion with an energetic gesture of both hands, before turning back to the engine and gingerly closing the bonnet. 'I always dread a patient's cat climbing in. They wouldn't thank me for that, would they? But then they don't thank me for much anyway, Joe, not in the blame and compensation culture. Civility's a thing of the past. Now it's suspicion and mistrust. They accuse me of failing to disclose side-effects, they tell me I'm trying to damage their babies with vaccines, they demand second opinions. They call me out late at night to tell me I don't know what I'm talking about.' He leant back against the side of the car with a cheerful shrug. 'There we are, Joe. There we are. Thank heavens for the very young and the very old. They're not interested in their rights, God bless 'em.'

'You've got some help, though, haven't you, Alan? You've merged with this other practice.'

'Trouble is, Joe, they do things differently. I'm a great believer in letting patients have a good moan. Does them no end of good. Saves on the drug bill. But now everything's about efficiency and work-sharing. Ten minutes a patient.' Distracted, he began a search of his jacket pockets, then opened the door of the car to peer inside.

Joe glanced towards the house, which was of solid thirties design, grey pebble-dashed with a two-storey tile-hung bay topped by a gable with black bargeboards. The faded curtains were half drawn or hanging aslant. Inside, there were no lights lit against the gloomy day, but through the smeared glass of the ground-floor window he could see, clearly outlined against the patterned wallpaper, the familiar form of the upright piano, a book of music open on its stand.

Alan abandoned his mysterious hunt with a last pat of his outer pockets. 'Joe, it's good of you to look in. Very good of you. The thing is, I called because – I don't suppose Helena told you—'

'She said you wanted to find Jenna.'

His eyebrows shot up. 'She said that? Well, well . . .' Resuming an expression of great seriousness, he said, 'Normally I wouldn't bother you with such a thing, Joe. Of course I wouldn't! Absolutely not. Not when it's going to be such a lot of trouble, not when it might all be for nothing. But it's Marcus, you see. He'll never forgive me if I don't give it a try. He'll never – well, let's put it this way, Joe, I don't want to lose a *second* child. *One* could be termed bad luck, *two* carelessness!' He forced a loud chuckle, but neither of them felt like laughing.

'Helena said something about a legal matter. Something to do with a property.'

'A property? That's far too grand a word. Goodness gracious – a *property*! No, it's a tiny terrace house, one up, one down. Damp, decrepit, no view. Down by the river, next to the coal tip – what used to be the coal tip – behind Myersons.'

Myersons were the builders' merchants, but Joe had only the dimmest recollection of houses nearby.

'It was left to the kids by a patient, Edith Gutteridge,' Alan went on. 'No family of her own. Wanted to leave it to *me*, if you please. Can you believe it! I said not on your life. Not allowed! Not in my book anyway. Otherwise people would start thinking I had designs on my patients, wouldn't they?' His shoulders lifted in brief merriment. 'No, no – wouldn't do. So I thought that was that. Thought Edith would go and leave her pennies to a cat sanctuary – you should have seen her cats, Joe, eight, ten at one time, mange, fleas, you name it – but no, not a bit of it. No, without a by-your-leave she went and left it to the kids. Marc used to pop in on his way to and from his holiday job, you see. Did the odd jobs for her, gutters, light-bulbs, that sort of thing. And Jenna – well, Edith only met her a few times. That's the strange thing, Joe – no more than three or four times, at the most. But of course she heard her *sing* – that's what it was. Heard her sing at St Luke's one Christmas, and really took to her. Always talking about her ...' He ducked his head to peer into the car again, without success. 'And you know how Jenna was with old people – always sweet with them, always found time for them. They always adored her, didn't they, old people? So, anyway, there it was! Edith died six years ago and out of the blue we found she'd left them her house. But the place was a mess, Joe. Worth next to nothing, we thought. In fact the estate agent said it was a waste of time putting it on the market because there were so many problems. It wasn't just the damp, you see. There was a bulging wall. And cracks.'

He plunged into the back of the car with a grunt of triumph and re-emerged with a pipe and tobacco pouch. He shot Joe a mischievous glance. 'Don't tell me! I know – I should have given up by now. Helena gets very cross. She's got a nose like a bloodhound, smells it on my clothes.' He rolled his eyes in

mock despair and began the ritual of filling his pipe. '*Anyway*
there's been an offer for the place. That's the thing, Joe. That's
what Marc's in a tizz about. There's this offer and it won't go
through unless we can find Jenna.' He paused with an unlit
match in his hand. 'It's not a lot of money, Joe, not for a house
– forty-two thousand – but Marc could do with it just at the
moment. Badly. That's the thing, Joe. I don't want him to feel'
– he waved the match in the air while he found the word –
'cheated.' But he wasn't satisfied with this either. 'I don't want
him to think badly of his sister. That's what I couldn't take,
Joe.' Settling for this, he struck the match and drew the flame
into the bowl.

Marc was younger than Jenna by four years. Joe had seen
him once or twice in recent years, but he remembered him
mainly as an intense, rather taciturn schoolboy with an appetite
for junk food and video games.

'So, it's Jenna's signature you need.'

Alan looked at him sharply, as if he'd made an unexpected
and unwelcome distinction. 'Well, yes . . . But we have to find
her first, don't we?'

'Yes, of course.'

Alan was still looking for the catch. 'You can't have one
without the other, surely?'

'No, of course not. It was just my lawyer's mind.'

A last frown and Alan disappeared behind a wall of smoke.
'I never inhale, of course,' he commented. 'Ridiculous, isn't it?
It's the stink I go for, I suppose. The *memory* of wickedness.'
When he spoke again it was hesitantly: 'I should tell you, Joe
. . . I took it on myself to . . . it must be a year ago now . . . I
got in contact with the Missing Persons Line and asked them
to have another look for Jenna.' Alan's face had always been
transparent, and now Joe saw the pain and disappointment
there.

'And nothing?'

He shook his head solemnly. 'I tried the Red Cross too.
Unlikely, I know – they deal with refugees, don't they? – but I

thought I might as well, while I was about it.' He added in a casual tone that didn't quite come off, 'Oh, and I didn't bother to tell Helena, by the way. No point.'

'No.'

'She hates any mention – you know.'

'She seemed all right when I phoned last night.'

'She wouldn't have minded talking to you, Joe.'

'She said something about some news. Something you got excited about.'

Alan looked blank for a moment. 'Oh, for heaven's sake!' he protested. 'It was nothing. Nothing at all! And way back when. Good gracious – months ago. *April*. And I wasn't *excited*, just curious. No harm in a bit of curiosity!' He gave a half-hearted laugh, only to pause, locked in some internal wrangle. 'Well, all right,' he admitted in a rush. 'It was my birthday. I thought Jenna might remember. My sixtieth, you see. I thought she might make the effort to get in touch. Just that once – you know.' His voice dipped suddenly.

'Your sixtieth, Alan – I had no idea!'

'For heaven's sake, why should you? We didn't make a fuss about it. Nothing to celebrate, I can tell you. *Sixty*.' He rolled his eyes.

'All the same. Many congratulations.' Joe gripped his shoulder affectionately.

'Hey ho. Old Father Time.'

'So . . .? Was it a phone call?'

'What? Oh . . . no, it was a card.'

'Any signature?'

'No, no,' he scoffed, as if arguing against himself. 'You see? Could have been anyone, couldn't it?'

'But you thought it was Jenna.'

'I *thought* all sorts of things . . . I thought . . .' He hung his arms, the pipe forgotten in his hand. 'I saw what I wanted to see, Joe.'

'The card was blank?'

'For heaven's sake, Joe – as good as. There was a single

kiss – an X – and a happy-face. You know, the sort kids do, with a circle and a smile and two dots for eyes. I was just being slow.' He tapped his temple in a schoolboy gesture of stupidity. 'Jenna used to draw happy-faces on her cards, but with lots of kisses – I mean *showers* of kisses – and always set in clouds, large clouds. Never one X on its own. Never without clouds. Not her style. Well, there you are!' He spread a hand, palm up. 'The happy-face went to my head. I wasn't thinking straight. There was no reason to think it was Jenna. None. But Helena . . . she doesn't let me forget these things. She told me I was a fool.'

Joe made an expression of commiseration.

'Can't blame her, Joe. She feels very angry.'

It was an odd word to use. Perhaps the word bothered Alan too, because he puffed aggressively on his pipe and Joe couldn't help noticing that when he pulled it away from his mouth he appeared to be drawing the smoke down into his lungs.

'You never found out who sent the card?'

From the side of Alan's mouth a stream of smoke shot out into the misty air. 'A patient, I imagine. They do, sometimes. Send things.'

'What about the postmark?'

'I don't know. Local, I think.' Again, he lifted a hand in appeal. 'You see, it was nothing, Joe. Really.'

The sounds of the weekend rose around them: a revving motorbike, kids playing, the beat of a hammer. Glancing round, Joe's eye caught what might have been a flicker of movement in the house, a person, a shadow, he couldn't tell.

He said, 'I haven't had time to investigate everything on the search front, Alan, but there are some checks that can be done straight away. They may duplicate the Missing Persons of course, but it's worth a try. Could you let me have Jenna's national insurance number? That might help. And her last known address.'

'Her last address? But, Joe, the only one I ever had was that place in North London. Grisham Gardens—'

'*Gresh*am, I think it was.'

'Yes, yes – Gresham Gardens. But *you* went there, Joe. You saw it for yourself.'

'Just the once.'

'Well, that was one more time than we did.' The bewilderment tugged at his voice. 'As for Jenna's national insurance number, Helena will have it somewhere.' He knocked out his pipe and straightened up. 'Now, if there's any cost involved, anything at all, Joe, I insist on paying,' he announced in a tone of great gravity.

'Well, let's wait and see, Alan.'

'No – whatever needs to be done, Joe. Advertising. Private investigators. Whatever you decide – that'll be fine with me.' Alan was incapable of a bitter thought, he'd never once blamed Joe for introducing Jenna to Chetwood, but when he laid his hand trustingly on Joe's arm, his touch contained all the unwitting reproach of a forgiving heart.

'Come and have a coffee, Joe. Come and see Helena. She's been asking after you.' Halfway up the path Alan halted irresolutely, eyes fixed on the ground. 'You don't think anyone's heard from her and not told us, do you, Joe?'

'A friend, you mean?'

'Someone in London.'

'There was Martha, but she would have let me know, I'm sure.' Martha had been Jenna's best friend at music college.

'She was the pianist?'

'The singer. With red hair.'

'Ah, yes,' Alan murmured. 'What about later, after she left college?'

This was the summer that Jenna had moved in with Chetwood; the summer she had turned down the place with the Welsh Opera chorus. 'I'm not sure what friends they had, Alan. There were a few in London, I think, at the beginning. Then in

Hereford, in the farmhouse days. Fellow escapees from city life. I tracked a couple of them down, if you remember, right at the very beginning.'

Alan was nodding furiously. 'Yes, yes. A musician, wasn't it?'

'Guitar player. Dave Cracknell. He and his girlfriend were up in Hereford all that summer but lost touch soon after. They said everyone had lost touch with Jenna and Chetwood.'

'You checked, Joe. Of course you did.' Alan flung him a grateful smile. 'And after Hereford? After the farmhouse?'

'They moved so often, I don't think they were in one place long enough to make friends, Alan. That was the impression I got anyway.'

'And she used to love her friends,' Alan sighed wistfully. 'What about Gresham Gardens?'

'I can't be certain, but I had the feeling they saw nobody. They didn't even tell Martha they were back in London, not that last time.'

Eyes back on the ground, Alan said in a voice that rose suddenly, 'No word at all, Joe. That's what I find so hard to understand. She must have known we'd be sick with worry. She must have known we wouldn't have a moment's peace. That's what's so hard, Joe – how she could know and not make contact. You don't think she's dead, do you?' he asked almost as an aside.

'I think you'd have heard.'

But Alan knew this better than anyone; he dealt with the bureaucracy of death all the time. 'Abroad then? The other side of the world?'

Joe thought of all the places Chetwood had been in thrall to over the years. The treks through Nepal, Laos and Vietnam; the spiritual pilgrimages into remote corners of India; the years of conscience in Bosnia and Somalia. 'It's possible,' he said unhelpfully.

'But still with *him*, Joe? Still with – James?'

'I'm sure, yes.'

With a resigned nod, Alan led the way into the house. In the hall Joe counted off the well-remembered clutter: the mirror scattered with Post-It notes, the small table with its tangle of dusty phones and answering machines, the bulging coat-stand with the array of country hats draped over its horns, the assortment of stout boots around its feet, the collection of rough-hewn walking sticks in the tall wicker basket. Alan was a countryman without land or space, who on his suburban rounds could only dream of the high moors and the open trails and the pheasant shoots that would fill the happy days of his retirement. Once, about ten years ago, the two of them had gone for a hill walk in the Peaks, and managed twenty miles, a distance that had left Alan scarlet-faced and panting, but utterly thrilled. They had been promising each other to repeat the outing ever since.

Alan's pager bleeped and, signalling a momentary hiatus, he reached for a phone.

Joe looked into the front room, a combined dining room, workroom and storage area, which in his memory was always the music room. Even as he pushed open the door he seemed to hear Jenna's rich contralto, to see her looking up from the upright piano and grinning at him. She practised here every afternoon after school and some evenings too. Now and again Joe would turn the pages for her, though she had to tell him when. For a while she had a singing teacher in Nottingham, then someone important in Manchester who she went to every Saturday, though it took hours. Finally there was the audition for the Royal Northern. The day the acceptance arrived she rushed at him as he came in through the door. She clasped his face in both hands and kissed him excitedly – the first time she'd ever kissed him on the lips – before dancing away across the room. She was almost mad with happiness. Weeks later, she was still flying high. She talked about going professional after graduation, trying for a place in an opera chorus, even, if all went well, a solo career.

Her diplomas hung on the wall. Piano, to Grade VI. Voice,

to Grade VII: one highly commended, three distinctions. Behind the piano was a cast photograph of a school *Mikado*, Jenna centre stage, and one from her days in the church choir. To the left, the usual graduation portrait, posed and over-lit, but which did surprising justice to Jenna's colouring: the pale violet eyes, so clear and vivid, fringed by dark lashes, the milky skin with its even dusting of freckles – she wouldn't have minded one or two, she used to complain furiously, but *all over her face* – and the dark rich hair.

On the piano a book of Mozart lay open, though no one else in the family played. At the far end of the room Jenna's old bicycle stood propped against the dining table. As kids the two of them had pedalled miles together, into town, up across the fields. Jenna wasn't allowed to bicycle alone; a young patient of Alan's had been attacked once, and he was haunted by it. From the large basket strapped to the handlebars it looked as though Helena used the bicycle now.

In the hall, Alan was calling for him.

From old habit, Joe left his coat hanging over the newel post before following Alan into the kitchen. Helena was standing silhouetted against the window, leaning back against the sink with her arms folded low across her waist. She was so still she might have been waiting there for ever.

'How are you, Helena?' As he bent to kiss her, she tilted her cheek a little towards him, but if she offered a reciprocal kiss he missed it.

'Coffee?' she asked.

She made no effort to talk as she pulled out the mugs and spooned the coffee, and Alan filled the silence with a stream of nervy chatter which rang too jolly and too loud.

Eventually Joe said, 'How's Marc, Helena?'

She looked up as if emerging from a dream. 'Oh, he's fine.'

'What's he doing nowadays?'

'Oh, this and that.'

From what Joe remembered, Marc had done little else but

this and that since leaving school. There had been a job in a video shop, he seemed to recall, and something with a homeless charity, though that might have been as a volunteer.

Helena added, 'He wants to train as a teacher.'

Alan chipped in, 'He was talking of doing medicine, but it's no good, he's twenty-seven and he hasn't got the A levels.'

Helena said in a tone of correction, 'It's not the qualifications, it's the time and the cost.' She passed Joe his coffee. 'Teacher training takes a year. He might just be able to do it.'

A look of understanding passed between them – this was what the sale of the damp house by the timber yard was about, this was why Joe was here.

'He can't go into student accommodation at his age. And he wants to keep his cottage going. We can help out a bit, of course we can,' Helena added, 'but you know us, Joe, we were never going to be rich.' In the moment before she turned away, she gave the vestige of a smile, her eyes flickered with brief light, and for an instant it might have been the old days again. Returning to the counter, she drew out a stool and by the time she eased herself onto it the abstraction was back in her face. Joe couldn't help noticing that she wasn't looking her best. Her hair, a dark pewter-grey, was dull and compacted around the crown, as though pressed down by an invisible hat, and sprang out around her face in an unruly halo of waves and spikes. He hadn't seen her for a couple of months, but it seemed to him that she was also dressing with less care. Her cardigan, in an indeterminate tone of beige, had a stain on the front and a frayed sleeve.

Alan was repeating an old refrain. 'No, my love, if you'd married me for my money, you'd have left me years ago, wouldn't you?' His forced laughter filled the room.

'Years ago,' she recited mechanically.

In the hall the phone rang a couple of times and was picked up by the answering machine.

'Well!' Alan rubbed his hands together, as if to summon everyone to the business in hand. 'Well!' His nerve failed him, he shot Helena an anxious glance before appealing to Joe. 'What was it you wanted exactly, Joe?'

'Jenna's national insurance number, if you have it.'

He feigned a look of surprise. 'Ah, *right*.'

'And a photograph, if that's possible.'

'Of course. I'll go and find them. Tell me where to look for the insurance number, my love.' He hovered in front of Helena, poised to do her bidding.

She put her coffee down and slid off her stool without a word.

Alan argued, 'No, no – let *me* go.'

She shook her head as she moved towards the door. 'I know where to look.'

After she'd gone, Alan muttered, 'She's in charge of all that sort of thing.' He wavered between pursuing her and staying put, shifting from one foot and back to the other in a pantomime of indecision. Pursuit finally prevailed, and with an apologetic flap of one hand he hurried out of the room.

Joe rinsed out his mug and stood it in the rack. Nearby, a pinboard hung askew. Amongst the sheaves of paper and postcards three photographs jostled for space. All were of Marc: Marc slumped in a chair, sporting earrings, garishly bleached hair and a scowl; standing on a path wearing a suit at least one size too small and a flower in the buttonhole, expression unreadable; and in a studio pose, stiff and self-conscious. All appeared to have been taken some years ago. The camera had done its best, but there was no escaping the fact that Marc had inherited Alan's physique. He was chubby, with a round face, broad nose and small eyes, but while Alan's looks were thoroughly redeemed by his lively benevolent expression, Marc had the sulky look of a someone who feels that life is failing to deliver.

Alan reappeared, followed by Helena, who was holding an envelope at arm's length, like something that was dangerously hot. Joe looked inside and saw a piece of paper with a number written on it and a long narrow photograph. The photograph wasn't one he'd seen before, but he knew instinctively what it was and his heart tightened.

'I thought you'd have had plenty of pictures of Jenna,' Helena remarked.

Glancing up, he couldn't make out if she'd meant this in a spirit of regret or accusation. 'Mine were all taken rather a long time ago, Helena.'

'Well, that's the most recent we have.'

The photograph showed Jenna on her wedding day. Joe hadn't been there to see her – none of them had – yet the cream dress, the flowers in her hand, the pose, the rhetorical stone doorway in the background, all pointed to the steps of a registry office. Her expression was difficult to read. She wasn't smiling, but her face had a tranquillity that suggested, if not happiness, then acceptance.

The picture was long and narrow because the left-hand side had been cut off; the only remnant of Chetwood's presence was the bend of an elbow, clad in grey, through which Jenna had hooked her right hand. This act of mutilation startled Joe because it had been achieved with savage scissor strokes.

Watching him, Helena remarked, 'I couldn't bear the look on his face.' Taking Joe's silence as a rebuke, she added, 'Too self-satisfied by half.'

It might have been Joe's imagination, but it seemed to him that Helena was still dark with suppressed anger when he kissed her goodbye.

Alan came out with him into the hall. 'The picture wasn't *that* bad,' he muttered under his breath. 'You know how it is with photographs. They can make anyone look a bit off-beam. He was looking down his nose a bit, that's all.'

'I never realised there were wedding pictures.'

'Oh yes. They sent it straight away.'

'Just the one?'

'Yes, yes. That's all you need, isn't it?' He scooped up Joe's jacket and helped him into it. 'Joe? Before you go . . .' He stood in front of the coat-stand, his head framed by the array

of sporting hats. 'The thing is, whatever's happened to Jenna –
and it could be *anything*, couldn't it? Illness . . . depression . . .
accident . . .' He paused, a little expectantly, a little nervously,
as though Joe might want to add some suggestions. 'Well,
whatever it is, there's one thing I'm sure about, Joe – that she
won't have given up her music. She could never give up her
singing. Somehow, she'll have found a way. I know it.'

'She'll have joined a choir, you mean?'

'Absolutely.'

Joe nodded thoughtfully, though he couldn't work out
where this was leading.

'Well, she'll be with a local church, won't she?' Alan
declared. 'Or a choral society. Or working with children. Yes
– a children's choir.'

Joe took his time. 'It's an idea.'

Alan peered at him. 'But you don't think so?'

'I can't see how to make use of it, that's all.'

'Well, we could send her photograph round to churches
and schools, couldn't we?'

'Well . . . I suppose so.'

'Nothing elaborate. A small flier.'

Joe was still trying to muster a response when Alan's pager
went off again and, imploring Joe not to rush away, he hurried
to the phone.

Joe wandered outside into a cold white sun. *Nothing
elaborate*. Even supposing it was possible to track down every
choral society in the country, even before adding the thousands
of churches and schools, and well before counting the phenom-
enal cost of mass mailing, Joe wasn't convinced that Jenna
would have the opportunity, let alone the wish, to sing in a
structured environment, rehearsals every Thursday night,
church twice on Sundays, and trouble for anyone who didn't
turn up regularly. You needed a settled life for that, and
whatever else Jenna's life had been with Chetwood, it could
never be described as settled. Anyway, he told himself, hadn't
her singing always been about joy?

He remembered the last time he had seen her, in the two-roomed flat in Gresham Gardens. No joy then, not in the dowdy décor, not in the worn furnishings with the musty smell, not in Jenna's silence, and not in her eyes, which had the faraway look of a traveller on a long and arduous journey with no end in sight. He saw her sitting on a low stool on the far side of the twilit room, close by the door, as if to steal away at the first opportunity. Joe kept trying to get her talking, but she left the conversation to Chetwood, who was at his sparkling best and in no need of encouragement to talk for the whole world. Then, just as Joe was beginning to despair of speaking to her alone, the doorbell rang and by some miracle it was Chetwood who got up and padded off to answer it. Even before his lanky frame was out of the door, Joe was up and crossing the room. He moved with such speed that Jenna gave a slight gasp and drew back against the wall. And what did he do next, for heaven's sake? The stupidity of it still had the power to make him shudder. Perching on the edge of a chair, he reached over and grasped her wrist, tightly as if to intimidate her. What was going on? Why hadn't she been in touch? Where had they been all this time? Not surprisingly, she stared at him open-mouthed, breathless, at this sudden onslaught. And then – worse still, if that was possible – he fired the same questions at her all over again, even more harshly, like some brainless bully. Jenna inhaled slowly and gazed solemnly at his hand on her wrist until he withdrew it. Then, fixing her gaze on a point just short of his face, offering a thin smile, she announced that she was fine, thank you very much, they'd been travelling a lot, that was all. He pressed her: but why hadn't she been in touch? Oh, she said, it was hard to keep in touch when they were so busy. Somehow they never seemed to have the time.

And then – a different sort of wretchedness at this memory – he lost his nerve, his mind seized solid, and he crouched there, staring at her helplessly, beseechingly, tongue-tied, like some teenager confronted by the woman of his dreams. Finally, he heard himself mumbling the first thing that came into his head. Was she doing any singing? Her eyes made the briefest pass across his face before hovering somewhere by his right shoulder. No, she said. Didn't she miss it? She had to think about that. Hardly ever, she said at last. Then, in her only unprompted offering of the evening, she said that if she wanted to sing she sometimes found the nearest church and went to evensong. At this, Joe had a ludicrous image of her in the flat shoes, sensible coat and headscarf of a devout church-going lady, a sad figure in the sparsely filled pews, singing softly under the discordant bellows of the elderly congregation, and he thought violently: My God, Jenna, has it really come to this?

The thought recharged his sense of urgency, but, just as he remembered all the things he'd meant to say, Chetwood's smooth irresistible voice sang out from the stairs.

Now, all these years later, the unspoken questions still reverberated mercilessly around Joe's head. Why hadn't he come straight out and asked her what was wrong? Why hadn't he made the speech of an old and devoted friend who wanted nothing more than to help in any way he could? Why hadn't he offered to do anything, go anywhere, keep any secret under the sun – or simply to shut up and listen if that was what she wanted. Why, for God's sake, hadn't he just asked her out to lunch?

As it was, Chetwood had spoken for both of them. Easily, amenably, seemingly unaware of any problem. They'd been travelling a lot, he said; they were going to travel a whole lot more. They felt bad about not seeing more of their friends; once they'd found a place to live they'd make more of an effort. They might settle in the country. Or abroad. Or half and half. They really hadn't made up their minds. Once they'd decided, they'd let Joe know, of course they would. Of course . . .

Then Chetwood was asking Joe about his life, question after question, no diversions allowed, and grinning his piratical grin. 'So you're a City shark-man, Joe. All teeth and bite. A limb-from-limb merchant.'

Then someone had been in a rush – he supposed it was Chetwood – and they were saying goodbye. At the door Jenna had kissed Joe lightly on the cheek before dropping her eyes and stepping back into the sanctuary of the room.

Reliving the frustration and the failure four years later, Joe wandered down to the road and back again between beds of bedraggled lavender and withered roses. A battered car distracted him as it drew up in front of the house. The driver was peering Joe's way, but it wasn't until he clambered out that Joe recognised Marc.

Marc's wave was so spontaneous that Joe felt sure he must have mistaken him for someone else and almost looked over his shoulder. Yet when Marc came striding up the path, a short purposeful figure on sturdy legs, it was to declare without hesitation, 'Ah, Joe. Glad to have found you.'

The brisk smile, like the wave, took Joe by surprise. At their last meeting two or more years ago he had been left with the firm impression that, so far as Marc was concerned, Joe was irredeemably damned by his association with Chetwood.

Marc was dressed in jeans, trainers and a puffy quilted jacket which, with his round face, gave him an unfortunate resemblance to the Michelin man. He had the plump boy's stance, legs braced, feet out-turned, and the plump boy's eyes, seemingly too small and close together for his face. His lips were thin and puckered with an air of fussy concern.

'Dad told me you were coming by,' he announced in his reedy voice, 'and I was just a little concerned.'

'Oh?'

'I fear that a few mixed messages may have entered into the equation somewhere along the line. And it would be unfortunate if they were not resolved at the earliest possible opportunity.'

The pomposity was new. So was the accent, located at some politically correct point between the North of England

and the Essex marshes, complete with a spattering of sludgy consonants and wide vowels.

'What's the problem?'

'Dad's asked you to help look for my sister, has he?'

'Yes. And I'll be glad to do whatever I can.'

Marc shook his head with a knowing little smile of derision. 'Kind of you to offer, but I really don't think it would be appropriate, do you? Because – correct me if I'm wrong – you don't have any expertise in this area, do you?'

'Well . . .'

'You're not qualified in the field of missing persons.'

'No. Is anyone?'

Marc smiled in the manner of someone who's prepared to be extraordinarily charitable under trying circumstances. 'It is a highly specialised area.'

'Well, your father seems to think I can help.'

'Yes, yes. But with him – well, wishful thinking tends to overcome reality, doesn't it? I did try to make him understand. I did point out that you didn't have the skills. You and others. In the last two weeks he must have asked the entire neighbourhood. The local MP. Some county councillor guy. The *vicar*.' A taut sigh of forbearance, a roll of the button eyes. 'It'll be the local psychic next. He's met her, you see, and that's all it takes. Immediately convinced they're going to be able to help. Though what they're meant to do is a total mystery. Pull off a miracle? Wave a magic wand? No, he can't seem to understand that they're never going to have the *first idea*.' This in a tone that left Joe in no doubt that he himself had been consigned to the ranks of these well-meaning inadequates. 'So,' Marc finished on a brisk note, 'I can only thank you for coming and apologise for any inconvenience that may have been caused. You didn't make the journey specially, I hope?'

Joe shook his head slowly.

'Good.' Marc tilted his head and pulled in his thin lips, in the manner of someone who has made his point.

Joe said, 'I may not be an expert – as you so rightly say – but I'd still like to help if I can.'

A tight smile. 'Much appreciated, Joe. But it's really not required.'

'There are a few checks I can get done. I was just telling your father. It's only basic stuff, but you never know.'

'*Oh?*' A elaborate display of bewilderment. 'What sort of checks?'

'From data banks, that sort of thing.'

'You mean the standard trawl through the police computer?' An undisguised smile of satisfaction. 'I instigated that procedure *months* ago.'

Marc had caught Joe by surprise, and he knew it.

'Alan didn't say anything.'

'No, *well*.'

'So . . . do I take it you've some other ideas, then?'

'I don't follow,' Marc said with deadly patience.

'Ways of finding Jenna.'

Marc frowned in a rhetorical expression of perplexity. 'Funny – I thought I'd made myself clear just now. Apparently not. The situation' – he went slowly, as though spelling it out to a child – 'is that we're going to handle this ourselves, Joe. In our own way.' In his most officious tone, he added: 'No help required.' This was delivered as a closing statement, with a tuck of the chin into the thick neck and a move towards the house.

'Who's the *we*, Marc?' Joe said to his retreating back. 'I'm a bit confused.'

He didn't reply and after a moment Joe followed him into the house. 'Who's the we, Marc, if it's not your parents?'

He was pulling off his jacket to reveal a seriously overstretched T-shirt. 'It's like I explained, Joe. Twice now, I think?' He sucked in his breath with exaggerated forbearance. 'Yes – *twice*. It's none of your fucking business.' He dumped his jacket on the stairs. Under the taut T-shirt, his large body was surprisingly solid. His muscles had the sort of tone that only comes from long hours in the gym. As if to emphasise his new vigour, he stood with his head thrust slightly forward and his hands hanging loosely at his sides in the stance of the fighter ready to spring. The button eyes glinted. 'Tell me, Joe,' he added darkly, 'don't you think you've done quite enough damage already, without wanting to do a whole lot more?'

Ah, thought Joe, here we have it. Is this what all this unpleasantness is really about? Just a golden opportunity to put me in my place? Is this the real agenda?

Joe let the remark pass with a small shrug: of acceptance or denial, Marc could make up his own mind.

A faint sound came from the kitchen, a footfall, a swish of the door, and Helena appeared. She greeted Marc with a swift kiss on the cheek. 'How are you, darling?' Ignoring Marc's lingering glower, she touched his arm. 'Would you be a dear and bring the bins in for me?'

Marc shot her a look of sharp resentment, as though he had far more important things to do with his life, before capitulating with bad grace and marching off with a last dark squint in Joe's direction.

Helena said, 'Alan's stuck on the phone, Joe. He said not to wait and he'll call you.'

Opening the front door, she led the way outside and with a backward glance pulled the door closed behind them. There was a sharp wind now, and she had no coat, only the frayed cardigan.

'Don't get cold,' Joe said.

'I wish this stupid house business had never come up,' she cried harshly. 'I knew it'd be nothing but trouble.'

'Marc's just warned me off.'

'I heard. Take no notice, Joe.'

'I appear to be the big bad villain.'

'Oh, it's not about *you*, Joe. No . . .' Her eyes ranged unhappily over the garden. 'It's about Jenna. I was always careful to treat them the same, Joe. No favouritism. Share and share alike. But however hard you try, they end up seeing things differently. Marc always felt like second best. It was the singing, of course. All that adulation for Jenna. All that praise. Always being the centre of attention. He felt he could never match up. Forever cast as Jenna's little brother. You must have realised that, Joe. You must have seen it for yourself. *Surely.*' She threw him a glance that was almost angry. 'So when *this* came up . . . Oh, he wants his share of the money, yes. But he's absolutely obsessed with organising the whole search. With taking charge.'

And with being centre stage, Joe thought. 'But what's he planning?' he asked Helena. 'What's he got in mind?'

'We've no idea. He's got some friends who're helping, I think. In the police? In the social services? I'm not sure. He won't tell us. He says to leave it to him. And quite honestly, Joe, I'd rather just let him get on with it. Anything for a quiet life. If I had my way we'd simply take out a second mortgage and hand him the money. But that's not allowed. No, we have to have this awful money all tied up with finding Jenna, so that we can all feel twice as bad if it doesn't work out. *Ridiculous.*' With a shiver, she pulled her cardigan tighter across her waist.

Joe slipped an arm round her shoulders.

'You will find her, won't you, Joe?'

He squeezed her shoulder. 'I'll do all I can – you know that.'

'Oh, not for me, Joe!' she announced dismissively. 'No – I gave up on Jenna long ago. Don't worry about me! And don't worry about Marc either. No, if you do it for anyone, Joe, do it for Alan. Do it for *him.*'

'Of course.'

Turning to face him, she grasped his arm, and her eyes were shining with a desperate light. 'No, no,' she argued as though he had missed the point. 'He's not well, Joe. That's why we have to find her. He's not at all well, and this is killing him.'

Joe stared at her, a cold feeling in the pit of his stomach.

'What do you mean, not well? What's wrong with him, Helena?'

She dropped her hand. 'Oh, chronic hypertension. Sky-high cholesterol. Other things he's probably not telling me about. Everything that comes from stress and overwork and not sleeping properly. But really it's Jenna. That's what's eating him up, Joe. He never stops worrying about her, not for a single second. It got to the point where I couldn't stand him talking about it any longer, I began walking out of the room every time he started, otherwise he'd go on for hours and hours. Just torturing himself. Going over and over the same old ground. And for what? To make himself ill. To kill himself. It was driving me wild!'

'Is he seeing someone about the hypertension?'

'The cardiologist, yes. Given half a chance, he'd forget to take the drugs of course. But it won't guard him against worry, Joe. That's what gets people in the end.'

Joe stepped forward and embraced her. The halo of unkempt hair lay close against his cheek, and he thought he caught a hint of the scent she used to wear when he was young.

'Take care, Joe,' she said, pulling away.

Walking away, he turned to wave but she had already closed the door.

He was just about to drive off when he heard a shout and saw Alan trotting rapidly down the path towards him. 'Joe! Joe!'

Catching his breath, laughing at the ridiculous amount of time it took him to speak, Alan passed a bright-yellow envelope through the window. 'Just – thought – I'd show you – this, Joe.'

Joe pulled out a birthday card with a happy sixtieth greeting on the front and a cheery little rhyme inside. Beneath the rhyme, a happy-face with a single X beside it had been drawn in black ink.

Still panting hard, Alan wheezed, 'See, Joe – just one X. Usually she covered the thing in Xs. Just covered it. She only ever drew one X when—' He paused, he gave Joe an awkward glance. 'Do you remember when she failed that scholarship, Joe? The one to the Royal Academy?'

'I remember.'

'Well, she gave me a card with a single X then. Just a small X under the happy-face, to show she was unhappy. And when she first went to college, when she was homesick, she sent me another one then. It was when she was unhappy.' He looked up again. 'What do you think, Joe?'

Turning to the envelope, Joe tried to make out the post-mark, but it lay immediately over the stamp and, apart from the letter E and what might have been an R, was too smudged to read.

Alan was watching his face anxiously. 'What do you think? Is it Leicester?'

'I can't tell.'

'If it's Leicester . . . Well, some of my patients work there.'

'Can you leave it with me?'

'Of course!'

'No promises.'

But Alan was incapable of hiding much in his face, certainly nothing as fundamental as hope. 'Thank you, Joe! Thank you.' He clasped Joe's hand before stepping back and giving a wave like a salute.

Joe started off then stopped again to call back, 'We'll go for that walk at Christmas, shall we?'

Alan's expression lit up.

'The Peaks? And lunch at a country pub?'

'You bet!'

When Joe glanced in his rear-view mirror, Alan was still smiling, his arms crossed over his chest, as if to resist the lure of the tobacco pouch.

Chapter Three

———•———

JOE HEARD her before he saw her: the murmur of a soft voice floating down from the landing above. Rounding the turn of the stairs, he saw through the wrought-iron banisters first the slim legs sheathed in tight black jeans, then the head of long pale hair and finally the mobile clamped to one ear.

Catching sight of him, Sarah said something into the phone and snapped it shut. 'Traffic?'

'Horrendous.' He dumped the shopping on the top step and went to embrace her. 'Why didn't you let yourself in?'

'How?'

'With the key.'

'I don't have a key.'

'What happened to the one I gave you this morning?'

'I posted it under the door.'

'You should have kept it.'

She looked appalled at this idea. 'Oh no, I couldn't have done that.'

As soon as he'd opened the door, and even before he'd turned on any lights, she scooped up the discarded key from the floor and placed it ostentatiously on the radiator shelf, as if to emphasise that she made no claims to it, either now or in the future, and that it had been an indignity to suggest she would.

Joe wasn't sure what law of relationship etiquette he'd broken but he was prepared to bow humbly to her judgement. At some point in the last twelve hours he'd decided that despite the mixed messages over Morocco he didn't intend to give up

on her. It seemed to him that her cool enclosed nature com-
plemented his own more variable temperament rather well,
that her practicality was a welcome prop in times of uncertainty, and that in an odd way they might rub along quite well
together. Armed with this thought he went to help her off with
her jacket, but she was too quick for him, slipping it off in one
rapid movement and throwing it onto the sofa.

'I'm gasping for some water,' she announced, heading for
the kitchen.

He followed with the shopping. 'How were your family?'
he asked solicitously.

'Oh, loathing the weather, the way they do.' Her parents
lived in Kent, he'd gathered, somewhere near Faversham, and
were old for parents, over seventy.

She helped him unpack the shopping. 'And your father?'

'Battling the world, as usual.'

'The negligence case?'

'Oh, *always.*'

With quiet efficiency, she began to organise the dinner
ingredients into groups: vegetables on the chopping board,
cheese and fruit to one side, chicken near the stove. 'What's his
legal argument exactly?'

'For the last two years it's been the Human Rights Act. I
forget which article.'

'And what are his chances?'

He drew the cork on the vintage Burgundy he'd bought on
a whim at a ridiculous price. 'None, so far as I can gather. But
to be honest I don't really know. I keep well out of it.'

'But it was what got you started, wasn't it? With the law.'

He had given Sarah the bare outlines of the story two or
three weeks ago because she'd asked about it, but it wasn't a
subject he ever chose to bring up. He was particularly uncom-
fortable when he saw a neat equation looming: filial loss added
to medical negligence equals a burning sense of injustice,
because it wasn't the way it was with him, never had been.

'The first lot of lawyers who got their teeth into my father were inept,' he said carefully. 'I sure as hell knew I wanted to do better than them.'

'But you didn't choose medical negligence.'

'Christ, no,' Joe shot back, wondering at how little she had understood him. 'When I had a missionary father? A man who lived, breathed, slept medical negligence? A man who'd give his right arm – his *soul* – to have his day in court? No, correction – *every* day in court. Who'd be looking over my shoulder every second of my working life, and probably my non-working life too, because there's no difference to him. Day, night, it's a vocation, you take your vows, you follow the gospel. No, I could never have been one of the faithful.'

'All the same, fighting for the underdog – wouldn't that have been more your style?'

'Why? Do I look like someone with a conscience?'

She regarded him in open appraisal. 'Yes. Yes, you do.'

He laughed. 'But we can't all take up worthy causes, can we?'

She said with strange intensity, 'But you've taken on the cause of Jennifer Chetwood.'

He made a business of opening the wine. 'I'm trying to find her, which is rather different. And she's not a *cause*.'

Sarah's face took on an expression he'd noticed before, a lowering of the eyes and a twitching of the mouth, which seemed to signal conclusions being drawn and carefully stored away. Looking up again, she said crisply, 'Well, I'm sorry to say that Mrs Chetwood is not going to be found very easily.'

Joe paused, corkscrew in mid-air. 'Why?'

'The searches have drawn a blank.'

'They're done already?'

'Sure. I said it wouldn't take long.'

'But you've been away.'

'I didn't do it myself, Joe. *Hardly*. But my contact – he was in his office all day, he had the time.'

'But what about the national insurance number? I was going to give it to you.'

'Oh, my man managed to find it off the computer, no trouble.'

The wine forgotten, Joe went and sat down at the hinged flap that served as his breakfast table. 'So ... No sign at all?'

Sarah brought the wine and the glasses and sat down opposite. The table was so small that their knees touched. 'A complete blank,' she announced in the measured tone of a report. 'Nothing under Jennifer Chetwood, and nothing under Laskey. Nothing active on the national insurance number. She hasn't claimed benefits, not for unemployment and not for sickness, she hasn't been admitted to hospital, not recently anyway, and she hasn't died and she hasn't had a baby. She last filed an income tax return four years ago. No telephone line in either of her names, no mobile phone, no gas or electricity accounts, no council tax, no entry on a UK electoral register, no outstanding debts or county court judgements against her.'

'Abroad,' Joe muttered, more to himself than to Sarah.

Still at full professional stride, Sarah continued her effortless display of memory. 'No credit cards either, none that have been used anywhere in the world in the last four years at any rate. She hasn't appeared on the news pages of any newspapers, either national or local. She hasn't incurred any penalty points on her driving licence. She hasn't acquired a criminal record. There's no car registered in her name, nor any other motor vehicle.'

'The last trace, then?'

'The address in Gresham Gardens. She's still registered with a local GP there, but it's probably by default. Just because her name's never been transferred to another doctor's list.' Sarah added wistfully, 'For a moment I thought we might have got something when the utility records for Gresham Gardens showed the occupier of the flat to be someone called Marsh. I thought it might be a name the Chetwoods had used, but this Marsh, whoever he was, had been there for some time beforehand and went on paying the bills for two years after the Chetwoods left, so I would imagine he was just the landlord, subletting.' She poured the wine, and went on with the same air of concentration. 'So, after drawing a blank on *her*, my contact tried *him*. James Robert Chetwood. Family home Weston Manor Farm, Coln Rogers, Gloucestershire.'

'And I said Wiltshire.'

'Oh, but it was easy enough to find. Chetwood's an unusual name. It's the Joneses and Patels that cause all the problems.'

'So?'

'Nothing in any of the data banks. Though *he*'s been off the map for longer than *she* has. Five years without filing a tax return. Last occupation, director of a company called Amrita. Fellow director, Mr Asif Ebrahim. Stated business: import, goods unspecified. You said rugs, I think?'

'And other ethnic stuff. Fabrics, pots, lamps, that garden furniture – what is it? – wicker? Cane? Anything he happened to see on his travels, really.'

'Well, the company's moribund now.'

'My God, he's been bloody thorough, hasn't he?' Joe's anger came out of nowhere and took him by surprise. 'Gone and fallen off the edge of the bloody planet.'

Ignoring this outburst, Sarah said, 'Was his business a success?'

Joe gave a bark of a laugh. 'I wouldn't have said business was Chetwood's strong point. He put in the minimum of effort. Only ever wanted enough money to keep the wolf from the door.'

'And did the company have a base? A warehouse? An office?'

'Don't think so. I always had the feeling he ran it with a mobile phone and the back of an envelope. He was allergic to paperwork, ignored it on principle. I'm surprised he got around to setting up a company at all.'

'Perhaps Mr Ebrahim was the commercial half of the partnership.'

'I never met Mr Ebrahim.'

'But Chetwood travelled to buy the stock?'

'He travelled all the time, yes.'

'Did he go on his own or with her?'

Suddenly Joe was back five years, to a summer day at the farmhouse outside Hereford. He was standing in the kitchen, watching Jenna unfold a length of Indian silk. The silk was ruby red. It fired with gold when it caught the sun. As she pulled it higher into the air, the sun caught her dress too, cutting through the flimsy cotton until she might have been standing there in naked silhouette. She was talking, but it was a while before he heard what she said. *I could have stayed for months, Joe! Oh, the beauty of the place, and the people, and the crazy music, just like a treeful of birds, and the way everyone looks as though they've found the secret of life.* Then her mischievous laugh. *But I didn't love the sanitation, Joe. And the stench. They haven't found the secret of that yet! Which makes me a bit of a poser, doesn't it? A bit of a fake.* She'd laughed again, almost naked in the sunlight.

The image was still clear in his mind as he answered Sarah. 'They went to India together a few times in the early days. But then Chetwood began to go on his own, I'm not sure why.'

'When you say the early days?'

'I mean the first couple of years they were together.'

'That's when you still saw them?'

'Not often – but yes, I still saw them. They rented this farm-house near Hereford.'

'What was it called?'

'Pawsey Farm. Funny name.'

'And later?'

'Oh, I never saw them then. Apart from that time in Gresham Gardens.'

'Well, I can tell you one thing, for what it's worth. If she's still living in this country, she can't have done any travelling in the last eighteen months. She hasn't renewed her passport, you see. It's out of date.'

Joe stared at her while he tried to make sense of this. 'They can't be abroad, then?'

'I'm not sure that quite follows, does it? She could be living abroad, and unable to leave. Forced to stay put. Or perfectly happy to stay put.'

Groaning, Joe rubbed both hands down his face. 'Oh well. I never thought it was going to be easy. I sort of knew they weren't going to turn up just like that. But thanks all the same, Sarah. And thank your man, will you, for covering so much ground in such a short time.'

'Oh, it's no skin off his nose. Makes a change from his usual suspects.' Getting up, she went to the counter and began to unwrap the vegetables. 'But I certainly wouldn't give up yet, Joe. Family and friends are still your best bet, you know. Historically. Statistically. People usually get found because they've kept in contact with someone from their past.'

'Jenna hasn't kept in touch with anyone, I know she hasn't. And Chetwood – well, I'd have heard.'

Sarah turned, knife in hand. 'Are you sure about that? It could be anyone. Childhood friend, drinking mate, business associate, favourite granny, brother, sister, travelling companion. What about Mr Ebrahim? What about Chetwood's family? His old friends?'

'Not his family,' Joe declared unhesitatingly. 'No love lost there.'

'But they might know of someone. You'd be surprised.'

'Would I?'

'It's definitely worth a try.'

Joe watched her chopping the carrots, working the knife like a professional, sweeping the slices expertly off the board into the wok, and felt a fresh wave of gratitude.

Coming up behind her, he looped his arms round her waist. Half joking but half serious too, he said, 'What would I do without you?'

But, for Sarah, praise belonged to the same category as

tenderness, it was definitely suspect, and she frowned disap-
provingly as she reached for the potatoes.

'Okay,' Joe announced brightly, 'if it's a family connection
you're looking for . . .' He went and fetched Alan's birthday
card.

Wiping her hands on a towel, Sarah examined the card.
'There's no obvious reason to think it's from *her* though, is
there?'

'Except she always signed with a happy-face just like this.
And a single X when she was unhappy. And the postmark
doesn't seem to be local.'

She took the envelope from him and peered at it closely.

He asked tentatively, 'No chance of your contact getting it
unscrambled, I suppose?'

'Forensic stuff is farmed out, requisitioned, *accounted for*.
It's not like running something through a computer. No, it
won't be possible, I'm afraid. No chance. Sorry.'

'Okay.'

'It's really too difficult,' she said, as though he'd continued
to argue the point. 'Too many *procedures*.'

Nevertheless, before they went to bed he saw her examining
the envelope again, holding it up close to a table lamp and
moving it this way and that. And the next morning, before she
left to do her Christmas shopping, he found her wrapping the
envelope in a plastic bag and putting in her handbag. She said
in a curt tone, 'There's an expert witness we used in a benefit
fraud the other day. No promises though.' Then, as if to cover
herself: 'I still say *his* family's your best bet, Joe. By a long
way. Why don't you go and ask them?'

She made it sound straightforward, but nothing about
Chetwood had ever been straightforward, certainly not what
he chose to represent as his history, an ever-shifting mixture of
fact, obfuscation and downright fantasy. Only once had Joe
heard him talk about his family in any serious way, and that
was barely an hour after they'd met. The conversation, like

everything else about that night, was emblazoned on Joe's memory, forever fixed by the image of a tall figure balanced on a parapet, a feather's touch from death.

It began with a shout.

He was lying on his bed where he had fallen, half-undressed and drifting towards sleep. It was a Saturday night in the hall of residence, five weeks into his first term at Bristol, and for once Joe had managed to stay the manageable side of drunk. In every other way, though, the big night of the week had followed the usual pattern. The party had begun in the ground-floor bar soon after six with the cheapest drinks, the more the better, beer and throat-stripping Bulgarian red which left stains on your teeth and time-bombs in your head, then, following some immutable timetable, the crowd had gravitated upstairs, into the corridors and communal kitchens and rooms that boasted low lights and music systems, until every doorway seemed to disgorge smoke, illegal and otherwise, the stink of spilt beer and the murmur of prostrate bodies, glimpsed darkly through the fug.

The shout actually sounded twice. The first time, it barely registered on Joe's consciousness: just another drunken yell in the general din. The second time, though, it came at a roar from bang outside his door with no possibility of missing a single word.

'Some stupid bastard on the roof!'

Joe might still have ignored it if the same voice hadn't laughed raucously, 'For Chris' sake, I'm telling you for real – there's some guy doing a fucking balancing act on the fucking parapet.'

Even then, Joe emerged from his soporific haze with huge reluctance. It had to be a joke. No one would laugh like that unless it was a joke. And a parapet didn't necessarily have to be perched over gut-dropping infinity to be a real-live authentic parapet, especially when described by a giggling wine-head.

He got up before he could change his mind, rolling out of bed and pulling on some trousers and reaching for the door in one unified movement. He found the owner of the voice propped against the wall opposite and extracted some slurred directions which led him up to the next floor, to the end of a corridor where six or seven people were gathered tensely around an open window. Outside, holding on to the frame, a girl was crouching in a gutter behind a low parapet, pleading with the rooftop wanderer, somewhere out of view to the right.

The girl came to a despondent halt and, looking back at the waiting group, shrugged helplessly. A ginger-haired guy with an angry high-pitched voice announced that he was going to phone for the emergency services and strode off self-importantly.

The group was clustered tightly round the window. A girl backed out to let Joe in, gesturing him forward as if to hand over responsibility. Thrusting his head out of the window, Joe saw the parapet-walker just three or four yards away, clearly visible against a near-full moon, standing immobile on the ledge. He also saw the bricks sitting at intervals along the parapet, but didn't realise their significance. Instead, he took in the stillness of the tall figure, the straight back, the hands hanging loosely but precisely at his sides, the up-tilted face and seemingly absorbed gaze, and said, 'Good view tonight?'

'Absolutely,' came the soft unhurried reply. 'Really remarkable.'

'And if someone's called the emergency services?'

'Oh *shit*. Have they really?'

'Afraid so.'

A groan. 'No innocent deed ever goes unpunished.'

Even then he took his time. He stretched both arms out very wide, palms down, fingers rigid, like someone preparing to dive, and took a long slow breath before lowering his arms and stepping backwards into the gutter.

From somewhere far below, a ragged cheer went up, some

voices shouted friendly exhortations, and the walker raised a hand in salute, like a sportsman leaving the pitch.

Joe stood back. The knot of spectators unravelled itself to let the girl clamber in through the window, then drew back still further as Chetwood appeared and dropped lightly down onto the floor. There was a silence, a moment of almost farcical suspense, before the group realised that Chetwood's quizzical smile was all they were going to get by way of an explanation, and then the recriminations began, a couple of jibes that rapidly ballooned into a display of collective anger. Chetwood stared at them with an air of bafflement before catching Joe's eye and gesturing him away with a tip of his head.

Chetwood set a fast pace until they reached the gates, when he slowed to take a backward glance over his shoulder. Following his gaze, Joe saw a home-made banner hanging from the recently occupied parapet. *Druce Money is Blood Money.*

'Who's Druce?' Joe asked as they continued into the town.

'*What* is Druce. An arms company. I wanted to hang it on the science building, but the roof's locked.'

'What's the deal?'

'The *deal*?' He winced painfully at the word. 'The deal is that Druce kills more people in Africa than malaria and old age put together, and the university's colluding in a disgusting PR whitewash by letting them endow the new science block.'

This kept Joe quiet for some time; he didn't even know there was a new science block.

They reached shops and brightly lit windows. 'I thought they were going to lynch me back there,' his new companion commented without apparent resentment.

'You frightened them. They thought you were going to jump.'

'Which just goes to show how wrong people can be when they think in narrow formulaic terms.'

'Without better information you can't really blame them.'

'But I told them I was okay.'

'Come on. Not a lot of people could do what you did

without running a high risk of being very *un*-okay. Ending up as a nasty muddle on the ground. Especially after a few drinks.'

His fellow walker shot him an approving look, and Joe had the feeling he had gone some way to redeeming himself for his ignorance of Druce.

'A *muddle*. Yes, that's good. A muddle it is. But you see, I never drink.'

'They weren't to know that though, were they?'

'Well, I've never fallen yet. And I certainly don't intend to start now.'

Joe slowed. 'You do this regularly?'

The tall figure walked on for a couple of yards before turning and standing in the fluorescent glare of a chemist's window, which leached all colour from his skin. With his mass of wavy dark hair, his striking eyes and strong features, his eyebrows like two brush-strokes, he might have been a still photograph in black and white. 'Look, I stayed up there to rescue a cat, that's all. I heard the thing crying and I thought it needed help, and when I got to it of course the bloody thing laughed in my face and hopped away over the roof. So on my way back I decided to look for a star or two. Wanted to find Altair, but no go. Too many street lights.' He turned up one palm in a gesture of having made his case. 'So, you see, I was a consenting adult, doing my thing in private. No need for everyone to go ballistic.'

It wouldn't be the last time that one of Chetwood's explanations left Joe with the suspicion that he'd been presented with something colourful that boiled down to rather less than the truth. 'You were playing to the crowd.'

'On the contrary – I was ignoring them.'

Feeling the need to argue against his complacency, Joe said, 'You knew they were worried though. You could easily have come in before you did.'

Chetwood considered this with apparent gravity. 'You're right,' he said at last. 'What a bad person I am.'

And with that he came forward almost shyly and proffered a hand. 'I'm Chetwood. And you're?'

'Joe McGrath. Reading law.'

'*Law*.' He sucked in an admiring breath. 'How very . . . upright.'

'You?' Joe asked automatically.

'Ah well, the university and I seem to disagree on that. I—'

He broke off as a siren whooped, coming closer. They turned to see a fire engine shoot across an intersection that led to the hall of residence.

'Oops,' Chetwood said.

'We should go and tell them.'

'I think not. Explanations, Joe – they never do any good.'

The night was cold, Joe's T-shirt was thin. He would have turned back then but Chetwood wouldn't hear of it. 'You saved me from the mob,' he said. 'The least I can do is buy you breakfast.'

Joe wavered. For years afterwards, he would remember how close he had come to heading home and how different his life might have been if he had. As it was, Chetwood turned and walked on and began to talk to Joe as if he was right behind him, which, after striding fast to catch up, he was.

'In the East, you know, they regard outer balance as a sign of inner harmony. Of equilibrium and spiritual peace . . . Nice if you can get it.' With more along the same lines, delivered in a discursive style, Chetwood led the way unerringly to a steamy all-night café at the bottom of town, where they sat at a table patterned with cigarette burns and the milky smears of a hasty cloth, and ordered bacon and eggs.

Sliding an elbow onto the table, propping his head low on one hand, Chetwood fixed Joe with a benign gaze and began to ask questions in a desultory way. Where did Joe came from? What sort of school had he been to? What family did he have? Out of habit or caution, Joe kept his replies short, but Chetwood weighed each at length, as if fitting them into an altogether larger picture. 'Just a father,' he repeated back to Joe. 'No mother?'

'No. She died.'

'No sisters or brothers?'

'No.'

'Stepmother? Second family?'

Joe shook his head.

Chetwood sat up a little and scrutinised Joe afresh. 'Get on with him?'

'My father? Oh, you know . . . So-so.' Joe asked quickly, 'And what about you? What family do you have?'

'Mine? Ah, I'm like you, Joe. We're two of a kind, with only a father to our poor orphan names. Though mine's what you might call *absentee*. Absent in mind and spirit, that is. The bodily part makes the odd nightmare appearance now and again.' At this, his slightly hooded eyes took on a rather demonic slant.

'Sisters and brothers?'

A pause during which Chetwood seemed to lose focus. 'Oh, enormously,' he murmured at last.

Moving on uncertainly, Joe asked Chetwood where he lived. But this subject didn't seem to sit much more easily with him than the one before.

'I don't live anywhere,' he announced at last. 'If I do anything at all, I probably camp.'

The conversation halted as the food was slapped down onto the table in front of them. Chetwood plunged a knife straight into his egg yolks. 'Tell me something, Joe,' he asked in a voice that had regained all its former thoughtfulness, 'what do you hope to get out of your time in this place?'

'Apart from a decent degree, you mean? Well—'

'I have to say I'd count a degree as one of the more dubious benefits.'

Joe gave an unconvincing laugh. 'Trick question, was it?'

'Not at all. No, if you say that's the main purpose . . .'

Upending the ketchup bottle, Chetwood traced an elaborate crimson ribbon over his food. 'Okay, so apart from this degree, what else will you get from being here?'

'Hell . . . I don't know.'

'But you must know.' This was delivered in a tone of polite rebuke.

'Well, I suppose I'm hoping to enjoy the course. And to have a good time. Play some football. Meet a few people. And waste huge amounts of time. All the things students usually do.'

At this, Chetwood abandoned his knife and fork and said in a tone of pained reason, 'But, Joe, just a generation ago students felt bound to question society's assumptions. They didn't arrive at college like they do now, deeply middle-aged and deeply middle-class, with a complete set of received values picked up at Comet, along with the new TV. They didn't pride themselves on being moral apostates. They didn't come to university with the sole ambition of getting jobs that would make them obscene amounts of money, exhibiting their greed like a badge of honour.'

Trying to remember what apostate meant, Joe said, 'But most of us have got to get good jobs to pay off our loans.'

'Sure. But does that mean leaving all the important issues to the multinationals and the drug companies and the arms traders and the stock market? Because don't kid yourself, Joe, we're letting the robber barons shape our society, take all the important decisions.'

It was a long time since Joe had tasted such good bacon, and it was all he could do not to exhibit unrestricted greed, albeit of a non-mercenary kind, while Chetwood progressed his argument through Africa, India and the developed world via the scandalous patenting of life-saving drugs, the short-termism of the City, and Western support for corrupt regimes.

'We've lost our spiritual values,' Chetwood concluded with passionate despair. 'People are happy to live in a moral and ethical void. They've lost all sense of mystery and gratitude and wonder. They talk about fulfilment when they mean self-gratification. They talk about balance when they mean having it all. They talk about love when they mean control.'

'But there're plenty of people who care about the world,' Joe ventured at last.

'*Are* there, Joe?' Chetwood asked earnestly. 'Just tell me where they are, because *I* don't seem to meet any of them.'

'Well . . . Greenpeace has a huge membership.'

'That's just Middle England getting cosy about whales, surely?'

'What about the huge numbers of people who do voluntary work then? The thousands who do something for nothing every day? You don't have to have a formal belief system to be a good person.'

In one of those rapid changes of mood that was to be so characteristic of him, Chetwood blinked and gave the ghost of a smile. 'So it's enough to *do*, is it, Joe? Is that what you're saying? That we should all stop our whingeing and go out into the world and *do*?'

'I suppose.'

'*By your deeds shall you be known.* Is that it?'

'Well, yes.'

'What should I go and do then?'

Joe shrugged and wolfed down his bacon. It wasn't until a couple of days later, when he found Chetwood waiting in his room, picking unenthusiastically through his small collection of novels, that Joe realised he was serious.

'You're right, Joe,' he remarked, as if no time had passed since their last talk. 'The doing is everything. But the *what* — that's everything too. And that's the bloody problem.'

Over the next few weeks Chetwood returned to the idea spasmodically, usually late at night after a party or a meal at the local curry house, after the rest of the group — nearly always Joe's friends — had drifted away. Joe couldn't remember their conversations now; only that, once launched on the subject, Chetwood worried at it like a loose tooth, coming at it from different angles, unable to leave it alone. Even at his most gregarious – and, stone cold sober, Chetwood could be as silly as the rest of them – Joe sensed that the issue of 'what to do' was never far from his mind.

Two other conversations from that autumn stuck in Joe's memory. The first when Chetwood glanced down at Joe's open wallet and saw, among the concertina of photographs, a picture of Jenna.

'Girlfriend, Joe?'

'More of a sister. We grew up together.'

'A sister. Will we meet her?'

'Probably not. She's in Manchester. At the Royal Northern.'

'Ah. And what does she play?'

'She sings.'

'She *sings*.' He seemed enchanted by the idea. 'So, not just the face of an angel, but the voice too.'

'We think so,' said Joe, laughing, though he couldn't have said why.

'But trapped in the cold north.'

'She might come down in the summer. She wants to go to Glastonbury.'

With a last look at the photograph, Chetwood appeared to lose interest. 'Perhaps it's better if angels don't travel.'

The second conversation came in the all-night café, when they were eating egg and chips after a late film. Chetwood announced he was going climbing in the Lake District at New Year.

'What, parapet-walking on sheet ice?'

Chetwood frowned at him. 'Parapets have never been my thing.'

'You said you'd done it before.'

The dark eyes narrowed. 'It was roofs. When I was a kid – roofs.'

'Star-gazing?'

'At seven? Don't be ridiculous. No, it was the only place I

could be sure of not getting any stick. I'd go up there in the evenings. Though I did an all-night stint once, as a protest against being sent away to school. Problem was, no one knew I was there, even at bedtime, so the point was rather lost. All that happened was I got pneumonia.' Then, in the closest he would ever come to a confidence, he muttered, 'The crazy thing was, I couldn't wait to get away. I can't imagine why the fuck I made such a fuss about it now.'

'So you went to school?'

'Oh yes.'

'And?'

The frivolous expression that Joe was to recognise so well slid across Chetwood's face. 'I became a disgustingly amenable little schoolboy, I'm afraid. Quite outstandingly repulsive.'

Five minutes after leaving the main road Joe was lost in a tangle of twisting lanes and unmarked crossroads. It was past three, and already the dusk was thickening around the hedge-rows. Reaching a signpost at last, he found no mention of Coln Rogers, nor indeed any other Coln, of which the map boasted at least three, and in the absence of any other information drove straight on.

He'd set off from London at noon, fifteen minutes after making the decision to come. Persuaded by Sarah's argument to pursue the family connection, prompted by the realisation that he wouldn't have another opportunity to get out of town until Christmas, he had paused only to get the Chetwoods' number from directory enquiries. Even the airy response from Mrs Chetwood – 'I can't *absolutely* promise who'll be around' – hadn't put him off, not till now, as Chetwood's roof-sitting conversation came back to him, and he began to think of several reasons not to have made the journey.

He came to a junction with signs to two of the Colns, and, entering a small village which he took to be Coln Rogers, turned left only to find after two miles that he'd reached a main road going the wrong way. He turned left again, onto a switchback lane that rose gently onto higher ground. Rounding a bend, he almost missed the farm entrance. Only a glimpse of a sign reading Weston Manor Farm in blue letters above a trio of wheatsheaves prevented him from shooting past.

He had been here once before, on the way back from a party near Oxford. Chetwood had wanted to pick up some belongings – books or papers, he had been characteristically vague. At the start of the journey, Joe had put Chetwood's silence down to lack of sleep and his meandering driving to inattention, but as they'd got closer to the house Chetwood's face had become increasingly grim and his driving positively erratic.

There was a tall gate with a cattle-grid, which Joe had forgotten, and an unmade track between white paddock-rails, which he remembered quite well. The track continued straight for a hundred yards or so before dipping away into a fold of the hills. It was at the end of this straight that Chetwood had said, 'Best wait in the car.'

As the track dropped gently away, a cluster of barns and stables came into view, and beyond, the roofs and chimneys of an L-shaped house, set amid a landscape of ploughed fields. On that first visit, Chetwood had roared into the stable yard and stopped with a jolt. 'If you do get dragged inside, you should be warned – this is Indian territory. No hostages taken.'

But no one had dragged Joe inside, and the only person he'd seen was a girl of thirteen or fourteen in riding boots and quilted jacket, who appeared from a loosebox with an armful of straw. She was fair-haired and pretty and shy; when she caught his eye she blushed and walked quickly on.

Passing the yard entrance now, he saw no people and no horses. Ahead was a stark windswept garden, with stone pathways and beds of raked earth and clumps of harshly pruned roses and a gaunt pergola supporting a tangle of bare twigs. Rounding the end of the house, he saw a traditional farmhouse, perhaps a hundred and fifty years old, built of flint and brick, with white paintwork and bare-stemmed climbers reaching up to the eaves. Three cars and a mud-spattered four-wheel drive stood on the gravel. Walking towards the door, Joe saw people huddled around a dining table and caught the muffled babble of conversation.

The door was answered by a slim woman in her forties, well-groomed in the high-shires style, with no obvious makeup, greying blonde hair worn in the simple shoulder-length fashion of her youth, and a cashmere sweater with a single row of pearls.

'Oh, yes, of *course*,' she said in a studiously cordial voice. 'Won't you come in? I'm Susan Chetwood.' Closing the door, she gestured with a gracious unfurling of one hand for Joe to follow her across a low, flagstoned hall with raspberry-coloured walls and oak furniture and sporting paintings in heavy gilt frames topped by brass picture-lights. A pass-door led into the more austere regions of the kitchen quarters. At the end of a short passage Susan Chetwood paused in a doorway to switch on some lights before ushering Joe into a study. 'My husband will be along in a moment,' she said.

'I'm sorry if I'm interrupting your lunch.'

'Not at all.' She gave the smile of an accomplished hostess for whom nothing short of complete catastrophe could ever justify the slightest show of bad manners.

She made a graceful exit, and Joe looked around a low ceilinged room dominated by furniture made for a much larger house: a huge kneehole desk that would have satisfied the ego of a dictator, and, taking up almost the entire length of two walls, matching mahogany bookcases in the monumental style, with columns, pediments, and diamond-paned glass doors. Beyond the desk, on either side of the window, were photographs of three golden-haired blue-eyed children, two girls and a boy: on ponies, with and without rosettes; running around a swimming pool; in school photographs and sports teams. In a couple of the shots Susan Chetwood appeared with her children, and you didn't have to be a genealogist to spot the likeness.

Beside the door were pictures of smiling fishermen standing on river banks, and shooting parties with shotguns, panting dogs and dead pheasants.

There were no photographs of Chetwood.

The sharp rap of heels resonated in the passage. Joe stood back as the door opened and a moth-eaten golden labrador waddled in followed by a tall figure of about sixty, of upright bearing, with a long mottled face and lugubrious slightly bloodshot eyes. He wore a tweed jacket, twill trousers and country-check shirt, a little tight around the collar. His thin greying hair was combed back, with no attempt to disguise the bald heavily freckled crown, and his boots shone like chestnuts. His handshake was brisk and distinctly hostile.

'*McGarth?* Never met, have we?'

'McGrath, actually. No. I was a friend of Jamie's. We were at university together.'

'University? But he only stuck it a week.'

'Well . . . a couple of terms.'

The hooded eyes measured Joe unenthusiastically. 'My wife tells me you have some idea of finding him.' He made this sound like a thoroughly offensive proposition.

'I'm going to try. I was wondering if you could suggest anyone he might have stayed in touch with.'

'What exactly is the *purpose* of this search?' There was something in the way the older man spoke, a slight sibilance, a peculiar emphasis, that made Joe suspect he was well fortified from lunch.

'Jenna's family have asked me to look. They're desperate to find her.'

Mr Chetwood lifted his chin and narrowed his eyes. '*Jenna?*' Then, affecting to hazard a guess: 'Ah, the *wife* – is that it?'

Joe was careful not to dignify this with an answer.

'She stuck it out then, did she? Well, well.'

Selecting a neutral tone, Joe asked, 'So . . . is there anyone you can think of?'

Mr Chetwood slotted both hands into his jacket pockets, bar two precisely angled thumbs, and canted his elbows backwards like a turkeycock. 'I don't follow you.'

'Anyone Jamie might have kept in touch with, anyone he was particularly close to?'

'Can't help on that score. In fact, not on any score. James was a stranger in this house.'

'What about when he was growing up? Friends in the neighbourhood?'

Mr Chetwood raised a scornful eyebrow. 'None that he didn't offend or insult at the earliest possible opportunity.'

They stood facing each other across the gloomy room. Somewhere in the passage a door banged, a woman gave a rich laugh.

'What about at school?'

'I have no idea.' Whenever he spoke, the older man had a way of lifting his chin and squinting down his nose, as if sighting down a barrel.

'His housemaster then. Could you give me his name?'

'Never met the man.'

Joe made an incredulous face. 'Never?'

'He had his job to do. I assumed he got on and did it.'

A stubbornness came over Joe then, a determination not to be bullied. 'Friends who came to the house, then? Who came to visit him?'

'*Here?*'

'Yes.'

The chin came up double quick. 'James went his own way from a young age. I didn't care to meet his friends.'

Choosing to take this as a compliment, Joe gave a slight bow. 'What about his brother and sisters?'

'He has no brothers or sisters.'

Joe corrected himself diligently. 'Well, *half*-brothers and -sisters.'

The drooping warrior-eyes regarded him unblinkingly. 'James has no place in this family,' he announced with biting precision. 'He forfeited it many years ago. He does not belong here. He is not welcome here. I'd turn him away if he came begging at my door. I think that answers your question!'

Joe gazed into the stony face and said, 'But he *used* to be a member of your family.'

'In the sense that he was fed, housed and educated by me. One does one's duty. In my case, one does substantially *more* than one's duty.' Mr Chetwood snapped his mouth shut with something like fury, and, dropping his hands from his pockets, braced his shoulders. 'I think that concludes the matter, Mr . . . Mc*Carthy*. I have guests waiting.'

He made a move towards the door, the dog scrabbled to its feet and lumbered forward, but Joe in his indignation was there before either of them. 'Perhaps you could tell me, Mr Chetwood – I'd really like to know – what did Jamie *do* that was so bad? What was his *crime* exactly?'

The old man's eyes seemed to bulge a little. 'Not something I choose to discuss!'

'But tell me – I'm curious – did he hurt someone?'

The old man's stare hardened.

'Did he rob a bank? Make off with the silver?'

The chin rose, the watery eyes glowered from under deeply hooded lids, and in that instant Joe was startled to see in the ravaged face a disturbing resemblance to Chetwood.

'What did he do?' the old man repeated with a deathly pleasure. 'What he did was to be a bad lot from the day he was born. From the day he was brought into this house. Devious. Disruptive. Dishonest. Lazy. Took every privilege and repaid it with ingratitude. Took every chance and threw it back in my face.' He added, 'In the blood, you see. Always will out.'

'I'm sorry?'

'Bad blood. Always will out in the end!'

Joe said, 'I'm not sure I understand,' though he feared he did, all too well.

'His mother's son. Contaminated by her. Tainted through and through.'

'You're saying he was no good because of his *mother*?'

'No escaping the genes.'

Joe whispered, 'You have to be joking,' though everything in Mr Chetwood's manner suggested otherwise.

'It's a known fact! You city people haven't a clue. What d'you think bloodstock's all about? What d'you think farming's all about? It's about genes. Good genes, bad genes.' He stabbed a forefinger into the air. 'And the bad will always out.'

'I have to say that words completely fail me.'

'In which case we have nothing more to discuss, do we?' With a final lift of his chin, he marched out into the passage.

The anger raced through Joe's veins like a drug. He felt hot and sick and close to violence. Following hard on the other man's heels, it was all he could do not to shout out, *No chance this had blood came from your side of the family? No stray relatives who don't quite match up?* Instead, he said in a voice that was all over the place, 'What about Jamie's mother, Mr Chetwood? Perhaps you could tell me where to find her family?'

The older man strode on into the hall, heels tapping a furious tattoo on the flags.

'His mother's family?' Joe demanded at something approaching full volume, not caring if the entire house, the entire world, could hear him.

The front door was flung open. 'Good day, Mr McCarthy.'

'It's McGrath with a *G* and no *y*. Okay? McGrath. And I was asking about his mother's family.'

'Get out!'

'Just a simple question.'

The mouth quivered, the eyes bulged. 'Try the sink holes of South America. That's where she came from. And doubtless that's where she returned.'

Abruptly, Mr Chetwood's focus shifted, his eyes fixed on a

point beyond Joe's right ear. Following his gaze, Joe saw a girl standing in the dining-room doorway, a tray of glasses in her hands. She was a grown-up version of one of the pony-riding girls in the photographs. Utterly motionless, she was staring at her father with an expression of exasperation.

When Joe got into the car he found he was still trembling. He gripped the wheel so hard he might have been trying to wrench it off. 'You bastard!' He tried the words at different pitches and in different voices, roaring them, hissing them, growling them. 'You absolute bastard!' Then, starting the car with a violent twist of the key, he muttered, 'You poor damn bastard,' and this time he was talking about Chetwood.

Reversing out, he left plenty of gravel on the flowerbeds and was already touching a stupid speed by the time he shot through the cone of a floodlight fixed high on the corner of the stable yard. He caught a flicker of movement somewhere beyond the light, but in the heavy dusk he couldn't make it out until he looked in the driver's mirror and saw a figure running out onto the track and staring after him.

It was the girl.

He stopped and reversed back to her.

She came to the passenger window and said simply, 'I'm so sorry.' Her face was in shadow.

'I don't think I've ever heard anything quite like it.'

'No – it's his blind spot.'

'That's fairly obvious.'

'Look, there's tea and coffee in the tack room, if you'd like some.'

Joe drove into the yard, catching the eyes of the ancient labrador in his headlights.

'My mother told me who you were,' the girl announced as he climbed out. 'And why you'd come.'

The labrador lumbered alongside her as she set a cracking pace along a line of looseboxes. Joe caught the smell of horses and the rustle of shifting hooves. The girl opened a door and turned on a bright overhead light to reveal a neat tack room, with bridles and reins and various other horse apparel hanging in orderly rows around the walls. With a bubbly laugh, she called, 'The coffee's disgusting, I'm afraid.' Striding across the room at the same determined pace, she crashed a kettle into the sink. 'Unless you want tea – workman's grunge.' Turning, she bounded back with an apologetic grin. 'I'm Kate. Jamie's sister, in case you hadn't guessed.'

He had guessed all right; what he had failed to appreciate was how pretty she was in a china-doll-like way. She had smooth clear skin, a small upturned nose, wavy golden hair cut short, and a bow-shaped mouth, while her big blue eyes rolled with fun and gaiety.

She laughed, 'He used to talk about you.'

'Good, bad or indifferent?'

She giggled infectiously, and he had the feeling she giggled a lot. 'Certainly not *bad*, anyway.'

Joe said, 'I have to say he never told me anything about you. Any of you.'

Matching his mood instantly, she made a troubled face. 'That doesn't entirely surprise me. He had a miserable time of it here, I'm afraid. He and Pa were always getting on each other's nerves. They were always having rows.'

'But your father – he was so utterly scathing.'

'I know! He's completely off the planet about it, just won't listen. I did try to talk to him about it once, I did try and tell him how much we hated having Jamie banned from the house, but he absolutely refused to talk about it. He just got into the most terrible state. Shivering and shaking. I thought he was going to have a heart attack. Mummy did try to warn me. She said the subject was dynamite.'

'But this talk of genes and bad blood – I thought that went out with the Third Reich.'

The big blue eyes widened further, the eyelids fluttered uncertainly. 'Absolutely. Coffee all right?' She went back to the sink and took some mugs off a shelf. 'Look, I'm not making any apologies for Pa. No way. But for him it's all hopelessly wrapped up with Jamie's mother and their break-up. Milk? It's only powdered.'

'Black, thanks.'

'Look, I don't know the full story. Only what I've picked up over the years. The one thing Mummy told me – apart from saying I must never *ever* talk about it – was that Pa's heart had been broken very badly. That it took him years to get over it. But then someone *else* told me it was Pa who'd behaved badly. Well, she said "like an idiot" – which boils down to the same thing, doesn't it?' Kate brought the mugs over to a work-bench under the window and, pulling out two stools, waited for Joe to climb up next to her. 'But if I believe *anyone*, it's my godmother Rosie. She's a writer, you see. About plants. But she's terribly clever with people too.'

Watching her in profile, Joe thought how strange it was that Chetwood should resemble his father, while Kate, in all her china-doll prettiness, bore not the slightest likeness.

Kate turned her huge eyes back on him. 'Evidently Pa adored her, was absolutely besotted by her. Her name was Catarina. He met her when he was nineteen, working on a ranch in Brazil.' From the awe and enchantment in her voice, it might have been a fairy-tale, and for an instant, imagining the pampas, it almost was for him as well.

'She was very beautiful,' Kate continued breathlessly. '*Warm* and *passionate* and *outgoing*. Quite dazzling, according to Rosie. It was love at first sight for Pa. He pursued her, absolutely wouldn't let her go, and they married when Pa was twenty-one. Grandpa still ran the farm in those days, so Pa and Catarina went and managed a farm near Gloucester. Then when Jamie was only one it all went wrong.' Two tiny furrows sprang up between her eyebrows, her voice sank to a sigh. 'Rosie says that Pa put Catarina on this pedestal and he couldn't forgive her for not living up to this impossible dream he had of her. She was very quick and funny, Rosie says, but she used to tease Pa, and he couldn't take it. She used to tell him he was being silly and laugh at him, and he went and turned against her. And ended up hating her.'

'What happened to Catarina?'

'She went back to South America. Rosie thinks Grandpa gave her money on the condition she never came back. She ended up marrying some incredibly rich guy anyway, with lots of houses and yachts.'

'And Chetwood – why didn't she take him with her?'

'Is that what you call him – *Chetwood*?' The laughter threatened to bubble up again.

'Always have.'

She shook her head and giggled.

'So he was left behind?' Joe prompted.

Instantly, Kate was serious again. 'I think it was part of the deal, that she should leave him behind. Poor Jamie – it would have been far better if he'd gone. Look, I have no idea how true this is,' she said with elaborate caution. 'I was told by someone who isn't always totally reliable, but' – the luminous eyes came up to meet Joe's again – 'this person said that everything was fine between Pa and Jamie at the beginning, after Catarina left, that Pa was really sweet with him, but when he reached three or four and got rather cheeky and began to look like Catarina, then Pa couldn't stand it. He saw it as the worst of Catarina coming back to haunt him. And, well . . .' Her eyes grew rounder still. 'According to this friend, Pa began to tell everyone that Jamie wasn't even *his*.'

'But the likeness – you can't miss it.'

'I'm afraid Pa isn't very logical on the subject of Jamie. All I remember when I was very young was this big *cloud* that seemed to hang over poor Jamie's head. He always seemed to be in trouble.'

'But he had you, at least.'

'Oh, we were pretty useless, I'm afraid. For one thing, he was hardly ever here. He was away at boarding school. And in the summer holidays he used to go to an aunt's in France. The only time we saw him was at Christmas and Easter. And of course there was quite an age gap – five years between him and me, more for the others – and that's a huge difference when you're young, isn't it? Most of the time he just ignored us. Went off with the local lads, or hiked off to see schoolfriends. And when he *was* around, well' – she bit her lip and made a rueful face – 'I have to say we were rather terrified of him. He used to play tricks on us. Chase us and hurt us and scare us half to death. But, Joe, I can tell you all this now because when I got to know Jamie properly, when I was grown up enough to understand, I realised what a *lovely* sweet person he was. How under all that horrible older brother stuff he was just a *sweet* kind person who'd had a hard time.'

Preoccupied with the more distant past, Joe missed the significance of what she was saying. 'This aunt in France – was he close to her?'

'Oh, very. She was called Lucia. She was Catarina's sister – elder, I think. She lived somewhere near Nice. That's where Jamie always used to fly to, anyway. But the last I heard, she was ill. Jamie said she had cancer. But I could probably find an address somewhere, if you want it.'

And still Joe failed to realise what she was saying. 'I'm amazed your father let Jamie go to France, with the risk of genetic contamination.'

Kate blinked again. 'Oh, it was a relief for both of them. They got on each other's nerves so much. And Lucia was very different to Catarina. That's what Mummy used to say, anyway. Much more *practical*.'

A car sounded in the distance and they glanced up in time to see lights passing the yard entrance.

'So . . . France,' Joe murmured. 'I'm just trying to think of places Chetwood might have gone to live.'

'The best person to ask is probably Ines.' Catching his look, Kate explained, 'That's Jamie's cousin – Lucia's daughter. She was closer to Jamie than anyone.'

Ines's name stirred a memory, though Joe couldn't immediately remember when or in what context he'd heard Chetwood speak of her. 'Where would I find her?'

'I'm not sure. I've rather lost touch. The last I heard she was living in Rio. But I think she's still working for the same bank she worked for in London. It was the Banco Popular of Brazil. Or should it be Banco Popul-*ari*?' Her eyes danced with fun. 'Spanish isn't my thing.'

'Portuguese, I think you'll find.'

'What?' She hunched her shoulders, her hand shot up to her mouth to cover her giggles. 'Oh my *God*! Hopeless!'

'You met Ines in France?'

'What? Oh, no, no. London.'

Finally, the fragments that Joe had missed began to resonate in his brain. *When I got to know Jamie properly, when I was much older ... the last I heard, Jamie said she had cancer ...*

'You used to see Jamie quite a lot then? Before he disappeared?'

'Not as much as I'd have liked. But yes, two or three times a year. When he was on his way to India or somewhere like that. I lived in South Kensington then. He used to phone, and we'd meet up before he went to catch his plane. It was just *wonderful*!' She clasped her hands close against her chest, like an excited child. 'As though we were making up for lost time! Like finding a brand new brother. Of course he only called me when Ines wasn't free or was cross with him. But I didn't mind a bit. Not a bit! I was just thrilled to see him.'

Joe didn't hurry the thought that was forming slowly in his mind. 'He saw a lot of Ines, then?'

'Oh, yes.'

'Could she still be in touch with him?'

Kate pouted her pretty mouth in concentration. 'I don't know. For a while after he disappeared I think she was still hoping ... But then she finally gave up on him.'

'Still hoping . . . what, to find him?'

Kate blinked. 'Yes.' Reaching for her coffee, the blinking accelerated to a nervous flutter. 'And to win him back,' she whispered, risking a glance at Joe. 'I think she was sort of – well, definitely – in love with him, you see.'

Joe said nothing, letting the silence carry her forward.

'In fact, she adored him,' Kate said, gaining momentum. 'And you know something – I always thought he adored her too. He always seemed so happy when they were together. So un-frazzled. So funny.'

And still Joe kept silent.

'Ines was sure that the relationship with Jenna wouldn't last. Even after he moved in with her. Even after they married. That's what she told me. She was sure it wouldn't last. And Ines is such a cool person, she always knows everything. She's about the coolest person I know. I thought she must know something I didn't. Even after they disappeared she didn't give up hope, not for ages. She used to ring me and talk about it. She was sure Jamie would come back to her.'

'And this love affair – whatever it was – between Chetwood and Ines, how long had it been going on?'

Kate's eyes grew large as saucers. 'Since they were eighteen, Ines told me. For ever and ever.'

Chapter Four

———

'WHAT ARE you telling me, Joe? That he was being a pain – the Ritch? Or should I say the *filthy Ritch*?' Harry Galbraith, the senior Litigation partner, gave a satisfied smirk as he sifted through the papers on his desk. He was at his expansive Monday-morning best, fresh from overseeing the re-landscaping of his country garden, which, he liked to complain, was costing him arms and legs and parts of his anatomy he didn't care to mention. He was a big man with a double chin and a large belly, which he concealed under expensive suits and bright ties. In a less original moment, the office wits had dubbed him Flash Harry.

'He beefed about almost everything,' Joe replied. 'About what we were doing, why we were doing it, the costs. Oh, and not having a full team on the case.'

'Well, he can hardly expect *me* to be involved in the nuts and bolts.' Harry sat back in his chair to cast a more critical eye at Joe. 'But he had you, and he had Anna and Ed?'

'Until near the end, when I let Anna and Ed go.'

'As in depart?' said Harry, who liked to tie these things down. 'Why did you do that, Joe?'

'It was late. We'd been at it for two hours. We'd covered the ground at least twice. Anna and Ed were tired. And Ritch was starting to get difficult.'

'Tired? I'm sorry, we all get *tired*, Joe. Part and parcel, isn't it? And if they can't take the heat at *their* age . . .'

'It was my decision. Entirely mine. Ritch was getting offensive. He implied we were trying to jack up our fees unnecessarily.'

'*Implied?* How implied?'

'Said straight out, actually. To one of his henchmen.'

'You mean, as an aside?'

'Oh, he meant us to hear. No doubt about that.'

'But it wasn't actually *directed* at us,' Harry said briskly.

'Well, no, but . . .'

'Not an issue then.'

Harry Galbraith had several faces. There was the gung-ho team leader, disciple of the bonding and motivational techniques absorbed on expensive management courses, there was the astute lawyer, quick as they come, no dawdlers tolerated, and there was the senior partner of twenty years' standing, the consummate corporate manoeuvrer and keen watcher of his back. He was in lawyer mode now, alert, canny, not in any mood to curb his natural impatience. '*And?*' he demanded.

'Then Ritch and his guys started munching on hamburgers. Didn't apologise, didn't say a word, just turned their backs on us and started to eat.'

'Hell, Joe, they're the clients. They don't have to apologise for getting hungry.'

'It was just so incredibly rude.'

Harry started to drum his elegant fingers lightly and quickly on the desk, like a pianist polishing off a *con brio* section. '*And?*'

'Ritch said he thought I was rubbish basically, so I ended the meeting and told him we'd reconvene when the rest of the team were available. I followed up with a fax this morning, asking them to name a day and a time.'

The drumming stopped, Harry's expression hardened. 'You didn't include *me*? For God's sake, Joe, what were you thinking of? I've got a hell of a week.' He thrust a hand in the direction of his diary. 'I may not be free.'

'I think you should try and swing it.'

'Hang on, hang on. What am I hearing, Joe? Am I hearing that Ritch is seriously angry with us? Am I hearing *crisis*? Or is he simply in need of TLC?'

'He was angry all right.'

'But *annoyed* angry? *Furious* angry? About-to-take-his-business-elsewhere sort of angry?'

'I don't know.'

'But, Joe, what's your judgement on it? What's your reading?' For Harry, not knowing was a serious enough failing, but not taking a flier was even worse, and when Joe gave a shrug the last of Harry's good mood vanished behind a look of thunder. 'Well, find out, will you?' he snapped. 'And quick.'

Joe got up to leave but Harry halted him with an irritated wave. 'Amend that. You're making me nervous, Joe. I'm beginning to think I'd be safer to call Ritch myself.' Increasingly irritated, he looked at his watch. 'When do they open up shop?'

'Two thirty our time.'

He peered at his diary. 'God. *Client* meeting. That's all I need – *two* lots of clients getting temperamental.' He flipped his diary shut and gave Joe a searching stare. 'Not like you, Joe, to go and lose the plot like this.'

'It'd take a saint to deal with Ritch.'

'Well, *I've* certainly never had any trouble.'

At some point in prehistory the Litigation floor had been open-plan, but a rethink had brought in a series of glass cubicles whose walls had quickly accumulated a patchwork of calendars, postcards and lawyer jokes which blocked off much of the view. Starting down the central aisle, Joe could see someone moving around his cubicle, but he was almost at the door before he realised it was Anna. She was leaning precariously over the front of his desk, phone held loosely to one ear.

Spotting him, she capped the mouthpiece. 'How'd it go? Harry not in flesh-eating mode?'

'He's calling Ritch himself.'

'I should bloody well hope so.' She handed him the phone

like a relay runner, already halfway to the door. 'The Banco
Something of Brazil, returning your call.'

Sitting down, Joe gave his name.

A female voice responded, 'How can I help you, Mr
McGrath?'

'I was wondering if you could give me a number for Ines
Santiago.' He said the name slowly, so there should be no
mistake.

'You are speaking to her.'

'I am?' he exclaimed. And then just as stupidly: 'You're
Ines?'

'Yes.'

'I didn't realise the bank were going to contact you. Thank
you for calling back.'

'So, how can I help you?' The voice was cool and softly
accented, with a hint of breathiness in the *h*.

'It's about Jamie Chetwood. I used to be a friend – I don't
know if he mentioned me?'

'Yes, he did.'

Joe wondered: Why is it I never met you? Why was
Chetwood so careful to keep you out of sight? Possessiveness?
Guilt? Or whatever else a man feels at running two women at
the same time?

'I'm trying to find him,' he said. 'And I was wondering if
you had any idea where he might be.'

'I can't help you, I'm afraid.'

'No idea of the country he might be in? The continent?'

'I'm sorry.' A silence. 'Why do you wish to know?'

He tried to explain, and did it badly. He started with Marc,
then jumped to Jenna, to the property, and back to Marc. 'It's
rather complicated . . .'

'So I realise.'

'But you can't help?'

'No.'

'Oh, well.' Joe couldn't bring himself to ring off without
asking, 'We've never met, have we?'

'No.'

'Strange.'

She didn't answer that.

'Perhaps when you're next in London.'

Another pause, longer than the one before. 'I finish at six.'

For the second time in as many minutes, Joe was ridiculously slow. 'You're in *London*?'

'In Moorgate,' she said, which was three streets away.

He spotted her as he came through the revolving doors of the bank: a still figure in black, dwarfed by the marble columns and arches of the grandiloquent lobby. She stood watching him as he walked the length of the floor towards her.

'How do you do?' she said formally. When she shook hands, her arm was at full stretch, as if to establish a distance.

'I'm glad to meet you after so long . . .' Joe was immediately in awe of her, though he couldn't have said why.

'There's a coffee shop next door.'

She walked beside him in silence. She was short, not much more than five foot one or two, with dark, very shiny hair cut into a bob. In the coffee shop she slipped off her coat to reveal a plain black business suit over a generous but well-shaped figure. In a more frivolous woman, the word would have been voluptuous. Her face, however, was pure Modigliani: long and olive-skinned, with fine arched eyebrows and almond eyes. She was not conventionally beautiful – her nose was long and thin and set noticeably off-centre – yet her poise and her exquisite eyes made her utterly arresting.

'Kate was sure you were in Brazil.'

Ines stirred her coffee. 'I have not seen Kate for some time.'

'Have you been back long?'

'Three months.'

'And you lived in London before?'

She nodded without volunteering any details.

'Yet we never met.'

'No.' The almond eyes were unreadable.

'You never came to see Chetwood in Bristol?'

'I was abroad that year.'

'Ah! That explains a lot.' Joe heard himself laugh unnaturally. 'Chetwood always seemed at a loose end when he was
there. He complained that most of the students were hopelessly
retrograde. Though I have to say he was a bit lame-brained
himself that autumn. Trotting along parapets, frightening us
all to death.'

Ines looked at him as if he were the one who was slightly
lame-brained and Joe realised he had been jabbering. There
was something about Ines that made him feel off-balance: her
composure, the sense that nothing escaped her, the unwavering
gaze, the feeling she had lived a hundred lives before.

'So,' he said, 'when did you last see Chetwood?'

She took a moment to think about that. 'When was it that
he went away?'

'Four years ago.'

She nodded slowly: this was her answer.

In the pause that followed, Joe noticed her hands, which
were neat and well-manicured, and the plain pale-gold ring on
the third finger of her left hand. For some reason it hadn't
occurred to him that she would be married.

'Have you any idea why he should go and vanish?' he
asked.

A lift of one shoulder. 'No.'

'He never said anything about wanting a change? Or going
travelling or anything like that?'

'No.'

'He gave no hint that he was planning anything at all?'

'No.'

'What about Brazil? Could he be there, do you think?'

'No.'

Joe couldn't make out if her reticence was habitual or
reserved for talk of Chetwood. 'You're sure?'

She gave a slight nod.

'Not with his mother?'

'No.'

He gave a laugh of exasperation. 'Any particular reason?'

Offering a gaze that was fractionally more approachable, she volunteered, 'He never knew his mother. He never wanted to know her. He had no wish to go to Brazil.'

'What about your own mother? He was close to her, Kate told me.'

'Yes.'

'Might she have heard from him, do you think?'

Ines looked down at her coffee. 'My mother died four months ago.'

'Oh,' he said hastily. 'I'm sorry.'

She was very still, her face expressionless except for the downcast eyes, which seemed to contain a wealth of thought.

She broke the silence first. 'When we spoke earlier I did not understand exactly why you want to find him. Could you tell me again, please?'

Joe made a more logical job of it this time. He started with the property and Marc's need for money, and went on through the difficulties of selling something in joint ownership when one of the owners can't be found.

'So a document needs to be signed?'

'Well, yes. But there's more to it than that. It's Jenna's parents – they're desperate to know she's safe.'

'Why should she not be safe?'

'Well, it's been so long. Anything might have happened.'

'They don't believe he is taking care of her?' Then, and afterwards, Joe noticed how she tried to avoid the use of their names.

'It's not a question of what Chetwood might or might not be doing. It's the not knowing. It's always thinking the worst.'

'You don't believe she has made a choice in this?'

'For what it's worth, I think she has, yes. But it's no good saying that to Alan and Helena. It won't make them sleep any better at night, it won't stop their health from suffering.'

Ines regarded him quietly. 'You are good friends with her family?'

'Alan and Helena gave me a home from home when I was a kid. Kept me out of trouble.' In a moment of inspiration, he added, 'Like your mother did for Chetwood.'

The almond eyes did not waver.

'I went down to see Chetwood's family yesterday,' Joe went on. 'Which is how I met Kate of course, and got to hear about you. But the father – what a nightmare! It's a wonder Chetwood survived at all.'

This subject prompted her first spontaneous offering of the evening. 'A bad man,' she agreed. 'With a bad heart. Consumed with the hate and envy of a mean spirit. Sometimes he would try to stop' – she brought herself to say his name at last – 'to stop Jamie coming to us. He would refuse to pay the fare at the last moment, or he would cancel the arrangements, and then my mother would have to travel to England to collect Jamie herself.' She pronounced Jamie in the Latin way, with a soft J that was almost an H.

'It must have meant a lot to him, having a real family to come to.'

The wariness returned to her face.

'Having you as a friend.' Joe was pushing her, but he didn't know what else to do.

She slid her coffee cup to one side and for a moment he thought she would make her excuses and leave. Instead, she said, 'Tell me something . . . *Joe*.' She might have been trying his name for size. 'Did you visit them – Jamie, her – when they lived in the country?'

'Once, for a short weekend, it must be six years ago. No, a bit less. Five and a half.'

'And?'

'They seemed fine.'

'Tell me.' Her shrug invited whatever impressions he cared to choose.

'It was summer. June. Lovely weather. You never went there?'

She shook her head.

'It was a rented place, a bit shambolic, a bit overgrown, but magical at that time of year. I got up there in time for lunch on Saturday. We ate outside. Late. Went for a walk at about five. Then supper – also very late – with a few other people, maybe ten of us. And I left before lunch the next day. It was all very relaxed. Chetwood and Jenna both seemed okay.'

'Who were the other people there?'

'God, now you're asking. There was certainly a musician called Dave Cracknell, plus girlfriend. Then there was a neighbour, a farmer – organic, that's all I remember. And some other locals. An antique dealer, I think. The rest ... no, I'm afraid it's gone after all this time.'

'Not someone called Sam?'

Joe shook his head doubtfully.

'Nineteen or twenty. Fair-haired.'

'I don't think so. Why?'

She blew a small puff of air through her lips, like an audible shrug. 'Something that was said once. And the next time you saw them?'

'It was in London, a year or so later.'

'And?'

'Jenna seemed ill. Depressed. Chetwood seemed ... the same.'

'He said nothing about what was wrong?'

'No. And to you?'

Ines paused, as if to debate the wisdom of what she was about to say. 'I think they had come to London for her to see a doctor. A – what do you say? – specialist.'

'She was ill then?'

'I cannot be sure, I can only guess. But I think she had a problem here.' She tapped the side of her head.

'Physical? Mental?'

'Mental. I think something bad happened.'

Joe felt a small surge of tension. 'Bad in what way?'

Ines made a more eloquent shrug, a lift of both shoulders, a flicker of an arched eyebrow. 'It was winter. Jamie called me from the farmhouse to say he could not leave. I thought it must be snow, but he said it was not snow. He would not explain. He would not say why. He said only *I cannot leave*. And he did not leave for a long time. Usually he was away every two weeks, three at the most, to Bombay, Jakarta, Shanghai. But after this he did not travel for four months. And he did not say why. I thought maybe she wanted him home. That she was making him stay. That she was having – what do you say – a nervous *attack*?'

'A breakdown?'

'A breakdown. But when I said this to Jamie, he was angry, he told me this was not true.' Lost to this memory, clearly troubled by it, it was a while before she worked her way free. 'At last he began to travel again,' she resumed distractedly. 'To be busy with his work. But nothing was the same after that. Nothing.'

Joe wanted to ask: And your relationship, was that never the same either? Did Chetwood tell you it was over? Because it seemed to Joe that Ines was being a touch ingenuous about all this, that she was rather conveniently ignoring the possibility that Jenna had found out about their love affair and forbidden Chetwood from seeing her again, or even travelling through London. It would not have been the first time that a wife had issued a drastic ultimatum.

'Chetwood never explained what had happened?'

'You know the way he was. He could talk about so much, but in the end he only said what he chose to say.'

And what about you? Joe wondered. Are you telling me only what you choose to tell?

She might have been reading his mind. 'Oh, do not think I did not try to discover what had happened. I wanted more than anything to understand. I saw so little of him after that, you see. I lost my best friend.'

Joe wasn't sure what best friend meant any more. When you were a kid your best friend was the person you went cycling with, like Jenna, or kicked a football with, like his schoolfriend Paul, but when you got older a best friend became something much more confusing, anything from a drinking mate of either sex to a superior kind of lover, a sort of kindred spirit, life traveller and sexual partner all rolled into one.

Finally he asked: 'You mean best *friend* or . . .?'

'I don't understand.'

'More than a friend?'

Ines's eyes darkened. It was a while before she whispered, 'Is this what Kate said to you?'

'Sort of.'

Ines shook her head coldly at the absent Kate.

'Oh. It's not true?'

In slow motion, with an air of injured dignity, Ines reached for her coat and pulled it onto her lap. 'He married *her*. There you have your answer.'

She turned in her seat, on the point of getting up, only to stop and fix Joe with a long appraising look. 'I will tell you something. I will tell you that in that last winter before they left the farmhouse they were going to split. To separate. He was ready to leave. In his mind he had already gone.'

A number of thoughts went through Joe's head just then. That this could explain a great deal. That men don't usually leave without a good reason. That the good reason might well be facing him across the table. That it was nothing like that at all: that Ines had merely talked herself into believing what she wanted to believe, that at the end of the day intelligence was no barrier to love and delusion.

'*Yes*,' she said as though he'd spoken these thoughts aloud, 'I hoped he would come and live with me. But *no* – nothing was arranged between us.'

'Why was he leaving?'

She dropped her eyes briefly. 'He did not say.'

'What, no reason at all?'

'He spoke only of . . . difficulties.'

'Had he told Jenna he was going?'

'Oh yes.'

Joe felt a stab of sympathy for Jenna, but also unmistakeably a small glimmer of vindication.

'Well, there's your event,' he suggested. 'There's the reason Jenna was depressed. The reason Chetwood stayed at home.'

Ines stood up, and he hurried to help her with her coat. It had a long row of buttons down one side, Cossack style. Fastening them with swift fingers, Ines declared, 'People do not get so badly ill for love.'

'Oh. I thought they did.'

'I think, only in romantic books. Besides . . .' Again she seemed to weigh Joe up, to decide if he was worthy of her trust. 'She had someone new already.'

Joe stared at her.

'Oh *yes*,' she insisted. 'This younger guy called Sam.'

It wasn't until they reached the door that Joe asked, 'Chetwood told you this?'

She nodded.

She seemed to catch some criticism in his face because she was suddenly very formidable. 'He would not lie about such a thing to me.' She pulled the door open before he could do it for her. 'He never lied in the important things.'

Standing in the street Joe said, 'Well, I'm glad to have met you at last.'

'Yes.'

'Typical Chetwood, to have kept us from meeting.'

'He liked his friends in different compartments.' She added, 'Though we almost met once.'

'We did?'

'There was a party he talked about. In the summer after he was in Bosnia. It was going to be in a strange place. A castle that had fallen down? A place with holy stones? Do you remember? He said you would be there. But then he cancelled. He argued with the person giving the party – something like that. We did not go.'

A police siren screamed and Joe tracked the squad car as it raced past. 'Oh, but I didn't go either,' he said. 'So it wouldn't have made any difference.'

But Chetwood had gone all right. He had gone with Jenna.

Making his way back to the office through the December darkness, Joe relived the heat of the summer day nine years ago when the sun had been too strong, the air too close, and his chest so tight he could barely breathe. He was with Jenna, and they were climbing the side of the Cheddar Gorge. He had planned to take her to Cadbury Castle and Queen Camel, both claimed to be the site of Camelot, but in his jealous misery he had lost the stomach for romantic legend, and on the spur of the moment they had set out for Cheddar, without much of a plan, certainly without anything as practical as water or sun-block or hats. Arriving at the foot of the steps, they had found most of the county already there: rows of parked cars, chatter-ing groups, and a chain of bobbing figures zigzagging up the steps above them. If Joe'd had any sense he would have suggested they turn back, but his sense had been lost under the weight of aching pride.

They walked single file, occasionally forced to halt as people bunched up ahead. By the time they reached the top of the ridge with its far-ranging views over the Somerset Levels, they were hot and thirsty and blind to any view, spectacular or otherwise.

Joe led the way across the grass, to a clump of gorse which offered precious little shelter, not from the sun, and not from the pain of their disharmony. The moment they sat down, the heat seemed to pulse down onto Joe's head and the tension to claw at his heart.

Jenna groaned, 'It's baking.' She sat with her forearms

draped over her knees, funnelling air up through her lower lip over her face. 'No chance of an ice-cream van, I don't suppose?'

He stared doggedly out over the hazy landscape.

Speaking into his silence, she sighed, 'Joe? What is it, *please*?' Then, in a murmur, 'For heaven's sake . . .'

And still he couldn't speak.

'I shouldn't have come. I had no idea . . . It would have been far better if I hadn't come.'

'No, I wanted you to come.'

Joe had been planning the weekend for months; the thought of it had carried him through the drudgery of revision and the exhaustion of finals: it was to be a celebration of everything that was to come.

'You're cross with me,' she said. 'I've done something, or *not* done something.'

He could only gesture tightly.

'Not the holiday? I've said I'm sorry. I had no idea you were *fixed* on it. I had no idea you'd booked it.'

'I hadn't booked it. How could I book it?' For years they had talked about walking in the Lakes. In the spring, Joe had got as far as buying maps and walking guides and listing the best hostels.

'You do understand, don't you?' Jenna cried. 'I can't turn down the opportunity of working with Sherer. She hardly ever gives master classes, and all of the most important agents will be there.'

'Of course I understand. Of course.'

After a while, she sighed, 'Well, *what* then?' They were sitting side by side, and she dropped her head to try and see his face better. 'Not that thing with Chetwood again?'

His silence was her reply.

'For heaven's sake, Joe, I've already told you – you're making something out of nothing.'

He found his voice at last. 'You start seeing a friend of mine without telling me and you call it nothing?'

'Perhaps I didn't tell you because I just knew it would be like this, I just knew you'd get the whole thing out of proportion!'

'What proportion am I meant to get it in, then?'

He heard her suck in her breath, like someone needing a heroic level of patience. 'I told you – Chetwood just appeared. He turned up and asked if I'd like a glass of wine. So we went to a wine bar and had a glass of wine. And that was it. End of story. I'm not going to see him again and I don't know what makes you think I am.'

'He turned up unannounced in Manchester? No one just turns up in Manchester.'

'How should I know why he was there, Joe? It was none of my business.'

'But he must have said why he'd come.'

'He may have said something about a business meeting. But quite honestly, I didn't pay much attention. I didn't realise I was going to be interrogated on it afterwards.'

'And after this one glass of wine he wants to take you to Eddie's party.'

'And I've said no.'

'Well, he seems pretty damn sure you said yes.'

She touched his arm. 'Listen to me, Joe.' She waited until he half turned his head towards her. 'I'm not going. Okay? I can't put it any plainer than that.'

And still Joe couldn't stop himself. 'You'd go if it wasn't for me though? You'd say yes all right?'

'For what it's worth, Joe, I don't think so. No.'

'Well, you gave a good impression of thinking he was pretty damn fantastic. Laughing at all his jokes.'

'So he makes me laugh. So?'

'He was putting on an act.'

'Well, all right then, his *act* made me laugh, but that doesn't mean—'

'He was just trying to impress you.'

'People are always trying to impress each other, Joe. It's what people do. It doesn't have to *mean* anything.'

She was pulling at the grass and shredding it in her fingers. He noticed the smoothness of her forearm and the light covering of down that glinted gold in the sunlight.

'Well, whatever happened, he thinks you've agreed to go to the party with him.'

'It simply isn't true, Joe. How can I get through to you? He's not my type.'

'You could have fooled me.' The childish jeer made him wince inwardly; he would have taken it back if he could.

'Joe. Joe. I don't know what to say any more. You're my best friend. You always will be. But . . . oh dear, I didn't want to have this conversation, not this weekend, not when you've gone to so much trouble. But, Joe . . . we're friends, aren't we? I mean, isn't that where we are at the moment? Friends.'

His head was aching from the sun and from the knowledge of what was to come. 'Ah, *friends*.'

'Maybe we'll see more of each other one day. If that's what we both want. But not now, Joe. I've still got another year at the Royal Northern. I need to concentrate on my music.'

'So it's not possible to do both?'

'I really don't think so, Joe.' She laid her hand on his arm and her voice was sweet and kind. 'Not with someone like you. You're an all-or-nothing person, Joe. A real romantic. I never dreamt you'd go to so much trouble this weekend. Dinner last night. The trip to Camelot. *Camelot*, Joe. I realised then . . .'

She shook her head. 'I thought we were just going to have a bit of fun this weekend, go to a few parties. I had no idea it was going to be like this – just the two of us. It shows the sort of person you are, Joe. Lovely. Thoughtful. Romantic. But if we started going out together you'd expect it to be like this all the time. You'd want us to see each other every weekend. And it just wouldn't be possible, not when you're going to be in London and I'm going to be in Manchester.'

Where her hand lay on his arm, there was an unbearable heat. He felt the sweat on his body like a river.

Finally he looked at her. Her face was flushed from the climb, sweat shimmered around her nose, and strands of hair clung damply to her forehead, yet looking into her wide-set eyes, seeing the upturned mouth, he thought he'd never seen her more beautiful or more desirable.

He said, 'Other people manage to have long-distance relationships.'

She took her hand away. 'Well, maybe I'm not as clever or well-organised as other people. It would be another pressure, Joe, and I don't think I could take more pressure at the moment. It's hard enough getting through the course, achieving the grades, without feeling responsible for someone else's happiness.'

He forced a laugh. 'But you wouldn't be responsible for my happiness!'

'Oh yes, I would, Joe. With you I would. And you'd feel responsible for mine, because that's the way you are. And it wouldn't work.'

He stared into the distance again, and the heat pricked at his eyes. 'So, on the same basis, you won't be seeing anyone else?'

'Joe, I can't say I'm not going to see anyone at all. That's just not realistic. I'm going to go out now and again, of course I am. But casually, without getting serious.'

'I get the idea.'

She sighed wearily. 'Oh Joe, Joe . . . it's far too hot to talk about this now. Can't we leave it alone?'

He stood up. 'I think you should go to the party with Chetwood.'

'Don't be silly.'

'Why not? I'm not going to go. You might as well. You'll enjoy it.'

'Joe, don't do this. Please.'

'No, I mean it. You want to be free. Well, then, of course you must be free. Totally free. I wouldn't want to stand in your way. God forbid.'

He walked off a short distance to catch his breath. After a time she came and stood a few feet away.

'Perhaps it would be best if I went back to Manchester tonight,' she said.

'If you want to.'

'I don't want to, Joe. I just think it would be best.'

'Fine.' He began to walk back towards the steps, fast, and she had to hurry to keep up.

'Joe, this is crazy. Why am I feeling bad about something I haven't done, something I haven't any intention of doing?'

'Only you can answer that.'

Angrily, she pulled on his arm until he stopped and turned to face her. 'What are you trying to do, Joe? What are you trying to achieve? Because if you're trying to make me mad with you, you're really succeeding. At this rate, I'm going to go to the damn party, with or without you.'

'You can do what you like, Jenna. I don't care too much either way.'

Time is meant to heal most things, but it seemed to Joe that it did very little for the torment of self-inflicted wounds. As he met the stream of people leaving the Merrow building, he felt a fresh shiver of shame and mortification.

Anna must have been watching for him because she shot out of her cubicle the moment he walked onto the floor. 'I thought for an awful moment you'd gone home. Harry's been screaming for you. Calling your mobile every two seconds.'

Joe reached for his phone and looked at it. 'The battery must be flat.'

But Anna was already wearing the stern expression that told him this excuse wouldn't wash. 'He's waiting for you. He's held off going to some important bash.'

Harry's door was open. He was sitting at his desk in his shirtsleeves, bent over a thick document. Without looking up, he grunted, 'Where have you been?'

Joe sat down. 'At a meeting.'

Harry took his time finishing his reading. Usually he was gone by seven. If he had work to catch up on, he came in early, before eight. He had an ex-model wife who spent her mornings in Harvey Nichols and her afternoons on fundraising committees. According to the rumour mill, they went out almost every night.

'Ritch is seriously pissed off,' Harry said, still without looking up. 'You're going to have to go out there and whisper sweet nothings in his ear.'

'What, before Christmas?'

Harry's eyes rose at last and seemed to bulge a little. 'Yes, before Christmas. That's not a problem, is it, Joe?'

'No.'

'Christmas is still on the twenty-fifth, isn't it? Or have I got my arithmetic wrong?'

Joe chewed his lip.

'So what's the issue?'

'It's not an issue. It's just that I've got a Basis of Claim to do before Wednesday for GPG, and a—'

'Good.' Harry gave a shudder, as if to throw off superfluous talk. 'Ritch is expecting you tomorrow morning, bright and early. I suggest you use the flight to prepare your pitch.'

'I'm not sure the flight'll be long enough.'

'Well, perhaps it's your attitude that needs the work, Joe.'

'I'll have a go at that too, then. On the flight.'

Harry heaved the document closed. 'Joe, it's no good getting faint-hearted in this game. Not if you're going for the long haul.'

Joe supposed he was talking about a partnership.

'Sometimes you have to tough it out with the client, lay it on the line, take no nonsense. Sometimes you have to treat them like kids, hold their hands, pat them on the head. Other times, well, you have to treat them like a lover' – warming to the analogy, his eyes narrowed conspiratorially – 'fuss over them, take them out for a nice meal, listen to their problems, tell them all the things they want to hear.'

Joe muttered under his breath, 'Like a gigolo.'

He must have said it louder than he'd intended because Harry snapped, 'For Christ's sake, Joe!'

'I know. My attitude. I'll work on it on the plane.'

Harry shook his head with an appearance of genuine concern. 'What's got into you, Joe?'

'Perhaps Anna should have gone instead.'

'No, you're the right person, Joe. Of course you are.' He stabbed a finger at him. 'You're the man.'

Joe laughed aloud. 'You *have* been talking to Ritch, haven't you?'

'What?' Harry didn't get it. He finished rather crossly, 'No, your work's been fine, Joe. It's just on the presentation side that you seem to have lost your edge.'

On the way home, Joe thought about the edge he was meant to have lost, and decided that Harry had got it the wrong way round, that his problem wasn't too little edge, but way too much.

Sarah called from the kitchen, 'So you're expected to go and smooth things over.'

'I think the word is grovel.' Joe was rooting through his shelves, looking for the white shirt he had last worn at a funeral and probably forgotten to collect from the laundry.

'I'll drive you to the airport, shall I?'

'That's very kind, but I've got to check in by five. No point in both of us going without sleep.'

'But I've got my flatmate's car. It wouldn't be any trouble. I could go straight on to the office and make an early start.'

He went through into the kitchen. She had prepared a salad and beaten up some eggs, and was cutting smoked salmon into narrow strips.

'I thought we were having a sandwich.'

'Scrambled eggs with smoked salmon, and a side salad.'

'Hey.' It was more than he wanted or had time for. 'Look, er . . . I'm going to have to get down to work straight after supper, I'm afraid.'

'The thing for tomorrow? The Basis of Claim? Of course. Do you want me to get it couriered over to your office first thing?'

'What I mean is, it could take me all night.'

She stiffened. The knife paused for an instant in its journey across the salmon. 'You mean, you don't want me to stay? Well, why didn't you say so? Hell, you only had to say. It was never going to be a problem.'

'I'll work better on my own, that's all.'

'But it's fine. Why wouldn't it be fine? I'll leave straight after supper. You only had to say.' Then, seeming to hear the tension in her voice, she announced in a voice that was unnaturally soft, 'But I wouldn't mind some wine first.'

When he handed it to her, she struck a pose, mouth shaped into a flashy smile, eyes in an expression of apparent uncon-cern, and he thought how badly this role suited her, and how very fragile was her confidence.

'Oh, I almost forgot!' She went into the living room and reappeared with her handbag. Reaching into a pocket, she pulled out the envelope from Alan's birthday card. 'We have a result.'

'The postmark?'

She was like a conjurer, spinning out a trick. She bran-dished the envelope in the air. 'A city – which covers a large rural area.' She cocked her head challengingly: it was to be a quiz. 'No?' She brought the envelope down with a flourish. 'Over towards the west?'

He made the effort to play. 'Cornwall?'

'Higher up.'

'Wales?'

'Not quite.'

He said in disbelief, 'Hereford?'

She placed the envelope in his hand. 'Hereford. Or rather, the Hereford postal district, which is large, geographically speaking. Stretches over the border into Wales and halfway to Birmingham.'

Glancing at her watch, she swept a saucepan off its hook and slid it onto the stove. 'You look doubtful.'

'Just surprised.'

'Not a likely spot for your friends?'

'They used to live near Hereford four years ago. But everyone who knew them there was quite sure they'd left.'

'Perhaps they chose a more remote spot.'

'But for no one to have seen them . . .'

Sarah took a swig of her wine and an equally hasty look at the wall clock. 'Sounds like they're doing a good job of keeping out of sight. Look, why don't you do some more packing while I get on with the food? That'll save a bit of time.'

Her voice was still a fraction high and a fraction sharp, and he put a steadying arm around her shoulders.

'The time thing,' he said. 'It's not that desperate.'

'But you must do your work. Of course you must. I understand completely. Don't I always understand about your work?'

'Yes.'

'Well, then.' She shot the brittle smile at him again, she leant her head briefly against his shoulder before returning to the food, slicing some butter off the block and lobbing it expertly into the pan.

Five minutes later, she called him in to eat. Ten minutes after that, she was rinsing the last plate and standing it in the rack. 'There,' she declared, whipping off her rubber gloves with a snap. 'No time at all!'

She had picked up her handbag and was halfway out of the kitchen before Joe could say, 'Hang on!'

Only her head was visible round the door.

'I wanted to ask you something.'

He beckoned her to sit down again, but she would only

come a few inches back into the room, and he got up and joined her by the door.

'It was an idea Alan had. About contacting every church and choral society in the country, to see if Jenna was singing there. Crazy of course – every last church! But I was thinking that it might just be possible with a single county. What do you think? There can't be *that* many churches in Herefordshire.'

Sarah held up a hand. 'Hold on, Joe. You're way, way ahead of me. What's this singing business?'

'Well, that's what Jenna did. That's what she trained to be – a classical singer. A mezzo. Well, more of a contralto, really. Shades of Kathleen Ferrier. But there aren't too many parts for contraltos, so officially she was a mezzo. She could have made soloist, everyone said so, but choral was her real love.'

'I still haven't got the church connection.'

'That's the best place to find a choir. In fact, it's the only place if you live in the country. And she loved to sing. It was her life.'

Sarah absorbed this idea slowly, as though it was rather alien to her. 'Okay,' she said at last. 'But at the end of the day this is just supposition, right? Just a guess?'

'Well . . . yes.'

Sarah's Nordic eyes wore their most professional gleam. 'It has to be a non-starter, Joe. I've heard of a long shot, but this would be . . . well, like looking for piss in a pond, as the CID guys would say.'

This time when she started for the hall he didn't try to stop her.

He saw her down to the street. Her flatmate's car was a spanking new Ford, not top of the range, but definitely not the cheap end either.

'Your flatmate on the sweeteners, is she?'

'Sorry?'

'Getting a little encouragement from the defence.'

'Corruption jokes don't go down a bundle in our office, Joe.'

'No, I can see that.'

She gave a last frown as she got into the car.

'Oh, about your missing friend,' she remarked through the window. 'Why don't you try something in the *Hereford Gazette*?'

'There's a *Hereford Gazette*?'

'I've no idea. But there'll be some sort of county rag, won't there? Every Thursday.'

'A small ad, you mean?'

'Worth a try.'

There was one Thursday left before Christmas and the two-week close-down. He said, 'If I scribbled something now, would you be able to phone it in for me?'

She hesitated, her hand on the ignition, but he could see that she was quite glad to be asked. She dropped her hand. 'Sure.'

She gave him paper and pen, which he took back to the rickety ring-stained table inside the hall of the apartment block. Pushing aside the stacks of circulars and letters addressed to mysterious long-forgotten residents, he stared at the sheet for a full minute before writing: *Jenna, ex-Laskey. Anxious for news. Please call. Joe.* But even as he wrote it he knew it wasn't right. Too categorical. Too demanding. Crossing it out, he wrote on the other side: *Jenna? Missing contralto for Messiah. Just call to say you're singing elsewhere this Xmas. Joe.* It was far from ideal. With more time he might have thought of something better. Adding his mobile number, he took the paper out to Sarah.

'It's all I could think of.'

She glanced at it before storing it in her bag. She offered up her lips for a last kiss. 'No one can say you haven't tried.'

Joe lay awake in the darkness, a long way from sleep. He had finished the Basis of Claim at midnight in the knowledge that it could have been better constructed, and undoubtedly a lot crisper too, then persuaded a reluctant cabbie to deliver it to Merrow at the end of his shift, when there would be someone there to receive it. For some time after that, he'd fretted over the document bundle he'd put together for the trip to Houston, worrying about a couple of papers he'd left behind. When he'd finally made it to bed, it was to hear the sounds of the night magnified: the ticking of the pipes, the low thump of amplified music from the flat of the lovelorn actor above, and, from beyond the windows, the street musak of sirens and car alarms.

He was certain he wouldn't be able to sleep, yet when the phone rang it seemed to drag him from a deep and irresistible coma. He seemed to hear in rapid succession the jangle of the dormitory bell from the hated boarding school, the four a.m. wake-up call for the airport, though when he managed to focus on the bedside clock it displayed a resolute one forty, and finally, while reaching for the receiver, to presage the brutal words that only ever come in the early hours: his father ill, the house burnt down, a death.

A male voice said, 'Joe? How are you?'

'Who is this?'

'Well, it's me, of course '

And the crazy thing was that Joe knew straight away. 'For Christ's sake . . .'

'Not a bad moment?'

Struggling with a brain that was simultaneously wide awake and half asleep, Joe propped himself on one elbow and reached for the light. 'No, no. What the hell.'

'So, how's life with you, Joe?' Chetwood's voice was perfectly relaxed. It might have been a month since they'd spoken; it might have been a civilised hour of the day.

Joe heard himself give a short laugh. 'Me? Oh, for God's sake, I'm fine, Chetwood! But what about you? What about Jenna?'

Chetwood hummed a little. 'Can't complain. But, look, Joe – a couple of things first, okay?'

Pulling himself upright, Joe leant forward with his elbows on his knees, wondering how to play this. Friendly? Tough? Conciliatory? 'Sure!' he said too brightly.

'Just need to establish the rules of engagement.'

'Right!' Too anxious now. *Slow down, slow down.*

'Need to ask that this goes no further, Joe. Need to have your word.'

'If that's what you want. Sure.'

'No one will know we've spoken – right?'

'Okay.'

A snort of amusement. 'It's not as bad as it sounds, Joe.'

'I'll take your word for it.'

'I wouldn't do this if it was anyone else, you know.'

'Do what?'

'Call.'

'Well . . . you've called. So now you can tell me – is she all right, Chetwood? Is Jenna okay?'

'Yeah, she's okay.' His voice was unreadable.

'Really okay?'

'Yeah, really.' He might have been talking about the weather.

'Thank God. It'll be a huge relief to Alan and Helena. They've been frantic with worry. Alan especially . . .' Joe trailed off, aware that the silence at the far end of the line had taken on a life all its own. 'You're not saying I can't tell them? For God's sake, Chetwood, they're sick with worry. They're making themselves ill.'

Another silence before Chetwood replied, 'You can tell them. But not yet.'

'When?'

'When this legal thing's out of the way.'

It was late, one half of Joe's brain was still way behind, and in a ludicrous moment of confusion he couldn't think what legal thing Chetwood was talking about. 'Fine. Sure. How are we going to do it?'

'Listen, if it was up to me . . .' But Chetwood didn't finish this thought, and when he spoke again it was hastily. 'Here's a once-and-for-all offer, Joe. Not to be repeated. I'll meet you tomorrow night at nine—'

'Not tomorrow. I'm going to America.'

'For God's sake, Joe. Why *America*?' A sigh. 'Okay. My final offer – Saturday morning.'

'Saturday's fine.'

'Ten o'clock at the Watford Gap Services. Only the most glamorous places, Joe.'

'It'll have to be a power of attorney,' Joe said, thinking aloud. 'There's nothing else I can prepare in the time.'

'You're the lawyer.'

Before he could ring off, Joe said hastily, 'Chetwood?'

'Hello.'

'Jenna will be there, will she?'

'No, Joe, she won't be there.'

'I'd love to see her.'

'She doesn't travel.'

'Can't I come to her?'

'No. She doesn't know about this yet. I haven't even worked out how I'm going to tell her.'

This time, when Joe became aware of the silence on the end of the line, it was because there was no one there.

He dialled last number recall knowing, before the mechanical voice began its chanting, that the number of the last caller would be unavailable.

Chapter Five

———•———

EVEN AS Joe dropped his bags on the floor, he was scanning his desk for a note from Anna. But there was no note – she'd been too discreet for that: there was a sealed envelope marked 'Private'. From the size of it, and the bulk, she'd done everything he'd asked for, and he thanked her aloud. 'Star, Anna.'

It was three thirty in the afternoon, though it could have been midnight Chinese-time for all Joe knew. He felt as if he'd been travelling for ever, and perhaps he had. Following the normal pattern with Ritch's team, the last meeting had overrun badly, and he'd missed the direct flight back to London. Re-routed, he'd been trapped by a twelve-hour blizzard in Chicago, and at Heathrow his bag was last onto the carousel. The Heathrow Express worked well, the Tube badly, and by the time he emerged on to the streets of the City it was already dark. The nine-hour journey had taken more than twenty-four, but Joe wasn't really counting. He'd got home before Saturday, and that was all that mattered. Through the interminable meetings and snow-bound airports and foreshortened days, Chetwood's words had whispered hauntingly round his head. Sometimes the tone seemed friendly, sometimes cool, now and again the sequence had got completely jumbled, but the final message had never been less than clear. *A once-and-for-all deal, Joe. Not to be repeated.*

And now, in what seemed like a concerted effort to disorientate him, Joe had arrived back at Merrow to find the litigation floor deserted. He'd checked his watch, but unless every clock in the entire city had got it wrong, London was still six hours ahead of Chicago. Bomb scare? Fire drill? Strike? Though it was a considerable challenge to whistle up grounds for a lawyers' strike: too much business? too much income? The cards plastered over the glass partitions and the token mistletoe finally nudged his memory: it was the day of the Christmas lunch.

The envelope yielded a two-page power of attorney on heavy legal paper, a duplicate on lighter paper, a computer disk, and a handwritten note. When he'd called Anna from Houston and asked if she could spare some of her own time to draw up the power of attorney – 'Glad to help, Joe: anything that keeps me out of the shops' – he'd left her to ring Alan and get the details, and he saw now that she had inserted Marc's full name and address and the address of the jointly owned property. The only blank was the one immediately after Jenna's name, the one they would all like to fill. Next to it, Anna had stuck a Post-It note: *Last known address – "formerly of"? Or c/o her solicitors? We need to put something here.*

The scribbled note read: *Dear Joe, Well done with the beastly Ritch. You deserve a medal. We're at the office lunch getting drunk and disorderly. You'd best escape before Tamsin from Accounts gets back and pins you to the desk (for some reason she thinks you're okay – did you fiddle her expenses?). Serious matters: Power of Attorney attached. If you want to make changes it's on the disk as: Laskey.wps. But, Joe, I should tell you that when I last spoke to Dr Laskey (Thursday 4.00 p.m.) he seemed upset about something. He couldn't (or wouldn't) say what it was, but I got the impression it was serious and somehow involved with this. Anna.*

With a sense of foreboding, Joe dialled Alan and Helena's private number and got no reply. Trying the listed number, he found himself transferred to a central doctors' pool where a hard-voiced female told him they didn't pass on messages to the off-duty doctors and to try Alan's surgery. The surgery was answered by a recorded female voice only marginally less fearsome. It recited the surgery hours and referred urgent calls back to the doctors' pool, adding pointedly that the machine did not take messages.

Joe thought of asking his father to go round to Alan and Helena's, and rejected it almost as quickly as the idea of trying Marc.

There might have been a worse time to try to get out of London by car but the Friday evening before Christmas took some beating. Stopping at the flat only to shower and stuff some clean clothes into an overnight bag, Joe nosed the car out into traffic that was moving by the inch or not at all. The half-mile across the river took twenty minutes, and when he got to the other side all the north-bound routes out of Chelsea were solid.   ·

Twice he tried Alan and Helena's numbers, listed and unlisted, and twice he rang off at the click of the automatic transfer. Then, sitting in a three-lane jam south of the Crom-well Road, as he was starting to dial Sarah's mobile, a figure in a tracksuit with a raised hood jogged past the car, brushing against the wing mirror. The figure wove nimbly through the gridlocked traffic, ducked briefly out of sight, then with a huge burst of speed sprinted away into a side street. A horn blared, long and loud, a woman screamed, and by the time Joe registered the connections it was all too late. He jumped out of the car and ran to the street corner, but the bag-snatcher was long gone and the horns were beginning to blast for him. Driving on again, he came alongside the woman leaning against the door of her car, talking tearfully into a mobile phone. He called out, 'Are you all right?' and got a raging gesture for his trouble. Closing the window, sealing himself off against the world once again, he thought: So much for the Christmas spirit.

At West Hampstead the traffic finally began to move, only to bunch up again the other side of Brent Cross. When his mobile rang, he answered it rapidly, hoping for Alan.

Sarah's voice said, 'So you're back.'

'You got my message okay?' He'd called from Heathrow.

'Five minutes ago. Where are you?'

'That's the thing. I'm on my way to see Alan and Helena. Very slowly.'

A pause that seemed to contain reproach. 'I thought you weren't going north till Christmas Eve.'

'I'm not. I'm coming back again tomorrow.'

'Oh.' The difficult moment, if that was what it was, had passed. 'Has something happened?'

'I'm not sure. But since I have to be up north anyway, I thought I'd better go and find out.'

'I see.' If she was curious to know the reason for his trip, she didn't say so. 'But back tomorrow?'

'Lunchtime. You free later?'

'Sure. Shall I cook?' Before ringing off, she added, 'Oh, I caught the deadline at the *Hereford Times*. The ad appeared yesterday.' Then, as an afterthought: 'Could that be the problem with your friends?'

Joe had forgotten about the ad, or at least relegated it to the future. 'Go on.' He was getting there, but slowly.

'Maybe she saw the ad and when she couldn't reach you she rang her parents instead.'

The traffic had begun to move again. Keeping one eye on the road, Joe held the phone up to the wheel and scrolled through the list of messages and missed calls. There were no new numbers showing, though this, as he hastily reminded himself, didn't mean Jenna hadn't tried, only that she preferred a real person to a tape, a phone that was answered to one that rang and rang. So had she called Alan instead? The more he thought about this, the more likely it seemed, and the greater was his foreboding.

The glaziers had repaired the broken window at Shirley Road, but the builders, whose promises had from the first had a doubtful ring, had failed to fix the drooping fence, which had collapsed into three sections, one twisted on the pavement, one concertinaed into a broken fan, and one flat in the front garden, as if deposited there by a disgruntled passer-by. A light was showing behind the drawn curtains of the front room, but when Joe knocked there was no sound and no movement. Returning to the car, he scribbled a note saying he'd like to stay the night if that was okay and could his father possibly leave a key on the nail in the shed. Before posting the note he called a bright greeting through the letter-box, and before he turned away he thought he heard the shuffle of a footfall in the hall.

Alan and Helena's house was in darkness except for a bare bulb in the porch, which flickered and dipped in the blustery wind. There were no cars on the garage apron and none parked along the front. The curtains were open in the front windows, top and bottom, and in the back ones too, as though the house had been deserted all day. The kitchen door was locked, but when he tried the handle a dark shape came streaking out through the cat flap, frightening him half to death. In the old days the house cat had been a haughty marmalade called Tiggy, but this one was black and brazen, rubbing its back furiously against his leg.

The surgery was a quarter of a mile down the road, at the end of a narrow tarmacked apron, tucked behind a dingy pub. The single-storey building was made of breeze-block and ply-wood held together by thirty years of white paint. It could have been an engineering shop except for the powerful flood-lights and barred windows and the red-eyed blinks of the twin burglar alarms.

From the road the parking area looked empty, but when Joe drove in he found Alan's car hidden round the corner formed by the rear of the pub.

He rang the bell three times before Alan's voice came cautiously over the intercom.

'It's Joe.'

'*Joe?*' It was a gasp of surprise and agitation.

The door took a lot of unbolting. When Alan finally appeared, it was to stand uneasily in the darkened doorway, not barring Joe's way, but not exactly welcoming him in either.

'You all right, Alan?'

He made a small circle of one hand, a lift of a shoulder that was a greeting, a shrug and an expression of dejection all rolled into one. 'Fine, Joe.'

'Can I come in?'

'Of course!' With a nervous laugh, Alan took a jerky step backwards and closed the door behind Joe, plunging them into a gloom relieved only by the reflection of the floodlights through the barred window.

Joe would have moved towards the consulting room, but Alan showed no signs of following.

'My friend from the office,' Joe began. 'She explained that I was abroad? She told you why I couldn't call?'

'Yes, but listen, Joe,' Alan said in a headlong rush. 'The business with the property. I did try to explain to your lady. I did try to tell her. We're grateful, very grateful, but we've decided we don't want to be bothered with that just now. I'm sorry if you've gone to any trouble, Joe, I really am, but we can't be dealing with it at the moment. We really can't!'

'What is it, Alan? What's happened?'

In the dim light Alan made the same lost gesture as before, but now the hand spun wildly, in a wheeling motion that came down against his thigh with a thud.

Joe said, 'For heaven's sake, Alan,' and, putting a hand on the drooping shoulder, led him down the passage.

The consulting room had an undulating plywood ceiling and fluorescent lighting which revealed chips in the wooden desk, fading in the blue vinyl floor and gleams of condensation on the metal window-frames. The same brutal light exposed the pouches under Alan's eyes, the tension around his mouth and the frown-lines that crisscrossed his forehead like ravines.

'Trying to catch up on the paperwork.' Alan indicated the stacks of files on his desk. 'Every day new government initiatives and targets and funding schemes. Alice in Wonderland stuff!' He lowered himself into his chair like an old man, taking most of his weight on the chair arms.

Sitting down opposite, Joe asked, 'What's happened?'

Alan cast around uneasily before brightening suddenly. 'I almost forgot! I was going to ring and tell you. Your father's window? It was like I thought. Some boys from the estate. Not bad boys, Joe. Just kids who took a joke too far. Throwing stones. Larking about. And, well' – his face creased up ruefully – 'your dad might have antagonised them a bit. Shouted at them for riding their bikes on the pavement. You know.'

Joe knew.

'I've had a word with them. Explained the situation. I don't think they'll bother him again.'

'Thanks. You're a miracle worker.' But the real miracle was that the kids hadn't reported him for harassment, that he hadn't been spat on by the parents or had his tyres let down, that there was still a corner of the world where communities managed to sort out a few of their own problems.

'So?' Joe prompted him.

Alan's eyes hunted around the room once more before venturing up to meet Joe's. 'A call.'

'Jenna?'

When he nodded, the dread stirred in Joe's stomach. 'What did she say?'

'Things aren't good, Joe.'

'Is she ill?'

Alan blinked a sudden brilliance from his eyes. 'Not ill. Well, I don't *think* she's ill. I don't know! Maybe she *is* ill.'

'What, then?'

'Fear. She's living in a state of fear, Joe! That's what she said. Fear!'

'Of what? Who?'

They exchanged a look of mutual incomprehension.

'Well, of *him*, Joe. Of *him*.'

Joe made an exclamation of disbelief, partly to hide his shock, partly to give himself time. 'But that's ridiculous, Alan. I simply don't believe it. Not Chetwood!' Even as he said this, he was wondering if it could possibly be true. 'Why on earth would she be frightened of him? It doesn't make sense.'

'You're asking me, Joe? You're asking why anyone would want to hurt my beautiful girl? You're asking me how he could do this to her? If I knew. *If I knew.*' Alan made a gesture straight from his European roots, a reaching up of one palm, as if to demand an answer of God himself.

'Well, I can tell you straight away, Alan, Chetwood could never be violent. He's just not the sort. He always loathed violence in every shape and form. Really, Alan – it can't be that.'

But Alan wasn't listening. He had propped his elbows on the piles of paper and buried his head in his hands. 'All these years she's been desperate for help. All these years she's needed me, and I've done *nothing*.'

Joe got up and reached across the desk to squeeze his shoulder. 'But there's nothing you could have done, old fellow. Even supposing this is true. Really – what could you have done?'

'I could have searched for her.'

'But you did search. You did all you could.'

'Not enough, Joe. Not enough.'

Sitting down again, Joe said firmly, 'Tell me about the phone call. What did Jenna say exactly? How did she sound?'

Alan lifted his head again. 'Sound? I don't know. You'd have to ask Marc.'

Joe was very still. '*Marc?*'

'He took the call.'

It was all Joe could do not to snort aloud. 'I *see*. And how did that come about?'

'He was in the house, waiting for us to get back. He picked up the phone.'

'Well, that explains a lot, doesn't it?' Joe muttered, just loudly enough to be heard. 'In fact, that probably explains everything.'

Alan looked at him with a pained expression.

'Well, forgive me, Alan, but we only have Marc's word for what was said. And he's hardly likely to play it down, is he?'

'You're quite wrong, Joe,' Alan said in a voice that quivered slightly. 'Marc was careful to write everything down. Straight after Jenna called. Every word. So there'd be no mistake. He was determined to get it right, you see. He knew it was important to get it right.'

Several thoughts occurred to Joe. That it was typical of Marc to be so meticulous. That it was remarkably convenient that he had been the one to take the call. That Marc wasn't going to be too upset if the whole episode got blown up out of all proportion.

'Okay,' Joe said. 'So according to this immaculate record of Marc's what did Jenna say?'

'Well, I'd only be going by memory . . .'

'As close as you can.'

'She said . . . let me think, Joe, let me get it right.' Alan pressed the fingertips of both hands to his forehead. 'What she said was . . . that she didn't dare speak for long. That she was taking a terrible risk even calling. That he would' – Alan stalled abruptly, eyes brimming – 'he would *kill* her if he found out.'

Somewhere beyond the window an animal screeched in eerie lament: cat, fox, bird, Joe could never tell.

'What else?'

'Oh . . . I don't know.'

'She didn't ask for help?'

Alan looked up sharply and shook his head.

'She didn't ask to speak to you or Helena?'

Alan was getting flustered. 'No. I . . . I don't know.'

'She didn't send you her love?'

This earned Joe an open glare of reproach.

'Or ask if you were well? Or how you'd enjoyed your birthday? Anything apart from this speech that Marc has managed to record in perfect detail? I'm sorry, Alan, but if we're going to talk about people being seriously frightened, I think it's important to get the facts straight.' Not caring for the badgering note in his voice, he added in milder tone, 'Look, is Marc around? Can we get him on the phone?'

'But what other facts do we need?' Alan cried. 'She's under duress. That's all we need to know!'

'Duress?' Joe took an instant dislike to this word, which smacked of a thousand cheap American TV dramas. 'I'm not even sure I know what that means, Alan.'

'Well, that's the term they use, isn't it? I'm sure that's what Marc said. That's the term the police use.'

Joe stared at him. Now he understood everything. 'The police are involved?'

Alan nodded mutely and began to shuffle papers.

'Marc's idea, by any chance?'

'Yes. No! It's what we all want, Joe! It's the only way to find her.'

'It's going to be a full search?'

'That's what they said. That's what they promised.'

'Starting when?'

'Now. Already. Yesterday.'

And still the implications were sinking in. 'On the premise that Jenna's in danger?'

'Yes, Joe. Yes!'

'So Chetwood's going to be under suspicion of – what? – assault? For God's sake, Alan – this is mad. This has gone way too far. An accusation like that – it could ruin people's lives.'

'Don't talk to me about ruining people's lives,' Alan stated with ragged dignity.

Joe nodded in rapid surrender. 'I'm sorry. You're right. Of course you must find her. You're right.' Getting up, he paced the room and found himself looking at a stack of children's picture books. 'For what it's worth, Alan, Jenna seems to be back in Hereford. I didn't bother to tell you before because – well, to be honest I never dreamt she'd get to see the thing – but I placed an ad in a local paper, asking her to call me.' He explained about the postmark and the *Hereford Times*.

Alan seemed to absorb this information with difficulty; he asked Joe to repeat every detail. The postmark. The name of the paper. 'And when was this again, Joe? When did this advertisement appear?'

'Yesterday afternoon.'

Alan shook his head and kept shaking it while he said, 'No, no, Joe, it can't have been your advertisement she saw. No, it's not possible. You see, the call came some days ago.'

For the second time in as many minutes, Joe stared at him. 'When?'

'Four days ago? No, three.'

'You're sure?'

'Yes, I . . .' He cast around the room as if for confirmation. 'Tuesday?'

Joe understood then. Immediately after his coffee-house meeting with Ines on Monday night, she'd called Chetwood and told him. And Jenna had found out. Maybe Jenna had overheard the phone call, maybe Chetwood had lied about not having told her. Either way, she'd decided to call home, to make contact again, to cry a little over lost time, to talk about a reunion. But instead of her parents she'd got her brother. Yes – he was beginning to like this story – she'd got Marc, who'd started to get difficult, demanding to know where she was, making her thoroughly defensive, and she'd told him she was taking a risk even speaking to him because . . . He was stuck for a while. Because they were on the run? The old-fashioned phrase appealed to him. On the run. Or – almost as good – in hiding. Yes: they were in hiding and Chetwood would give her hell if he caught her on the phone. He would 'kill' her if he found out. Yes, this had to be the story, surely: it was neat, it fitted the facts, and, best of all, the plot demanded no villains.

'Tell me,' Joe said, 'after Jenna called, did Marc try last number recall?'

Alan seemed confused.

'Did he dial 1471 to find out where the call had come from?'

'No idea.'

Joe looked at the punished face, the baffled expression of injury, the way Alan's breath was coming in short gasps, and said gently, 'Why don't you leave the paperwork, old fellow? Go home and have some rest?'

'Sure.'

'Have you had any dinner?'

'Helena's left me something.'

'She's not at home?'

'Her evening at the community centre. She organises sing-alongs for the pensioners.'

'Come on, then. Why don't I pick up a takeaway and the two of us find ourselves a nice bottle of wine?'

They ate curry and cold meat with a bottle of Australian Shiraz. By the end of the meal some of the life had come back into Alan's face; he laughed at the memory of the summer holiday in Torbay when it had rained every day, he talked about Jenna with some of his old pride. They promised they would go on their much-postponed hill walk over the Christmas holiday. Only at the door did his smile falter.

When Joe reached his father's house no lights were showing, but a key had appeared on the nail in the shed. Inside the house the temperature was icy. In recompense, an ancient hot-water bottle had been placed on Joe's old bed. He knew better than to leave this token of hospitality unused and, going down to the kitchen, filled it through an alarmingly perished neck to the sweet smell of ripening apples.

The day was dark with low scudding cloud. Dawn had glimmered into uncertain life an hour before, but for all the light it had brought it could have been dusk already. Through the murk, the motorway service area blazed with the jaunty illuminations of retail festivity. Flashing lights chased around the shopping arcade, dwarf Christmas trees spiked the roof, while inside the entrance an ungainly youth in a Santa outfit tried to force leaflets into unwilling hands. The tinny treble of 'Jingle Bells' set up a feeble accompaniment to the rumble of the traffic heading away for the holiday.

It was five to ten when Joe stationed himself on a corner of the sprawling car park, within sight of the arcade entrance. He had set off before seven, driving across country on minor roads, and arrived an hour early. Over a cup of coffee and a spongy croissant, he'd skimmed a newspaper and watched the motorists traipsing through the arcade, a shuffling band of Lycra pilgrims in tight-fitting tracksuits and scruffy trainers.

When he took up his position outside, the wind was skirring sleet around the arc-lights, the racing clouds seemed barely to clear the trees, and the only colour that pierced the gloom was the rear lights of the manoeuvring cars.

At ten past ten, Joe walked along the edge of the car park and back again, before stationing himself a little closer to the arcade entrance. The sound system was croaking 'White Christmas' and by the doors the scrawny Santa had stopped someone to ask him the time. A party of senior citizens streamed past, twittering and whooping in the wind as their hair and coats were swept before them. A child in a pushchair howled at full volume, an adult shouted to be heard, and down the embankment six lanes of traffic thundered past.

At twenty past ten, Joe told himself Chetwood wasn't coming. Five minutes later, he decided to give him ten more minutes, knowing full well he'd make it thirty. Chetwood's grip on time had always been tenuous. Only planes and films had ever brought him close to punctuality. Though once – a small stab of memory – he'd actually been early. When Jenna first came down to Bristol Chetwood had arrived at the pub well before anyone else. Joe saw him now, waiting in a corner seat, deep in some esoteric reading matter, looking up with surprise, clambering awkwardly to his feet to greet them, gazing at Jenna with an oddly diffident smile. Later, when the rest of the gang arrived and the meal began, Joe had a picture of Chetwood watching Jenna, listening with quiet attention, letting other people do most of the talking, casting an occasional smile in Joe's direction, as if to say: lucky man, good choice. But she's not mine, Joe had wanted to argue. And in the next instant: I'm not sure she ever will be.

He couldn't remember how the meal had ended, but he had the impression that Chetwood had vanished before the party broke up. At the station, when Joe saw Jenna onto the train, she'd said, 'I liked your tall friend.' He had a memory of her giving a jokey wave, a neat imitation of a windscreen wiper, from the train as it gathered speed.

The wind seemed to have reached storm force. Wires were strumming, and, somewhere close by, metal was vibrating in intermittent crescendo. Joe's feet had gone numb, and the feeling was going in his nose.

It was ten to eleven. Chetwood wasn't coming; perhaps he had never intended to come. It wouldn't be the first time he had stood Joe up. Even as he thought this, he heard a quiet voice at his elbow.

'Watcha, Joe.'

He spun round. 'For God's sake,' he laughed.

They embraced.

'Where the hell did you spring from?' Joe demanded with another laugh.

'Good to see you, Joe.'

'And you.'

'Too long.'

Chetwood seemed taller, or at least thinner, an effect of his haircut perhaps, which was positively short by past standards, close at the sides and not much longer on top. His eyes had gathered a few lines, and his forehead too, and there was a faint patch of colour high on each cheek, like skin scoured by long exposure to the wind. But his face was as striking as ever, with the steady black eyes and the dark eyebrows that swept out like paint strokes and the fine-drawn mouth over white teeth. 'Come on!' Chetwood beckoned with a shiver, as if Joe had been the one keeping them from the warmth. Walking down the arcade, he declared, 'The places we meet, Joe. Never let it be said I don't bring exotica into your life. Where was it last time?'

'Gresham Gardens.'

'That tandoori house in Cricklewood,' he said, talking across Joe's words. 'The place with the curried dog meat and those suspicious raisins. A little too black for comfort, didn't you think? And what about Bristol? That caff with the teeth-curdling tea and the anaemic eggs and the brassy bacon. Yes, Joe, never let it be said we don't hit the gastronomic high spots.' He led the way into the Happy Wayfarer and up to the servery. 'And *here* we have the best of British cuisine. Isn't that right?' – this to the girl behind the counter.

'Yes?' She held her spatula like a weapon.

'Your very best breakfast, please.'

'The Great English?' With a stabbing motion of the spatula, she gestured towards the bill of fare on the wall over her head.

'Is that what you recommend?'

'It comes with everything.'

Chetwood threw out a hand. 'Well, everything's what I've always wanted.'

The girl's eyes flickered dangerously.

Chetwood said, 'He'll have the same.'

'No, no,' Joe said hastily. 'Just coffee for me.'

'Townie habits, Joe. Won't do you the slightest good.'

Chetwood picked up the tray and carried it unhurriedly down the length of the restaurant. He was dressed for the country in a green waterproof jacket, well-worn and frayed along the hem, and khaki trousers, also far from new. But it was his shoes that caught Joe's attention. They were brown and thick-soled, and there was a deep rim of dried mud around the heels, topped by a jagged water-mark.

They sat in a corner booth with tartan seats and tinsel pinned diagonally across the walls. There was a family of four at a table opposite and an elderly couple in the booth behind, but hardly anyone was talking. Overhead, Harry Belafonte was wending his way through 'Mary's Boy Child'.

'So, Joe, how's it going?' Chetwood pulled his jacket off to reveal a dark blue sweater with the shapeless weave of a hand-knit. 'How's the big bad city and the big bad world of the law? Are you successful? Are you rich? Are you heading for great things?'

'No chance.'

Above the faint smile, the dark eyes examined him unhurriedly. 'But you enjoy it?'

'Increasingly uncertain.'

Another thoughtful gaze and a sudden grin that didn't entirely reach his eyes. 'And what about the rest? Is there a person in your life, Joe? Is she beautiful and clever and wise?'

'There's . . . someone, yes.'

'Special?'

'Early days yet.'

Another speculative glance, before Chetwood began to eat as though he hadn't seen a proper meal in a long time. Between mouthfuls he produced a fast and furious stream of questions: what did Joe's work involve, what did he dislike about it, where was he living, what did he do in his spare time. From Chetwood's manner, the two of them might have been old friends whose lives had diverged through an accident of geography. He listened intently, with regular exclamations of surprise, interest and outright astonishment, sometimes exaggerated for effect, sometimes heartfelt. How could Joe live in London, how could he work such long hours, how could he travel without seeing anything of the countries he was visiting. 'God, Joe, what a bloody treadmill!' Yet all the time Joe had the feeling that the dark eyes were watching him, missing nothing, perfectly friendly, a little nostalgic even, but ultimately wary, and that when the grins came, sudden and broad, they were as much a means of maintaining distance as showing pleasure.

By the time Chetwood was finishing his breakfast he had
run out of questions, which was probably the intention.

'And you?' Joe asked into the first available silence. 'You're
busy?'

'Oh, busy enough. But you know me, Joe. I was never
going to kill myself from overwork, was I?'

'Travelling a lot?'

'Enough.'

'Still involved in the orphanage?'

He shook his head. 'Too much corruption, too much
thieving, and the kids still ended up on the streets. You
can't change the system in a place like that, and it's crazy to
try.'

Joe must have let the surprise show in his face because
Chetwood added, 'Human nature untamed is a pretty stinking
thing close up, Joe. Pity is no weapon against corruption. Not
in a place where no one knows the meaning of shame.'

'I see.'

'What the hell. Can't take on the entire world. We've each
of us only so much to give. It's a fact of life. You've got to
keep centred, or you'd bleed yourself dry.'

'Sure.'

He grinned. 'Lawyers keep centred, right?'

'You bet. You're still importing rugs?'

The grin faded. 'Not so much rugs nowadays.'

'Other things?'

'This and that.'

'Business good?'

'You know how it is.'

It was all Joe could do not to growl, no, he didn't know
how it was, not at all, and why the hell did they have to play
these bloody stupid games, but he bit his tongue and said
lightly, 'It was good to meet your sister the other day.'

Chetwood lifted his eyebrows in an expression that could
have meant anything. That he knew about Joe's visit. That he
wasn't terribly interested.

'I went to see your family because I didn't know where else to start.'

'You met my father?'

'Yes.'

'My God. What bravery! How d'you get on?'

'He threw me out of the house.'

Chetwood roared with strange intense laughter. 'Classic! God Almighty, what a player!'

'Kate picked up the pieces and put me back together again.'

But Chetwood was still caught up in his dark laughter.

'She's a great girl.'

'Mmm?'

'Kate.'

'Oh yeah.'

There was a pause while Joe waited for Chetwood to ask after Kate's welfare and Chetwood conspicuously failed to do so.

'She told me about Ines.'

'Ah.'

'The incredible thing is that I found Ines working just a couple of streets away from me in London. Kate thought she was in Brazil.'

Chetwood maintained a restless silence.

'I liked Ines very much.'

Another deliberate pause while Chetwood stirred his tea.

'It was Ines who phoned and told you about me, was it?'

Chetwood flashed him a narrow look. 'Well, someone phoned and told me, didn't they?'

It was like a gust of cold air and a call to order, all in one. As if to underline the start of the official agenda, Chetwood pushed his plate to one side and tidied the debris from the table. When he looked up again, his expression was noticeably cooler.

'So! This thing that needs signing, Joe. You've got it?'

Joe took the rolled envelope from his jacket pocket and extracted the document.

Chetwood scanned it fast, then went over it again more carefully. Ridges sprang up between his eyebrows, and grew more pronounced as he flicked back and forth between the pages.

Joe said, 'If you're worried about the address for Jenna, you could make it care of a solicitors' firm. And the witness – you could use a solicitor for that too. In fact, under the circumstances I would strongly recommend it. To avoid any problems.'

'Uh huh,' he murmured, reading again. 'Are there likely to be problems?'

'Normally, no. But in a situation like this, where the signatory' – he corrected himself very deliberately – 'where *Jenna* hasn't been seen for a long time, where her family haven't spoken to her for over four years, it's best to have a lawyer to vouch for the fact that, well . . .'

'She's still alive?'

'That everything is as it should be.'

'That I'm not trying to pull a fast one?'

'It's not a question of—' Spotting the sardonic glint in Chetwood's eye, Joe broke off with a smile.

'That I'm not standing over her with a gun, getting ready to make off with the money. Is that it?' He was grinning dangerously.

'Absolutely,' Joe agreed, forcing the joke. 'But, look, it's just my lawyer's mind at work, Chetwood. I'm just trying to anticipate problems before they arise. That's all.'

But Chetwood said with ominous calm, 'What else might I be up to? Tell me, do. I'm really interested.'

'In theory, you mean?' Joe said, careful to interpret the question in general terms. 'Help . . . this isn't exactly my field. But if I remember rightly, problems can arise if there's any question of the signatory not understanding what he or she is signing. If there's a possibility of mental incompetence or confusion. Any question of coercion. Or – I've forgotten something – yes, forgery. I think that's it.'

'But if we get a solicitor to witness Jenna's signature I'm off the hook?'

'It's not about getting you off the hook,' Joe laughed awkwardly. 'But if you like – yes.'

'Unless I find a bent lawyer. Right?' Chetwood pointed a gleeful finger at Joe, as if scoring a point.

'Right.'

Chetwood's strange suppressed anger evaporated. 'This gives Marc power of attorney?'

'But only for the sale of the house. Nothing else.'

'Why Marc?'

'Because it makes things that much simpler for the nego-tiations and the paperwork. But, look, if Jenna would like to nominate someone else it's not a problem. She can nominate anyone she likes. I would point out, however, that the nominee would have to be available to discuss the terms of the deal with the other parties, and to sign on the dotted line when the time comes.'

Chetwood shot Joe a wolf grin. 'You sound just like a bloody lawyer, Joe.'

'Guilty as charged.'

Returning to the document, recharged by a nervous energy, Chetwood tapped a finger rapidly against his mouth, and Joe noticed that his nails were short and chipped and that the skin round the edges was rough and stained, by soil or paint, it was impossible to tell.

'But if we wanted someone else as our nominee or whatever you call it we'd have to start all over again with this thing, would we?' He chucked the document onto the table.

'No way round it. But any solicitor should be able to draw one up in a matter of hours.'

'And what about the money? Would that go through this nominee person too?'

'Not Jenna's half, no. That would be paid direct to her by the conveyancing solicitor. That's one of the reasons there has to be an address.'

With the air of moving on to the next item, Chetwood straightened up and laid both hands flat on the table. 'Okay, so what's the deal? How much are they offering, these developers?'

'Forty-two thousand.'

'Each?'

'In total.'

Chetwood's mouth drew up into a grimace of disbelief. 'You're telling me that a house on a prime site in the middle of town is going for forty thousand?'

'It's a tiny place, with structural problems and damp. It isn't worth anything as a house.'

'Sorry, Joe, there can't be a place in the entire country that goes for forty thousand, let alone one the developers are hungry for. We're in the middle of a property boom, for God's sake.'

'But it's not for housing, it's for an industrial unit. And it's in a bad part of town.'

Chetwood wasn't having any of this. 'It's one of a terrace?'

'I'm pretty sure, yes.'

'Well, how many have the developers managed to get hold of so far? Is this one of the last? How badly do they need it? Is this their best offer?'

'I don't know.'

'Well, if it's one of the last houses, I can tell you it's going to be worth a lot more than forty thousand. It's simple arithmetic, isn't it? Who's been handling the negotiations? Or,' he added heavily, 'is that a stupid question?'

Still adjusting to the vision of Chetwood as a commercial operator, Joe was slow in answering. 'Marc, I suppose.'

'Well, has he tried to jack the price up at all? Did he turn down their first offer?'

'I don't know.'

'I tell you, Joe, if it was anyone else I'd suspect I was being conned. I'd be smelling a huge and extremely niffy rat. But with Marc it's just going to be pig-headedness, isn't it? And there's no arguing with that.'

'I could try and find out what negotiations have gone on, if you like.'

Seeming to lose interest, Chetwood sank back in his seat and muttered, 'All this trouble for twenty grand.'

'Marc needs it to study. He wants to qualify as a teacher.'

'A teacher? Right – power without responsibility. That'll suit him down to the ground.' He rolled his eyes. 'For twenty grand I'm beginning to think it'd be easier to give him the cash.'

'What about Jenna? Doesn't she want to sell the house?'

'Now you're the one who's being stupid, Joe!' The rebuke came out of nowhere, sharp and not at all contained, and there was a startled pause while Chetwood drained his tea and Joe tried to work out what he'd said to touch such a nerve.

'So, do you want to go ahead with this or not?' Joe asked at last.

'I guess so.'

'Any idea when you can get the power of attorney back to me?'

Chetwood slid the document a little closer, then away again, then lifted his hand clear in a gesture of wanting to be rid of the whole thing. 'I suppose it'll have to be Marc,' he sighed doubtfully.

Joe waited until he made up his mind.

'Yes, the crazy Marc! What the hell.'

'It'll be okay with Jenna?'

'Yeah, yeah.'

'You're sure?'

The black eyes shot Joe a warning glance. 'I'm sure.'

But Joe was in no mood to be put off any longer. 'Does she know anything about this yet?'

'I'll tell her when the time is right.'

'Why hasn't she been in touch, Chetwood?'

Chetwood leant his elbows on the table and made a steeple of his hands. 'It's just . . . not been practical.'

'That's not an answer.'

Chetwood regarded Joe for what seemed a long time before appearing to come to a decision. 'She likes a quiet life, Joe. She needs . . .' He chose each word with care. 'A life . . . that's uncomplicated. A life without . . . distractions.'

'But why, Chetwood? What reason?'

'She has the life she wants. Believe me.'

'But is she ill? Has she had some sort of breakdown? Is she depressed?'

'I'm not going to get into guessing games, Joe. I told you before, there's nothing wrong with her.'

Joe took a deep steadying breath. 'So, this hiding away – it's her decision, is it?'

'Of course. Who else's would it be?' He looked at his watch, then back to Joe. He gave a sudden smile. 'Hey. I've got to go.'

'Wait.'

He was reaching for his jacket and pulling it onto his lap.

'I need your word that you're taking good care of her.'

'My *word*.' He almost laughed. 'Long time since anyone asked for my *word*.' The idea amused him. 'Yes – for what it's worth, *fine noble Joe* – I give you my word.'

'And that she's happy.'

'Happy's a bastard word, Joe.' There was an edge to his voice. 'Got hijacked by Hollywood. Like *love* and *fulfilment*. Turned into candyfloss. But if you want me to say it, I'll say it. She's happy. Okay?' He slid to the end of the bench.

'She's not frightened of anything?'

Chetwood paused in profile, his eyes on the family in the opposite booth. He was still staring in their direction a couple of seconds later when he stood up and began to pull on his jacket. 'What would she be frightened of, Joe?'

'You tell me.'

He shrugged the jacket up onto his shoulders. '*Fright-ened* . . . What made you ask that all of a sudden, Joe? Where the hell did that come from?'

Joe hesitated as two parallel and opposing narratives ran through his mind, one written by Marc in which Chetwood must not on any account be told about Jenna's call for fear of what he'd do to her, one written by Joe's instincts and mem-ories which told him that the truth was not going to do anyone any harm.

'Where the hell did that come from?' Chetwood repeated.

'Marc. He says he spoke to Jenna on the phone.'

Chetwood's gaze lost focus. 'When was this meant to be?'

'Monday or Tuesday, I think.'

Another pause, almost as long as the one before. 'No,' he announced with finality. 'No, that's not possible.'

'That it was Monday or Tuesday?'

'That she made a call. On Monday or any other day.'

'Marc seemed pretty sure.'

'Then he's lying!'

The family at the opposite table looked round.

'Well, whether or not—'

'No, let's get it right – he's lying!'

Joe acceded with a gesture.

Chetwood turned away, only to turn straight back again. 'And what was this call meant to be about? What was she meant to have said?'

'I don't know.'

'But you know she was meant to be frightened?'

'According to Marc she was frightened to come to the phone. She was scared of what might happen to her if she was found out.'

Chetwood gave an awful smile. 'Ah! I'm getting there now. She was frightened of the big bad husband, is that it? She was married to the monster?'

Joe gave a rueful shrug.

'Well, what a bad boy I am, Joe. I spirit her away, I cut her off from her family, I frighten the hell out of her. For Christ's sake, nothing to be said for me at all!'

The next moment he was gone, leaving Joe to snatch up the document and hurry after him. In the arcade Chetwood strode ahead, until without warning he swivelled round, stopping so abruptly that a small kid cannoned into him. 'What else did she say, *according to Marc?*' he demanded, disentangling himself from the child.

'I don't know.'

The speakers were reprising 'Jingle Bells' as a clatter like scattering marbles sounded around their feet. Joe looked down to see Maltesers bouncing and rolling in every direction, and the child frozen in disbelief.

'No calls for the police?' Chetwood scoffed, oblivious.

The child sucked in a shuddering breath and began to scream. A man, scarlet in cheek and garb, scooped the kid up and, thrusting his face close to Chetwood's, started to hiss abuse.

Chetwood backed away, looking astonished. '*Hit* your child? I didn't hit your child!'

This seemed to goad the father to greater fury, and Joe rapidly placed himself between the two of them. 'An accident,' he said in a reassuring voice as he dug in his pocket for some coins.

'I didn't *hit* your child,' repeated Chetwood on a rising note of bewilderment.

'Here.' Joe beamed at the screaming child. 'Enough for a bumper packet!'

The father snatched the money. 'Soddin' disgraceful, people like you.'

Taking a firm grip on Chetwood's arm, Joe hauled him away. At the doors the teenage Santa was about to thrust a leaflet in front of them when he read Chetwood's expression and thought better of it.

Outside, Joe called on Chetwood to slow down, but he didn't slow down, not until he was into the car park and halfway across the first lane, when he halted restlessly, muttering to himself. Joe caught 'aggression . . . as *if* I wanted to . . .'

Finally he stopped his aimless circling and glanced sideways at Joe with a dark laugh. 'Never did like bloody Maltesers.'

Headlights pierced the gloom and a car manoeuvred past them. The sleet had gone, but the wind was racketing over the tarmac, pulling at their clothes and snatching at their breath.

Sensing that Chetwood was about to leave, Joe moved round to face him. 'It's not enough,' he said sternly. 'What you've given me. It's not enough for Alan and Helena.'

'What, to persuade them I'm not a danger?'

'They need a reason for all this, Chetwood. They need something they can understand.'

He started to shake his head. 'Sorry—'

'No, Chetwood!' Joe checked his anger, but not a lot. 'Sorry's not good enough. Not any more. Alan's not well. I can't go and give him this quiet life rubbish – it'll kill him. What – his daughter's fine but she just doesn't want to see him again? He deserves better than that. For Christ's sake, Chetwood – Jenna can't want him dead of a broken heart.'

Beside them, a car started up, its rear lights sprang into life. Joe touched Chetwood's sleeve to draw him away, but he didn't move. Instead he went on staring at Joe in an intense, reproachful way. The driver began to reverse, then stopped, waiting for them to take the hint and get out of the way.

Joe tried again, jerking his head towards safety, but Chetwood stayed rooted to the spot. 'You're right,' he said at last.

The driver resorted to his horn, a quick beep, but Chetwood wasn't listening or didn't care.

'You're right,' he announced again. Then, in a voice so tight and low it was almost lost to the wind, Chetwood said, 'All right, Joe, I'll tell you. I'll tell you, and hope to God we're doing the right thing.'

The horn sounded again, for longer this time, and as
Chetwood began to speak Joe took him bodily by the arm and
pulled him away.

'She had a breakdown,' he was saying. 'She had a breakdown, Joe, and she's not over it yet. I'm not sure she'll ever get
over it.'

Keeping hold of Chetwood's upper arm, Joe kept him
walking. They were heading into the full blast of the wind and
Joe had to bend close to Chetwood to hear.

'Something bad happened. A friend of ours died and Jenna
blames herself. It was an accident, but she feels responsible.
She's never got over it.'

They reached a landscaped area with spiky black ground
cover and low shrubs and dwarf trees which thrashed and
shivered in the storm. Beyond it, the embankment dropped
down to the motorway and the droning traffic. Stopping,
Chetwood hunched his shoulders against the cold.

'She's just about okay when we're on our own. We've got
animals. A dog, a pony . . . She loves all that. But she can't
deal with people, Joe. She needs to talk about it sometimes
and, well' – he gave a dry laugh – 'people don't understand.'

'Has she had professional help?'

'Sure.'

'No good?'

He shook his head.

'A therapist?'

'She was the worst. A nasty devious mind. Did more harm
than good. No, Jenna's fine on her own, Joe. I mean, as fine as
she'll ever be.'

'This friend . . . who was it?'

Chetwood's eyes hunted across the horizon. 'Sam Raynor.
Just a kid. Twenty.'

'And what happened?'

Chetwood's mouth turned down, he stared at the ground.
'He drowned. Crazy, crazy boy.'

After a time, Joe prompted, 'How?'

Chetwood studied the sky before casting Joe a sideways look. 'Craziest thing of all, Joe. A river in full flood. Got swept away.'

This was so unexpected, so startling, that Joe could only stare dumbly at Chetwood as a series of images chased across his mind. He saw cascading water, rocks, a savage undertow that would not release its grip on the struggling man. He saw the body found miles downstream, bloodless and cold. Then, drawing back from this, he pictured the unknown Sam before his death, young – youth seemed to be his defining feature – yes, a paradigm of youth: fresh-faced, smooth-skinned, golden-haired, sitting at the table in the garden where Joe himself had sat. And then the final thought – no image attached to this – Sam and Jenna. And the memory of Ines's voice: *She had some-one new already.*

'But how did it happen?' Joe asked.

Chetwood gestured mystification.

'Why did Jenna blame herself?'

'She felt she could have stopped him.'

'You mean . . . it was suicide?'

'No, an *accident*. I told you.' His voice had developed a nervy ring. 'Look, the whole thing's crazy, okay, Joe? There's no reason. No reason for any of it. But it happened, and she can't get it out of her head. And the only way she keeps going is to have her animals and her music and her quiet life. Okay?'

Not okay, thought Joe. Not okay at all. Why vanish with-out trace? Why bother to go to such lengths? But he saw the old restlessness back in Chetwood's face and the warning flash in his eyes, and knew this was as far as he was going to get, for the moment at least.

They began to walk back. Ahead of them, the wind picked up a beer can and sent it clattering over the tarmac.

'There wouldn't be any harm in Jenna seeing the family though, would there?' Joe asked. 'They'd understand. They'd bend over backwards to help.'

'Best not.'

'Just a phone call.'

'No,' Chetwood snapped. 'She'd end up in pieces. I'm telling you, Joe, it would set her right back.'

Joe gave a weary sigh. 'Okay.'

'And what I've just told you – only Alan and Helena. Okay?'

'Marc?'

'Not Marc.'

'It might be an idea to tell him, Chetwood.'

Chetwood looked unconvinced.

Joe hadn't planned to hold back on the bad news, he told himself there simply hadn't been an obvious opportunity; but now he braced himself rather guiltily to say, 'He's taking the search for Jenna very seriously. In fact . . . he's called in the police.'

Chetwood stopped, his face puckered in disbelief. '*What?*'

'After the call from Jenna – the *alleged* call, rather – he decided to report it.'

'Report *what*?'

'I think . . . that she seemed to be frightened.'

Chetwood looked shocked. It was a moment before he managed to speak. 'Why didn't you tell me this before, Joe?' And now his voice was cold. '*My God . . .*' He began walking away. 'Thanks a million, Joe! Thanks for nothing!'

Catching up with him, Joe said, 'So the police find you. Does it matter that much?'

'It matters! It matters like hell!'

'Well, why don't you call Marc and sort it out?'

Halting again, Chetwood asked roughly, 'Tell me something, would you say that Marc was stupid or clever? On balance, I mean.'

'The strange thing is I'm not absolutely sure about that.'

In a move that was so slow it was almost hypnotic, Chetwood reached for the rolled document sticking out of Joe's pocket and held it up. 'Well, tell him this, will you? Tell the little shit that if he wants an absolute guarantee that Jenna will never agree to sell this house, if he wants to be absolutely sure that there's not a cat in hell's chance of her signing this or anything else, then he's going about it exactly the right way.' Chetwood came closer, and it seemed to Joe that he was trembling. 'And you can tell him another thing. That this crazy search will only cause huge grief. To Jenna. To himself. To everyone.' He turned away, only to turn straight back again. '*And* you can tell him that if the police are going to be involved I'll come and kill him. In person. With my bare hands.'

Slowly, Chetwood ripped the document in two, and again and again. 'As for giving him power of anything, you have to be kidding. I wouldn't trust him further than something nasty I'd picked up on my shoe.'

He held the shreds up in one hand and opened his fingers. The wind snatched the fragments away and carried them fluttering across the tarmac.

As Chetwood strode off, he spun round, walking backwards, and called, 'He was lying about that call, Joe. The little shit was lying.'

Chapter Six

———·———

THE VILLAGE straddled a busy trunk road. The pavements were so narrow, the cottages so bent that, when juggernauts thundered past, whole rows of dwellings seemed to teeter on the brink of demolition. Hand-painted notices on the approaches read: *Where's Our Bypass?* and *Children Killed By YOUR Speed*, but nobody slowed down.

Driving into the village, Joe found himself sandwiched between two lorries and swerved off at the first available opportunity onto the forecourt of a pub called the Belvoir Arms. The barmaid told him he was on Nottingham Road all right, but hadn't a clue where number two was. The lone occupant of the public bar, an old boy with rasping breath, jerked his head towards the far end of the village and muttered the word 'newsagent'. Taking his life in his hands, Joe went on foot, pulling in against the grime-encrusted walls whenever anything large roared fire at him. He found the newsagent all right and, three doors beyond, number two. It was a cottage, a century younger than the ones in the heart of the village, and set a yard or so further back from the road, though not far enough to avoid the caking of dirt which covered the walls, doors and windows to a height of six feet or more, as though sprayed on with a paint gun.

The door had no bell and no knocker, so he rapped with his knuckle. During a lull in the traffic, he thought he heard music. He rapped again, harder. After a time, a window opened above and Marc's head appeared, a mobile phone to his ear, a look of annoyance on his face. He made a circular gesture, which took Joe around the side of the newsagent's and into a small back lane to a gate marked 2.

Pushing it open, he entered a narrow garden with a slimy stone path flanked by layers of mouldering vegetation. The back door had frosted glass and a bell. After a while, Joe pressed the bell, but it was either silent or broken because no buzzer sounded. Finally, he heard leisurely footsteps approaching and Marc opened the door, talking ostentatiously into the phone. With barely a glance at Joe, he turned and wandered back into the house. Following, Joe passed through a long kitchen extension which smelt of frying and vinegar and gas, into a living room with speckled terracotta wallpaper, a Romanesque dado frieze, a low sofa with a cream fake-fur throw that had seen cleaner days, and a hi-fi playing easy listening.

A large frizzy-haired girl with pencilled eyebrows and hard eyes sat slumped on the sofa, picking at a bag of crisps. She met Joe's 'Hi' with a long expressionless gaze before returning to the magazine on her lap.

Joe glanced out of the window and saw a murky area formed by a wall and the back of the kitchen extension. Removing the *Guardian* appointments section from a wooden chair, he sat down and felt the traffic vibration resonate in the chair frame.

Continuing his phone conversation, Marc strutted backwards and forwards across the room, clad in a sweater which showed the breadth of his shoulders and the solidity of his stomach, an effect somewhat spoilt by the thigh-switching plumpness of his legs, which gave him a slight waddle.

It was impossible not to overhear what he was saying, nor to realise this was the intention.

'Denial of due process, Steve – that's grounds for constructive dismissal. Their refusal to address the issues – that definitely amounts to harassment. You have the right to go straight to tribunal, you know. And if they try to block you then they're in breach . . .'

When he finally rang off, he snapped the phone shut with a smooth flick of the wrist, like a trick he'd seen in the movies and been practising ever since.

Joe got to his feet. 'Thanks for this.'

Marc tightened his lips to show he thought he was being pretty generous too, and shifted his stance into something more comfortable for the trying time ahead.

'Okay to talk now?' By which Joe meant in the hearing of the frizzy-haired girl and to the accompaniment of the sound-track from *Gladiator*.

Marc let his eyelids droop for a moment, and in the absence of other information Joe took this as a yes.

'Your father said you'd spoken to Jenna.'

Marc liked that. It allowed him to say, 'That's not something I'm prepared to discuss with anyone outside the family.'

Apart from the police, Joe thought. 'Can you tell me when she called?'

Marc did the eyelid droop again, though this time it seemed to signal a no rather than a yes.

'Was it on Monday night?'

A grim little smile gathered at the corners of Marc's mouth. This was proving to be far more fun than he'd dared hope. The silence that followed was all about who was going to give in and speak first.

'Okay,' Joe said in his most reasonable tone. 'Can you confirm that the police have got involved?'

'Correct.'

'On what basis exactly?'

'Couldn't say.'

'Well, what are they doing exactly?'

'They have the facts. I couldn't say what conclusions they might choose to draw, or indeed what actions they might choose to take, if any.'

It wasn't often that Joe was driven to thoughts of violence but for a tantalising moment he imagined what it would be like to punch Marc in the centre of his dough-like face, to deliver a neat little jab straight to the fleshy nose.

'You don't worry what might happen once the police turn up on Jenna's doorstep?'

'I don't follow you.'

'You don't think she'll look on it as an unjustified invasion of her privacy?'

Marc folded his arms and went through a pantomime of restraining himself with the greatest difficulty, puckering his mouth and flaring his pudgy nostrils and taking long noisy breaths through his nose. '*Really*,' he declared in a voice that sang with righteous indignation. 'You've got a nerve!'

'Look, I don't want to interfere – believe me – but supposing I had it on good authority that she doesn't want to be found?'

A series of expressions flitted across Marc's face, but the one that lingered longest was a sort of triumphant disgust. 'I get the picture. I get it. You're in *contact*.' He made it sound like a contagious disease. 'Yes, yes . . .' He nodded furiously, as if this explained everything that was wrong with the entire planet. 'You're in contact with them. Or' – he gave an unpleasant little snort – 'should I say *him*? Now why do I think I don't need to ask that question? Why do I think I know the answer?'

'They don't want the police involved, Marc.'

'Says *him*, right?'

'I think he speaks for both of them.'

'Says *him*.'

'Whichever, there's no way they're going to agree to sell the house, Marc, no way they're even going to discuss it, while the police are involved.'

The *Gladiator* music had moved on to the arena theme, the bit where the tiger tries to eat Russell Crowe, and the room was filled with the bass crescendo of cinematic tension.

'How was that again?' said Marc. It might have been Joe's imagination, but he looked shaken.

'Can we kill the music first?'

Maybe the girl was waiting for the chance to hear better, maybe she had the remote control in her hand, but the music stopped almost immediately, and the silence gave way to the rumble of the traffic two walls away.

'What I said was they're not prepared to sign anything while the police are clumping about.'

Marc had heard all right the first time, but he'd wanted a bit longer to prepare his speech. 'Well, I've got news for you,' he declared in a virtuous tone. 'Your friend can make all the threats he likes. It won't make the slightest difference. This isn't about the house, this isn't about the money, and he's making a big mistake if he thinks it is.'

'What is it about then?'

'It's about my sister's welfare! And her right to self-determination!'

Joe thought he had kept all expression out of his face but Marc quickly added, 'You seem to be having trouble with that idea, Joe. You seem to think *I'm* the one who doesn't care about Jenna. That *I'm* the one who started all this trouble. Well, you didn't see the way he treated her up at the farmhouse, did you? You didn't see her on the point of an overdose.' Watching Joe's reaction, he said with quiet relish, 'Didn't know about that, did you? No, well, I tell you, you never knew half the things that went on up there.'

The jetlag seemed to hit Joe with all the force of a sleeping drug. He felt a sudden and overwhelming tiredness. He went back to the chair and sat down again. 'Any chance of a strong coffee?'

Marc hesitated suspiciously, hackles still at full alert, before turning to the girl and jerking his head towards the kitchen. She threw him a don't-expect-me-to-wait-on-you face and, his mouth drawn into a tight pucker, Marc stalked off to make the coffee himself. When he came back balancing a full mug in both hands, his hostility seemed to have given way, if not to open co-operation, then to guarded neutrality.

Joe said, 'I didn't realise you'd been to the farmhouse.'

'Oh yes!'

'I'd no idea it was like that,' Joe said, with a show of being suitably impressed. 'None at all.'

'Oh yeah, it was bad all right.'

Again, Joe seemed overawed by the information. 'What happened?' he asked humbly.

Marc pulled a matching wooden chair away from the wall and placed it next to the hi-fi, not too close to Joe but not too far away either. Sitting down, crossing one sturdy leg over the other, Marc considered Joe with an air of studied indifference that didn't quite stretch to his eyes, which contained a gleam of anticipation.

'I've never told Mum and Dad.'

'No, of course.'

'I've never told anybody.'

'I promise it'll go no further,' Joe said deferentially.

This seemed to remind Marc of what a huge favour he was doing Joe, and he gave a condescending sniff.

'I hadn't seen Jen in an age,' he began at last. 'Six months maybe.' He glanced at Joe, as if to gauge the reaction so far. Apparently satisfied, he went on: 'It was Easter, I was meant to be going to France with the college, but there was a ferry strike, the trip was cancelled, and Dad was keen for me to go and see if Jen was okay. They hadn't heard anything for weeks, Mum and Dad, and they were getting worried. So I offered to go up there, to Hereford.' Another pause to read Joe's expression. 'Couldn't get through to Jen to begin with. Rang dozens of times, and then of course it was him who answered, and he wouldn't put her on, not till I made it clear I wasn't going to give up. Took for ever before she finally came on the line, and then it was like, it's a long way to come, are you sure you want to come all this way, that sort of thing. And all in a dead voice. Like she was brainwashed or something.'

A heavy vehicle lumbered past the house, shaking it to the

foundations, and it seemed impossible that any mortar could survive the continual barrage.

'Anyway, so I got there and of course there was no one to meet me at the station—'

'Sorry, Marc – when was this? How long ago?'

'Must be five years? Yeah, four and a half, five at the most.' Marc crossed his meaty arms and settled back in his seat. Apart from the occasional glances at Joe, he kept his button gaze fixed on the window beyond Joe's chair. He spoke in a squeaky monotone of disapproval. 'So, I wait for the best part of an hour at the station – can't get them on the phone of course – and eventually *he* turns up. No apologies, needless to say. Then he runs around town, picking things up, shopping, generally farting about. Like he's trying to waste time. Must have been two hours he kept driving around. I could see what he was up to, of course, but there was nothing I could do. Just had to sit it out. He kept talking all this crap. India, Buddhism, the state of the world – as if *I* was interested in hearing *his* views on the subject.'

'But you got there eventually?'

It didn't take much to make Marc bristle, and he bristled now. 'I'm explaining what happened, okay? I'm telling you it was all a scam, that he was trying to keep me away from her for as long as possible. I'm explaining, okay?'

'Sorry.'

With a tight sigh, Marc went on, 'So when we finally got there he announced Jen was upstairs resting. That she'd be down soon. Well, it wasn't soon, it was hours, and all the time I had to listen to him rabbiting on while he made this meal. It was evening when she finally came down. She looked like death. I mean, terrible. Skin and bone. Dark shadows. If it hadn't been Jen, I'd have thought she was on substances.' Answering Joe's frown, he snapped, 'I'm not saying she *was*, okay? I'm saying she *looked* like it.'

Joe nodded. 'Sure.'

With a last indignant glance, Marc settling his gaze on the window again. 'She hardly said a word at dinner. She hardly had the chance. He was too quick. Watched us like a hawk and every time I tried to talk to her he cut in and spouted all this crap. And when she did manage a word he'd pick her up on it. Sort of rubbish whatever she said. So I tried to find a way of getting her on her own—'

Joe interrupted gently, 'Sorry, Marc, but when you say he rubbished her, how? What sort of things did he say?'

'Hey, we're talking five years ago. I can't give you chapter and verse after all this time.'

'No. But roughly?'

Grudgingly, Marc searched his memory. 'I suppose it was things like, "You don't mean that, do you?" and "You're talking nonsense." Stuff like that.'

'And what was she trying to say when this happened?'

'Well . . . nothing. Anything.'

'I see. Thanks.'

'So . . ' Marc said in the tone of getting back to the business in hand. 'I tried to get her on her own. It wasn't easy. He was like an effing shadow. But in the end I managed to catch her on her way upstairs. And of course she'd been longing to talk. Sort of pulled at my arm and broke down and begged for help. Wanted right out. There and then.'

'What do you mean, wanted out?'

'Said she couldn't go on. Said she couldn't live like that any more. Asked me to help get her out. Get her to the police. Otherwise she was ready to jack it all in. I might not have got the exact words, okay? But near enough.'

'But . . . why the police?'

'For protection,' Marc replied as if it was glaringly obvious. 'To keep him away.'

'She actually said that?'

He looked at the floor. 'Well, yeah,' he argued with sulky ferocity. 'She wanted the police. She wanted protection.'

There were times when Marc stared unflinchingly at you
and times when he couldn't meet your eye, but Joe couldn't
decide which, if any, went with the truth.

''Course, I said she could rely on me a hundred per cent,'
Marc resumed with bad humour. 'That I'd get her out straight
away. Right there and then. And I would have too. But the
moment I said it, she began to panic. Started saying it would
be difficult. That *he* wouldn't like it. That *he* would try and
stop her. Basically, she ended up doing a complete U-turn. No,
no, she didn't want to go anywhere. No, I wasn't to take any
notice of what she'd said. No, she was fine. No, she was just a
bit stressed, that was all. The real reason she was backtracking,
of course, was that she'd heard *him* coming to look for her.
That's how much he scared her! She only had to hear him
coming.'

Joe tried to imagine Jenna in the role of oppressed wife,
but the image wouldn't form and it seemed to him that after
all this time he couldn't even conjure up her face with any
accuracy.

'I tried to keep her talking,' Marc declared with a hint of
pride, 'but he hustled her off to bed. Then he came back and
insisted we have a brandy together. You know, man-to-man
stuff. Tried to pump me on what Jen had said. Gave me all this
junk about her not being well and the best thing was peace
and quiet, that she'd been upset over the death of a friend and
needed time to get over it, that he was looking after her all
right and not to take anything she said too seriously. Well, I
thought, he *would* say that, wouldn't he? But I wasn't going to
be put off that easily. No way. And I wouldn't have, either,
if—'

Joe risked an interruption. 'Did he say how this friend had
died?'

'No.'

'Did Jenna?'

Marc tightened his prim mouth. 'I'm coming to that.
Okay?'

'Okay.'

'*So* . . .' He took a moment to find his thread. 'I was ready to get her out, no question. But the next morning, Jen was – well, not sweetness and light exactly, but sort of through the storm. Still not like the old Jen, still quiet, but no sign of panic, and sort of smiling serenely. I asked her if she was on medication, because that was what it looked like to me, like she was on uppers and downers and everything in between. But she said no, she just had bad patches, that was all, and she was sorry I'd been there at the wrong moment and happened to see one, because it looked much worse than it really was. I told her it couldn't have looked much worse if she'd tried, and she mustn't put up with *him* a second longer, not if she had any self-respect, that she must pack her bags and I'd order a taxi and we'd leave straight away. But she said she didn't want to do that, she said she was fine, she wanted to stay right there. Well, I wasn't going to give up that easily. No way.' Marc gave an emphatic snort. 'I argued with her. Gave her a hard time. But I was never going to win, I knew that the moment she began making *him* out to be a frigging saint. Talked about how good he was to her, how he took care of her, how lucky she was to have him. Lucky, for shit's sake! She went on like that, I mean for a long time. Talking as if *she* was the bad person. I looked it up on the Internet. Victim mentality. Battered wife syndrome. They always think it's their fault, that they're not trying hard enough, that they're no good, that they're unworthy. And you can't tell them otherwise. They won't listen. It's like an addiction, a need to be punished, a sublimated desire for abasement.' He said abruptly, 'No need to look at me like that, Joe. I'm only telling you what it says on the Internet! I'm only giving you the medical definition.'

Joe picked up his coffee and drained it before he could say something he might regret.

'You can read it yourself!' Marc insisted.

'Sure.' Joe got to his feet.

Marc stood up too, but irritably, like someone who's about

to be denied his punchline. 'Well, there was nothing more I could do, was there? There was no way she was going to leave, and that was that. I thought of calling the police but it wouldn't have done any good. She'd only have said everything was fine and made me look like a prat. So—'

'And this guy who died? What did she say about him?'

On the sofa, the girl, evidently despairing of the conversation ever coming to an end, gave a sharp sigh and reached for the remote control.

'Not a lot,' Marc said. 'You know the way Jen was – liked everything in the garden to be rosy. Couldn't take rain on her parade. She didn't want to talk about this guy. Said something like, *it was terrible*, then blanked it out the way she did with anything nasty. Can't say I entirely blame her, the way he died—' The hi-fi came back on, blaring pop music, and Marc snarled at the girl to keep it down. Then, with an air of getting back to the real agenda: 'So when I got home I had to face Mum and Dad. Had to find something to tell them. Said Jen was wrapped up in her life, very busy, and was going to do her best to come and see them when she had the chance. They couldn't understand it of course, but I took a judgement that anything was better than the truth. After that . . . well, I did what I could to keep in contact with Jen. Tried calling – oh, once a week? Till she disappeared. But it was like this wall. She never answered. Never returned my messages. *So* . . . that was it! Done all I could!' he finished on a note of self-justification.

'Yes.'

'Don't see how I could have done more.'

'No,' said Joe obediently. 'But then she rang on Monday. Thank God you were in the house when she called.'

The old caution clouded Marc's face. 'Yeah.'

'How did she sound?'

'Like I told you, it's all with the police. I can't discuss it.'

Nodding absent-mindedly, Joe asked casually, 'But it *was* Monday?'

Marc gave a foxy look to show he wasn't going to be caught out as easily as that. 'I told you. I can't say.'

'Ah' – as if understanding at last. 'Right.'

Either the CD had skipped a track or the girl had notched up the volume, because a blast of music suddenly filled the room and this time Marc didn't tell her to turn it down. Taking his cue, Joe made his way through the kitchen to the back door, feeling Marc's eyes boring into his back as he came along behind. 'Oh, this guy Sam,' Joe began, as if the question had just occurred to him. 'Did Jenna say how he came to drown?'

Marc scowled at him.

Joe tried again. 'How he came to be so close to the water?'

It might have been a trick question for all the suspicion Marc was showing. 'What the shit are you talking about?'

'The river . . . how he came to be swept away.'

'She didn't say anything about drowning. He fell from a dam. That's what she told me.'

Joe didn't let anything show in his expression. 'A dam?'

'Yeah. He was prancing around on some sort of dam and he fell onto rocks. Crash. Splat. She didn't say anything about drowning.'

Joe found himself nodding. 'Right . . .' Then, as Marc continued to stare at him as if he was a lunatic: 'I must have misheard . . . before.'

Joe would have started off down the slimy path, but Marc cried in a scornful tone, 'So it's going to be no sale, is it? Jenna's not going to be allowed to sell the house?'

'I think there's likely to be a problem while the police are involved.'

'Well, you can tell your *friend* I don't give a monkey's about the house. It's Jen I care about. Tell him that!'

Wearily, Joe replied, 'Sure, Marc. Sure. I understand.'

The alarm sounded from a dark and cruel place. Waking, Joe registered several things. That he'd slept for barely an hour, that if he was to have any hope of sleeping through the British night he must make the effort to get up and stay up for at least three hours. That he had set the alarm on snooze, which meant he could doze for a while longer. That Sarah was moving around the kitchen, getting the dinner ready. That in normal circumstances this would have been enough to get him straight out of bed and into the shower, but when she'd arrived she'd been in a strange mood, stressed and a little short with him, and said she needed time to unwind. He supposed she'd had a bad week, and made a mental note to ask her about it. His final thought was that the central heating was clunking like the Anvil Chorus and he should complain to the managing agents, though with only three days to Christmas there wasn't a hope in hell of getting anything done about it.

The jetlag had dragged at him all the way back to London. He drove with the windows wide open and the heating off. Even then, he had to stop somewhere near Peterborough and force down more coffee and douse his face in water. On the road again, he listened to the radio and played some music, but mainly he drove to the thrumming of the wind and the cold air against his face while he tried to make sense of his day.

He could get no perspective on Chetwood at all. He had seemed both the same and quite different. Philosopher, joker, commercial operator, conscience of the world; each image fitted him as effortlessly – or as badly – as the one before. For every moment that he'd seemed like his old self – the sparks of humour, the intellectual meanderings, the easy manner – there'd been a moment when he might have been a stranger, cool, detached, abrupt.

And what to make of his explanations? That Jenna was happy with her strange isolated life, that she didn't want contact with 'people' – all people? some people? particular people? – that she wasn't able to forgive herself for something that had happened over four years ago. How much did you have to love someone to grieve for that long? How could you feel such a huge weight of responsibility for what was, after all, an accident? Perhaps her need for solitude owed more to a nervous breakdown than a crisis of conscience, but, fearful of the stigma, no one wanted to call it by its proper name.

In the past, Jenna's bouts of unhappiness had been short-lived if intense affairs. What was it Marc had said? *Couldn't take rain on her parade.* Joe remembered a day when Jenna's rain had come in a thunderburst. It was spring, April or May. They were both seventeen. Joe was sure about that because, against all his own expectations, he'd passed his driving test that morning and, as with every landmark event in his life, he'd gone straight to the Laskeys to tell them. As he hurried round to the back door, the congratulations were already resounding in his head, the celebratory cake – a speciality of Helena's – was already sweet in his mouth. He found Helena in the kitchen, just as he'd hoped, but there it ended. Her smile was perfunctory, she made a rueful face as she reached for the phone to make a call. 'We're in a state,' she remarked heavily. 'Jenna didn't get the part.'

In the hall Joe met Marc coming in from school with a crash of the front door. They would have passed each other with nothing more than a glance, but they were both halted by the sound of Jenna crying in the front room and the murmur of Alan's voice as he tried to comfort her. 'She didn't get the part,' Joe explained.

Marc's eyes rolled expressively, his face puckered in cold scorn. He looked down at the sheet of art paper in his hand, some painting effort with a gold star fixed to one corner, and, letting it fall against his leg, trudged off up the stairs.

There was no consoling Jenna. When Joe put his head round the door, Alan beckoned him in with relief. 'Here's Joe!' he exclaimed. 'He'll tell you! Won't you, Joe? He'll tell you it's *nothing* to do with your abilities. *Nothing* to do with your talents. They just felt it was time to give someone else a turn. Isn't that right, Joe?'

But Jenna wasn't having it. 'The whole *school* thought I

was getting the part,' she sobbed from inside her hands.
'*Everyone!* Just everyone! And now they'll all laugh at me.'

'Not if you walk tall,' Joe said. 'Not if you show you don't
care.'

She glared up at him through red-rimmed eyes. 'But I do
care! I do! They gave the part to *Kim Newton*! And she can't
even *sing*! Why do they hate me so much, Joe? Why have they
done this to me?'

'No one hates you, Jenna. But they know you have a
brilliant future. They think of you as different. I'm sure Alan's
right, I'm sure they just wanted to give someone else a
chance.'

'But I don't want to be different, Joe. I want to be like
everyone else!'

Days later, when school had been endured and more bitter
tears shed, she said in a rare moment of calm, 'I don't want a
brilliant future, Joe. Not if it's going to be like this. Not if
people are going to hate me for it.'

They were walking home from the bus stop under the
violent pink of the cherry blossom. He slipped a hand behind
her elbow, trying to hold it unobtrusively. Even then he
dreaded gossip and the risk it would get back to Jenna's ears.
'You're wrong,' he said. 'They'll love and admire you for it.'

'Only if I'm a success,' she said.

'Of course you will be!'

She looked at Joe strangely, and afterwards it occurred to
him that it wasn't what she'd wanted to hear.

He must have dozed because the next thing he knew the alarm
was sounding again. He opened his eyes to see Sarah silhouetted in the doorway.

'Hi. Dinner's almost ready.'

'Give me five minutes.'

'And your mobile just rang.' She came and put it on the
table beside him.

'Thanks.'

He thought she might bend down and kiss him. He reached out to touch her, but it was dark and she was already moving out of range. She paused in the doorway. 'It's fish. I thought you'd probably be fed up with T-bone steaks.'

'Great.'

It might have been his imagination, but he thought he caught a note of tension in her voice.

When he came into the living room he found what passed as his dining table pulled out into the middle of the room and laid with all the things he would have forgotten, like candles and napkins. There was even a single flower in a makeshift vase.

Sarah appeared with the first course. 'I opened some white wine,' she said. 'Was that all right?'

'Of course.'

As she took her seat, he asked, 'How was your week?'

'Oh, fine.'

'No one escaped?'

'Sorry?'

'Metaphorically. Or literally, I suppose.'

'No.' She offered a sudden smile which didn't quite reach her eyes.

'Done your Christmas shopping?'

'This morning. In two hours flat. The benefit of having a small family. My father likes books, my mother likes silk scarves.'

'Do you open presents on Christmas morning? Or are you Christmas Eve people?'

Sarah put her fork down and gazed at him, and for an instant Joe thought he'd missed something. He gave a questioning smile.

'Joe, I've booked a holiday. Starting on Boxing Day.'

His heart squeezed uneasily. 'I see,' he said, though he didn't see at all. 'When did you decide this?'

'Three days ago.'

'Rather sudden.'

'I always forget how much I hate Christmas. Just hate it. And I didn't realise how tired I was.' She gave a little shrug that didn't quite come off.

'I thought your office needed lots of warning about holidays.'

'I'm lucky. They're going to be able to cover for me.'

'How long are you going for?'

'Two weeks.'

His mouth was dry as he asked, 'With someone else?'

'No,' she said, 'I'm going alone.'

He took a swig of wine. 'Destination?'

'Jamaica.'

'A real holiday then.'

'I got a cancellation on the Internet. Well, I imagine it's a cancellation. A really good deal, anyway.'

'I thought all the resorts there were for happy couples.'

'Not all.' She faltered. 'Obviously.'

Under his gaze, she looked down at her plate. She fiddled with her fork. 'I'm sorry but it's going to use up the last of my holiday allowance.'

'No Morocco?'

'No.'

'I get it,' he said, hating the sarcasm in his voice.

'Just for the record, Joe, it was my boss who suggested I take some time off. He thinks I need a break.'

'Odd boss, to give you leave at a moment's notice.'

'He thought I was overworking.'

Joe took another gulp of his wine and heard the devil pipe up in him again. 'Quite sure there won't be anyone joining you?'

'Quite sure.'

'I shouldn't take this as a coded message?'

She waited for him to spell it out.

'Is this a way of saying we're over?'

In the bedroom, his mobile chose that moment to start

ringing. Sarah looked down at her plate while they waited for it to stop. After the fifth or sixth ring, there was silence. Sarah's gaze met his. Then, after a moment in which she seemed to be steeling herself, she opened her mouth to speak.

'Joe, I—'

The phone began to ring again.

Joe hissed, 'For God's sake!'

'Perhaps you should answer it.'

Joe strode into the bedroom and snatched up the phone. He checked the display to see if it was anyone he knew, but there was no caller ID and no clue.

His aggressive hello was met by a long pause and what sounded like an intake of breath.

'Hello?' he barked again.

Another pause. He was about to ring off when a woman spoke. The voice, when it finally came, was soft and hesitant. 'Joe?'

He felt a violent lurch, followed by a sharp sense of disconnection. One part of him knew what he was hearing; some other part refused to take it in. His throat seized and for an instant he couldn't find the breath to speak. At last he whispered, 'Jenna?'

Her voice was so faint it might have been coming from a long way away. 'I just wanted to say . . .'

Then nothing. The fear knocked at his ribs. 'Jenna?' Silence. 'Jenna?'

'I wanted to say . . . I sang Messiah tonight.' Then a sudden exhalation of breath, like a soundless laugh.

He whispered, 'You did?'

In the pause that followed, he thought he could hear her breathing.

'So . . . you see, Joe.'

'Yes, I see. Yes!'

The rush of breath against the mouthpiece again, and what was unmistakeably a short broken laugh. Then, hastily: 'Goodbye, Joe.'

And she was gone.

He felt a slight nausea, a clammy feeling. He was exhila-
rated, but he was also sick with the feeling he had missed his
opportunity. Why hadn't he *said* something? Why hadn't he
asked her if she was all right? Why hadn't he come right out
with it and asked her to meet him?

He was still clutching the phone to his ear. Hastily, he
thrust the display up to his face and saw the station indicator
light up again. He was still staring at it when Sarah appeared
at the door.

'Okay?' she asked.

'It was her,' he said.

Sarah was quick, but not that quick. 'Who?'

'Jenna.' And saying it, he finally believed it.

'My goodness, Joe.' She came closer. 'That's wonderful.'

'Yes.'

'Well . . . Is she all right?'

'I think so.'

'That's great. I'm so pleased for you.'

'Yes.'

'What did she say?'

'She said she'd been singing again.'

'There you are. She must be all right.'

'Yes.'

'Did she say where she was?'

He shook his head.

'Did you ask?'

He shook his head again, more unhappily.

'Perhaps the phone recorded her number.'

'I was going to look.'

But he was too frightened to look: in case he pressed the
wrong button and erased it, in case he was faced by 'number
withheld'.

Sarah disappeared and came back with a pencil and paper.
'Do you want me to have a look?'

He sat down on the bed. 'No.' He scrolled carefully through

the phone's menu to received calls and, pressing select, saw a number come up that he didn't recognise.

He read it out and Sarah wrote it down. For safety's sake, he read it out a second time, and Sarah confirmed it.

He said, 'Just remind me, if she'd withheld her number it would have said so, wouldn't it? Wouldn't it?'

'Should have done, yes. But take a look at missed calls. Because it was probably her the first time, wasn't it?'

Sarah was right: the same number came up under missed calls.

'My God,' Joe said, and still he couldn't think straight.

'Do you want me to get an address for it?'

The number had an area code he didn't recognise. His head began to clear at last. 'Yes, please.'

Sarah touched his shoulder lightly with her fingers. 'I'm so pleased for you, Joe.' And she took the slip of paper out of the room. When Joe followed a minute later he heard her in the kitchen, murmuring into her mobile.

'Could be as soon as half an hour,' she announced when she came back to the table.

'Right.' Remembering his manners, he said, 'Thank you. And thank your police friend too, would you?'

She nodded mechanically.

He tried to eat but couldn't. He tried to drink but didn't want to.

'Sorry,' he said.

'I'm not too hungry myself,' Sarah said. 'I haven't started cooking the fish yet. I could put it back in the fridge, if you like.'

'She must have seen the ad,' Joe murmured to himself.

'It would look that way.'

'So it's definitely Hereford.'

'I hope you're not thinking what I think you're thinking.'

'How long would it take? If I left now.'

'Don't be crazy, Joe. You've had no sleep. You'll kill your-self.' Then, with a sigh: 'Three hours? Maybe less. But Joe, don't even think about it till you've had some sleep.' She slid his plate back towards him. 'And some food.'

Obediently, he picked up his fork and, tasting something delicious, rediscovered his appetite. Sarah cooked the fish, and he found himself eating that too.

Watching her washing up afterwards, he said, 'I don't want us to be over.'

She slid a plate slowly into the rack. 'I'm not sure I'm the right person for you, Joe.'

'Why?'

She dunked another plate into the water, began to scrub it, then abandoned it. Her eyes fixed on the sink, she said gravely, 'Because I'm no good at sustaining relationships. Because I start to push people away if there's a risk of getting too close to them. I get stifled.'

'But we've been fine so far, haven't we? Given each other plenty of space?'

'I need to be free. I have to be free.'

'But I don't know what you mean by free.'

'Whatever it is that I haven't got now.'

There was no answering that, and he didn't try. 'Perhaps if we leave it till after Christmas. Think about it again then.'

'Perhaps.'

But meeting her gaze, he had the feeling she had done all her thinking already.

Her mobile rang five minutes later. She went and answered it in the bedroom. When she came out she had another slip of paper in her hand. 'On one condition,' she said, holding the paper out of reach. 'That you promise to get some sleep before you go.'

'Promise,' he said, because he would have said anything just then.

'And you'll want to take a photograph of your friend to show around, because it's not going to be that simple.' She handed him the paper. 'It was a phone box.'

He went to the car to fetch a map and found the town west

of Hereford, west of Pawsey Farm, on the edge of the Welsh mountains.

'Black hills and sheep,' Sarah said.

He slept fitfully until five, with Sarah at his side. He hadn't thought she'd stay, but without a word she'd led the way into the bedroom and made love with solemn intensity. He had the suspicion it was her way of saying goodbye.

Chapter Seven

———

HE DROVE through a night of clear skies and dark frost until, nearing the distant country, the land turned white. The snow was thin, it barely covered the open ground, but it reversed the landscape into a photographic negative, white on black. He passed conifer plantations like ink, and bare-limbed woodland like waiting armies, and luminous white fields crisscrossed with black-lace hedgerows. In the distance the border hills were hunched like sleeping ghosts. Once, when he pulled up to read the map, he climbed out into harsh silence and saw a dome of stars so deep and so wide that the universe might have been turned inside out.

He found Pawsey Farm before dawn. It lay off the bend of a lane, up a short track. Leaving the car in the lane, he walked up the rutted track and heard ice snapping beneath his feet. The house was in darkness, but behind the sturdy five-bar gate he saw the outline of a parked car. Unlatching the gate, he trod on thick gravel and in the stillness each footstep sounded like a pistol shot. The car was a four-wheel drive, very shiny in the starlight. An alarm winked a warning from the dashboard. He went up to the front door of the house and again had the impression of newness, this time from the paint, which glimmered softly. It was almost seven. If there'd been a light showing he would have knocked. As it was, he decided to wait for daybreak. Turning away, he put his nose to a window and saw what looked like a pair of candlesticks on the sill, and, close by, what might have been a chairback.

He remembered this room. It was here they'd had supper,

late, round a rickety pine table, with candles that guttered and formed huge spikes. They had eaten roast lamb, almost raw in the middle. They had laughed a lot, they had drunk a lot. Jenna had been dressed in blue: vivid, beautiful, smiling, but also – the word that came to him was watchful. He saw her sitting at one end of the table, looking down the length of it to Chetwood, alert to everything he was saying, her feline eyes never leaving his face for long. At the time, he had taken this for love.

He was halfway down the track when he glanced back and saw a bright square of curtained light showing in an upstairs window. As he retraced his steps, a glow appeared in the dining room, the diffused reflection of a light in the back of the house. Approaching the front door again, Joe paused by the dining-room window and saw a table in silhouette and a connecting door framing a rectangle of brightly lit kitchen. He waited, and after a while a woman in a dressing-gown passed across the doorway. She was brown-haired and she was holding a baby against her shoulder. A minute later she passed again, this time with a kettle in one hand.

It wasn't Jenna, and a part of him argued that he'd never expected it to be.

He thought of asking the woman if she knew anything about the previous inhabitants, but the Chetwoods had only rented the place, it had been more than four years ago, and the woman had a baby to feed.

He drove on north-west in the gathering light, through rolling hills and valleys ruffled with mist. The snow lay thicker here and to the west the Black Mountains were more white than black. There were no cars about, the hamlets showed no lights, and Joe had the impression of going deeper into a deserted land.

For miles the road ran alongside a meandering river which issued vapour like a hot spring, before snaking over a hill and down the other side to join a faster-flowing river. Finally, as both road and river took a long bend to the west, a sign in

Welsh and English announced the place from where Jenna had made her call.

It was a small market town, little more than two main streets on the lower slopes of a bluff dominated by a fine castle, half abandoned, half occupied. The houses were small and ancient, or tall and Victorian, in contrasting shades of grey stone or white roughcast with black-rimmed windows and bargeboards, and roofs of grey slate. There was woodland to the south, the bluff close above, and a line of snow-dusted hills to the west, which he supposed to be the Cambrian Mountains.

He followed the one-way system along narrow streets, past a handsome church, and parked in an open square with a small covered market and a free-standing clock-tower, which was stone, Victorian, and built to last. Sweeping away from the clock tower was the appropriately named Broad Street running east and parallel to the river. The south side of the street was set higher on the hill, with a raised pavement and railings and a line of shops. On the north side the pavement was two steps down from the road, with a chapel, a dark hotel, and a scattering of houses which backed on to the river just below.

The place had the stillness of a winter Sunday: no cars and no people.

He walked back to the handsome church along a gritted pavement. The church notices made no mention of a *Messiah*, only carol services and Midnight Mass and services for Christmas Day. Three services were advertised for today, an ordinary Sunday: communion at nine thirty, family service at eleven and evensong at six thirty, all promising carols. Returning to the square, Joe went to the dark hotel, which had dark wood and dark carpets and a smell of yesterday's beer. Waiting for his coffee and scrambled egg, he asked the sleepy waitress if the manager could spare a moment, and was met by a spotty blank-eyed youth who introduced himself as the duty manager. He'd not lived in the town long, he announced quickly, he had no idea if it possessed a choral society nor could he suggest anyone who might know, though when pressed he thought there was no harm in trying Mrs Hopkins, the housekeeper. Mrs Hopkins, who didn't look too pleased at being called away from her work, shook her head. Not that she'd heard of, she said. Not in the town itself. She suggested Joe ask at the church.

After breakfast, Joe took a quick walk around the town, and found a visitor centre displaying literature on Offa's Dyke and the Brecon Beacons National Park, shops with knitwear, china, and gifts, and a Co-op, all closed, and a newsagent's which was open. A sturdy couple in their fifties were manning the counter. Between them, they seemed to know most of the customers who trickled in. Joe inspected the postcard rack until there was a lull in trade, when he asked the man about a choral society.

The man frowned and immediately referred the question to his wife, who said there was a choir in the church all right, but not a choral society as such. She thought you'd have to go to Hereford or Abergavenny for that.

'I heard there'd been a performance of the *Messiah* somewhere hereabouts,' Joe said.

'A proper performance? Not that I've heard.' And from her tone Joe was left in no doubt that she would have been sure to hear. 'There's the school put something on. What was it, George?' George shook his head and got on with stacking cigarettes. 'The school,' she repeated more decisively. 'They always put something on at Christmas.'

Joe said pleasantly, 'I'm trying to contact an old friend who used to sing in our local choir. She's come to live somewhere around here. She's called Jenna – Jennifer – Chetwood.'

'Chetwood?' The woman was starting to consider the name when she saw Joe pull the photograph from his pocket, and he might have been offering her a rotten fish from the speed with which she recoiled. 'Can't help you,' she said firmly, and without even glancing at the picture retreated behind the counter.

Joe risked: 'It's her family who want to find her.'

But the woman's face confirmed her earlier message: she had no truck with enquiries of an intrusive nature, and a photograph was an intrusion too far.

The church was called St Peter's and the guidebooks would probably describe it as mediaeval with later additions. It had a stocky tower, square with a clock face on each side, and no spire. Inside, there was a Christmas tree, a crib, and draped foliage with candles. Two churchwardens were tucking carol sheets into hymnbooks, while another moved around the altar.

'Good morning.' The churchwarden who greeted him was a tiny lady with a voice like a bell.

'Good morning. I'm admiring your church.'

'You're most welcome,' she said.

'You have a choir?'

'We do indeed. Just eight, but voice enough to be heard twice over.'

'Does Jenna sing with them?'

'Jenna?' Her little head cocked to one side. 'I don't believe so. What would her surname be?'

When Joe told her, she thought about this with the conscientiousness she undoubtedly applied to every task in her Christian life. 'No,' she said. 'I don't believe anyone of that name has ever sung here, not in my memory.'

Joe thanked her and took a seat in the back pew where he could keep an eye on the door. The younger generation were too busy inheriting the earth to thank heaven for it, for apart from one or two families with young children the congregation that assembled for nine-thirty Communion were all middle-aged or elderly.

Once the service began, Joe slipped quietly away. Walking west this time, he came to another church, United Reformed, in dark grey stone, but there was no service till later and he wasn't sure Reformers sang anyway. Turning east, he climbed the slopes of the bluff, up narrow cobbled streets with tightly packed cottages and an arts centre and an ancient timbered pub, which promised a quiz on Tuesdays and live music on Saturday nights. Dropping down towards the square again, he found a fine Georgian hotel called the Royal Oak which smelt of woodsmoke and the beginnings of lunch. Mention of a choral society brought frowns from the staff, and no one had heard Jenna's name. A couple of the female staff were prepared to inspect the photograph, however; both were sure they'd never seen her before.

One of them eyed the jagged scissor-marks down the side of the print and gave Joe a hard stare. 'Didn't work out, then?'

Finding a quiet corner, Joe folded the photograph once down the edge to hide the scissor-strokes, and again across the bottom to conceal the bouquet in Jenna's hand, before sliding it back into his pocket.

Exploring the considerable length of Broad Street, he came to a bridge and heard the water before he saw it. Standing on the bridge he looked west and saw a strong river flowing steadily towards him, its surface burnished with cold metallic light, woods down to the water's edge, and, above, heavy clouds streaming in from the mountains. Fifty yards downstream on the other side was the source of the muffled roar: a weir in the form of a well-defined step, straight as a die and marked with a line of posts, over which the water slipped in an otherwise unbroken line, to reappear as churning foam below.

When he turned away, the cloud was fast covering the sky, a wind had sprung up, and it felt cold enough for snow.

He got back to the church in time for the end of the sermon and the last two carols. The choir sang a good descant and there was at least one fine soprano among them, a plump thirtyish woman with glasses. When the service ended, Joe went up the side aisle to the robing room and heard voices chattering. He knocked on the open door. The soprano with the glasses and two of the men looked round, and Joe apologised for bothering them.

The soprano was in a hurry, pulling on her coat, running a comb through her hair, but she listened attentively and by this time most of the others were listening as well.

'No one's done a *Messiah*,' the soprano said. 'Not this year.'

'The school did *Jesus Christ Superstar*,' said the alto.

'You'd have to go to Hereford for a *Messiah*. There's at least one choral society in Hereford, maybe two.'

Joe explained about the old singing friend he hadn't seen in a long time, how she always sang alto in *Messiah*, and how anxious he was to find her. He gave plenty of detail this time, about Jenna being his childhood friend, the daughter of the family doctor, how by chance and a huge amount of bad luck involving name changes and house moves and lost addresses they'd managed to lose touch. 'Oh, and I brought a photograph,' he said, making it sound the most inoffensive thing in the world.

The soprano had hoisted her bag over her shoulder and was moving purposefully towards the door, so he showed it to her first. She peered at it, shook her head and moved away, only to come back for a second look. She stared at the picture for much longer this time, then reached out to take it from him with a 'May I?'

She showed it to the second soprano, and they conferred for a while, apparently without result. Then, marching past Joe without a word, the first soprano took the picture into the body of the church and when Joe followed he saw her holding it up to the tiny lady churchwarden who'd greeted Joe on his arrival.

'Ah, it's you,' tinkled the voice as Joe came up. 'Did you enjoy our service?'

'I did,' Joe said, allowing himself the lie.

'We've seen her all right,' declared the first soprano, handing back the picture. 'But we don't know her name, do we, Mrs Evans?'

'Not her name, no,' piped Mrs Evans. 'But she used to attend here.'

'Not now?'

'Not for, oh, six months, I'd say. But' – the tiny voice dropped so low that Joe had to bend to catch her words – 'I think you might find her at the other place.' Now the whisper took on a pained note, as though it offended her to utter such words in the true house of God. 'The Roman Catholic church. You'll find it at the far end of Broad Street, right at the fork, just there on the left.'

'Thank you.'

The first soprano was in a hurry now. As she moved away, she called back over her shoulder in a ringing tone that caused Mrs Evans to close her eyes: 'You'd best be quick if you want to catch the Romans. They come out about now.'

Joe ran to the car with the photograph still clutched in his hand and almost slipped on ice or slush. He drove the length of the street, past the dark hotel and the bridge until, coming to the fork, he took the right-hand road as directed. He saw the church even as he turned into the tiny lane. It was a low-built rectangle with a steep gable-end topped by a cross, perched over a sharp downward slope. Knots of people stood outside, others were walking away. Joe stopped rather suddenly, blocking a car that was trying to leave, and in his haste began to reverse before he'd taken a proper look behind, causing a man and woman to pull back against the wall, their arms flung protectively across their children. Joe stopped and waved them across with an apologetic smile, and took the time to examine the people outside the church. The priest stood in the porch taking leave of his congregation. He was a short man with a thatch of grey hair who smiled a lot and, from the sound of the laughter, joked a lot too.

There were ten or twelve people left outside the church. Jenna was not among them.

Making sure the family had safely negotiated the road, Joe

reversed slowly alongside a wall. He looked up the rise ahead and he looked back towards the village centre, then climbed out for a better view. He realised the service must have finished a good five minutes ago and that in his dash down Broad Street he had almost certainly passed people coming away from the church. Passed, but not thought to see. The street was long, one pavement raised, the other low. Had he missed her? He wanted to think it was impossible, that even from an acute angle her outline, her walk, would have brought him up short.

Thoroughly annoyed with his own ineptitude, he looked around fretfully, but there was nothing more to be seen. The people strolling away up the hill or back towards the village walked in pairs or family groups, while the few on their own looked elderly. Those who'd parked on Broad Street were opening car doors and helping each other in.

Soon there were just three people left outside the church. Joe walked quickly down to the fork, where he could see almost the entire length of Broad Street. Cars passed, pedestrians walked by: he examined them all. The wind was bitter now, and when he looked out over the rooftops the hills had been consumed by cloud.

Turning back towards the church, Joe found the priest loading a bag into the boot of his car.

'Good morning, Father. Have I missed the service?'

'You have indeed.'

The smile was quick but with a hint of reserve, and it occurred to Joe that he should have said Mass.

'Visiting for Christmas?'

'Yes.'

'Well, there's Midnight Mass at eleven tomorrow night. For Mass today, you'll need to go to Hereford.'

'I was meant to join a friend for your service' – he stuck with the word – 'but obviously I got the time wrong.'

The priest slammed the boot shut and offered a bright nod of commiseration before moving round to the driver's door.

'And now I seem to have missed her as well.' Joe looked

around as if searching for her even now. 'Jenna. You know who I mean?'

'Jenna,' the priest repeated contemplatively, his hand on the open door. 'I would say that you've certainly missed her.'

'But she was here?'

The father cast another glance over Joe. Beneath the thick grey hair, which stood short and bristly as a brush, were fierce eyebrows and sharp eyes that missed nothing. 'Would that be Jenna Macintyre now?'

If it was a trick question, the father carried it off well.

Joe took a gamble and said, 'Yes.'

'In that case you didn't miss her because she wasn't here today.' With a small salute – and possibly a gleam of disapproval – the father got into his car and drove away.

Joe wandered back to his car, now alone in the road. His restlessness had given way to indecision and despondency. To trawl the streets, to question strangers, to give up now and drive back to London, to find a bed for a couple of hours: just then, he could have taken his pick.

Driving up the lane, he found a place to turn, and headed back into the centre of the town. The sky was darkening steadily, and pinpricks of snow settled and melted on the windscreen. Parking near the clock tower again, Joe was in time to see a couple hurrying down the lane to St Peter's, ten minutes late for the eleven o'clock service.

He began to walk back towards the Royal Oak. At some point in the last few minutes, he'd decided quite arbitrarily that if they had a room available he'd stay another twenty-four hours, but if they were fully booked he'd leave town in the evening, no later than six.

Crossing the square, Joe glanced across to the opposite side of Broad Street and registered the fact that some of the shops had opened. A woman was coming out of one that sold woollens or general clothing or both, a couple were going into another, which looked like crafts. He registered the presence of more people on the periphery of his vision: a strolling window shopper, a bustling figure with a pushchair, a pensioner with a stick. Then, with a sense of *déjà vu*, or maybe it was premonition because the two things seemed the same just then, he jerked his head up and stared.

She was some way off, diagonally across Broad Street on the higher level, walking rapidly away. Momentarily she was hidden by a tall vehicle, then by a couple of men walking; but there was no mistaking her. Joe's heart gave a thud of recognition, he felt an idiotic excitement, a great leap of joy, quickly damped by the fear of losing sight of her.

Not daring to call out, he half ran across the road and, reaching the upper pavement, half ran along that too. She was still quite a way ahead, a slim figure in a long tweed coat, with a hat that could have been wool or fur, a rucksack on her back, a cream scarf over one shoulder, and a plastic carrier bag in each hand. Suddenly she was going down steps to the road and leaning down to unlock a car. She unlocked it the old-fashioned way, with a key not a remote, because it was an old-fashioned car, an ancient Volvo a bit the worse for wear.

She chucked her bags onto the back seat and got into the front fast, and it was this, along with the fact that the Volvo was facing in the opposite direction, that warned Joe against running after her. In a tiny snapshot of possibilities, he saw her looking into her rear-view mirror, spotting this frantic running man and feeling, if not panic, then something pretty close to it. Whichever way he played the scene – whether she recognised him or not – he saw her starting the engine and shooting off before he could run back to his car and follow.

Ducking his head slightly, wheeling rapidly around, he strode back in the direction of the market square, like one more parishioner late for family service. He didn't look back until he was safely inside the car, when he spotted the Volvo at the far end of Broad Street, turning towards the bridge.

Driving as fast as he dared, he reached the bridge and, starting across, spotted the Volvo heading away towards the west along the opposite bank. He felt a surge of elation that

was quickly overtaken by an emotion altogether less comfortable, something closer to shame. He was following her like a
spy.

At first he was cautious, hanging so far back that he lost
sight of her at the bends, then, fearing he might lose her, he
closed the distance to thirty yards or so. They were driving
along a valley side that was first gentle then steep, then gentle
again. To their left the river had lost its placidity and was
rippling angrily over a stony bed. They came to a small village,
grey-stoned and grey-roofed. The Volvo slowed to under thirty,
and Joe remembered a time when Jenna had been entirely care-
less of speed limits.

Suddenly the Volvo was indicating right and slowing still
more. Joe lowered his sun visor and also began to indicate.
The Volvo stopped on the crown of the road for an oncoming
car. Joe checked his mirror and braked, eking out the time
before he must pull up behind her. The oncoming car was
some way off and travelling slowly: the Volvo could easily
have turned across it. As it was, the Volvo waited for what
seemed an age but was probably seven or eight seconds before
the oncoming car dawdled past. By the time the Volvo finally
began to turn, Joe was within five yards of it, driving at a
trickle. To gain distance again, he took his time with his own
turn, stopping on the crown of the road as if to wait for
another car. The precaution was almost certainly unnecessary;
he'd watched her eyes in the mirror and not once had she
looked his way. He'd watched her eyes and had no doubt they
were Jenna's.

She turned again at a fork, left this time. Now, they were
on a smaller road, which rose steadily onto higher land, where
hardy sheep grazed between patches of snow. The river was
lost to view to the south. Ahead, the flat-topped mountains,
now darkened with cloud, suddenly looked quite close, and he
wondered how far they were going. The pasture was wide and
open, with only an occasional farmhouse snugged down
against the wind, which fanned and rippled across the exposed

tussock grass. One car passed them, otherwise there was nothing. The sky was blackening steadily, the land too, and it began to snow, abruptly and heavily. He could make out the Volvo only by its tail lights.

After a while, the road dropped down to a hamlet at the mouth of a deep valley, and he saw a seething river, maybe the same one as before, maybe another. He followed the Volvo over a hump-backed bridge then right, onto a road that led, he thought, west or a little north of west. For no reason he could have named, he hung back a little further.

The snow was falling steadily, and settling. The valley was steep on one side, less so on the other, and heavily wooded; where trees overhung the road, the curtain of snow would momentarily vanish, the road surface turn black, and the Volvo seem much closer. They passed a sign to some priory ruins, then to a castle, also ruined. There was a hamlet on the far side of the river, just three cottages, then another beside the road, barely much larger, and all the rooftops were white with snow. This, with the Welsh place names, added to Joe's growing sense of unreality.

He lost all sense of distance, but after what might have been ten miles, they came to a bridge with a village on the far side, then a fork in the valley where two tumbling rivers converged over stony beds. He thought they were taking the northerly fork but, coming to another bridge, the Volvo crossed over and almost immediately they were entering a third valley, hidden in the cleft of the fork. Here the snow was thick on the trees and the road, as if it had been falling for some time. The road had not been gritted, and he was glad when the Volvo slowed right down.

The road ran low in the valley, to the right of a boisterous river; sometimes the leaping water seemed very close. He glimpsed the occasional dark-stone cottage among the trees or huddled low on a promontory where the river swung wide, but for the most part there were no houses and no turnings, so that when the Volvo lost speed it caught him by surprise. He could see no reason for her to slow down; no signpost, no gate, no break in the trees. He slowed uncertainly, wondering whether to pass or stay behind and risk alarming her. Then she was indicating left and, slowing to a crawl, pulling in towards the river side: it was an invitation to overtake.

A last moment of hesitation and he made up his mind: it was time to come clean. He pulled out and, drawing level, ducked his head, the better to show his face, and began to wave. But the falling snow was thick, the light gloomy, and after giving the briefest of glances in his direction, enough to register the fact that he was passing, the woman's head continued to turn until she was looking back over her shoulder. The woman: in the eerie half light the face, blurred, indistinct, seemed to belong to a stranger.

Pulling up, he looked in the mirror and saw the Volvo swinging across the road in a tight arc. Hastily, he stuck his head out of the window and watched it make not a complete U-turn but just short of it, taking a narrow lane that Joe had missed among the trees.

By the time he'd turned round the Volvo's tail lights had disappeared, but the tyre tracks lay in the snow like long interweaving ribbons. The beginning of the lane was steep, he felt the wheels spin, he only just made it to the brow. The road wasn't too steep after that but it was single track and for all he knew sheet ice on the bends, so he took it slowly. It meandered upwards for half a mile or so before levelling off, when he found himself in a valley with gently sloping sides of snow-filled fields and dark hedgerows, the fields so small and the hedgerows so magnificent and so numerous – row after row of mature craggy-limbed trees, dense walls of shrubs and saplings – that the valley might have been a glorious parkland, one of Capability Brown's most accomplished efforts, an Arcadia painted in black and white.

There was a fast-running stream that snaked beside the road and a series of small bridges, stone or wood, and then, as the valley narrowed and began to rise, the fields fell away and there was just a woodland of naked oaks bathed in white. He had noticed one cottage further back, now he saw another, but still the tracer ribbons of the tyre tracks wound on.

A last bend, a last rise, and the ribbons wove to the left onto a track that led upwards through dark enclosed woods. The track was rough and potholed, the trees dense. But then the trees began to open out, the sky to grow a little lighter, and he entered a clearing.

Ahead, on a rise, was a cottage with the Volvo parked alongside.

He stopped in the clearing and climbed out into a profound and unearthly silence accentuated by the hush of the whirling snow and the muffled rush of water, near or far he couldn't tell. He began to walk, and the faint squeak of his footsteps was quickly swallowed up by the silence.

The cottage was squat and dark-stoned. There was a window on either side of the door and two narrow dormers in the roof; the glass was as dark as the stonework, reflecting nothing. Snow had settled on the roof and there was no smoke coming from either chimney; as Joe approached he had the sense of a place abandoned. Footprints led from the Volvo to the door however, and someone had walked around to the side of the cottage, though from the covering of snow this might have happened earlier.

He knocked, and the sound seemed to be sucked up by the snow. He knocked twice more before he moved self-consciously to the right-hand window and, peering in, saw a room with old-fashioned floral wallpaper tinted resin by age or smoke, a Baxi fireplace, fire unlit, surrounded by chipped amber tiles and topped by a black mantelshelf, two tall-backed easy-chairs covered in threadbare coffee-coloured velvet, and various side tables and rugs that might have been scavenged from a car boot sale. After knocking on the door again, he moved to the left window and saw a room with faded white walls, a fireplace that had been boarded over, and a floor almost entirely covered in packing cases and cardboard boxes.

Following the faint footprints around the side of the cottage, he passed an outhouse with an open door and saw a freezer, fairly new, which was humming gently and showing a green light. At the back, he came to a small yard with outhouses on two sides and would have turned away but for a shuffling sound which took him to a stable door with a grille over the top half, where a bright equine eye met his gaze. It was a shaggy pony, which snorted a little and came closer, nose outstretched, nostrils twitching curiously.

A lean-to ran the full width of the back of the cottage, with a frosted glass window at one end and a door with four panes of glass, opaque with dirt, at the other. Joe put his nose to one of the panes and saw gloom. The door was unlocked though, and pushing it open he stepped into a ramshackle kitchen with an ancient stone sink, a wooden draining board, sagging shelves and the rank smell of damp. Water had stained the side wall and mildew speckled the ceiling, and the areas of lino that hadn't rotted through to the concrete were scored and crumbling. The air was freezing, with the added bite of the damp. Standing there, Joe felt a wave of fury. No one could be expected to live like this. No one could live like this and be happy. Then, in a parallel thought which brought a different sort of anger: these conditions might be designed to break a person's spirit.

He wandered through into a tiny hall and, standing at the bottom of the staircase, called out, but there was no reply.

Retracing his steps, he went round to the front of the cottage again and listened, but all he heard was the breathless hush of the snow as it wafted against his face, spiralled away, and fell with infinitesimal softness to the ground. The flakes were larger or falling more heavily; when he looked across the clearing he could barely make out the dark cleave of a brook running through the trees. The valley rose gently towards, he supposed, open moorland, while behind the cottage the valley side was steep and thickly wooded, carpeted with bracken and rock supporting fragile cornices of snow.

He went to the Volvo and examined the footprints again.
They were getting faint now, but there was no doubt they
pointed towards the cottage. Beginning to despair, he looked
up the valley once more and saw what might have been a path
leading away through the trees. He made directly for it,
plunging down into a dip and up the other side, his soles
slipping on the steep slope. It was a path all right; looking
back, he realised it snaked around from the outhouses, hugging
the contour of the hill, then – heart lifting again – he saw that
there were footprints on it, like the ones next to the Volvo. A
few yards further on, he came across more prints – dog paws,
medium-sized – and almost laughed.

The path rose gently through the woods. He walked as fast
as his shoes, the tree roots and the icy patches would allow.
Now and again he spotted the tracks of the dog leaving the
path or returning to it, zigzagging this way and that. He felt
the cold pinching his nose and ears. The trees became sparser
and, whether from this or a sudden worsening of the weather,
he became aware of a blurring of the light and a sharpening of
the wind as the snow drove in closer around him. He wasn't
sure how far he could see, probably less than ten yards. In one
blast of wind the path ahead seemed to vanish altogether and
he paused to get his bearings. He carried on cautiously, eyes
down, alert to the feel of the ground under his feet. When he
glanced up, it was to see shadows that were trees and trees that
were shadows, shifting and fading in the circling snow.

The wind eased suddenly, the snow as well, and looking up
he saw her standing directly in front of him. Even then he
doubted his eyes, and it wasn't till a black labrador rushed
down the path and bounded up to him that he finally stepped
forward and called her name.

She didn't move at first. Then she put a hand to her mouth
and let out a long gasp of disbelief.

As he stopped in front of her, she stared at him as if he
were a ghost, before reaching out and putting her fingers to his
hand as if to confirm he was flesh and blood. '*Joe?* For

goodness' sake.' She gave a choked cry of excitement. 'How on earth!'

The next moment she had looped her arms gravely around his neck and pressed her head to his neck. He would have hugged her back but his arms got tangled up in her rucksack.

Pulling away again, she stared intently into his eyes. 'Joe, for God's sake.' And then she was stepping backwards, looking past him. 'Did you come with Jamie? Is he with you?'

'I'm alone. Completely alone. I followed you from town. No excuses, Jen. I saw you in town and I'm afraid I followed you back.'

She laughed oddly. 'I never saw you.'

'The snow. I followed the tracks.'

'Like a paper trail!' She gave the strange laugh again, like a shuddering gasp.

He wished he'd planned what to say. 'How are you, Jenna? Are you okay?'

Her gaze strayed over his shoulder again. 'Just you, Joe? No one else?'

Was she hoping for her father or mother? Or scared of someone else he might have brought?

'Just me,' he said in a reassuring voice. 'No one knows I'm here.'

'Oh, Joe . . .' She came closer again. Her hat was pulled half way down her forehead, her scarf up to her chin. In the eerie light, her skin was bleached of all colour, a pale mask in which her eyes seemed to float softly. The snow fell between them like an impenetrable layer of gauze, and she seemed both close and a long way away.

'But what are you doing here, Joe?' she asked. 'Why did you come?'

'I came to see *you*, of course.' And now it was Joe who reached out and touched her arm.

'You came all this way? To see me?' From the way she spoke, it might have been Siberia. She smiled through glistening eyes. 'Only you, Joe. Only you.'

He felt his throat tighten, he blinked uncertainly. 'But every-one's been desperate to find you, Jenna. The whole family. Your dad, your mum – they've been so worried.'

She dropped her head a little, she couldn't or wouldn't speak.

'They want to know if you're all right.'

'I'm all right,' she murmured, her voice almost lost in the whispering snow.

'Can I tell them that?'

She gave a troubled nod.

'What else can I tell them, Jenna?

'Nothing, Joe.'

'No message?'

Her eyes came up to his. 'Sometimes it's best to leave the past behind.'

'What, including the people who love you?'

'It's hard – to give things up,' she said with difficulty. 'But sometimes – to find peace – to find a way of living – a reasonable life – sometimes there's no other way – to find peace.'

'Okay,' he said with a slow nod. 'But to cut yourself off from everything and everyone – so hard, Jenna. So hard on everyone.'

Her eyes were a little wild now, her voice too. 'I have to make my own journey, Joe. I have to make it as best I can.'

'Your father would give anything to see you. Anything in the world.'

He had meant to push her, and he was succeeding. Her lip trembled, she bowed her head.

'How is he?'

Joe could see no point in holding back. He told her about Alan's workload, his heart problems, the worry that wore at him constantly, and she flinched a little, she screwed up her eyes, and when she opened them again they were glittering with tears.

'So why not speak to him, Jenna? What possibly harm could it do?'

Pulling off a glove, she dug a handkerchief out of her pocket and wiped her eyes with punishing strokes. Seeing this, Joe felt a rush of tenderness. He might have retreated then, he almost did, but something made him press on: his love for Alan; an obscure exasperation.

'A call every now and then? A letter?'

She shot him a pained glance, she made a gesture of hopelessness. 'But I'd only talk, you see.'

He didn't get it. 'So?'

She blew her nose hard. 'I'm not allowed to talk.'

'Says who?'

'I mustn't talk,' she repeated like a mantra.

'Says Chetwood?' he scoffed. 'For God's sake, Jenna.'

'That's what I promised – not to talk.' She spoke like a child who must keep reciting the words to bolster her resolve.

'Look,' he said almost roughly, 'is this to do with the death of your friend? Because if it is, nobody has to talk about it. Nobody has to even mention it.'

'Oh, but *I* would have to talk about it!'

'Jenna . . .' He stood in front of her, he gripped her upper arms and felt how thin they were under the layers of clothing. He waited for her restless eyes to come up to his before saying, 'Chetwood told me all about your friend. I'm deeply sorry. It must have been a shock. Awful. But it's no reason to keep away from your mum and dad. They love you. They want to know you're all right.'

'But I'd have to tell them!'

And then Chetwood's words came back to him. *She needs to talk . . . and people don't always understand.* 'Okay . . .' he said soothingly. 'Okay. But your parents would understand. Of all people. They wouldn't blame you. Not in a million years.'

She gave him a baffled look, as though they had been talking at cross-purposes. 'But of course they'd blame me.'

Joe had finally got there. He dropped his hands. 'Right.'

'I did a terrible thing.'

'Right.'

'I couldn't hide it from them. I couldn't – *not* tell them.'

'But it was an accident, right?'

'Is that what Jamie told you?'

'Yes.'

'What did he say?'

Hearing the sudden rise in her voice, Joe went cautiously. 'That he fell? Into a river?'

She shook her head in despair.

Her face had grown blotchy from the cold and the tears, her nose was red. He could see faint lines fanning out from the corners of her eyes and tiny frown-marks between her eyebrows. But it was the same face for all that, a lovely face written over by time and unhappiness. As he looked at her, a snowflake settled on her eyelashes and she made no effort to blink it away. In that instant it seemed to him that she was gripped by a weariness so deep she would never recover from it.

'We killed him, Joe. That's what he doesn't want me to say. We both killed him.'

Her breath had emerged in a plume of vapour, and he watched as the wind sucked it away. He heard a soft whistling in the treetops as a gust approached and saw the falling snow change direction and spiral upwards. He tried to juggle two thoughts, one that didn't bear thinking about, the other that had him grasping at Chetwood's words. *She blames herself. The whole thing's crazy, okay, Joe? There's no reason. No reason for any of it.*

He chose a natural tone to say, 'You don't have to tell me any of this—'

'But I do.' And now her eyes were luminous and fervent. 'That's the whole point. I'll never be able to achieve grace, I know that. But I must be allowed my guilt, Joe. I must be allowed remorse. I must be allowed to carry the burden of mortal sin. To acknowledge that I took someone's life, a life that was sacred and innocent and loving. I won't be denied that, Joe. I'm not like Jamie, you see – I can't pretend.'

They stood in the falling snow and it seemed to Joe that the space between them contained an unbearable heat.

'You understand, Joe?'

He nodded rapidly. 'Yes. I think I do.'

The dog had returned from a hunting expedition and was circling round them. The sight of him seemed to engender alarm in Jenna. 'You must go now. Jamie mustn't find you here.'

'I don't give a damn if he finds me here!'

'Please, Joe.' She took a step towards the cottage. 'For me. Please.'

He gave a sigh of capitulation.

As they started off, she seemed to stumble and he reached out for her hand. She would have pulled it away, but thinking better of it, she let him tuck her arm into his and cover her hand with his.

'Joe . . .' She murmured with a kind of puzzlement. 'All this way . . .'

'What shall I tell them when I get back, Jenna? What shall I tell your dad?'

'Tell him . . . I'll write.' She said it once more as if to convince herself: 'I'll write.'

Reaching the denser woodland, the wind subsided a little and he was aware of the silence again and the faint squeak of their steps on the snow.

'Marc told me he spoke to you on Monday.'

She was bemused. 'No . . . No, I haven't talked to him in ages.'

'How long ago? Can you remember?'

'I don't know. A year? No – more like two.'

Joe allowed himself a grim satisfaction at having caught Marc out in the lie.

'I wanted to speak to Dad,' Jenna continued in a tense reminiscent tone. 'It was his birthday. It took me weeks to decide what to say, to summon the courage – and after all that he wasn't there. I got Marc.'

'What did you say to Marc?'

'Oh, I don't remember. Nothing much.'

'Could you have said anything to make him think you were – well, frightened? That you were feeling threatened?'

Jenna jerked to a stop, she stared at him with a kind of horror. The next moment she seemed utterly confused, she opened her mouth to speak and nothing came out. Finally she gasped, 'What sort of a threat? What do you mean?'

'He said you seemed to be *living in fear* – I think that was how he put it.'

'But I never—' She shook her head as if to bring herself to her senses.

'He said you rang off because you were frightened of what might happen to you if you stayed on the line.'

'Oh – maybe,' she said vaguely. 'Yes . . . maybe.' Then: 'For a moment I thought . . .' But she never managed to articulate what it was she had thought.

'So, he got it wrong?'

'Yes.'

'I rather thought so.'

He drew her arm back into his and they walked again, Jenna distractedly.

'On the subject of Marc, he wants to sell the house you were left by the old lady – Edith Gutteridge, wasn't it? There's an offer. He wants to know if you'll agree.'

She was still dazed. 'If that's what he wants.'

'He needs the money to study. He wants to train as a teacher.'

'A teacher?' For an instant her expression lifted with surprise and pleasure. 'Yes . . . he'll make a good teacher.'

'He's keen to get it tied up as quickly as possible.'

'To get what . . . ?'

'The sale of the house.'

'Ah.'

'If you agree.'

'Yes, yes,' she said uncertainly. 'Of course.'

'The easiest thing would be a power of attorney. I could get something drawn up in the morning and drop it over at lunchtime.'

Her pace faltered again.

'We could meet in town if you'd prefer.'

Suddenly she seemed to realise what she'd been drawn into. She stopped and looked around, as if for escape. 'Can't you do it for me? Sign this thing?'

'Not possible, I'm afraid. But there's nothing after this. You don't have sign anything else.'

They walked on.

'Shall I come here, then?'

She shook her head, so he suggested the Royal Oak at twelve. He repeated it to be sure, and this time she gave a small nod.

Twice, her breath emerged in a plume as if she were about to speak, and twice she stayed silent.

'And what about lunch afterwards?'

She glanced up at him as if he were mad.

'Nothing elaborate.'

Her eyes hunted across the ground. 'If you like.'

'I'd like it very much.'

They rounded a corner and the cottage appeared as a smudge beyond the curtain of snow. Remembering the chill kitchen, Joe's anger pricked at him again. 'How can you live in a place like this, Jenna? How can you stand it?'

'Oh, but I like it here, Joe.'

'But to have no *heating*?'

'We light fires.'

'And the damp. The mildew. The *lino*.'

'We've been happy here,' she said firmly, and there was a ring in her voice that warned him against discussion.

The path narrowed and slipping her arm free of his she went on ahead.

'Did I see you in London one day?' Joe asked. 'In Oxford Street, in the rain?'

Her head turned a little, but she kept walking.

'Did I frighten you? You probably thought it was some lunatic.'

'No, I . . .' Silence.

'But you were there?'

'I've only been to London once . . .' She stopped and swung around impatiently, as if she had no more time for pretence. 'I did see you,' she confessed. 'But I couldn't believe it was you. I . . . ran away.'

'I don't blame you.'

'I couldn't face you, I'm afraid. I couldn't face anything then.'

She walked on and they didn't speak again till they reached the cottage.

'You sang the *Messiah*?' he asked kindly.

For the first time, she smiled faintly. 'At a friend's house. Four of us. Just a couple of the quieter choruses. It was lovely. But your advertisement, Joe . . .' She shook her head, not at all displeased.

'You saw it all right?'

'One of my friends saw it.'

She walked down to the car with him. As they came within sight of the front of the cottage she glanced towards the windows a couple of times, nervously it seemed to Joe, and he wondered if Chetwood was back, though there was no sign of another car and no smoke from the chimneys.

In the end he asked her straight out: 'Is he back?'

'No. But any minute.'

'Wouldn't it be easier if I just waited?'

She shook her head adamantly.

'What about my car tracks?' he said, more to point out the absurdity of the situation than to alarm her.

'I'll say it was our neighbour.'

'But what would it matter, Jenna? I only saw Chetwood yesterday.'

She turned to face him, wide-eyed. 'Because he'll know that I told you about Sam. He'll know straight away. And he'll be very angry.'

'So what?'

'I couldn't do that to him, Joe. Not after all he's done for me. He's been so good to me. You can't imagine.'

'He looks after you, Jen? He's kind to you?'

'Oh yes,' she said unhesitatingly.

When he bent to kiss her, her cheek was like ice.

He smiled, 'Tomorrow at twelve then?'

She took a step backwards and immediately the drifting snow seemed to put an impossible distance between them.

They found him a small overheated room at the back of the Royal Oak – he was lucky to get anything this close to Christmas, the manager informed him crisply – and he slept badly to dreams of snow and darkness, and to the clatter of food deliveries well before dawn.

After a cooked breakfast that sat uneasily on his stomach, he called Anna and told her to report him off sick. 'Shall I say you've got a bad case of flu, Joe? Because so far as Harry's Christmas spirit is concerned, it might as well be Easter. We think he's had his wife's credit card bill.' They settled on a bad cold. 'Happy Christmas, Joe.'

He remembered with a sinking heart that it was Christmas Day tomorrow and he had nothing to give his father, and no food.

It had stopped snowing in the night, the wind had dropped, and a high mackerel haze covered the sky. He found a solicitors' firm by the simple expedient of walking the town till he saw a brass plate. The firm had two partners and, it seemed, plenty of business to wrap up before the Christmas break starting at one o'clock. It was almost an hour before he emerged with a power of attorney, correctly spelt – the secretary had typed Marcus with a *k* first time round – and the assurance that the office wouldn't shut a second before one o'clock if he needed someone to witness the signature.

In the hall of the Royal Oak, people spoke in festive voices, loud and forced. Some joked about the snow – if a white Christmas came with the booking, they'd certainly be coming again next year – some complained excitedly about the dangerous driving conditions, some laughed hugely for no apparent reason; and their voices seemed to grow more raucous as the morning went on, though Joe knew it was only the effect of waiting.

He left it till two before making a move.

The gritting lorries had been out as far as the forked valleys, but the road turned white as he crossed the bridge into the small middle valley. Driving low alongside the dancing river, Joe twice felt the wheel go dead in his hands and the back wheels slip.

The angled turn-off to the Arcadian valley looked disturbingly steep under three inches of snow. He saw a sign he hadn't seen yesterday which read 'Nant Garth'. Performing his U-turn twenty yards up the road, he took a run at the lane and made it to the first corner before the wheels spun uselessly. Trickling back down the hill, he tried again and didn't even make it to the first corner.

He reckoned half an hour on foot, but quickly amended this to an hour because of his shoes and the drifts coming off the fields. There were recent vehicle tracks along the valley road, some of them tractor-sized, others car-width but with deep treads. One of the cottages had smoke coming out of the chimney and a four-wheel drive outside, but he pressed on.

He reached the woods at last and saw fresh car tracks running on ahead of him. Coming to the left turn, the car tracks branched off towards the cottage and one moment it seemed to him the tracks were leaving, the next coming, and only logic told him it was impossible to tell the difference.

He climbed on, and in the unobscured light saw the clearing long before he reached it. Through the last of the trees, balanced on the brilliance of the white slope, the cottage appeared solid and empty. No smoke, and no Volvo.

He paused and heard a silence that was muffled and unresonant. Nearing the cottage, he saw that curtains had been drawn across the lower windows, and when he went round to the back the kitchen door was locked. The snow in the yard was heavily trampled and scored with tracks – human, car, pony, dog – but it wasn't till he went to the door of the stable and saw the padlock that he faced the possibility they had gone for good. The path leading up into the woods had seen at least one human and one dog since the snow stopped falling, but no pony. He looked for a gap in the curtains at the front and, through a minute crack at the left-hand window, thought he saw bare floorboards where packing cases had been.

Back in the valley he trudged up the track to the cottage with the smoking chimney. The woman who came to the door was fortyish with a shock of prematurely white hair in a utilitarian bob and a pleasant scrubbed face. She was wearing an apron and brought with her the smell of baking. With her quiet voice and ready smile, she might have come straight out of one of those amber hued advertisements for Mr Kipling's Cakes.

'All I know,' she said, 'is that they're called Evans.'

When he laughed from sheer disbelief, she laughed with him, a little uncertainly. 'Oh, you mean, as opposed to Jones!' she cried, delighted to have got the joke.

They were standing on the front step in the cold, but she didn't seem to mind. She was quite happy to talk.

That was all she knew about the two of them, she said: their name. 'They always kept themselves to themselves. Polite, oh very much so, but not people to socialise. Not at all.' She

couldn't remember exactly how long they'd been up the hill. A
year? Maybe a little more. Oh yes, they were renting the place,
that was definite, because, you see, it had been her mother-in-
law's home until she passed away two years ago, God bless
her, and now it had come to her husband. But the letting itself,
that was done through an agent in Builth Wells, who took up
the references and collected the rent. She couldn't tell Joe any
more than that.

Then she hesitated. 'Strange you should come asking today,
though, because I think we might have seen the last of them. It
must have been midday I saw them leaving. I noticed especially
because they looked loaded up, like. Both cars they had, and
the estate car sitting very low, like it was full to the brim. Oh,'
she added, 'and the horsebox hitched on behind.'

He left his phone number and asked if she'd be good
enough to tell him if his friends came back.

'Delighted,' she said. 'To be quite honest, we were surprised
they stayed this long. We thought they'd be gone once winter
came. It's prone to damp, that cottage. Always has been.'

She waved him off as though it had been a real pleasure to
see him. So far up the valley, he supposed she didn't get many
callers.

Chapter Eight

IT WAS two months before Joe and Alan achieved their long-promised walk. Christmas had been too busy and perhaps too troubled, though neither of them would have admitted to that. Then Alan had weekend duties he couldn't avoid, and Joe had to fly to Hong Kong on business. Finally, after some confusion over dates – Alan had it down for the wrong week – they were set for the last Sunday in February.

Joe spent the Saturday with his father, food shopping, unclogging gutters, sweeping a couple of floors. The employment agency had provided a cleaner who had thus far fulfilled the main requirement of the job, which was not to walk out, and if she left more dust than she picked up she was still a long, long way short of dismissal.

It was Joe's first visit since Christmas, and the sprigs of holly which he'd brought in from the garden and stuck in a mug on the dining table had dried to paper. Christmas lunch had been just as scrappy, the product of Joe's trawl through a smugly empty-shelved supermarket late on Christmas Eve: a battery chicken which bled its weight in water, some frozen vegetables with no taste, packet gravy, and roast potatoes which refused to crisp. They finished the meal with stewed apple and custard out of the store cupboard. But if Joe had failed on the food he made up for it on the wine, with a fine Burgundy and some vintage port. Whether it was the wine or the remembrance of Christmases past, but his father didn't rush back to his computer after the meal. Instead they talked, or rather his father reminisced about the old days and Joe

jogged his memory now and again. At one point, talking of
Joe's mother, the old man's eyes sparkled with tears, he pulled
out a handkerchief and lifted his spectacles to dab furiously at
his eyes. 'She was an extraordinary woman,' he breathed in an
unsteady voice. 'There's not a day I don't miss her. Not a day
I don't remember the last time I saw her alive and well. Smiling
as they wheeled her away.'

After two glasses of port the old man fell asleep in front of
the television. When Joe brought tea and cake a couple of
hours later, he had woken in an altogether more acerbic mood.
'Not off to the Laskeys yet?' he asked with a pointed look at
the clock. Joe said he'd be going over later if that was all right.
Then, to mollify the old man, but also from a need to talk it
through with someone, Joe told him about the search for
Jenna, and how, once found, he had succeeded in losing her
again. He mentioned the drowning accident and Jenna's
anguish. But not killing or confessions. Like a secret accomplice, he held those words guiltily to his heart.

The old man listened with his usual air of touchy disdain,
scoffing under his breath, lifting his eyebrows in a show of
weary amazement; none of which quite succeeded in hiding his
considerable interest. He demanded details, protested at Joe's
sloppy reporting, pounced on inconsistencies and batted them
straight back for clarification. Repetitions were treated to an
impatient wave. 'Yes, yes – you said that.' Joe felt as if he were
in court.

The observations, when they came, were delivered crisply.
He'd never heard of a development down by the builder's
merchant. The houses around there were still in private ownership, people were doing them up, spending money on them.
And worth far more than forty thousand, he thought. In fact,
closer to sixty, he was willing to bet on it. 'No, someone's
having you on, Joe. You and the Laskeys.' His tone, which
bordered on the sympathetic, suggested this wouldn't be difficult. As for Wales, well, it was an obvious spot to hide, wasn't
it? Dark, damp and all those valleys. In the next breath, he

proclaimed the inoffensiveness of damp, that there was nothing wrong with it in the kitchen, it was in the nature of kitchens to be damp, certainly nobody ever died of damp, not in a kitchen, and it was ridiculous to talk about it in the same breath as bodily neglect (not in fact the term Joe had used). Inconvenient it might be, but not neglectful. 'Only children and plants suffer from neglect,' he declared. As for the pony being moved, this was no indication that the Chetwoods had left the place for good. Welsh ponies were bred to live on the hills all year round, surely Joe knew that. The Chetwoods might simply have been transporting the animal to a winter pasture. As for the heavily loaded car, there was only the neighbour's word for that, and how long was the neighbour's drive? A hundred yards. The snow thick? *Quite*. No, this talk of doing a moonlight flit was a bit overdramatic – one of the old man's favourite rebukes. No, they'd just wanted to escape for the day so as to avoid Joe. They'd probably got back that very evening. 'And this false name,' he sneered. 'Evans, indeed. Obviously, he owes money. I always said he'd turn out to be a scoundrel. What else could it be? You say Jenna couldn't offer a reason for all this hiding up valleys?'

Joe framed his evasion carefully. 'She said she wanted a quiet life.'

'There you are – he owes money.'

Finally, the handing down of the judgement, delivered in a brisk professional tone. 'Well, I don't know what you mean by the search going *wrong*. You found her. You saw her. She didn't want to have anything to do with the outside world. I'd say the case was closed. Nothing more to be done. Nothing more to be said.'

This speech certainly seemed to close the subject for the old man. He didn't mention it again over Christmas, nor in the following weeks when they spoke on the phone. These conversations were anyway sporadic, not because Joe didn't call regularly – twice a week when he was in London, once a week when abroad – but because his father left most calls to the peremptory tones of the answering machine. The few times when the old man snatched up the phone and barked his own distinctive greeting, it was to make it clear that he was far too busy to chat, and after a few one-sided enquiries Joe gave up.

Now, as Joe balanced on a chair, changing an outside light-bulb in the darkness and drizzle of the February night, he became aware of his father peering up at him from the kitchen door. It was the first time the old man had left the computer since Joe's arrival.

'Never use that light.'

'The more lights the better. Next time I'll bring one of those bulbs that comes on automatically when it gets dark.'

Normally this would have been enough to provoke a frown, but the old man let it pass. He hovered for a while, staring out into the garden, before vanishing again. A minute later, he was back.

'Did you say you were going walking with Alan tomor-row?'

'Yes.'

'No news on the Jenna business?'

'No.'

'Didn't manage to find her again?'

Joe had fitted the glass back onto the light-casing but was having trouble getting the fixing screw to grip. 'I haven't been looking.'

'Oh?'

'The Laskeys didn't want to go on with it.'

'Ah.' A small grunt of satisfaction. 'That's what I said, wasn't it? No point.' Then, in a tone that attempted to be casual: 'So what's happened to the famous house sale?'

'It must have fallen through, I suppose.'

The old man had been laying the ground patiently, and now he had his reward. 'Well, of course it's fallen through! With good reason!'

If Joe was to get the rest of the story within a reasonable

space of time he knew better than to show less than total interest. He looked down. 'You've heard something, Dad?'

'No more than anyone could have found out with a simple phone call.'

Joe climbed down from the chair. 'And what was that, Dad?'

'I checked with the planners, that's all. Nothing elaborate. Just phoned the council and asked. Couldn't have been simpler.'

'And?'

'There's no development planned for anywhere in that part of town. Nothing. It's zoned as housing. Just as I told you.'

'Right.'

'Wasn't that what I told you?'

'You did.'

Joe tackled the screw again and wondered what Marc's game could be. Why bother to invent a developer? What was wrong with a private buyer? Perhaps he was trying to set up some intricate deal and wanted to cover his tracks. Joe seemed to remember some scandal about a bent estate agent who got an accomplice to buy a property cheap, only to sell it on the following week at a vastly improved price. But all that bother for what? The only person Marc could defraud was himself. And of course Jenna.

His father had reappeared in the kitchen doorway. 'I told you, didn't I?'

'You told me, Dad. And you were absolutely right.'

After a delay in setting out – Alan had phone calls to make, he couldn't find his special walking socks – there wasn't time to go as far as the Peaks, not with dusk at four, so they settled for the Vale of Belvoir half an hour away. Here the trails were narrow, muddy, and interrupted by gates and styles, but the instant Alan struck out along the path, in tweed jacket, tweed hat, errant knee-socks, walking stick swinging jauntily in one hand, map jutting from his pocket, he pronounced himself happy.

'What's life about if it isn't this, Joe? We're all mad, you know, every single one of us – the life we lead! We have it all wrong!' The Christmas snow had long since thawed, it had rained for most of February, and now a winter gloom hung over the sky. Alan took long breaths of the damp air and declared, 'Wonderful! So fresh!' The hedgerows were almost bare but Alan found enough to catch his eye, identifying each plant with if not the expertise of a botanist then certainly the enthusiasm. He extolled the beauty of the seed-heads, the last shrivelled blackberries hanging off the brambles, toadstools that he pronounced edible – though on second thoughts maybe not: 'I wouldn't like to swear to its bona fides without my book, Joe.' Nearing some woods, he pointed to some circling crows, then, halting, begged silence for the tap of a wood-pecker. 'What a world, Joe!' he sighed rapturously. 'What more could one ask?'

Reaching the brow of a low hill they paused to look out over damp fields dotted with sheep.

'Don't you long to live in a place like this, Joe?'

'Half of me. I'm rather schizophrenic about it.'

'When you have a family, then you'll see the point. Children do better in the country, no doubt about it. The free-dom. The innocence – what's left of it anyway.' Then, shyly: 'Nothing in sight yet, Joe?'

'Sorry?'

'A special girl?'

'Oh. Not yet, no.'

He hadn't had any contact with Sarah since she'd returned from her Jamaican holiday, and then it had only been on the phone. She'd wanted to meet and talk face to face, but hearing the message in her tone he'd opted for immediate pain over prolonged uncertainty and asked point blank where they were. The conversation that followed was a model of a modern breakup. On her side there was much talk of career demands, personal space and her inability to commit. She stressed it was all her fault, she said how sorry she was it hadn't worked out. For his part, he produced the stilted politeness that reveals more about dented pride than it ever manages to conceal: he wished her well, he was sorry it hadn't worked out, he wasn't sure he understood why, but if it wasn't right for her, well, there was nothing more to be said, was there? For two weeks he drank too much and was slow to get jokes, but then, apart from the small ache of loneliness that took him unawares every time he walked into the flat, he began to put Sarah out of his mind. When work allowed, he saw friends; when it didn't, he went to the gym and started a couple of good books. A month ago, Kate had called him for news of Chetwood and they'd had dinner together. When the subject of Chetwood had been exhausted – he'd told her about the damp cottage and the sudden disappearance – he was surprised to find himself having a good time. Whether it was Kate's giggly nature – he'd never known a girl laugh so much or so easily – or her irreverence, which fell just the right side of silliness, he surprised himself a second time by suggesting they have dinner again soon. With the trip to Hong Kong he hadn't got round to calling her yet, but whether it was Kate or someone else – and in all likelihood it would be someone else – he realised that he had opened himself up to the possibility of someone new.

'Good women are hard to find,' Alan said. 'And then you have to persuade the object of your affections that she's not going to do better elsewhere, even when she's surrounded by dozens of blokes with more money and better looks!'

It was good to see Alan's round face split by a wide grin, his little eyes rolling with laughter, and Joe laughed with him.

They walked on for a while, single-file, then as the path broadened out, abreast. As soon as Joe drew level, Alan said in a tone of careful preparation, 'I'm sorry about Christmas, Joe.'

'Nothing to be sorry about.'

'Marc takes these things to heart.'

'Of course.'

'I want you to know – we never had any doubts about what you told us, Helena and I. No doubts at all.'

'I only wish it could have been different.'

'Not your fault if she was determined to make off. Not your fault if she didn't want to be found. No, you did your best, Joe. More than we could ever have asked for.' The swing of the walking stick had been describing smaller and smaller arcs until it barely matched his next stride. 'And Joe?'

'Yes?'

'Now I know Jenna's in good health, now I know there was nothing to stop her contacting us . . . well, it's made me realise. It's her choice, and there we are. Nothing to be done about it. Life moves on. Got to accept that, haven't you?' He flung a brief barren smile at Joe. 'You bring them up, you do your best, but then – well, you have no right to expect anything after that. They must go their own way. They must do their own thing.'

They came to a style, and with a puff and a pant Alan clambered over.

'Things might change.'

'No, no!' Alan declared firmly. 'Got to respect her choice. And that's all there is to it.'

'The police were okay about dropping the search?'

'Oh yes. Got enough on their plate. To be honest, Joe, I don't think it was ever very high on their list of priorities. I got the feeling they hadn't taken it very seriously.'

'You saw them yourself?'

'With Marc,' he said quickly. 'We went together.' Something in his tone spoke of difficulties and tensions.

'And what about the money? Will Marc be able to manage?'

'We've lent it to him. No, no – what am I talking about? We've *given* it to him. An outright gift. One way and another we gave Jenna quite a bit over the years. Lessons, master classes, dresses for concerts, this and that. So now – well, it's only fair.'

Joe remembered Helena's call for sanity over the money issue, and wondered if she'd persuaded Alan to take out a loan.

Coming to a bend in the path, a wide view opened out before them, a reach of fields, a distant undulating horizon, but Alan didn't appear to notice.

'One thing, Joe.'

They were single file again, Alan leading.

'Yes?'

Alan was walking doggedly, head down, no longer swinging his stick but clutching it under one arm like a military baton, so that when he stopped abruptly Joe almost walked into the mud-caked tip.

'Marc went to Wales.' He turned and offered an unhappy glance.

'He went to look for them?'

Alan answered with a small sigh.

With a surge of irritation, Joe made a swift inventory of the information he'd given Alan and Marc: the name of the Arcadian valley – Nant Garth – an approximate position for the cottage – what was it he'd said? Something like *at the far end* – and the name Evans. In fact, pretty much everything.

'And did he find anything?'

'I don't think so.'

'So what was it about? He thought I was lying?'

'You know how Marc is, Joe. He has to do everything his own way.'

Joe thought: You can say that again. 'But he didn't find them?'

'No, no. He'd have said.'

Joe's irritation was replaced by a bafflement that was an echo of the one he'd felt yesterday. What had driven Marc to go to all that trouble? Was it just the money? Or was it something else altogether, something to do with his easily provoked sense of righteousness?

'The offer for the house, Alan – how did it come about? Was it an agent who approached Marc?'

Judging by the time it took Alan to answer, it wasn't something he'd thought about very much. 'I'm trying to remember,' he said at last. 'I'm not sure Marc told me. Why?'

'No special reason.'

A little later, Alan waved a hand in the air: it had come back to him. 'A solicitor's letter – that's what Marc said. A firm somewhere in Nottingham.'

After two hours they stopped at a village pub and had a trencherman's lunch, roast beef with all the trimmings followed by steamed sponge pudding.

'I think I've scttled a bit lower in the water,' Alan puffed on the way back.

They reached the car at dusk. Alan sank heavily into the passenger seat. 'Done me good,' he gasped with a laugh. 'Cleaned out the arteries.'

Nearing home, he said with a touch of anxiety, 'You'll come and have some tea before you head back, won't you, Joe? Come and see Helena?'

'Of course.'

'She always loves to see you, you know that.'

They lapsed into a preoccupied silence. Joe needed no reminding that it was Sunday evening, and another long week stretched before him. A video link with Ritch and his team had been booked for Tuesday. Ostensibly it was a progress meeting, but no one at their end had any doubts it was a shoring-up exercise. Harry was going to sit in, and Harry never sat in unless he felt that his massaging skills were going to be put to triumphant use.

Making the final turn into the Laskeys' road, Joe asked, 'Got any plans for Easter, Alan? Shall we try for a day in the Peaks then? Arrange to leave a car at our finishing point?'

When Alan didn't answer, Joe glanced across and saw him staring intently ahead with a deep frown. Following his gaze, Joe saw nothing, just the dark road interspersed with pools of light around the infrequent street lamps, and outside the house some cars, one white. Only as they got closer did he make out what Alan had perhaps already spotted: that the white car had bright stripes down the side and a blue bubble on top. It was a small police car, the sort used for community policing.

Joe grimaced sympathetically as he parked. 'Is this going to mean work for you, Alan?'

Alan shook his head, still frowning, and climbed out.

As Joe closed the car door he saw Alan's walking stick lying on the back seat. Having retrieved it, he arrived in the hall a few seconds after Alan. He remembered the walking stick for a long time afterwards because he was still clutching it when the policewoman took Alan a couple of steps to one side and told him that Jenna was dead.

Chapter Nine

THE ORDERLY tapped in a key-code and opened the door to let them through. Craig, the senior police officer, went first, then the younger detective whose name Joe hadn't caught, while the family liaison officer, WPC Jaffrey, hung back, waiting to follow up behind. Alan got as far as the threshold and faltered. Joe tucked a hand under his elbow. After a moment, they entered together.

It was a small bare room, dominated by a large interior window with curtains drawn back. Through the glass another small room was visible, also empty but for a corner of a white-draped trolley. Joe felt his stomach bunch, a sudden breathlessness.

They walked to the middle of the window and looked through the glass at Jenna's body. The white sheet had been pulled up to her ears and chin. In profile, her face might have been an effigy, timeless, untouched. But when Joe brought himself to look more closely he saw the unnatural tautness of her skin, the hollowness of her cheeks, the eyes which seemed almost too deep in their sockets, the lids tinged with grey.

Craig moved up to Alan's shoulder.

'Are you able to confirm that this is your daughter, Dr Laskey?' he murmured in a low voice. 'A nod will be sufficient.'

Alan took a sudden breath. 'Yes,' he whispered, 'it's my daughter.' Then, as if breaking free from a trance, he stated in a stronger voice, 'I'd like to spend some time with her. Alone, please.'

'Of course, sir.'

'But in there. I'd like to go in there. With her.'

'I'm sorry, sir, but that won't be possible at this point in time.'

Alan trembled visibly. 'But I'm a doctor. There's nothing I haven't seen – nothing I don't know.'

'I regret, sir – it's a matter of procedure.'

Alan shot Joe a look of appeal.

Joe whispered, 'Why don't we go back to the other room? I'll see if there's anything that can be done.'

'I'll wait here,' he replied firmly. 'On my own.'

The rest of them filed out. When Joe glanced back, Alan was standing at the window, staring into the white reflected light.

The liaison officer stationed herself outside the door while Joe followed Craig back to the room where they had assembled what seemed a long time ago but was no more than five minutes. The young detective came in after them and closed the door, though this did nothing to shut out the mortuary smell which seemed to pervade every corner of the room.

Craig said, 'Do sit down, Mr McGrath.' He moved two chairs either side of a low table.

As Joe sat down he made a conscious effort not to hold too much against Craig before they started: the fact that he and his colleague had only just made an appearance, the fact that Alan and Joe, having arrived the previous evening, had been left all night without information; that even this morning things had got off to an unbearably slow start. The liaison officer had done her best, but nothing could dispel Joe's angry suspicion that they'd been forgotten for the last four hours.

'You came up last night?' Craig asked.

'We arrived at ten.'

Craig seemed to feel no need to apologise for the fact that they were only meeting now, fourteen hours later. 'And you found somewhere to stay all right?' he enquired.

'Well, yes.' Irritated by Craig's polite nod, Joe added sharply, 'I have to say it would have been a considerable help to Dr Laskey if some basic information had been available last night. If there'd been someone – *anyone* – on duty.'

'But you were seen by a liaison officer?'

'Who had absolutely no information whatsoever.'

'The officer should have been able to give you a few basic facts. I'd be concerned if she hadn't done that.'

'The name of the river, the name of the nearest village – that was it. Nothing about how the body was found, if there was a suicide note, did she leave a car somewhere, was it far from where she was found, does her husband know what's happened, does he need to be contacted? Just for starters.'

Craig took this on board with a solemn nod. 'It takes time to establish the facts, Mr McGrath, and last night there weren't that many facts available. But perhaps we could come to those matters in a moment?'

He was a man of about forty with a broad face, strong features, and a steady benign gaze. There was no hurry about him, and no menace. His voice, which had only the mildest Welsh accent, was low and considered, and it was this, together with his air of quiet professionalism, that made Joe retreat a little. 'Okay,' Joe said. 'Okay. What about Dr Laskey having time with his daughter? Is there no way he can go into the room with her?'

Craig folded one arm over the other, then swung a hand out as if to divert the conversation onto another track. 'Before we start, could you tell me in what capacity you're here, Mr McGrath?'

'What? As a family friend.'

'Ah. It was just that someone mentioned you being a lawyer.'

'Purely coincidental.'

'I see.' His hand swung in again. 'To answer your question, there will almost certainly be a point when Dr Laskey can have time alone with Jennifer. But it will not be possible until the formalities are complete.'

Joe bristled at his use of her name. It was as though Craig

were claiming a gratuitous and rather offensive intimacy. 'The formalities,' he echoed coolly. 'With the coroner, you mean?'

'The next of kin will have to make contact with the coroner's office in due course, yes.'

'Is there anything the family need to be doing right now?'

'Not at this time.'

It was many years since Joe had acquired the few dry facts on family law required to pass his finals, and almost as many years since he'd forgotten them. Everything that would have been useful now – a working knowledge of the procedures, the paperwork, the family's duties after a death – was at best sketchy in his memory. 'What happens next then?'

'We have to complete our investigations.'

'But she drowned.' He had meant this as a question. When Craig didn't reply, he tried again. 'It was suicide?'

'Nothing can be assumed till we have the results of the post-mortem and the other investigations we have in hand.'

Joe did his best to keep all expression out of his face. It hadn't occurred to him that there would be a post-mortem, though now he came to think about it he realised the procedure would be obligatory in cases like this. 'Right,' he said, trying to shut unholy visions out of his mind. 'Right. The post-mortem – that's happened, has it?'

'The autopsy was carried out last night.'

Looking into the pleasant but unreadable face, Joe was struck by a thought that caught him like a blow. This man – maybe, God help us, the youth by the door as well – had stood in on the autopsy, had watched the pathologist at work, had discussed the case over her open body.

He pushed the visions behind him. What the hell did it matter now? Dignity is a luxury we all forfeit in the end.

Yet no sooner had he broken free of this thought than another began to form, disturbing in some other way he couldn't quite identify. He tried to grasp the idea, but it remained tantalisingly out of reach.

'Has her car been found?'

Craig named a place he'd never heard of, adding, 'It's two miles up river from where she was found.'

'There's a dam there, is there?'

Craig's hesitation was minute, barely a beat, but it was enough to make Joe realise his mistake.

'A large weir.' Then, with what seemed the mildest of interest: 'Why do you ask?'

Joe held his gaze. 'Well, suicides often choose to jump, don't they? From a high place.'

Craig looked at him without comment.

'Was there a note?' Joe asked.

Passing over this question with a slow lift of his head, Craig said, 'What would be most useful to us at this time, Mr McGrath, is any background information you might have. About James and Jennifer Chetwood. Their life, their interests . . .'

By the door, the young detective shifted in his seat. He had been sitting with his head leaning back against the wall, but now he sat forward and rested his forearms on his knees. Glancing at him, Joe was once again pricked by the half-formed thought that remained stubbornly out of reach.

'They lived very quietly,' he told Craig. 'They didn't have much contact with people from their old life.'

'But *some* contact?'

Joe signalled his error. 'Actually, no contact at all. In fact, Dr and Mrs Laskey hadn't heard from Jenna for a long time. That's why they were so worried.'

'How long?'

'Four years.'

Craig gave what Joe was coming to recognise as a characteristic response: a faint nod and a twitch of the mouth that was as much an acknowledgement of information received as a humourless smile. 'Any particular reason for the long silence?'

'Not that the Laskeys knew of, no.'

'But you yourself had kept contact?'

'I managed to find them about two months ago. Living in a cottage up the Nant Garth valley. That was when she told me about wanting a quiet life.'

'You found them?' Craig lifted his eyebrows, ready to be impressed. 'Was that difficult?'

'An ad in the local paper. Jenna replied.'

Craig gave a sage nod, and Joe noticed the crispness of his smoky-blue shirt, the well-cut jacket and silk tie fastened with a wide knot. Clothes from the better end of the high street; clothes that cost money. Again, he groped for the significance of this; again, he was too tired to grasp it.

Craig said, 'They were using another name, of course.'

'Evans.'

'Any reason for that, do you know?'

'They wanted a break with the past, I think.'

'Because they fell out with someone? Because they wanted to draw a line under something?'

'I think it was more of a lifestyle thing.'

'Ah,' Craig said immediately, as if this were the most reasonable explanation in the world.

A mobile warbled. The young officer scrambled to his feet and, pulling the phone from his pocket, left the room.

In the pause that followed, Craig's eyes seemed to lose focus; when he spoke again it was absently. 'And what was your opinion of Jenna when you saw her two months ago? Her frame of mind?'

Joe had no idea what triggered it, but in a cascade of reasoning that took him in several directions at once – Craig's air of authority, the long wait to see him, the post-mortem, the presence of the young officer – he finally stumbled over the thought that had eluded him for so long.

'Sorry – Detective *Inspector*, was it?'

'Detective Chief Inspector.'

'Aren't you rather senior?'

'I'm not sure I follow you.'

'It's just a suicide.'

'A sudden death is a sudden death. It has to be investigated.'

'But at your rank?'

'It happens.'

'But in what circumstances?'

Craig's eyes creased up in consideration, his mouth twitched, his expression took on a cooler edge. 'When there are elements of doubt.'

'There wasn't a note then?'

For a time Joe thought he wouldn't answer. 'A note was found, yes.'

'So where's the doubt?'

Craig sat forward and jammed his hands together, fingers interleaved like the teeth of a zipper. 'Mr McGrath, I'm not at liberty to divulge the particulars of our inquiries at the present time. I can only assure Jennifer's family that everything will be investigated most thoroughly.'

Joe studied him for a moment before nodding abruptly. 'Sure.'

Craig sat back again. 'So . . . Jenna's frame of mind when you saw her?'

'She seemed fine. A little subdued maybe.'

'Not depressed?'

'Hard to tell. She said she was happy. She said everything was fine. Though I have to say I was shocked by their living conditions. Fairly basic.'

'In the Nant Garth valley?'

'But I think they moved from there. Didn't they?'

Again choosing not to answer, Craig asked, 'Was Mr Chetwood there when you made your visit?'

'No. But I'd seen him the day before. At a motorway service station. We'd met to deal with some legal business. Jenna's brother Marc wanted to sell a property they owned jointly. We met to discuss it.'

The young officer slipped back into the room. Craig exchanged a glance with him.

'And did Mr Chetwood talk about his wife and their life together?'

Joe said uneasily, 'A little.' He was being led somewhere and it was a place he wasn't certain he wanted to go.

Craig spread a hand, inviting elaboration.

'He said the same thing, that they preferred a quiet life. Particularly Jenna. That she loved being with her animals. Look, he does know about Jenna's death, doesn't he? He's not abroad or anything?'

'He knows.'

'Where is he? I'd like to go and see him as soon as possible.'

Craig turned to the young officer. 'Turner? Did the desk manage to arrange that transport?'

'Yes, sir. He'll be back home by now.'

So that was what they'd been doing for the last few hours, Joe thought: taking Chetwood's statement. Very likely Chetwood had been only yards away from them in the police station while they'd waited through the long morning.

'What's the address?'

'Like you said, the Nant Garth valley.'

Joe was momentarily thrown. 'Right. And there're people with him, are they? He's not alone?'

'There are people with him.' Then: 'You were a friend of his then, were you? As well as Jennifer's?'

'We were at college together.'

Craig looked at him with new interest. 'I see. Did you see him when he came through London on his travels?'

'Not recently. We'd lost touch.'

Craig absorbed this slowly, but with no diminution of interest. 'Do you know someone called Ines Santiago?'

So now we have it, Joe thought: the trawling for dirt, the apportioning of guilt. 'She's his cousin.'

'You've met her?'

'Yes.'

'Close, were they?'

'I've no idea,' he said firmly.

Reading his tone, Craig moved on. 'And Jennifer. Nothing else she mentioned when you saw her, apart from wanting a quiet life?'

'No.'

'Did she say if she travelled abroad with her husband?'

'She said she preferred to stay at home with the animals.'

'What about holidays?' he suggested lightly.

'I don't think so. She didn't even have a passport.'

'Ah.' A look of enlightenment came over Craig's face. 'That would explain why we couldn't find one.' Then: 'She told you, did she? About the passport?'

Something in the way he said this caused Joe a sudden misgiving. 'Does it matter?'

Craig shrugged. 'It would be useful to know, Mr McGrath. That's all.'

Joe wrestled with the impulse to lie. 'It was something I discovered when I was trying to find the two of them. I checked with the passport office. I discovered her passport had expired.'

Craig bowed his head in a gesture that was not in the least ironic. 'Thank you.' He placed his hands over his knees, elbows braced as if to get up, but did not move. 'One last thing, Mr McGrath – did Jennifer mention a man called Sam Raynor?'

'Yes.'

'And what did she say about him?'

'She said he'd died in an accident some years ago. She said she'd never quite got over it.'

'Did she say that she considered herself to blame?'

Joe answered carefully, 'I think everyone feels to blame after an accident, don't they? They tell themselves they could have done more to prevent it. They forget that the whole definition of an accident is something that's unforeseen and unforeseeable.' He was making too much of this; he might have been stalling. 'Is that what she said in the note? Is that the reason she gave for killing herself?'

'It was mentioned.'

'For God's sake.'

'Did you know Sam Raynor yourself?'

'No.'

'Well. Thank you for your help, Mr McGrath.' Craig slapped his knees lightly and stood up. 'Shall we go and see how Dr Laskey's getting on?'

This struck Joe as the first stupid thing Craig had said. Alan would not be 'getting on', not now and not for the foreseeable future. Perhaps it was the lack of sleep, perhaps the tension, but the remark continued to rankle as he followed Craig into the corridor, and it wasn't till they were half-way to the viewing room that Joe thought to ask, 'The weir – was it the one where Sam Raynor died?'

'We believe so, yes.'

'When did they find her?'

'Yesterday morning.'

'How long had she been there?'

Craig stopped two yards short of WPC Jaffrey, who was waiting outside the viewing room. He pulled back against the wall and with a flick of his eyes commanded Turner to walk on. He crossed his arms and regarded Joe intently, as though making some judgement which could still come down either way. Finally he said in a low confiding tone, 'Probably best not to mention it to the family at the present time, Mr McGrath, best to avoid distressing them, but it looks like she was in the water some days. Could be as much as a week. Her body was caught up in some overhanging branches, in a remote spot. It wasn't till some kids happened by that she was found.'

'But wasn't she missed?'

'Mr Chetwood was away. It was the neighbours who raised the alarm when they realised they hadn't seen her for some days.'

Joe felt the bite of anguish; but mainly he felt anger. To have no one miss you, to have no one fretting because they can't get any reply: this struck him as the most unforgivable crime of all.

Chetwood, he thought. You bastard.

They followed a path of mouldering leaves through bare woodland. Below them, a bank fell steeply down to the river which appeared as a sheet of shimmering light through the dark web of the trees. Even before the uniformed officer began to glance down the slope, Joe spotted the signs of a path hastily hacked through the undergrowth: the flattened bracken, the broken branches, the muddy gashes on the woodland floor. They went down the hill single file, ducking under sagging boughs, climbing over fallen branches, stepping over roots, until they reached the water's edge.

'Just there,' the uniformed officer said.

He was pointing to an area of racing water under a black-fringed dome of overhanging trees. At first Joe couldn't imagine how anything could have been caught up here, how any object, whatever its size, could have resisted the sheer speed and power of the current, but then he noticed the way the water surged and bucked under the trees, the way it seemed to be squeezed upwards, and taking a step closer, looking downwards through a surface unobscured by reflection, he saw that the water was racing over a shallow gravel bed. Lifting his eyes, gazing out through the tracery of overhanging branches, he gauged the sweep of the river and realised they were standing on the outer reach of a long bend, and that everything – water, debris, more substantial cargo – would be flung out against the long curved rim of the bend by the force of the current.

She had been swept in here by the water and beached on the gravel bed.

Joe imagined her lying here in the days and nights before she was found, he saw her lying face-up under the canopy, and the image was strangely reassuring. Hidden from the world, out of reach of the land, cleansed by the fast-moving water,

with stars and dappled sunlight overhead. He thought senti-
mentally: Not a bad resting place.

He caught the eye of the uniformed officer and, leaving
Alan alone, they climbed to the top of the bank to wait for
him there. Back at the cars they split up, the uniformed man to
return to Llandrindod Wells, Joe to drive Alan on up the
valley.

It was only a couple of miles to the weir, but it was one of
the longer journeys of Joe's life. He drove slowly, giving Alan
plenty of time to examine the river as it ran below them,
sometimes in full view, occasionally lost behind a rocky out-
crop, but most often flickering behind a screen of trees, the
water white or dark, ruffled or sleek, but never less than fast-
flowing. The valley steepened on either side of them and the
tangled trees, black and bare, interspersed with the occasional
stand of evergreens, seemed to rise above them on both sides,
darkening everything, until the sky was like a pale river running
high above.

The weir was marked by a sign with a picnicking symbol.
There was a small car park with no cars. Choosing the slot
nearest the river, Joe wondered if this was the one Jenna had
chosen, and whether when she climbed out of the car she had
been determined on her course or whether she'd had doubts;
whether she'd been crying or calm; whether one small event
that day could have swung her decision the other way; whether
when she started towards the weir she was clear-headed or
desperately confused. Perhaps she'd taken some tranquillisers,
perhaps she'd had a drink or two. He hoped so, because he
couldn't imagine her starting down the path to the river with
nothing but the knowledge of what she was about to do.

The path led diagonally down the wooded slope through a
small cut whose banks hid the river for a distance so that they
heard the weir before they saw it, a muted roar that seemed to
come at them from the valley side, to move slowly around
towards the river and retreat a little, until, descending a series
of shallow curving steps, the sound rose up ahead. They were

low in the valley now, and the opposite side seemed to loom blackly above them.

Alan hung back and gestured Joe to go ahead. Joe saw smooth dark water first, a slipping sliding black mirror marked by the occasional ripple as the river flowed towards the weir. Next he saw a paved area opening out before him, a viewing platform with seats, then, beyond it, reaching out to span the river, a stone footbridge which straddled the top of the weir. The water, channelled by elegant buttresses, slipped through its arches and vanished smoothly over the brink.

The footbridge was a Gothic fantasy, with towers at either end, crenellations and arrow slits. The tower at the near end had an iron gate which was chained and padlocked. He continued past it, down four steps to a lower viewing platform, and watched the water storming out over the weir, an orderly curve which diffused into air and spray and white water as it cascaded down the wall to the maelstrom below. The water was white for quite a way downstream. Even when it darkened again it seemed to churn and heave, and he couldn't make out a point where it was calm again.

He went to the edge of the platform, wondering if she had jumped from there, but it was set back from the river, there were mossy rocks below, and he thought it unlikely.

Joe joined Alan by the locked gate. A notice read 'Not Open to the Public', but the gate was not that high, there was no barbed wire, and anyone reasonably agile could have climbed over. Beyond, the footbridge was long and straight, the parapet chest-high to a woman, and fairly narrow, just wide enough to sit on before slipping over.

Alan said the Lord's Prayer. Then, after looking out over the roaring water for another five minutes, he turned away.

Alan wanted to head home and, though he couldn't bring himself to spell it out, he wanted to go on his own. Joe would have hired a taxi for him, but Alan insisted on taking the train. They found one from Hereford, changing at Birmingham. On the platform, Alan squeezed Joe's arm before climbing in. Neither of them had anything left to say.

Joe reached the Arcadian valley in the early evening. It was pitch dark. There were no lights and no moon, though one bend was marked by a row of reflective lights which turned out to be sheep looking his way. Without the snow to define them the hedgerows were a blur, the trees an unstructured avenue, and the stream might not have been there for all he saw of it. Passing the cottage of the landlord-farmer, he saw a dim light, then nothing till he was on the track up through the woods, when one light then another glimmered through the trees. Reaching the clearing, he saw lights in and around the cottage, and cars: two of them, three. Getting closer, he saw still more cars around the side of the cottage and in the yard: in all he counted seven, at least two of them marked Police.

Someone was moving around in the kitchen. Through the glass he saw a shock of prematurely white hair and a stocky female figure. When he knocked, a dog barked and the woman shushed it. She opened the door wide and he met the gaze of the landlord-farmer's wife from down the hill. 'Hello,' she said calmly. She might have been expecting him: without a word she picked up a glass of wine from the side and held it out to him.

'No, thanks.'

'He's in the front room,' she said.

'How is he?'

She shrugged as though it would be futile to explain.

'Are the police with him?'

'No, no. Go straight in.'

Joe found Chetwood in the dingy room with the browning wallpaper. He was sitting hunched over a wood fire that smoked damply without flame. The room was lit by the unforgiving glare of a single overhead bulb; when Chetwood glanced round, his face appeared as a mask of harsh black shadows and sudden lines. Seeing Joe, his expression seemed to collapse gently, his mouth to drop.

'I'm so very sorry,' Joe said.

Chetwood clambered to his feet and in one swift movement came forward and, throwing an arm around Joe's neck, embraced him in a bear hug, the sleeve of his heavy waxed jacket pushing into Joe's face. Pulling away rapidly, Chetwood paced back to the fire and made a gesture of appeal or welcome: a brief lift of both arms. 'Good of you to come, Joe.'

'I came with Alan.'

Chetwood's gaze sharpened, he glanced towards the door. 'Is he here?'

'He's gone. He's on his way home.'

With a slow nod, a dulling of the eyes, Chetwood sat down again on the edge of the seat, shoulders bowed, forearms resting heavily on his knees. Joe sat opposite on an easy-chair whose springs threatened collapse so that like Chetwood he took refuge on the edge.

'Sorry about the cold,' Chetwood muttered. 'Absolute crap, this fire.' He pushed irritably at the logs, before retreating deeper inside his jacket, hunching the collar up around his ears.

'How're you doing, Chetwood?'

Chetwood gazed at him distractedly. 'Me? Oh, I've done my crying, Joe. Done it all yesterday. All cried out.' He reached for the glass of wine standing on the tiled hearth and took a long swig. 'Now I'm just angry.' He had spoken flatly, but now he went on with something approaching the genuine emotion. 'Angry that she didn't call me. Angry that she was such a great actress. Angry that she fooled me, because fool me she did, Joe. Good and proper.'

'She gave no sign?'

'Oh, she gave signs all right – but all the wrong ones. Never seemed better. I mean, better than for a long time. Not a hint. Not a whisper. Not even a phone call, for Christ's sake.' He took another swig of wine, draining the glass, and Joe had the feeling it wasn't his first drink of the evening. 'We had a deal, you see. We had a deal that she'd always tell me if she was feeling low. Didn't have to be a big speech, a word was enough, but she had to tell me. And she'd *always* told ~~be~~ me in the past. *me* Always.'

'Had she talked of suicide?'

'Oh, in the early days, yeah. A couple of times. Sure! But not for years. Not recently. No, she was happier than for a long time. I mean, she was full of plans.' He gestured into space with his glass. 'Plans to sell some paintings. To buy some more ponies.' The glass described a circle of the shabby room. 'To do this place up. I mean, *serious* plans.'

The dog trotted in and, lifting its nose to identify Joe's scent, ignored him and went to Chetwood's side. Pulling the dog close, Chetwood buried his face in the broad black neck, and stayed there for quite a while. 'Hey, boy. Hey.' Emerging at last, he said in a tone of disbelief, 'She left the animals, Joe. That's what gets me. She left the animals without food or water. She couldn't stand the thought of suffering, it drove her mad – and then she went and left the bloody animals.'

'Perhaps she thought she'd be found straight away and someone would come and take care of them.'

The fierceness of Chetwood's frown said he wasn't persuaded, not by a long chalk, and Joe tried again.

'Presumably she wasn't in any state to think too logically.'

'But I spoke to her! I spoke to her on the phone. She sounded fine. She sounded great! Christ, we were talking about holidays and going abroad together. I tell you – she sounded fine!' In the next breath, Chetwood swore at the fire, and punched at the logs with the side of his fist.

Looking into the sullen glow of the fire, Joe wondered how far depressives were prepared to go when planning their suicides, how elaborate was their subterfuge, and he guessed that the resolute ones derived some final satisfaction from leaving nothing to chance.

'When did you last speak to Jenna?' Joe asked.

'God, you sound like the fucking police!' Chetwood barked. Instantly, he withdrew the remark with a flick of his hand, a grimace of contrition. 'I was in there all morning. Three, four hours. I tell you, Joe, I thought they'd never stop. Talking like a bad film script. *How did you get on with your wife?* – that sort of thing. As if I took her to the dam and helped her over the edge myself, for God's sake.'

Remembering the cars parked outside, Joe said, 'But what are they doing here now? What are they up to?'

But Chetwood chose not to listen, or not to answer. Holding his glass up to the baleful light, as if to check it was empty, he stood up abruptly and started across the room. 'Drink, Joe?' Hardly waiting to catch Joe's nod, he went out and returned almost immediately with a wine bottle and a fresh glass. 'You've met Pym, haven't you?' he said expansively, as if it was a drinks party.

The farmer's wife had appeared in the doorway. 'Hello,' she said again to Joe.

'We met the other day.'

'No – you met at Pawsey Farm,' Chetwood corrected him. 'You met at dinner.'

With a jolt of memory Joe looked at Pym again. She had looked very different then, dark-haired, even black-haired; he supposed it must have been dyed. The style had been different too: long with a fringe. And he seemed to remember her in bright reds – dress, scarf, lipstick; possibly all three. As the memory took shape, he positioned her at the dinner table, sitting on Chetwood's right: Pym, the organic farmer's wife. She had laughed a lot, she had said something heartfelt about the state of the planet, she and her husband had left at midnight because they had to get up early to tend the animals.

'I'll be a couple of hours at the most,' she was saying to Chetwood. 'But I can come back sooner if you need me.'

Setting the wine down, Chetwood went and wrapped his arms so completely around her short frame that for a moment she seemed to disappear. His eyes were tight shut, his mouth clamped with fierce emotion.

With a nod to Joe, Pym left, only to put her head back round the door as Chetwood was pouring the second glass of wine. 'The police say they've finished,' she announced. 'They're just leaving.'

By way of confirmation a car door slammed beyond the window, an engine started.

'About bloody time,' Chetwood muttered, and barged out of the room. Joe heard voices, a second engine coughed into life, revved and faded, then Chetwood was back in the room, scooping up the wine bottle, draining his glass and beckoning to Joe, all in one furious movement. 'Leave the glass,' Chetwood called over his shoulder as they sped through the kitchen. Joe paused to close the door and wondered if he should turn out some lights as well.

Two more cars were on the move, reversing or driving slowly away, as Joe followed Chetwood and the dog across the small yard to the woodland path. Plunging into the darkness, Chetwood's pace did not slacken. Joe's eyes were slow to adjust, and he had the sense of blundering into the unknown. At first the feeble light from the cottage illuminated Chet-wood's free hand as it swung back hastily in a pendulum, making a dim intermittent beacon, but then there was no light from anywhere and no hand to see, and Joe strained to make out Chetwood's form against the deeper darkness. Twice a branch reached out to brush Joe's face, now and again his feet stumbled and jarred on the sudden lifts and falls of the path; but he walked on blindly, trusting to the sound of Chetwood's footsteps.

'Okay?' Chetwood called.

'Fine,' Joe replied.

The path started to climb steadily, and Joe knew it was here or very close to here that he had found Jenna. Either his night-vision was improving or the darkness had relented a little, because soon after this he began to make out the occasional tree looming up like a tall sentry, and thickets like giant ink spots, while high above the dark canopy he caught the glimmer of stars.

After a time, the branches seemed to fall back and the stars to grow steadily brighter, while a faint blue glow appeared in the sky somewhere ahead, giving shape and distance to Chetwood's body. Finally, as the trees parted and dwindled and the sky expanded, Joe saw a quarter moon balanced above the line of a hill: new or old, he couldn't tell. They were approaching a clearing, or perhaps it was the tree-line, because now there was nothing in front of him but hills and a high dome of stars. It seemed to Joe he had never seen so many stars, the sky was milky with them, then he realised he could see them low down below the hills as well, reproduced in a perfect water-mirror. He could get no perspective on the water – one moment the hills seemed close, the next miles away – but however wide the water, however far it ran, it was utterly smooth and still and without sound. He felt he had never been in a place so remote.

'Watch out for the steps,' Chetwood called from away to the right, and Joe heard feet striking wood, once, twice, then the skittering of the dog's claws, before a handle turned, or a latch, and the footsteps receded a little, and shuffled.

A pitched roof rose up against the stars, then Joe made out the faint lines of a verandah. He had just found the first step when a flame flared and he saw through an open door Chetwood's face and hands illuminated by a match he was putting to a lamp. The flame caught, and a golden light spread its glow through the windows and out onto the verandah of a long wooden cabin.

'Not much heat left! The bastards!'

While Chetwood padded purposefully around – he had removed his shoes – Joe closed the door behind him, and stared. The cabin was built of pale wood the colour of honey and smelt sweetly of resin. It was the size of a large bungalow, the sort of thing you'd expect to see in Scandinavia, and perhaps that was where it had come from. At one end there was a kitchen built of reclaimed pine, old shutters by the look of them, and an antique pine table with ladder-backed chairs; towards the centre, a sitting area with two big sofas and a low table in front of a free-standing stove with a polished metal flue rising through an open-beamed roof; and, partitioned off at the far end, what he took to be the bedroom and bathroom. Behind the sitting area was an artist's easel and stacks of canvases, and hanging on the walls above, the paintings to prove it. There were bookcases jammed with books, silk wall-panels, and everywhere fine furniture, most of it antique, some in natural wood, some lime-washed, some french-polished: sideboards, dressers, console tables, decked with fabulous pieces of china, jade and marble: bowls, vases, orbs and carvings. The sofas had cotton throws in rich colours, the windows gauzy drapes and the floors huge rugs, all from the East, all exquisite. The effect was exotic, confident, and utterly enchanting.

Chetwood had been busy with his chores, riddling the stove, throwing in wood, opening vents. He lit two more lamps and adjusted the wicks, then, pacifying the dog, who had been slavering and dancing with excitement, opened a tin and fed him. All the time Chetwood muttered and grumbled under his breath: 'Bastards . . . For Christ's sake . . .' Once or twice on his rounds he saw something that made him stop in his tracks and shake his head or throw a hand in the air in a gesture of disbelief.

Then, catching sight of Joe by the door, Chetwood waved him forward impatiently. 'Sit down, for God's sake! It'll warm up in a minute. The bastards must have left all the doors open.' On his way back to the kitchen he looked down at his hand and gave a sigh of exasperation. 'For Christ's sake!' He attempted to brush something off his hands, and when that failed rubbed them furiously against his trouser leg. 'Fairy dust! Everywhere!'

As Joe took his jacket off he saw that it was true, that there was fingerprint dust on most of the surfaces and on his own hand from touching the door handle.

Chetwood clapped two glasses down on the table with a fresh bottle of wine to augment the half-empty one he'd brought from the cottage.

Joe said, 'Why were the police here, Chetwood? What were they looking for?'

Filling Joe's glass, Chetwood tipped the bottle so steeply that some of the wine shot up over the rim. 'I told you – they think I helped her to jump.' If his glare acknowledged the bluntness of this remark, it also affirmed his right to say it.

'Why? What reason?'

Chetwood would have shrugged the question off but Joe cut in firmly, 'Tell me. Everything.'

'Okay, okay,' Chetwood complained with a rhetorical sigh. He sat heavily on the sofa opposite, but not before draining his glass and pouring another. It occurred to Joe then and at several points in the next couple of hours to try to get him to slow down on the drinking front, but, inhibited by the enormity of what had happened to Chetwood, and by his own inability to offer much in the way of support, he said nothing. The man's wife had died; he had the right to drink himself into oblivion.

'Yeah . . . well, I was in London. Pym got hold of me. Said she couldn't find Jenna, said the animals had been left hungry. I came straight back. Found the note. Searched for her. Told the police. Thought of the weir. Went there. Found Jenna's car. The police began a search, and soon after that some kids found her a couple of miles downstream.' Sitting against the end of the sofa, Chetwood slid a little lower in his seat, the arm with the wine at full stretch, the other bent back over his head. His eyes were heavy and red-rimmed. For a moment they became vacant, as if he were miles away, and Joe remembered how characteristic this was of him, how he would do this even in the middle of a conversation, and how often in the past Joe had been caught between annoyance and the fear that he'd been boring him.

'When was she found?'

Chetwood rubbed his eyelids savagely. 'Ten o'clock? Yeah, that's what they said – ten.'

'Yesterday morning?'

'Yeah.'

'Then what?'

'Identified her.' This time when he paused his gaze was far from vacant. 'Told them what there was to tell. About Sam's death – all that stuff. Then they came back this morning. Asked me if I'd like to accompany them back to the station for another chat – as in it's time to call your lawyer!'

He gave a sardonic smile, but Joe didn't smile with him. He was too busy trying not to show his alarm. He leant forward in his seat and asked carefully, 'Is that what they said – that you should have a lawyer?'

'Something like that.'

'And did you ask for one?'

'Don't be stupid,' Chetwood scoffed.

Again, Joe made a conscious effort to appear calm. 'Did they tape this "chat"?'

'I didn't notice.'

'Look, Chetwood, I'm no expert on police procedure, but I'm damn sure they have to inform you if they're taping things.'

'Maybe they did – I can't remember.' Then, with a concili-atory gesture, a spreading of his fingers: 'I'd had no sleep, for Christ's sake. It was some God-awful hour – eight. I didn't get to sleep till five – six – I don't know. Okay, I think they taped it. I think they told me. So what? There was nothing I could tell them, was there?'

'What did they want to know?'

'Oh . . . everything about Jenna. Our lives, our history, who Jenna's doctor was, what medication she was on. What you'd expect.' The drink was getting to him, and the tiredness: he was fighting to keep his eyelids open, his voice was sinking.

'What did her note say?'

'What it was always going to say. That she blamed herself
for Sam's death.'

'No other reason?'

'It was plenty enough reason for her. So it seems.'

'It was in her handwriting?'

Chetwood cast Joe a disparaging look. 'For God's sake, Joe
– she wrote it, okay?'

'What exactly did she say?'

Chetwood deposited his glass on the table before sitting up
with a grunt of exertion. 'Only read it a couple of times before
the police took it away. So, not *exactly*. But I suppose' – he
might have been recounting a shopping list for all the life there
was in his voice – 'she talked about feeling responsible for
Sam's death. About what a lovely person he was – a beautiful
trusting human being, I think she said. About it not being right
to forgive or forget what had happened. And' – he narrowed
his eyes with the effort of memory – 'she said: *Allow me this.*'
He repeated it under his breath. 'Allow me this. Well, she
didn't give us much choice, did she?'

'How did Sam die?'

'He fell from the weir.'

'And why did Jenna feel responsible?'

'She felt she should have done more to stop him.'

'It was suicide then?'

Chetwood frowned at Joe as if he were being exceptionally
dim. 'I told you – he fell accidentally. He was an impulsive kid,
full of crazy ideas, and that night he was a bit drunk – probably
more than a bit drunk – and when he announced he was going
to walk the weir, Jenna didn't take him too seriously. And then
when she realised, it was too late. He'd gone.'

'Walking the weir – what was that, a joke?'

'A game. But best not attempted late at night with too
much drink inside you.' Without appearing to notice the irony,
Chetwood reached for the bottle and refilled their glasses. Then
the refrain: 'He was just a kid.'

'I still don't understand why Jenna should feel responsible.'

'She never felt *responsible* – not in *that* sense,' Chetwood corrected him, though the distinction rather escaped Joe. 'What she felt was the guilt of omission. That she'd failed to understand how vulnerable Sam was, how desperate he was to be accepted, to be part of the group, and how far he'd go to prove himself to us. He was very young for his age, you see. Very impressionable.'

'He was staying with you?'

'Yup. Sort of an adoptee. An orphan of the storm.'

'And walking the weir was . . . important?'

'He must have thought so.'

After this, Chetwood was motionless, lost in thought, but a tension lingered in the hooded eyes, a hint of darkness.

'So what else did the police want to know?'

'Nothing. Just . . . about our lives.'

'You and Jenna?'

'Yeah.'

'Whether your relationship was okay?'

'Mmm?' It was a moment before Chetwood tuned in fully. 'Sure.'

'Did they ask if you were seeing anyone else?'

'They asked, yeah.'

'And what did you say?'

'I said no.' He added suspiciously, 'Why?'

'Someone said you still see a lot of Ines, that's all.'

Chetwood's bleary eyes glowered at him. 'We're cousins. Of course I see her. I see her when I'm in London. We have dinner together. So?'

'There must be a reason the police have mounted this investigation.'

Chetwood rolled his eyes heavenward in a plea for divine assistance. 'So – I'm meant to be having an affair with Ines, is that it? And – God, I'm having trouble even *beginning* to imagine where we go from there – I drove Jenna to kill herself. Is that it?'

Joe shrugged. 'I'm just trying to guess what the police might be thinking.'

'I couldn't give a stuff what the police are thinking! I couldn't be less interested in their sad little investigation. Playing detective! Because nothing they do's going to make the blindest bit of difference, is it? Not a fucking thing!'

It was this speech that undid him. Leaning forward, he sank his face into his hands. At first Joe thought it was simply tiredness, the effect of no sleep and too much booze, but then he noticed the whiteness of Chetwood's fingertips where they pressed against his skull, the frantic working of his jaw muscles, and he hesitated, wondering whether to offer inadequate words of comfort or leave him alone while he went to see what the kitchen had to offer. He hadn't eaten since breakfast, and he didn't imagine Chetwood had done much better. But just as he was making a move, Chetwood lifted his head.

'At least she didn't get to see those prats blundering around the house,' he gasped. 'She would have hated that. Their clod-hopping bloody feet. Just hated it!' His voice was thick, his eyes were fierce with unshed tears.

'It doesn't look as though they did too much damage.'

'Bloody plonkers . . . bloody plonking about.'

Attempting to change the subject, Joe said, 'You built it yourselves?'

Emerging slowly from his anger, Chetwood rubbed his temples furiously. 'Yeah.'

'Quite a job.'

'Yeah. Came in kit form and we had to hike it up the hill.'

'And no one ever knew you were here?'

'Oh, people knew, sure. People in the valley. But if you mean the authorities – no.' He snorted, 'That'll be next, no doubt. The little Hitlers in the planning department will want to get their thrills by making us take it down again.'

The *us* resonated in the silence.

'Why did you vanish so completely?'

'Began as a sort of dream. We camped up here a few times and never wanted to go back,' he replied in a hazy reminiscent tone, failing to hear the question or deliberately choosing to misunderstand it. 'It was going to be a summer house, then we decided to go for it big time. Pym and Evan thought it was a great idea. And it was. Best thing we ever did. Water off the hill' – he angled a finger towards various points of the compass – 'wood from the trees, solar power off the roof. Only thing we have to bring in is gas for the fridge and the cooker.' He grunted, 'You get to talk when there's no TV, you know. You get to communicate. You get to read all the books you'd never've got round to reading in a million years. You . . .' He trailed off and his expression dulled.

'I meant more of the name change, the disappearing act?'

'I told the police I had money troubles. That I was on the run from my creditors. Now they think I'm a con man.'

'Why not tell them the truth?'

Chetwood knocked back the last of his wine. 'What, that Jenna was convinced she'd killed someone? That she should pay for it? I don't think so.'

'But she hadn't – it didn't mean anything.'

Chetwood held the second bottle up to the light to check that it was as empty as the first. 'She was happy up here. That was the truth. *I* was happy up here. We were . . . *happy.*' With this, he got untidily to his feet and set off for the kitchen.

After a moment Joe followed and started hunting for food. Chetwood found a fresh bottle of wine and paused with a corkscrew clutched in his hand.

'Me and Ines – is that what the police are saying?'

'They asked what I knew about her, yes. If you were "close".'

'For God's sake,' he declared with a heavy sigh, prowling back towards the sofa.

Joe found cheese, pâté and biscuits. As he put the plate and knives down on the low table, Chetwood murmured, 'Of course I see her. She's my family. She's my best friend.' He stared into the distance, for a while it seemed he wouldn't go on, then with a ferocious rub of the skin beneath his eyes, a kneading of the flesh that squeezed his eyes alternately into slits and red-rimmed orbs, he forced himself back to life. 'Okay, there was a time when we saw a bit more of each other. But that was when Jenna and I were going through a bad patch—' His head jerked round, he grumbled indignantly, 'Who the hell told the police about me and Ines, anyway? Who's been talking to them?'

Joe shrugged.

'For Christ's sake.'

'This bad patch – it wasn't recently?'

'No, no. It was way back in the old days, back at Pawsey Farm.'

Joe waited in silence.

Chetwood looked at him with vague unfocused anger before staring past him to the window or the darkness. 'Yeah, it was so bad we almost split up. In fact, if it hadn't been for the Sam business ... It started when we moved to Pawsey Farm. Jenna liked the country all right, she liked the life, but she didn't like me being away so much. Well, that wasn't a circle anyone was going to be able to square, was it? Had to go on my buying trips. Had to do the business. It was my *work*, for God's sake. It was what I *did*. She tried coming with me in the early days, she tried plenty of times, but she couldn't hack the heat and the dust and the insect life and the lack of hotels.' He sipped some wine, and when he resumed his voice was harsher. 'Then she started sounding off about the amount of time I was spending in London. Well, Asif was there – my business partner. And the warehouse. I *had* to go. But she used to grill me about it. Every detail – where I'd been, when the plane had landed, how long I'd spent with Asif – all that stuff.' He drew in a sharp breath, his neck bunched in a shudder. 'Incredibly destructive. It got to the point where we were slaying each other on a daily basis and I couldn't wait to get far, far away, and stay far, far away. While she – well, she wouldn't give up and she wouldn't let go. I used to tell her to get back to her singing. Why waste that talent? But she wouldn't, of course. No chance.'

'Why not?'

'Mmm?' He focused slowly on Joe. 'Oh, too scared.'

'I don't get you.'

'Scared of failing. Couldn't deal with it at all.'

Joe grappled with this idea. 'But she'd never failed, not in anything important.'

'Oh, yes she had! You never realised – why should you? She never got the Welsh Opera job. She couldn't bring herself to tell anyone. Silly – I mean silly not to tell anyone. She was short-listed or whatever it was, they told her to come back and try again, but she never did.'

'I'd no idea.'

'*That* was how she came to end up with me, of course. Nowhere else to turn.' The thought didn't seem to displease him too much because his lugubrious eyes gleamed a little, and he gave the ghost of a smile.

'So . . .' He fiddled with his wine-glass, then lumbered to his feet to open the doors of the stove and adjust the vents. 'So . . .' Making for his seat again, he misjudged the distance or the speed and sat down again with an unexpected roll to one side, and thrust out a hand to save himself. 'Shit . . .' he murmured, as though he'd only just realised how much he'd had to drink. 'Shit . . .' He went through an exercise of trying to get his eyes to open wider, blinking hard and making extravagant faces.

'So?' Joe prompted, sliding the food across the table towards him.

'Yeah . . . So . . .' Still blinking hard, Chetwood looked down at the plate. 'Then Sam died, and Jenna had a sort of breakdown. Well, no, it wasn't a *sort of* a breakdown – it was a *breakdown*, pure and simple.' He picked up the knife and prodded the pâté. 'Doctors, shrinks, the lot. Getting her through it was a nightmare – the police, the inquest, the relatives . . . Jenna kept wanting to tell everyone it was all her fault, I kept telling her to keep quiet because talk like that wasn't going to do anyone any favours, no one *at all*, quite apart from the fact that she had nothing to reproach herself for. In the end, we did a deal. She said she'd keep quiet if I helped her start a new life. She'd thought it all out.' A touch of pride crept into his voice. 'Knew exactly what she wanted. To make this journey. To lead a life that was directed, structured, uncomplicated. A contempl—' he was beginning to stumble over his words – 'a *contemplative* life. Reading, talking, animals . . . no people.' His hand indicated their surroundings. 'And she made the most of it, clever girl that she was. Began to study and read – comparative religion, you name it. I tell you, she ended up knowing more about Buddhism than I ever did.'

Joe waited attentively while Chetwood fought to keep his eyes open.

'*So* . . . the deal was, I would stay with her for three months. That was all she asked. Three months while she got herself on an even keel, got some simplified living under her belt, so to speak. Well, I didn't feel I had much choice to begin with. She wasn't in any state to be on her own. But then . . .' He pushed the food away untasted. He sank back against the cushions. 'That was the crazy thing, Joe. I got sold. On the life. On the journey.' A soft pause. 'And on her.'

He was silent, and this time he never got going again. He squinted up at the roof through drooping lids, he made one last effort to open his eyes, and then he was asleep.

Joe went out onto the verandah and switched on his mobile to find there was no signal. Back inside the cabin he hunted for a phone, wondering if the drive for self-sufficiency had gone that far.

He spotted it the moment he peered into the bedroom, illuminated in the rectangle of light from the door, a portable sitting on its stand. Going to pick it up, he saw a bed strewn with clothes, a desk littered with papers, and on the floor an open travelling bag, half-unpacked. When he checked the phone, the dialling tone sounded so faint it might have been emerging from a long tunnel, but it got no worse as he walked back into the main room and across to the kitchen table.

Before dialling, he took a last moment to consider whether he was doing the right thing. Perhaps he should just walk away and leave Chetwood to his unconcern, perhaps he should simply leave a large note telling him to get himself a good lawyer. But even as he thought this his eye caught the daubs of fingerprint powder over the arms of the kitchen chairs, and he had an urgent sense of time running out.

To find a good solicitor in a strange part of the country at nine in the evening offered a range of choices. He could go about it the hard way and trawl through friends of friends who might know of someone in Cardiff who was a partner in a firm which boasted a high-flier in crime. He could go through the phone directory, conducting what would amount to a series of phone interviews with those solicitors so hungry for business that they'd posted emergency contact numbers in the book, itself an indicator that they might not have reached the higher echelons of the profession. Or he could take the easy option, which as he began to dial, as he felt the tightness in his chest and the sweat on his palms, felt like the hardest option of all.

Sarah's mobile was switched off or out of range. He tried not to imagine where she might be, but the images came to him all the same: at the cinema, at dinner, in bed with someone else. Her home number was taking messages, and he decided to leave one. He began casually – 'Hi, how are you?' and 'Sorry to bother you with this' – before describing the problem and the urgency. He was beginning to explain that Chetwood had already given one taped interview to the police when there was a click and, thinking she had picked up, he stopped and called, 'Hello?'

Met by silence, he resumed his conversation with the tape. 'I thought we'd been cut off.'

Her voice said, 'It's me.'

It was her. She sounded a long way off.

'Hello,' he said.

'Has he actually been arrested?' It was her working tone: cool and businesslike.

'I don't know. He's not too clear on the details.'

'Is he on police bail?'

'He hasn't said so. But they suggested he might care to have a lawyer with him before he did the taped interview.'

'But he didn't take them up on it?'

'No.'

A pause while she absorbed this. Somewhere in the background, transmitting faintly on the bass notes, a TV was playing, or a music system.

She said, 'You think it could be serious?'

'Well, they were all over the house today, fingerprinting everything.'

'What was that? You're fading.'

As Joe repeated it he got up and moved closer to the base station. Passing the glass-paned door, he saw Pym climbing up onto the verandah.

'He really must not say another word without a lawyer,' Sarah was instructing. 'Whether they arrest him on suspicion or just request an interview, he must refuse to say anything until he can get hold of a good solicitor. It might mean waiting around, but it's very important. Do you understand?'

'Yes.'

'You want me to find someone?'

'If you could.'

'I won't be able to do anything before morning.'

'No.'

She was thinking again. 'When was the body found?'

'Yesterday morning.'

'When was the post-mortem carried out?'

'Last night.'

'That's it,' she said.

'What is?'

'They must have found something in the post-mortem. That's the only possible explanation for kicking off a major inquiry so suddenly.' In the background the music had stopped, or she had walked into another room. 'Your side will have to get your own PM carried out,' she said briskly. 'The sooner the better.'

'Okay.'

'How long was she missing?'

'They think days.'

The final pause. 'Why wasn't she found for such a long time?'

'He was away.'

'Well, that could give him an alibi. Get him to think about it. Get him to remember where he's been, and who with, and what proof there is.'

'I'll tell him.'

'Give me till ten.'

'I'll have to call you. I don't know the number here. And Sarah? Thanks.'

She rang off without reply.

Pym had put a blanket over Chetwood and dealt with the stove. 'Are you staying?' she asked, as she let the dog out.

'Yes,' he said, and she brought another blanket.

Joe had the impression of being awake for hours, but probably slept for longer than he realised. When he was awake he thought about the post-mortem and the police investigation. When he was asleep he had dreams of the office, a recurring scenario in which he tried to get to the next morning's conference against impossible odds, geographical, chronological, and plain nightmarish – cabs refusing to move, lifts getting stuck – only to arrive as the meeting was finishing and finding Ritch there in person, pointing his stubby finger at a point between Joe's eyes, like a man sighting along a gun, with Harry Galbraith at his side, looking daggers. In one of these episodes,

Joe had actually been sacked before he managed to get there, so that his security card wouldn't operate the turnstile and the security men came forward to eject him from the building.

When he was half-way between sleep and waking, he thought of Sarah, hazy drifting images of her eyes and her mouth and her trembling body. Not so bad. Certainly not bad enough to throw away, or deny, or resent; good enough to miss in fact, good enough to revive the small dull ache of loss.

He woke at dawn to find Chetwood gone. From the door he saw a pale luminous sky and a low mist with the ridge of a dark hill rising out of it like a surfacing whale. In time the dog trotted into view, followed by Chetwood at a slow walk. In that moment Joe saw it all: the beauty, the remoteness, the seductive possibility of change.

It was half an hour later, as they sat down to breakfast, that Craig and two of his men clumped up the steps. Dressed as if for the city in a long coat, polished shoes and a silk tie, Craig stood square in the doorway and, addressing Chetwood in measured tones, announced that he was arresting him on suspicion of the murder of Jennifer Helen Rosalind Chetwood.

Chapter Ten

A PAIR of cream leather chairs inspired by leaping antelope dominated the conference area of Harry's office. The bentwood legs formed two wave-like curves, while the arms described tighter but equally graceful arcs above. The seats were low and the backs sloped at a leisurely angle like steamer chairs. Harry had found them at an exhibition in Milan, a fact of which he was inordinately proud and mentioned often, as if to dispel incipient accusations of fogeyism. However, the chairs were hard to sit in without appearing to lounge, even laze, a problem visitors overcame by sitting forward over their knees. Harry, on the other hand, had worked hard on the art of maintaining gravitas at the near-horizontal. Sprawled in the opposite chair now, his large frame was skewed at an angle across the seat, one elbow propped on an arm, a knuckle pressed to his chin, brows furrowed in an attitude of concern.

'I want you to know straight away, Joe, that I'm going to try and cover your back on this. I simply won't tolerate one of these instant witch-hunts. I loathe the modern revolving door mentality.'

'Thanks, Harry. But not necessary.'

Without appearing to have heard, Harry ploughed on. 'I'm going to try and argue that Ritch's business was a poisoned chalice all along – which it was, God only knows. And I'm going to send you on holiday. No arguments. I understand stress, Joe. I know only too well what it does to people.'

'I don't need a holiday. Thanks anyway.'

'But this flu . . .'

Anna had tried to persuade Joe to request bereavement
leave but, dreading explanations, he had refused, and allowed
her to talk him into a marginally less awkward dose of flu. 'I'm
fine now, really. It's not a question of a holiday, Harry. It's
whether I'm the right person in the right job.'

'For God's sake, Joe, you're a hard worker, you're con-
scientious. It's just on the interpersonal front that you've been
selling yourself short. Nothing that can't be worked through.
In time.'

'We've definitely lost Ritch, have we?'

The baldness of the question caused Harry a momentary
shiver. 'Yes.'

Joe had got the story of Tuesday's video conference from
Anna on his return from Wales the previous night. In Joe's
absence one of the department's rising stars had been hauled
in to make up the numbers, a quick-talking Oxford First with
a brilliant intellect and a bypass in common sense, all gas and
no wind, as Anna put it. 'None of which would have mattered
a damn,' she snorted, 'if Harry had been on time.' But Harry
wasn't on time, he was held up in traffic on his way back from
another meeting, and in answer to a simple question from
Ritch the Oxford First had started spouting precedent and
appeal court rulings and all the things that Ritch was paying
the firm huge amounts of money not to hear. Every time Anna
tried to bring the discussion back to strategy and results – the
two subjects that generally held Ritch's attention – the Oxford
First began to expound on the nuances of recent case law.
'Chapter and bloody verse,' Anna sighed. She had tried everything, kicking his ankle twice, passing him notes, but he was
not to be deflected. 'No,' she moaned despairingly, 'he knew
his stuff backwards, and, boy, was he going to tell us!' By the
time Harry waltzed in beaming his ears off, Ritch was
smouldering quietly, she said, a bomb just waiting to go off. 'It
was painful to see, Joe. Harry in empire-conquering mode,
opening the floodgates of his charm, the full gamut, from A to
B, outrageous flattery, huge stinking dollops of it, calling Ritch

"one of the great business minds in oil exploration today", and saying things like "but I don't need to tell you that, Mr Ritch – you're the master negotiator". I mean, *please*. Reach for the vomit bowl! And guess what, not only does Ritch fail to respond to this charm offensive, he is *hugely* underwhelmed. And Harry can't see it! He can't believe that his tried and tested smarm and charm isn't going to save the day. He just digs himself in deeper and deeper. When Ritch finally says, "This man's a load of shit," honestly, Joe, I almost exploded there and then. Almost shrieked. It was only the sight of Harry being so deeply tragic, and the suspicion that you were going to end up carrying the can that stopped me stone dead.'

Recalling this, seeing the sweat that even now stood in beads on Harry's temples, Joe felt a passing sympathy for him. Charm, ease of manner, facilitation were his watchwords, and when they failed him he had nothing to fall back on.

Joe said, 'If we've lost the client, I think I'd rather walk before I'm pushed, thanks all the same.'

Harry slid forward until, like Joe, he was sitting on the edge of the chair with his forearms resting on his knees. 'But, Joe, I couldn't let you do that,' he said unconvincingly. 'I really couldn't. It was a team effort. We all bear some responsibility. Of course we do.'

Knowing the effort it must have taken Harry to say this, Joe reassured him. 'I think it's time for me to move on anyway.'

The light of deliverance crept into Harry's eyes. 'Well . . . if you're sure, Joe.'

'I'm sure.'

'These things can sometimes be for the best of course. If you're positive?' Without waiting for a reply, he added, 'And it goes without saying that I'll write you a reference. No question, Joe. Absolutely none.'

'Thanks.'

'Yes . . . You may be right, Joe. Not everyone's cut out for the long haul at the coalface.' Harry had never been too strong on his metaphors. 'There've been times when I've wondered if it's worth the hassle.' He held up a hand as if to ward off cries of disbelief. 'Oh, I may look as though I've never lost a night's sleep, but I've had my fair share of cold sweats at three in the morning, believe me. The risks, the end game, the big picture.' With these confidences his tone became positively avuncular. 'So where'll you aim for, Joe? One of the other big firms?'

'Something more low-tech, I think.'

Harry nodded rapidly, then, deciding he had missed the central thrust of this remark, raised his eyebrows enquiringly.

'More community-based.'

'Community,' he echoed uncertainly. 'You mean, private clients?'

'A small general firm, anyway.'

'Less money, Joe.'

'Yes.'

'Fewer prospects.'

'I'll take my chances.'

Harry gave a short laugh, as if he'd finally sussed it. 'Less pressure.'

'I don't know about that. But more pay-back anyway. More job satisfaction.'

This was one mystery too far for Harry. His eyes shaded over, he said briskly, 'What're your contractual terms, Joe? Without the proper three months' notice, it's usually just a month's salary, but I'll try for more. Can't promise, mind. You know how the contracts people are. Well, they would be, wouldn't they?' he added with a grin.

At the door, Harry shook Joe's hand, a double-handed sandwich in the American style. 'It's been good, Joe. Thanks for all your hard work. And, Joe? Half an hour okay?'

For an instant Joe thought he meant lunch.

'Okay.'

'I'll send someone along for your pass. You know how tedious Security are about these things.'

When Joe emerged onto the litigation floor Anna glanced up from her work so rapidly he knew she must have been looking out for him. Reading his smile, she offered a tentative grin, a questioning thumb up.

'Okay?' she asked, meeting him at the entrance of his cubicle.

'I'm out of here in' – he looked at his watch – 'twenty-seven minutes.'

'You mean—' Her face turned from sunny to stormy. 'The bastard!'

'No. It was me. I jumped.'

'The shit,' she hissed, unmollified.

'Believe me, I'm glad.'

'But *Joe*, it's not right! Harry should take some of the blame.'

'He did.'

'He *did*?' She was immediately reduced to pleading, 'But what about me? You can't desert me! Look at them all.' She gestured towards the bowed heads in the line of cubicles. 'Earnest to a man. Heading for mock-tudors in Carshalton. I won't survive this place without you.' Then, slumping against the desk in a pantomime of dejection, she gave a long sigh and said more seriously, 'I'm just jealous, of course.'

'Nothing to stop you, Anna.'

'Don't tempt me. What will you do?'

'I'm not entirely sure.'

'Well, if it's legal and exciting, will you let me know?'

Rooting through a drawer, looking for any oddments he could call his own, he said, 'How about a celebration lunch?'

'But you're already booked.'

'I don't think so.'

'Well, reception called and said your lunch appointment was waiting downstairs.'

She was wearing black and seated like a supplicant, knees and feet pressed together, head of wavy blonde hair bent low, forehead propped on one splayed hand.

'Kate?'

Her head shot up, her large blue eyes brilliant with resentment. 'Why didn't you tell me?' she cried.

'About Chetwood?'

'Of *course* about Jamie! What else but Jamie!'

'I'm sorry—'

'My brother gets arrested and you don't *tell* me!'

Joe moved to sit next to her, but she jumped up abruptly, she made a sweeping gesture as if to push his hand away. Taken aback by her vehemence, it was a moment before he managed to say, 'We thought it was best not to tell anyone unless absolutely necessary.'

'But it was in the papers! *Daddy* saw it. *Daddy!* How could you not tell me first!'

'Kate, I only got back yesterday. I was going to call you this morning. Really. I had no idea it was going to be in the papers. I thought they weren't allowed to publish his name.'

'But Daddy knew straight away! From the age, the way they talked. Straight away!' Then, moving on impatiently, she grasped his arm, she tugged on it hard. Her huge eyes seemed to bulge a little. 'Tell me they've got it wrong, Joe! Tell me they realise they've made an absolutely terrible mistake! Tell me they're going to let him go! *Tell me!*'

'Calm down, Kate. Just calm down.'

'No, tell me!' she demanded at fever pitch.

Something in Joe's past had long since cautioned him against scenes of emotional frenzy, and now he raised a staying hand. 'You really must calm down.'

Kate pulled away, she blinked hard, as though this implacability had revealed him in a new and rather daunting light. Controlling herself with an effort, she gasped obediently, '*Please.*'

'Okay,' he said in a voice that was deliberately unhurried. 'The situation is that Chetwood was arrested on Tuesday morning, but has not been charged.' He repeated it slowly, as though explaining it to a child, which was perhaps how he saw her just then. 'He has not been charged. They held him for as long as they were allowed to hold him, which was a day and a half, and then they released him on police bail.'

'You mean he's free? He's out of danger?'

'Not necessarily. They could still charge him.'

'But they can't!'

'I'm afraid there's still a possibility.'

'But you mustn't let them, Joe! You've got to stop them! You've just *got* to. It's *mad* to think Jamie could ever do a thing like this. He's simply not capable of it! You must do something!'

'We're doing our best, Kate. We've found the best lawyer in the area. The best lawyer for miles. He's doing everything he can for Jamie.' Aware of his own more immediate deadline, he said, 'Look, I've got to go and pick up some stuff from the office. Give me two minutes and we'll go and find somewhere to talk.'

But Kate was still in the grip of her wild undirected panic. She cried in a series of gasps, 'Ines said she was strangled! Ines said—'

'We don't know that,' he interrupted firmly. 'We don't know anything of the sort.'

'But someone killed her – that's what they're saying! Why couldn't it have been a burglar? Or a rapist? Why does it have to be Jamie? Why not someone she just invited in! I mean, she always had to have someone around, didn't she? Always had to have some adoring man at her feet, feeding her ghastly – her ghastly' – she groped furiously for the expression – '*self-obsession*. She probably got bored and asked someone in – a complete stranger. Why not? A man she just picked up somewhere. *Much* more likely than Jamie!'

Joe took a long breath. When he finally spoke, it was in a low voice. 'I'll be five minutes, probably less.'

Searching his face, finding the rebuke there, Kate seemed to become aware of what she had said, and gulped as if to take back her words. 'Yes. All right,' she whispered in a voice that was suddenly very small.

Back at his desk, Joe scooped the accumulated personal detritus of five years into two carrier bags, and hugged Anna farewell.

'Remember,' she said sternly, 'anything legal. No, on second thoughts make that *anything*.'

The litigation floor was sparsely populated. Most people were on their lunch break, and rather than put the few at their desks through the thankless task of finding something uplifting to say to him he decided to slip away.

When he returned to the front hall, Kate was standing quietly, shoulders bowed. 'I'm sorry,' she said. 'I didn't mean to . . . I'm sorry, Joe.' She touched her fingers to his lapel, she stroked it lightly like a child asking forgiveness. 'It's all been such a huge shock.'

The wine bars were crowded, the pubs not much better, so he took her to a restaurant. She wasn't interested in the menu so he ordered for both of them. He gave her wine and watched her drink it.

'I'm sorry,' she said again, and gave a sweet apologetic smile, a forlorn look from the round blue eyes. 'I just find the whole thing so unbearable, you see. I feel Jamie's got no one to care about him. No one on my side of the family anyway. Daddy pretended to be horrified when he read the paper – well, maybe he was – but I know he was secretly pleased as well, because it confirmed everything he'd ever said about Jamie. About the bad blood coming out. All his worst predictions come true! He phoned me specially. Wouldn't leave a message, except to say he had something to tell me. He knew I'd been meeting Jamie in London. He knew we'd got to know each other, and he just couldn't wait to rub my nose in it! Couldn't wait to tell me what a very wicked person Jamie was! It was just awful!'

In anger, she seemed petulant. The doll-like features which

had appeared so pretty when she giggled had taken on a sulky look, her wide mouth was pinched into a pout of indignation.

He said, 'When did you speak to Ines?'

'Oh, I tried her all last night. I tried *you* all last night. I finally got through to her this morning. But she was in her car and it was a bad signal and all I heard was that she'd been in Wales with you, and Jenna had been *strangled*. Then we were cut off.'

Kate wasn't entirely calm, but she was getting there, and Joe decided it was as good a time as any to take her through the rest of it. 'We managed to find Chetwood a good lawyer. He's Dafydd Elwyn Roberts, a specialist in' – he almost said 'murder' – 'serious crime. He thinks the authorities haven't been able to establish the cause of death with any certainty.'

'But Ines said—'

'There was bruising on her neck, that's all we've been told. But Elwyn Roberts is pretty sure the post-mortem must have been inconclusive because the police have called in another pathologist for a second opinion. And now Elwyn Roberts has called in his own man as well, a top guy from London, to do a separate post-mortem. So a lot rests on what these pathologists decide, whether they think this bruising indicates strangulation, whether it could have been one of several factors contributing to her death, whether it was simply a by-product of the fall.'

'Then . . . Jamie might be all right after all?'

'Can't say until we know what else the police have. Or think they have.'

Her face fell, and again he was reminded of a child: the speed with which her moods changed, and the transparency of her emotions. 'But what else *could* they have?'

'We don't know. Obviously they need to find a motive—'

'Well, that's right! He had no reason to kill her! He was so incredibly good to her! So incredibly kind! He put up with all her behaviour! How can they think he wanted to kill her!'

'Well, they seem to be fixed on the idea that he was playing away. That Ines was more than just a cousin.'

Kate met his eyes unwaveringly as she said, 'Well, that's ridiculous. Absolutely ridiculous.'

With the memory of their conversation in the tack room reverberating in his mind, Joe waited for a flicker of recognition from her, some acknowledgement of the need for present and future complicity, but there was none.

'Nevertheless, that seems to be the way they're going,' he said at last. 'Along with Jenna's mental health. They've been asking a lot of questions about her breakdown, whether it caused problems in the marriage.'

'Ridiculous!' Kate declared sweepingly. 'He was so loyal!'

'And then there's the matter of his alibi.'

'Yes?' She was urging him on.

'The problem is that no one's sure when Jenna died. There's a gap of four days between when she was last seen and when the neighbours got back from their weekend away and realised she was missing. For the first two days Chetwood was in Mexico or on his way back from Mexico. The next two days he was in London.'

'Well, there you are then!'

'The problem is, he was with Ines.'

'Well, why on earth shouldn't he be?'

'The second problem is that he can't find any way of proving it. No receipts or restaurant bills or fuel stops on the way home.'

'Oh.' Gradations of understanding, concern and pessimism filtered over Kate's face. Her eyelids fluttered, frowns came and went, until her expression settled into one of despondency. 'I see,' she said. 'Oh dear. Oh dear.'

The food arrived. They began to eat without enthusiasm.

Joe said conversationally, 'I didn't realise you'd met Jenna.'

Kate had been miles away. 'Oh . . . yes.'

'When?'

She shrugged. 'I can't remember. Ages ago now.'

'Up at the farm?'

'We met in London.'

'And do I get the feeling you didn't like her?'

'Not a lot, no.'

He asked lightly, 'Any particular reason?'

She had been prodding her food with a fork. Now she paused, eyes lowered, she took her time before saying, 'I thought she was incredibly spoilt, if you really want to know.'

Joe allowed this statement a moment to settle. 'And she liked to have men at her feet, you said?'

Kate said warily, 'That was what I heard.'

'From Ines?'

'No, all sorts of people.'

'I didn't realise you had friends in common.'

She raised a shoulder. 'A few.'

'And these men, she liked them at her feet as what – lovers? Admirers?'

Kate cast him a narrow sideways look. 'She was your friend, Joe.'

He wasn't sure if she meant this as a reproach for encouraging her to speak ill of the dead, or a warning against hearing things he might prefer not to hear.

'I'd be interested to know.'

Kate gave a neat little shrug. 'People say she flirted all the time. That she liked to win men over, other women's husbands included. That she wasn't satisfied until she had them eating out of her hand. That once she'd got them just *there*' – she pressed down on the table with her thumb – 'she cut them out of her life.' She gave another little shrug. 'That's what they say.'

Disturbed by Joe's silence, or inferring some criticism from it, she added sharply, 'That's what happened to the boy who died! That's what made him kill himself. That's what everyone said. She made him miserable and then he killed himself. And now Jamie's being made to suffer! Why should Jamie have to take the blame? If Jenna felt guilty, then she deserved it, if you

ask me. If she killed herself – well, I would have said she did
exactly the right thing!'

The cabbie double-checked the address with Joe, once as they
set off, and again two minutes into the journey, for the place
Joe wanted was a trap for unwary cabbies, a square named
after Kensington Gardens which was neither in Kensington nor
particularly close to the Gardens. It lay instead in that part of
Bayswater which is forever foreign. Early Jewish émigrés had
built a synagogue there, the Greeks a cathedral, waves of
Italians and Spanish had come and gone; now the area formed
the western boundary of an Arab enclave. The houses were
faded white stucco, their steps overlaid with thick asphalt worn
thin down the middle. Many had long ladders of bells, but
number eighty-five had only five and clean stone steps and a
gleaming front door. Ines lived on the top floor.

She was waiting for him at the door of the flat. She was
dressed in jeans and a heavy fleece zipped up to the neck, as
though she was on the point of going out, an impression
reinforced by the two travelling-bags sitting ready in the hall.

'You're going back to Wales,' he said.

'Yes. I've managed to negotiate some leave.'

'Are you sure it's the best idea?'

He had followed her into a sitting room painted stark white
with exhibition posters on the walls and sparse modern furniture. Despite the CDs, books and framed family photographs
scattered around the room, it had the impermanent look of a
place rented ready furnished by the year.

She faced him. 'What do you mean?'

'It may not look so good for Chetwood if you go and live
with him at the cabin.'

'I understand that. I am going to stay with Pym and Evan.'

'Yes, well, that'll go some way to ... I suppose.' The
awkwardness that seemed to mark his encounters with Ines

had returned. In the hours they had spent waiting for news in the grimy hotel lounge near the police station in Carmarthen they had talked spasmodically about Chetwood's predicament, nearly always at Joe's instigation, and he had struggled to find a tone, an approach, an argument that didn't seem inadequate in the face of Ines's austere rationality.

'You don't think it might be better to stay away altogether?' he ventured.

'I could not do that,' she retorted. 'He cannot be left alone. From every point of view it would be unthinkable. I am his family.'

From an Englishwoman this argument might have been questionable, from a Brazilian it was unanswerable.

'How did you get on with the police?' he asked.

Ines went purposefully to a small dining table under the window and sat down with a briskness that suggested pressure of time. 'I told them everything they asked me. What we did when Jamie was here. The restaurants, the shops we went to, the film we saw. But I think they did not wish to believe very much of what I said.'

He took a seat on the opposite side of the polished black table; they might have been at a business meeting. 'What about receipts, bills – have you managed to find any?'

'Sure. The shop where I bought food, the cinema tickets – there was never a problem with the things *I* bought. But the restaurant, the wine, the things Jamie paid for – he paid in cash. There is no proof for him. He did not use his credit card while he was here.'

'No one who might have seen you together? Be able to identify Chetwood?'

'In a city?' she threw back. 'People don't notice strangers in a city.'

'What about the restaurant? The waiter?'

'It was a Chinese restaurant. You know how they are. They have trouble knowing one Western face from another.'

She sat straight-backed, immobile, hands lightly grasped on the table in front of her. He noticed her wedding ring again and wondered if she wore it for Chetwood.

'What else did the police want to know?'

'The same as in the first interrogation.' She tilted her head. 'I have the wrong word, I think?'

'Interview.'

'Interview,' she repeated, fixing it in her memory. 'They asked what was our relationship, how often we see each other, how long we spend together, if we travel together, had we plans to go away together soon, had we plans to live together. And always – I don't know how many times they ask – was not Jamie my lover. They found it impossible to believe he could stay with me here and not be my lover. I think that is a very English thing – the idea that a man and a woman cannot be close friends without being lovers.'

'Particularly when they're first cousins.'

But she didn't seem to set much store by this point; she dismissed it in a very Latin way, with a twitch of her shoulders, a small twist of her head. 'They wrote everything down oh-so slowly,' she resumed. 'Each word, like a child, bent over the page. They left out many things. They only want the *facts*. So what can I do? I signed it. But I had the sense of wasting my time.'

Aware that time was pressing on her now, that she had asked him here for a reason, he waited expectantly. But, far from hurrying, she pulled off the hot fleece jacket, she placed it neatly on a chair, and regarded him for a full ten seconds before announcing, 'I spoke to Elwyn Roberts. The new post-mortem by the expert professor – he has the results.'

'And?'

Suddenly Ines's immutable poise wavered. Her eyes dropped. She breathed, 'I'm not sure if it is good or bad.'

'Well, what about the marks on her neck? The ones the police have been so excited about?'

'Yes, he found them. Yes – I asked several times to be certain – bruising. Symmetrical. Here.' She touched two fingers to either side of her windpipe, low down near the collarbone. 'Made by thumbs, from the front.'

Coolly, she mimed it, placing her hands around an imaginary neck, and the words, the image caught Joe like a blow. Shock gripped his stomach, he felt a sudden heat. He understood everything and nothing: that there was absolutely no chance of suicide, that something truly appalling had happened to Jenna.

He managed to gasp, 'Is he sure?'

'Yes. But he cannot say if this pressure was enough to cause her death. There was no damage to – what do you call it in the neck here?'

'What? Oh – cartilage?'

'The cartilage. So for this reason he cannot give asphyxiation as the cause of death.'

'A *deliberate* act, though?' And still the horror was growing in him.

'Yes. But, Joe?' She waited for him to meet her eye. 'There was something else. Something which I think can only be good for us. The expert professor, he found more marks – around her wrists. He thinks a cord – a thin rope.'

Joe felt another lurch of disbelief.

'The way the marks were formed – he thinks her wrists were tied, one on top of the other.' Again she mimed it.

'My God.'

Ines leant forward across the table. 'But this is good, don't you think? Because this is not something a husband would do if he wished to kill his wife! This is something a stranger would do. A deranged person. A person who has come to commit a terrible crime. Not a husband. In a moment of madness a man might strangle his wife – yes, okay – but tie her hands together? No. Why would he do that? No, no – it is not in the psychology of such a thing! Don't you think, Joe?'

But Joe was too shaken to follow her argument. His mind was still overwhelmed by images of Jenna bound and terrified, of powerful hands tightening around her neck.

'Don't you think I'm right?' Ines demanded again. 'Only a violent stranger could do such a thing.'

'My God,' Joe muttered again. Then, with a shot of anxiety: 'Poor Chetwood. How's he taken it? He does know?'

She nodded.

'There's someone with him?'

'He is with Pym and Evan. I have made him promise not to be alone until I return.'

And still Joe couldn't take in the enormity of what she had told him. Getting up, he stood at the window, he stared unseeing over the darkening square towards a murky pink sunset. She had been murdered, and he had doubted her. All of them had doubted her. She had not chosen to die. She had died loving life and Chetwood and her animals. She had not died easily or willingly. She had died in panic and terror.

Perhaps – he winced as the thought leapt ready-formed into his mind – perhaps she had been half-strangled first, then dragged to a car and driven to the weir, only to realise that it was here she was going to die for real. Or – worse still – perhaps she'd known at the beginning of the car journey that this was how it would end and had already died a thousand deaths by the time she was pushed into the water.

Gradually he became aware of Ines calling to him. 'Joe, listen to me.' She repeated it sternly, 'Joe, *listen*. I have something to say to you.'

Inhaling slowly, he turned to find her standing beside him.

'Listen,' she said again. 'There is something that Jamie told the police this morning. Something he is *mad* not to have told to them at the very first moment she was dead, the first instant she was found! But no, no – he did not. He did not tell them. And now—' She broke off with a sharp sigh. Close up, her almond eyes were a rich hazel, rimmed with dark lashes, the whites very clear, but where before they had expressed a rather intimidating composure, now they showed something almost defenceless, like fear. 'Yes, he has told them now. Yes, I drove him there and he told them. Yes! Fine! But Joe, I do not think they will believe him. I think they will find it too *obvious*, too *imaginative*, too *convenient*. They will wonder why he did not tell them before. And I think – well, I *know* that it does not look good for him!' She gesticulated with a graceful arc of one hand.

'He had his reason, *yes*,' she argued, staring past him at the window. 'This I understand. He wanted to protect her. Always to protect her. But once she was dead . . .' She rolled her eyes and, swinging away, took two angry paces across the room. 'To protect her – that was his obsession. He said, "But she needs me. And I cannot leave her." He could not see beyond this one thing! That she needed him.' Now Ines was a mass of gestures. Hands described patterns, shoulders lifted and fell, eyes sparked. 'He was like a man who has lost his will. Lost control over his life. Sometimes I think she must have some crazy power over him, because before, he always needed to be free. To wander. To discover. To search.' Turning on Joe, she declared, 'But you know how he used to be! You know how he was. He lived a life of the *mind* and the *intellect* and the *spirit*. A life of places and ideas. I think he would have been a great writer. The letters he wrote me – fantastic! Beautiful! Full of poetry and imagination! A great writer! A great intelligence! Instead – what? Instead, she makes him into this man who must be home for dinner. Oh yes, she intended from the beginning to – tie him down?' – she flung Joe a glance to check on the accuracy of the phrase – 'and she succeeded. First she tried one way. She tried to keep him from travelling, she demanded he stay close. But he would not explain himself to her all the time, he would not say where he was at every moment. He did not want to be *captured*.' Now she knew she had the wrong word, and she shot out a hand in appeal.

'Trapped,' Joe offered.

'*Trapped*. The farm – there he felt truly trapped. Oh, he

told me all this! How the dream was no longer a dream. How he was ready to leave. And he was almost gone, you know. When it happened, he was almost gone!' She raked the fingers of both hands through her thick hair, she held them there a moment. 'But *then* . . . after the boy died . . . suddenly the one thing he wants more than anything in the world is to protect her. To *save* her. She is in pieces and he wants to make her – build her – back into–' She gave up on this idiom with an impatient shrug. 'He needs more than anything to protect her. *Why?*'

She drew Joe back to the table and down onto the seat next to her. She opened an expressive hand towards him. '*Why?* Because she is feeling sad about this boy's death? I do not think so. Because she was unkind to this boy when he was in love with her? No. This cannot be the reason. No, it is more than that. I think she did something bad that caused his death, something that was heavy on her conscience, and she persuaded Jamie to share this guilt. She made him think that he – somehow–' Dismissing this argument, she moved rapidly on. 'What I think is that he was covering for her, Joe. That he was protecting her from what she did, though he will never say so. Even now he won't tell me what happened! But there was someone else who knew – and this is what Jamie has finally told the police – there was a person who believed Jenna had killed the boy. And this person sent threats to kill Jenna. *That* is why Jamie needed to protect her. *That* is why he took her to hide in the mountains. Because this person wanted to kill her.'

Joe digested this with a mixture of astonishment and unease. 'But who?'

'Jamie does not know.'

'Well . . . he must be able to guess.'

'No.'

'Friends of the boy? Relations?'

'They never discovered this. They thought perhaps someone who used to come to the farm. But they were never sure.'

'How were the threats made?'

'Letters.' Anticipating his next question, she added, 'They were destroyed.'

'So . . . there's nothing to prove the threats took place?'

Ines's eyes narrowed and darkened. 'That is exactly what the police think, of course. They are thinking he is inventing this story to try and save himself. But Elwyn Roberts said we must tell the police, because if we do not they will never look for another person. They will simply decide it is Jamie. He said we must tell them immediately, so that they are forced to make an investigation.'

Joe took a moment. 'Sorry – maybe I'm missing something – but why didn't Chetwood report these threats to the police at the time?'

Ines frowned at him as if he were being remarkably slow. 'Because he was protecting her. Because she had killed this boy.'

'I see.' Though as he said this, he felt he was seeing rather less than before. He risked what might be another stupid question. 'And this person making the threats – why on earth didn't he or she go to the police right at the beginning?'

'Maybe they tried the police and the police did not listen. Maybe this person is mad,' she added carelessly. 'Look, Joe . . .' She leant forward again. 'You are Jamie's friend – yes? You are his true friend?'

'I would hope so.'

'Because this is what he needs at this moment. More than anything in the world. He needs his true friends. He needs all of us. You will help him, won't you, Joe?'

'Well . . . if I can.'

'Will you help to find this person, Joe? This person who made these threats?'

Whether he was still shocked by the confirmation of the murder and the images which had imprinted so disturbingly on his mind, whether it was the sheer quantity of information that had come his way in so short a time, but only now did Joe manage to force some sort of order into his thoughts. He felt

the detachment come over him that was his way of confronting
unwelcome facts. He understood what Ines had told him, he
realised how it would look to the police, he felt sorry for
Chetwood; but he was also deeply puzzled, and the reason for
his puzzlement sent a small sliver of unease into his stomach.

'What about the note, Ines? The suicide note?'

She pulled back. She said rather coolly, 'What about it?'

'Well . . . how could Jenna have written it?'

'It is obvious she wrote it at some other time. A time when
she wanted to kill herself.'

He absorbed this slowly. 'But the note was found at the
house after her death.'

Ines conceded, 'Yes.'

'And if she wrote it months – years – ago, why would it be
found now all of a sudden? Why would it be lying on a table?'

Ines's expression hardened, she got to her feet. 'I understand. You don't want to help him. Fine. We have saved
ourselves a lot of trouble by establishing this now. Fine.'

'I didn't say I didn't want to help, Ines—'

'Oh, I think that is exactly what you are saying, Joe. I think
you are saying it very clearly.'

She walked to the doorway and stood in an attitude of
frosty impatience, waiting for him to leave.

He followed slowly. 'All I'm saying is – an old suicide note
isn't exactly something you leave out on a table, is it?'

'Who said it was found on a table?' she declared as she
moved into the hall.

'Where then?'

'When someone dies, the husband goes through her papers
– no? He looks for a reason she has killed herself, and he keeps
looking till he finds it.' She swung the flat door open. 'So that
is what he did – he found it!'

'So it was in among her papers?'

'Why not?'

'Well, I just find it incredible that she'd keep something like
that.'

'To remind herself of how near she had come to it?'

'Okay,' he conceded. 'Okay.'

But she was staring at him as if she despised him, and he knew she was not about to forgive him.

She would have closed the door hard on his heels, but he stopped on the threshold. Something else had been niggling at him and only now did he realise what it was. 'The car.'

Ines raised one eyebrow.

'How could she have driven her car to the weir?'

Ines tightened her mouth in barely suppressed anger. 'Please—' She gestured him out. 'I really have to go.'

Moving onto the landing, Joe paused again. He was going to suggest that the car made a good argument for suicide, that it could only be a strong point in Chetwood's favour, but as he opened his mouth to speak the door shut with a firm thud.

The actor upstairs had landed a new part or a new lover because the music suppurating down through the ceiling was loud and upbeat. Preparing to call Alan, Joe poured a glass of wine and went to the bedroom because it was quieter there. Sitting on the bed, he thought briefly, *no more job*, and raised his glass in a solemn toast. The corollary to this – no income, large mortgage – was a thought for another and braver day.

On his twice-daily calls to Alan, Joe had found it hard to gauge how well the old man was coping. Yesterday morning he had sounded a little monosyllabic, a bit breathless, but otherwise steady enough, apparently taking things in, making sense, giving his usual effusive thanks for everything that Joe was doing, though as Joe kept reminding him he was doing nothing at all. At the news of Chetwood's arrest three days ago, Alan had expressed disbelief and incredulity, he had cast doubt if not on the competence of the police then on their judgement, he had declared himself certain it was a terrible mistake. Then, yesterday evening and again this morning, Joe had noticed a shift in Alan's tone, not quite a cooling – Alan could never be as calculating or ungenerous as that – more of a pained hesitation, an overlying awkwardness, and it was clear to Joe that Alan, possibly under Helena's influence, was having second thoughts about the arrest, that he was confronting the possibility that Chetwood might after all have had something to do with Jenna's death.

If Alan thought this idea was going to offend Joe, then he was mistaken. At several times in the last few days, waiting with Ines in the dreary hotel lounge, or in the cramped reception area at the police station amid the odour of unwashed bodies, stale booze and disinfectant, or driving to and from the valley, Joe had slowly, almost furtively, opened his mind to the possibility of Chetwood's involvement. In his more bullish moments, he wondered if Chetwood had driven Jenna to suicide. What, after all, did he really know about their life together? Perhaps for all Chetwood's talk of love and new-found contentment, he and Jenna had fought. Perhaps, in the mysterious way of some couples, they had thrived on goading each other until without warning Chetwood had simply snapped.

This idea hadn't lasted long, however. Remembering Jenna's praise for Chetwood, the spontaneity of it, and the gravity, he couldn't believe it had covered some huge unspoken tension. No, the two of them had not fought. Rather – he was grasping for straws – they had struggled to create the longed-for idyll, they had staked all their emotional energy on the dream, only to find the living of it soul-destroying. And then – but here his imagination failed him, he had no idea what could have happened then. He realised, too, that his vision of grim disillusionment belonged more to the mouldering cottage than the seductive comforts of the cabin. And hadn't Chetwood said he loved the life up at the cabin? Hadn't he sworn it was all he'd ever wanted?

To this must now be added the bald fact of murder and brutality. It would be tempting to accept Ines's talk of death threats, but he baulked at the over-dramatic term. He could have accepted the existence of a few anonymous letters – it was easy to be a thug on paper – but the idea of some elaborate plan to harm Jenna: that belonged to films. Having settled this in his mind, his thoughts were immediately unsettled again by the memory of the immense trouble Chetwood and Jenna had taken to hide themselves away. How far did you need to go for a fresh start? Or, as Joe's father would insist against the available evidence, to escape money troubles? Didn't it prove, as Ines would argue, that the threats had been all too real?

Dialling Alan's mobile, Joe prepared himself in case Helena should answer, as she sometimes did when Alan was at home and on the house line. Twice in the last few days she had made no response to Joe's greeting, either handing the phone straight to Alan – who had to ask him to hang on – or ringing off without a word, leaving Joe to the censure of a dead line. The first time, Joe assumed she was too upset to speak; the second time, he realised it could only be deliberate, and felt the sadness when two old friends fall out.

But it was Alan who answered now. He was in his car, and he asked Joe to wait while he pulled over.

'The police came this afternoon,' he said in an expressionless voice. 'The liaison people.'

'What did they want?'

'They came to tell us it was definitely murder.'

'Alan, I'm so terribly sorry.'

A pause during which Joe heard the grinding and rumbling of the traffic. 'They said she'd been strangled.'

'Yes.'

'Is that what your man's post-mortem said too?'

'Partly,' Joe said cautiously. 'But he couldn't establish a definite cause of death.'

'But he found signs of strangulation?'

'Yes.'

'You have the details, Joe?'

The music over Joe's head stopped abruptly, leaving a sharp silence. 'I've only had a third-hand report,' Joe said. 'I need to check it with the lawyer tomorrow. I—'

'If you could just tell me what you've heard so far, Joe.'

'There were marks on her neck, Alan. Thumb marks. Either side of her windpipe.'

The pause was so intense that Joe thought he could hear the sound of Alan's heart breaking.

His voice was noticeably unsteady as he asked, 'Anything else?'

Even if Joe'd had the chance to speak to Elwyn Roberts, even if he'd got confirmation of the rope marks, he didn't have the courage to tell Alan just then. 'No,' he lied.

'Thanks for letting me know.'

'Look, I'll be down in the morning. All right?'

'See you then, Joe.'

'You all right to drive, Alan?'

'Oh yes. Not far from home.'

There were two moments on the journey to Shepherd's Bush when Joe almost turned back, once when snatches of his last conversation with Sarah sprang into his mind – *I really don't think there's much point, Joe, do you?*; *it'd just make it worse to drag things out* – and again when he reminded himself that you don't spring unannounced on your closest friends, let alone your ex-lovers. Every few minutes he told himself it wasn't too late to call, and every few minutes he left the phone untouched in his pocket. Parking three doors from her address, he gave himself one last chance, but something held him back: the wish to surprise her; the wish not to be turned away. And he had his excuse. He rehearsed it as he went up to the house and found the bell marked 'GODDARD/ELLIS'.

No answer. What else had he expected at eight o'clock on a Friday night? She would be in a bar, at a restaurant, partying after a long week. She would be all dressed up for her new man: skimpy black top, long hair, long legs. *Lucky bastard.*

He stood back a little from the door and looked up. The house was flat red-brick and semi-detached, three floors with the third storey hidden in the roof, and plenty of lights showing.

He tried once more. After half a minute the intercom crackled and hissed, then issued a clattering sound as though the person at the other end had dropped the handset. A muffled curse, then a sharp, '*Yes?*'

'Sarah?'

'Yes.'

'It's Joe.'

A long pause, then the door-release buzzed. He stepped into a pitch-dark hall which was suddenly flooded with light as she hit the switch somewhere further up the house. The stairs were narrow and dog-legged. Rounding the first bend, he looked up and saw her on the landing above, hair dripping, towelling robe pulled roughly around her. His chest felt very tight; she was as lovely as ever.

'What on earth are you doing here?' she said.

He offered a rueful grin. 'Just passing.'

'You shouldn't have come.'

'I know. But I was just at the end of the street, and I thought . . .' He trailed off.

Her eyes were glittering strangely. In a short-lived flash of optimism Joe wondered if she had missed him.

She said accusingly, 'You came specially.'

'Yes,' he admitted.

'You've heard, then?' She was using one hand to hold the bathrobe across her front, the other to keep the flat door open, with none spare to wipe the drips running down her face. Two rivulets had formed down her temples, and a single drop sat on the end of her nose.

'Heard what?'

She shot him a narrow look to see if he was playing games. 'Heard *what*, Sarah?'

With a last searching stare and a shake of her head, as if she was being forced into a discussion against her better judgement, she led the way into the flat. A short passage opened out into a small hall with four doors, all ajar. She pointed him towards the room on the right. 'Give me a moment.'

He glimpsed a small kitchen and a white bathroom with all the lights on, before going into a living room decorated in all those shades of off-white that designers have strange names for, like ivory and ecru and alabaster. There were uplighters on tall spindly stands and good modern prints and a beautiful frosted glass bowl on the coffee-table. However, the overall effect was spoilt by a huge and ugly wide-screen TV overflowing with video tapes which protruded almost into the centre of the room.

He gravitated towards some framed photographs and saw Sarah with a group of people somewhere sunny, Sarah with a dark good-looking bloke who Joe would have liked to believe was her brother, except she had no brother, and a sixtyish couple conservatively dressed – he in blazer, she in flowered dress – presumably her parents.

There were two piles of magazines. He tried not to notice that one was topped by *Motorsport*. The videos weren't much better. *Rocky*, *Terminator 2*, *Die Hard*. He had known as soon as he'd seen the hall, of course. Four doors, one kitchen, one bathroom. Maths had never been his strong point, but you didn't have to be a rocket scientist to work out that there was only one bedroom.

She came in wearing jeans, a sweater and a towel wrapped in a turban around her head. She was agitated or she was angry. She reached onto a side-table and, picking up a packet of cigarettes, tapped one out and stuck it in her mouth.

'You don't smoke,' Joe said.

'I do now,' she said, lighting it.

She didn't invite him to sit down, so they stood on either side of the low table, gazing at each other across the copy of *Motorsport*.

She said, 'You've got me into serious trouble.'

'What do you mean?'

'You told someone on the investigation that I helped you.'

It was strange to see her dragging on a cigarette, inhaling the smoke in a sharp snatch.

'Of course I didn't. Don't be ridiculous.'

'Think again, Joe.'

'I didn't say a word. I promise you. I—' A hollow feeling suddenly opened up in his stomach. 'Well, I may have mentioned something about Jenna's passport. Knowing it was out of date.'

Sarah closed her eyes in disbelief. 'Didn't you realise?' she groaned. 'Didn't you know that would be enough?'

'Well, no, I didn't. Of course I didn't. Otherwise I would never have said anything.'

'Didn't I tell you to be discreet? Didn't I?' Without warning, her eyes glistened, she clamped her lips together.

'Sarah, I had no idea. I promise. When you say serious . . .?'

She shook her head as if he couldn't begin to guess how serious it was going to be. 'My contact's career will be on the line. He could get disciplined, he could get demoted. It's *Pete*,' she declared fiercely, as if there'd been a conspiracy to deny him a name. 'And in case you hadn't guessed, he's in the CID. For God's sake, Joe – the Passport Office! It's all logged on the damn computer.'

'Sarah, I had no idea that they'd pick up on it. I had no idea they'd even be interested. Why should I? In fact, I find it incredible they bothered to check.'

Dropping her head, shielding her eyes with one hand, Sarah mumbled something under her breath.

He skirted the table and put an arm tentatively around her

shoulders. She didn't shrug him off, and she didn't pull away. Squeezing her closer, the memories came rushing back, and it seemed to him that he had loved her very much.

He said, 'I had no idea it could be traced back, no idea I could get you into any trouble. Believe me.'

She kept shaking her head, very slowly. 'Too late,' she gasped. 'Too late.'

'Isn't there something I can do? Somebody I can speak to?'

And still she kept her hand over her eyes, still she kept shaking her head. In her other hand the forgotten cigarette was forming a column of ash and, taking it gently from her fingers, he leant down and laid it in an ashtray. He still had his arm on her shoulder, but the move had taken him a little in front of her, and straightening up he came closer to her, he paused with his face just inches from hers.

'Sarah, believe me, I would do anything to undo it if I could.'

She dropped her hand, she looked up at him.

'Anything.' He had forgotten her eyes, the extraordinary shade of grey-green. He had forgotten her mouth and how much he had enjoyed kissing it.

She held his gaze, she seemed on the point of speaking a couple of times, then her eyes dulled, she said in a subdued voice, 'Only one thing.'

'What is it?'

'Leave before Pete gets back.'

Joe got her message, he got it loud and clear, but he still needed to hear it from her own mouth. 'You live together?'

'Yes.'

He moved back a little and crossed his arms. 'Since when?'

'Since after you.'

'Well.' He heard himself give a false laugh. 'No answer to that, is there?'

'It just happened,' she said dully.

He wanted to say, *But he was your contact, your source,*

you must have known him well before. Instead, he said, 'I'd better go then.'

At the door she said, 'Why did you come, Joe, if it wasn't about the passport thing?'

'Believe it or not, I was going to ask you another favour.'

She raised an eyebrow, her mouth formed a slow circle as she breathed, 'Oh.'

In a more sanguine mood he might have thought she was hoping for rather a different answer.

She said, 'What was it, this favour?'

'I'm certainly not going to ask you now, am I?'

'No, tell me. Something to do with Jennifer's death?'

'It was something that might – or might not – help Chetwood, that was all.'

'They're not going to charge him though, are they?'

'Oh, I think it's highly likely they will, yes.'

The professional prosecutor in her asked, 'But what evidence do they have?'

'I really couldn't say.'

'You must have some idea.'

'Only that it's serious.'

Suddenly he was desperate to be gone, he would have run away down the stairs there and then, but she held him back with a light touch to the arm, she said, 'I'll be glad to help, Joe. So long as it doesn't involve . . .' The proviso hardly needed spelling out. 'Really.' Her hand was still on his arm. 'If I can . . . It sounds as though your friend's going to need all the help he can get.'

'Kind of you to offer. But, you see, it was the evidence from an inquest I wanted.'

She withdrew her hand with a small jerk. 'Ah. *No*.'

'Outside the public domain, I think?'

'Yes,' she said firmly. 'Yes, I couldn't help you there.'

'I can get most of it from the press cuttings anyway.'

'This is the boy who died?'

'Yes. I might go and see the family if I can find them.'

'The family.'

He smiled at her. 'That's what you told me before. Remember? You said always go and talk to the family. And you were absolutely right.'

When he reached the turn of the stairs and looked back, she had lifted her hand in a small wave of farewell.

He came out of the house head-down and only glanced up because he heard a car door slam. In the instant he recognised the smart Ford double-parked in front of the house, he also recognised the man coming round the back, striding rapidly towards the house. The car was the one Sarah had borrowed from her flatmate to take him to the airport – at least Joe couldn't fault her on the word 'flatmate' – while the driver was the dark-haired man from the photograph upstairs. Pete, the Ellis of the doorbell, the policeman contact lover.

It seemed that Pete had spotted Joe coming out of the house because he glared at him, he slowed down as if to challenge him, before tightening his mouth and sweeping past.

Chapter Eleven

———◆———

THE BUILDER had finally put up the new fence. From a distance it was just another brilliant addition to the shiny prosperity of Shirley Road. Closer up, however, set against the faded paintwork, rusting gutters and smeared windows of the house, the bright unweathered wood stood out like a new hat on an old tramp.

Lifting the shopping out of the car, Joe started the automatic inventory. Front windows unbroken, old fence removed, side gate still hanging onto its post, though by the lurch of the hinges not for much longer, rubbish bin still more or less continent.

The back door was unlocked. From the kitchen Joe called a greeting and heard a brief response from deep in the house. Unloading the food, he was surprised to find the cupboards far from empty. The fridge too was reasonably well stocked, with milk and fruit juice and chicken legs, all within their sell by dates. The counters were smooth and clean to the touch, while nothing sinister crunched underfoot.

Going into the front room Joe was met by his second surprise of the morning: a temperature that while a long way from hot was most definitely warm. The source, a portable electric heater, stood against the wall. Following his gaze, the old man commented, 'Thirty five pence a day. I checked on the meter because they can run these bench-mark tests under artificial conditions, give misleading results. It's foreign, of course. But clever. High thermal efficiency.'

'Great. Where did you find it?'

'Oh, Tracey's husband Mick. Got hold of it at trade price.'

Joe gave it a long moment. 'Tracey?'

'She does for me.' He peered at Joe over his spectacles. 'That woman you arranged from the agency, I didn't like to tell you, Joe, but she was a complete waste of time and money. I had to let her go.'

'Fine, Dad. No problem. How did you find Tracey?'

'Well, Mick runs the DIY store,' he declared as if this should have been self-evident. 'I'm helping them on a case.'

'Ah. Med-neg?'

'No, no. Personal injury.' Then, conceding the need for some sort of explanation, he added, 'Mick got injured by a fork-lift, couldn't work for six years, lost the house, lost everything, and the insurance company refused to pay more than a pittance. I can't see much mileage in the case myself. In fact I think they're living in cloud-cuckoo-land if they're hoping for a pay-out after all this time. But they had bad advice. Got bogged down in the system. So I've offered to give it a go.' He gave a long-suffering sigh. 'As if I needed the extra work. Ha! Like a hole in the head.'

'Very good of you, Dad.'

He retorted, 'Not *good* of me. I'm not going to make any difference, am I? But at least they'll feel someone's tried.' He looked crossly at the computer screen, then back at Joe, before choosing to address the floor. 'The day we stop challenging the buggers, that's the day they'll walk all over us, isn't it?'

'I'm sure you're right, Dad.'

'You bet I am!'

'I brought some food.'

'What? Oh, Tracey does all that. Tracey buys the food.'

'Well, it'll be a bit extra then.'

The old man's eyes came up to Joe's and retreated just as rapidly. 'Sorry about Jennifer.'

'Yes.'

'I wrote. To Alan and Helena.'

'They will have appreciated that.'

'Must be terrible, thinking it's suicide, and then to find out that he killed her.'

'Nothing's clear at the moment.'

'I always said—'

'I think this is a situation where it would be a mistake to make any judgements in advance of the facts, Dad.'

'I was merely going to point out that so far as Jamie Chetwood is concerned, nothing would surprise me!'

'And I'm saying that opinions invariably benefit from some knowledge of the truth.'

'*The truth?* I don't think there's very much you can teach me about the value of truth, Joe!' He swung back to his computer, shoulders hunched as if to attack the keyboard. 'I've spent my whole life dealing with the truth. And if I've learnt anything it's that the truth isn't worth a damn. It's the argument that counts. It's the presentation. It's the *spin* that wins the day.' He jabbed a finger over his shoulder at Joe. 'You should know that. You lot invented all the best ways of suppressing the truth.'

Joe lifted a hand in defeat, and stood up.

But the old man rushed on. 'You talk about opinion as if it's a poor relation of the facts. Well, I tell you, opinion, instinct, whatever you like to call it – it's stood me in bloody good stead! If I hadn't had a feeling *here*' – he tapped his chest – 'if I hadn't known the bastards were lying – well! We'd never have got to the bottom of your mother's death, would we? Do you think anyone would have come forward and told us? Of course they wouldn't! No, they would have palmed us off with their own carefully edited version of events. That's what you get when you ask for the truth, Joe – nothing worth a damn.'

'I'll remember that.' Joe made for the door. 'Bye, Dad. Take care.'

'Joe?'

The old man followed him into the hall. A small spark of mischief gleamed in his eye. 'You want some unvarnished truth? Guaranteed. Well, how's this then?' He paused for effect. 'There was never a buyer for that house down by Myersons.'

'No?'

'It was all a fabrication. A con. A trick.'

If the old man had wanted to impress Joe, he had certainly succeeded. 'Who told you that?'

'Harris, the estate agent. It was just as I suspected – a load of nonsense. There! A situation where opinion matches truth rather nicely, I think.'

A thin bunch of flowers had been left on Alan and Helena's doorstep. Joe picked them up before ringing the bell, then held them down at his side in case they should be mistaken for a feeble and inappropriate offering of his own.

He heard a muffled voice, a door closing, then light footsteps. Helena opened the door. 'Oh, it's you, Joe,' she said matter-of-factly. 'I thought it was going to be more flowers. I don't think I can take any more flowers.'

Joe revealed the bunch in his hand and indicated the doorstep.

With a small sigh Helena took the thin bundle. She seemed composed, but her eyes were sunken and glazed. She looked as though she hadn't been sleeping. She was wearing old clothes again, but they were tidy, no stains and no frayed edges. 'Alan's around somewhere,' she murmured vaguely, before turning away.

As Joe stepped over the threshold he caught a movement on the periphery of his vision and stepped back again in time to see Marc emerging from the side of the house, heading for the road, arms pumping self-importantly.

'I'll be with you in just a minute, Helena.'

The instant Marc heard Joe call his name, his head went back, his pace quickened, he began to walk as fast as his plump legs would carry him. Reaching the footpath, he wheeled right and was lost to view behind the neighbour's hedge. Joe might have left it there if his anger hadn't got the better of him.

Joe caught up with him at his car which, intentionally or otherwise, he had parked some way down the road. Marc lost precious seconds fumbling with the lock, and trying to dive in too hastily so that his foot caught on the sill. By the time he reached out to yank the door shut it was too late, Joe had a firm grip on it.

'A word!'

'I don't think so.'

'You've been lying, Marc.'

Marc pointed a forefinger. 'I'll give you ten seconds to let go of that door or I'll call the police.'

'By all means.' Joe moved around to the inside of the door and leant against it with his hands in his pockets. 'Then we can tell them how you lied about Jenna's phone call. About the timing of it. About what she said. We can tell them how you spoke to her well over a year ago. How there was nothing wrong with her at all. We can also tell them how you lied about the sale of the house. How you invented a buyer.'

'Take your sick mind somewhere else, Joe.'

'Is that a denial?'

'I think your ten seconds has just run out.' Trembling self-righteously, Marc took out his mobile phone and began to dial.

'If anyone's sick, old pal, it's you.' Hearing himself say this, Joe's anger evaporated, he felt a stab of disgust. This was brawling talk, and at the end of the day he didn't want to fight with Marc, he wasn't even sure he wanted to argue with him. He held up a staying hand. 'Okay, okay.'

Marc's finger hovered over the dialling pad. It was a threat but also a postponement.

Joe dropped down onto his haunches. 'Okay,' he said. 'Tell it your way.'

'Get away from the door.'

'So you can drive off?'

'I'm not prepared to speak to someone committing a gross act of aggression.'

'So if I move away, we're having a discussion?'

'That's for me to decide.'

The keys were in the ignition, just inches from Joe's hand. The temptation was too great. Before Marc had time to realise what he was doing, Joe had snatched the keys and stepped back onto the path. He dropped the keys very deliberately onto the ground. 'Let's talk.'

The colour had drained from Marc's face. He was trembling again, but this time it looked like fear, though Joe could have put his mind at rest on that score.

'Jenna never said she was frightened of Chetwood,' Joe prompted. 'She never said she was frightened of anyone.'

Marc turned his face away and stared obdurately through the windscreen.

'The only thing she was upset about was getting *you* on the phone, Marc, instead of her father.'

Marc's profile was growing more smug by the moment, as if having fixed on silence as his most effective and irritating weapon he was becoming increasingly confident of it. He folded his arms slowly, no easy task when his stomach reached almost to the wheel.

Joe said, 'Did you imagine Jenna wouldn't tell me about it? Did you think we hadn't talked it through?'

Marc's head twitched, his eyes began to swivel towards Joe before he returned his gaze to the windscreen.

'So now we have the question, have you repeated this rubbish to the Carmarthen CID?'

Marc blinked slowly.

'Because if you have, then it's time to go back and tell them it was all a mistake. Time to say you got carried away, or however you want to explain it. Because you'll get caught out in the lie sooner or later, Marc.' Joe added in a tone that came close to pity, 'They'll only have to look through the phone records.'

Marc tried to look impassive, but the tension in his neck and the working of his jaw muscles told another story.

'The other alternative is one I'm sure we'd both prefer to avoid.' Joe didn't elaborate on this grim option, partly because it was more powerful unspoken, partly because he hadn't entirely worked out what it was. 'It's your decision, Marc.'

In the silence that followed, Marc's obduracy seemed to harden again.

'And the mystery buyer – that's the only thing I can't work out, Marc. Why bother to invent one? Why go to all that trouble?' Joe left another lengthy pause. 'Or did you simply want Jenna's power of attorney so you could flog the house off to some mate of yours and pocket the cash?'

When Marc's reaction came it was volcanic. His chest swelled, his shoulders heaved, his folded arms sprung apart in a burst of elbows and clenched fists, the colour shot into his round cheeks, his head swivelled round, he swung one foot on the ground and clutched the door frame, as if to leap out, he cried in a high-pitched voice, 'You say that again and I'll fucking kill you! You bastard! You come here, you create nothing but trouble, and you *dare* to talk crap like that to me! Well, let me tell you' – he raised his fist and shook it in a gesture that would have been comical if it hadn't been so fierce – 'you are way, *way* out of line.'

Keeping a weather eye on Marc, Joe bent down and picked up the car keys. He balanced them in his open palm as if to throw them to Marc: a distraction, or a gesture towards con- ciliation. 'Okay. Put me right, then.'

Marc seemed torn between attack and retreat. Finally, with as much dignity as he could muster, he climbed out of the car and stood tall. 'Cheat my sister?' he declared caustically. 'Pocket the cash? I find your suggestion *totally* out of order. *Totally* insulting. *Totally* offensive.' He threw out his chest, he thrust his little chin forward, as if he'd rather belatedly appreciated the value of his weight-training. 'I can't even imagine the sort of mind that could dream that one up. I think you need help, Joe. I think you have a serious problem.'

'So tell me – who was the mystery buyer?'

'Why don't you ask your friend Chetwood?' Marc snapped. 'Because if anyone was cheating Jenna it was that low-life creature she married. He was the cheat!'

Joe asked incredulously, 'Are you saying *Chetwood* was pretending to buy the house?'

'What I'm saying is, you have a good look at *his* values' – this with a stab of the forefinger – 'before you start making statements about *mine*!' – this with a prod to his own chest. 'That's what I'm saying!'

Joe had the feeling of aiming at a shifting target, of getting it in his sights only to find it had popped up somewhere else. He made a humble gesture, a simple appeal for truth. 'I'm just asking who this mystery buyer was.'

Marc took a step closer, and for the first time it occurred to Joe that he was in serious danger of getting punched. Joe was two inches taller, but Marc had the muscle, and he seemed confident of it now, because his body language had developed all the subtlety of a fighter entering the ring.

'You're not asking who the buyer was,' Marc cried on a rising note of injury. 'You're saying I'm a liar!'

'Marc, I'm perfectly prepared to accept that you're not lying. But why can't you give me a simple answer to a simple question?'

'You're saying I was trying to cheat Jenna!'

'I just want the truth.'

'No, no!' His button eyes were glaring; the irises appeared to be completely surrounded by white. He was shivering with rage. 'You're making totally offensive accusations!'

In the instant Joe understood that he had touched some deep nerve in Marc and that it was going to take a huge amount of time and tact to placate him, he also realised he wasn't prepared to go to the trouble of doing it just then; he didn't have the energy, and, more importantly, he didn't have the patience.

Joe pointed a forefinger of his own, a purely defensive tactic while he stepped backwards out of range. 'Okay – have it your own way. But remember this, Marc. I loved Jenna too. And if someone killed her, believe me, I'll be the first to put him behind bars. Right at the front of the queue. But if I have to go to the police and tell them what you've been up to, then I'll do that too, because I'm not going to stand by and watch them going off on the wrong track, wasting their time, having the whole investigation fucked up just because you're stuck on some sort of private agenda. So unless you have anything to tell me . . .'

Joe made to chuck the keys to Marc, but as he swung his hand forward Marc suddenly averted his eyes. Catching the keys again, Joe waited while Marc, caught in the throes of some fierce inner debate, swayed forward as if to whack Joe after all, then rocked back again, locked in fury.

Finally, he hissed, 'Okay, okay!' and gave a bitter sigh. 'All right, all right . . .' And still it was a moment before he could bring himself to spit it out. 'Okay, so I made a mistake about when Jenna called. Okay, so it was a bit earlier than I said. *So?* But she was definitely frightened – no way I was wrong about that. *No way!* I could hear it in her voice. And the things she said – all of that was dead true!' His eyes were darting up to Joe's face, searching for the slightest hint of disbelief. 'All that about not daring to talk for long. About him killing her if he found her on the phone. Absolutely one hundred per cent accurate. Okay?'

Joe nodded.

Apparently dissatisfied with this response, Marc glared belligerently. 'One hundred per cent. *Okay?*'

Joe nodded again.

'*What's more —*'

He was waiting for a sign that he had Joe's full undivided attention, and Joe gave it to him. 'Yes?'

'You are *totally* out of order if you think I'd sound off
to the Welsh police. I haven't said a word to them!' He spelt
it out emphatically. 'Not – a – word. And I'm not going
to either, not till they say for sure that it was *him* killed
Jenna.'

Joe said nothing and waited.

'I want them to decide on the evidence. Okay? I want them
to find out for sure. Because contrary to what you're suggesting
I have no ambitions to stir up trouble. I don't want any bad
stuff laid at *my* door! So you should be more careful with your
facts, Joe, before you go pointing the finger.' His own forefinger made a final accusing jab. 'Don't you go accusing me of
being irresponsible, because you're the one who's wide open in
that department!'

'So, if the police charge Chetwood you'll tell them about
the call?'

'Too right!'

Joe couldn't help thinking that Marc's reticence had more
to do with having exaggerated the original facts than any sense
of justice. 'Fine. And the house buyer?'

'We were conned, okay?' The words might have been
extracted from Marc under torture. 'The estate agent was
conned. I was conned. We were all conned. It was a try-on.
Okay?'

'But who by?'

'Well, if we knew that, we wouldn't have had a problem,
would we?' Marc flung back. 'For Christ's sake.'

'But surely there must have been a name, a contact phone
number?'

'A solicitor in Manchester,' Marc chanted in a tone of
exaggerated weariness. 'Instructed by a company he couldn't
trace. Okay? A complete try-on, *just* like I said. But if you
don't believe me, Joe, you can check with the solicitor. Okay?'
He cocked his head in a parody of the reasonable man sorely
tried. 'Because if anyone's got egg all over his face, it's him.'

Taking comfort from this idea, Marc said, 'Yeah, *he* was the one who got well and truly conned.'

Or the solicitor wasn't telling the whole truth, Joe thought.

Joe chucked the keys across. Snatching the keys out of the air, holding them in his hands once again, Marc seemed to remember that Joe had put him at a humiliating disadvantage. Straightening his back, puffing out his chest, he hissed, 'Totally out of order, Joe!'

'If you say so, Marc.'

Alan stood marooned in the centre of the living room. He had set off on some task a while ago and long since forgotten his purpose. Helena sat on a chair, motionless, watching Joe through narrow slow-burning eyes, her hand resting on the cat, which reclined imperiously on her lap. In the window behind her, the sunlight came and went under scudding clouds, flooding or darkening the room with the suddenness of a faulty electric light.

Joe had always loved this room, with its faded curtains, its sofa and chairs covered in throws and cushions of every vintage and style, the ancient well-worn Axminster in a muted floral design, the herringbone parquet floor with its water marks and ink-stains. For him it contained all the warmth and security of his youth, the games of Monopoly, the TV soaps watched with Jenna over toast and honey, the evenings of celebration, Christmases, birthdays, anniversaries, exam triumphs, musical performances; Helena would find the slightest excuse. But today Joe could find no comfort in memory, and the very familiarity of the room, the air of timelessness, was like the reproachful gaze of a puzzled friend.

'Death threats?' Alan said. 'I don't understand.'

'Someone thought Jenna was responsible for this boy's death,' explained Helena, who had understood immediately.

'But *how* could Jenna have been responsible?' Alan looked

desperately from Helena to Joe and back again; he didn't care who gave him an answer.

Joe said, 'There's a suggestion she may have encouraged him to walk the weir.'

Helena asked flatly, 'The same weir?'

'Yes.'

'Was she in *love* with him then, to be so overwrought?'

Joe realised Helena was back with suicide, that either she hadn't come to terms with the idea of murder or she had rejected it out of hand.

Alan was still struggling with his first thought. 'But *encouraging him* – that wouldn't make her *responsible*. You can't be responsible for another person's actions.'

'But it's what this letter-writer *believed*,' Helena relayed tightly. 'This person believed she was to blame.'

'So – so—' Alan clutched both hands to his head, as if to stop his thoughts from spilling out all over the floor. 'Are you saying that this poison-pen writer *killed* Jenna?'

'The police are going to investigate the possibility.' Joe thought quietly: Or simply go through the motions.

'I don't understand,' Alan said with a sweep of one arm. 'Someone waits for four years, then finds her, then . . .' He trailed off unhappily.

Helena said, 'What do you think, Joe?'

'To be honest, Helena, I have no thoughts. I've rather given up on thinking.'

'Well, do you believe Jamie could be using these death threats to try and save his skin?'

Joe gave a small shrug.

But Helena wasn't going to let him off that lightly. 'Do you think he might have killed Jenna?'

'I'm trying to keep an open mind.'

Helena searched his face as if she didn't believe him, or worse, didn't trust him.

Wounded, Joe said, 'I follow no line on this, Helena,' and saw her eyebrows lift very slightly.

Abandoning his self-imposed exile in the middle of the room, Alan sank into the chair next to Helena's. But sitting brought him no peace and after shifting back and forth in his seat he clambered to his feet again. Thrusting his hands into his pockets, he repeated mournfully, 'I don't understand.' Then, as if to contradict this, he delivered an insight that caused Helena to look at him in surprise. 'That's why she went into hiding! She was frightened of this person. They were *both* frightened.' He stood in front of Helena and cried triumphantly, 'That's why they hid away all this time!'

Helena drew her mouth down. 'Well, that's neither here nor there now, is it?'

'Of course it is! It explains everything. They hid away because they knew this person was trying to track them down!' Alan looked to Joe for support.

Joe said, 'It's possible.'

There was a pause during which Alan muttered something under his breath and retreated to the fireplace, Helena stroked the cat and stared blankly into a corner of the room, and Joe found himself thinking of Sarah at the door of her flat last night, of her eloquent expression which managed to convey everything and nothing at the same time. Sadness? Determination? Relief? In his more optimistic moments he saw her strange half wave as a move to beckon him back, an acknowledgement that there was unfinished business between them. He couldn't help wondering what she might have said if there'd been more time. That she felt regret? That at another time and place it might have been different? On a more troubling note, he wondered what sort of a relationship she had with the policeman. Not an easy one, surely – he had looked the stormy type. And not a deep one either, though Joe knew this was just his vanity speaking. He didn't want to face up to the possibility that she'd been living with the policeman all along.

'*Death threats*,' Helena said with disdain. 'But that belongs to the criminal world. To all these dreadful gangs and drug dealers. Ordinary people don't issue death threats. Ordinary people go to the police if they think there's something wrong. They go to lawyers.' The more she thought about this, the more indignant she became. 'They don't issue *death* threats! This is nonsense, Joe. Nonsense!'

Alan swung away from the fireplace with a fierce scything motion of one hand. 'But it's not for us to decide, Helena! It's for the police. We have to trust in the police!'

Meeting Joe's eye, Helena's gaze relented a fraction, only to sharpen as the doorbell rang.

Alan commanded, 'Leave it.'

She shook her head. Disturbing the sleeping cat, which flexed its legs and hissed in protest, she disappeared rapidly.

Alan said, 'Flowers, probably.'

'Helena said there'd been a lot.'

'People are very kind.' Glancing around the room, Alan seemed to notice the absence of flowers for the first time. 'I don't know where she's put them all.' He extracted a pipe from one pocket and a tobacco pouch from the other, and sitting down began to pack the pipe-bowl. 'But there've been lots of letters as well, Joe. Wonderful, kind letters.'

From the hall they heard the murmur of Helena's voice, then the sound of the front door closing.

'From patients. Friends. All sorts of people from the past. Jenna's classmates. Fellow students at the Royal Northern. They all wrote, Joe! They all talked about her singing! Her marvellous talent. How she had the power to move people, to touch their hearts.' He pressed a fist against his breast.

'Her voice was very beautiful, Alan.'

'It was, it was!' His eyes glistened, his face began to crumple, the pipe was forgotten. 'And they all said how much they loved her, Joe. How much they were going to miss her. How full of light and life and laughter she was. They all said so!'

'Not all of them,' Helena announced as she slipped back into the room.

Alan said resentfully, 'Well, *most* of them.'

'One of them talked about the boy who died and how unhappy Jenna had been.'

There was a short silence before Joe and Alan spoke at once.

Alan complained, 'You didn't show me that!'

Joe asked, 'Who was it, Helena?'

She had the letter in her hand. She thrust it at Joe before going back to her chair.

Joe read the signature on the back. 'It's from the guy at the farm,' he said to Alan. 'The one I traced before.'

'The guitar player?'

'Yes. Dave Cracknell.'

Alan fidgeted. 'Well, what does it say?' Almost in the same breath, he muttered reproachfully to Helena, 'You should have told me.'

'It was there with the other letters. I thought you'd seen it.'

She was watching Joe's face as he began to pick his way through the erratic handwriting.

I was sorry to hear about Jenna's death, the letter said. *My girlfriend and I stayed with Jenna and Chet up at Pawsey Farm five years ago. Great times. Great memories. It must be hard for you that she took the decision she did. But she was never the same after Sam died. He was a young kid she took under her wing and she felt really bad about his death. It was an accident but I guess she never got over it. I'm really sorry. She was a lovely lady.* The signature was round and confident, with a flourish that sent a line through the middle of the name, as if to cross it out again. The letterhead was a studio – recording, Joe supposed – the address in Manchester.

While Alan read the letter amid a cloud of smoke Helena picked up the cat again and, sitting sideways in her chair, back straight, began to scratch its head in a rhythmic massage that had the animal arching its back in pleasure. 'So, how are the police going to investigate these so-called threats, Joe?' Her eyes veered crossly towards him. 'Are they going to start looking into this boy's death after all this time? Try and blame

Jenna? Because if so I think it's a travesty, a disgrace, a complete misuse of their time! They should be finding Jenna's killer. Nothing more, nothing less. A complete travesty!'

Alan looked up from the letter. 'This chap says it was an accident. He sounds very sure. Do you think we should put him in touch with the police?'

'Why not? Can't do any harm.'

Sunlight burst through the window, plunging Alan's features into shadow, but not so quickly or so completely that Joe didn't see the doubt on his face.

'Unless you'd like me to go and talk to him first.'

The pipe smoke had drifted towards Helena and now she waved it away in a gesture of disgust. 'To hear *what* exactly? He says it was an accident. What more do you want?'

The sun went in again, rolling the shadows back towards the corners of the room. Alan met Joe's gaze and they exchanged a look of complicity. Intercepting this, Helena shook her head and stroked the cat so fiercely that it gave a small yowl of complaint.

Helena didn't look up when Joe left, and she didn't say goodbye.

Joe arrived in a downpour and missed his turning. In the city centre, he got thoroughly lost among the steel and glass that could have belonged to any place in the world, and it was only as he escaped into the side streets that he recognised the Manchester of his memory, with its grandiose architecture and dusty plum stonework, stained a morose shade of burgundy by the rain. He had come here a couple of times to hear Jenna sing in college recitals, and once, famously, to visit an orthopaedic specialist whom his father predicted with quiet satisfaction would be unable to help Joe's recurrent knee injury.

Finding himself at the wrong section of canal for the second time in five minutes, Joe readdressed the map and set off westward down decrepit shopping streets plastered with damp litter through an area of towering Victorian warehouses and sixties offices to the commercial area of the canal where a lone coaster sat disconsolately at the wharf. The studio occupied one end of an old stone-built factory. Inside, a notice read 'ALL CALL-ERS REPORT TO RECEPTION FIRST FLOOR'. Nearing the top of the concrete stairs he was met by a burst of rock music which came from nowhere and just as suddenly disappeared again, as though a heavy door had opened momentarily.

There was no one in the office, just a smoking cigarette stub. On the landing there was a ladies' room and a reinforced door with a code pad and a warning against entry, so Joe went back to the office and waited. Eventually a world-weary girl in tight leather trousers, a bare midriff and purple lipstick shuffled in on platform heels. She must have been all of sixteen. When he asked if Dave Cracknell was about, she announced in broad Mancunian that she was only here with the band. As to whether Dave was a member of the said band, she didn't think so, though from her shrug it was a detail she could well have missed. After some persuasion, she agreed to go and ask the production team if anyone knew Dave. Joe wrote the name down on a piece of paper, so there'd be no mistake.

She clumped back five minutes later and wordlessly handed the slip of paper back to him. A mobile phone number had been scribbled across it.

Joe called from the car. The number rang for a long time before someone yawned a greeting into the phone.

'Sure, sure,' Dave Cracknell said when Joe reminded him who he was. 'Come on down.'

The house was a two-up two-down in Moss Side, one of a long terrace in sooty red brick overlooking an overgrown football pitch. The pavement was cracked and sprouting weeds and so was the narrow strip of concrete between the house and the ragged course of bricks where a wall had been. The stained-wood door was new, however, and so were the heavy locks. The electric bell made no obvious noise, so Joe knocked.

He heard a voice humming, a latch turning, and the door was opened by a tall lean man in jeans and ragged T-shirt, with a pony-tail and a sleepy smile. 'Hey, Joe, how ya doing?' The hand that gripped Joe's was thin and bony. 'Come in out of the wet, man.'

As Dave closed the door, Joe was met by the odour of curry and a sharp smell like ammonia. Dave waved him forward with a curious twisting motion of the wrist and a contented chuckle as though life was a bit of a breeze just then and he was blowing right along with it. They passed an open door where a mangy mongrel of uncertain age and three legs stared at Joe through cloudy lenses before staggering back to a bed surrounded by newspaper. Joe saw an electric guitar on a stand and a gaggle of sound equipment with a tangle of wires along one wall. As they went towards the back of the house, the smell of curry grew stronger, along with the unmistakable whiff of pot.

'Hey, siddown, Joe. Make yourself at home.'

The room looked as though it had been furnished forty years ago on a tight budget. The two sofas were matching sixties-style mono-block foam, blue-covered and armless, the foam showing through the seams, the low table had the Mappa Mundi in formica for a top and metal strips with the brass effect worn off for its edges, the carpet, once patterned, looked as if it had seen a thousand nights of cigarettes and red wine and no Hoover. A doorway with no door led into a small kitchen extension, with an ancient cooker on tall legs and piles of unwashed dishes.

Cartons of half-eaten Indian food sat on the Mappa Mundi, and a loosely-rolled joint lay on a saucer next to a pack of Rizlas and a rolling-machine. The air was thick from an ancient gas fire which burnt unevenly and probably leaked fumes.

'Hey, tea, man? Coffee?'

'I'm fine, thanks.'

Dave lit the joint with an over-size match from a slimline

matchbox, the sort that classy restaurants leave on tables. After taking a slow contemplative drag, he offered it to Joe.

'No thanks.'

'Sure.' Dave smiled beatifically. He looked thirty going on infinity. His face was exceptionally bony and tight-skinned, long and narrow with high angular cheekbones, a long hawkish nose, and a forehead which showed every contour of his skull and every squiggle of the raised blue veins at his temple. With his centre parting and pony-tail, his earrings and leather-and-bead neckbands, he looked like an anaemic Indian brave.

'Hey, how's Chet doin'?' he asked. 'Holding on in there?'

'More or less. I don't think it's really hit him yet.'

'I must give him a call. Yeah, I must do that.' He nodded his bony head. 'Gotta number for him?'

'No offence, but I'm not sure he wants to speak to too many people just now.'

Dave gave an easy shrug. 'Sure. But tell him I asked, will you? Give him my best.'

'How did you two meet?'

Anticipating the joke, Dave gave a slow grin. 'School.'

Whatever Chetwood's father had denied him, it had not been a private education. If Dave wanted to believe he was an unlikely product of the system then Joe was happy to go along with it. He showed suitable surprise.

'I'm a credit to the place, right?'

'Right,' Joe agreed with a smile.

'We were like survivors from this shipwreck, Chet and me, sort of clinging to the wreckage. Till Chet got clever and started doing his sums. I never got the hang of two and two.'

After a short pause, Joe said, 'Jenna's parents very much appreciated your letter.'

'Sure.'

'They knew nothing about the Sam business, you see. Or the effect it had had on Jenna.'

This thought settled slowly around Dave. 'So they hadn't reckoned on why she'd wanna go and end the story?'

Dave obviously hadn't been keeping up with the newspapers, and Joe hesitated to put him right. But Dave must have
read something in Joe's face because he said, 'It was suicide,
right?'

'The police aren't absolutely sure yet.'

Dave dismissed the police with a lazy wave.

'You knew Sam yourself?'

'Sure. Sweet kid.'

'So what happened? How did he die?'

Dave sank back on the sofa and holding the joint between
finger and thumb brought it up to a point just short of his
mouth. 'It's the family wanna know, right?' he asked benignly.

'Right,' Joe agreed in unconscious imitation.

'It's just . . . well, you might want to kind of edit the thing
down, know what I mean? Sometimes there're things family
don't need to hear. Right?'

Joe felt a small beat of dread; perhaps there were things he
didn't need to hear either. 'Right.'

Dave took a pensive drag. 'Okay, so . . .' He pursed his
lips, he exhaled gently, he gazed up at the ceiling. 'I guess
looking back I'd say it was kind of an accident waiting to
happen. Yeah . . . one way and another, things were heading
for trouble, looking back now. Don't get me wrong' – his eyes
came down to meet Joe's – 'Sam was a sweet kid. Quiet.
Intense. Sort of deep, you know? Into the meaning of life.
Poetry. Drawing. Truly wicked with the sketching pencil.
Flowers, trees, people – he could draw the whole damn she-
bang. He'd be there for hours, working away with his pad and
his pencil, never a sound, sort of lost to the world till he looked
up and hit you with this big wide smile. I tell you, that smile
was quite something. You couldn' help but smile right back.
Same when there were people around. He'd be there listening
and watching and saying nice things, just finding reasons to
smile, and people couldn' help but smile right back. And if
things got sort of edgy he'd just go and get one of his drawings
and give it to whoever was getting steamed up and they'd

loosen up and he'd be happy again. That's all he wanted, I guess, just to be part of this big happy family. Yeah . . .' Dave murmured as if the truth of this had only just come home to him. 'That's all he ever wanted.'

'He was staying at the farm?'

'Yeah.'

'He'd been there a while?'

Dave sucked idly through his teeth while he thought about this. 'Two months? Three?'

Joe waited silently.

'Yeah, a sweet kid,' Dave went on reminiscently. 'But deep, you know what I mean? Under the easy-going style, under the smiles, all the stuff was going on up here.' Dave tapped the side of his head. 'Thinking. Watching. Listening. You could see it all churning away.' He made a circling motion with his finger. 'And sort of hyper-touchy. You had to tread real carefully sometimes. He took things to heart, know what I mean? Wars, animals, cruelty, abandoned kids – anything mean or cruel – he'd just clam up and sort of look like he'd been hit in the face.'

Dave took another pull on the joint and, leaning over sideways so as to avoid the effort of sitting up, reached to the saucer and pinched out the end. '*Then* Chet goes away on this trip and things start to get moody. Sam'd always sort of had a thing for Jenna, right from the start. But it was kid's stuff, know what I mean? He was nineteen, twenty, sort of young for his age, a virgin I guess, and here was Jenna, beautiful, sexy, all cosied up in the same house but safely out of reach. It was your dream-lover fantasy, right? Your classic unattainable object of desire. Jeese, we've all been there, right? Mine, you will never believe, was the science teacher. Huge boobs, sexy eyes and a voice that shouldn't have been allowed out unattended.' He gave a dry chuckle. 'For chrissakes, I used to get off just regulating the old Bunsen burner.'

A quiet footfall and a swish of silk announced the arrival of a woman who walked rapidly through the room and into the kitchen. She was wearing an oriental wrap and her dark hair was cropped so close to her head you could see her skull through it.

'Sure you won' have a beer, Joe?'

'Not for me, thanks.'

Dave seemed on the point of stirring himself but eyed the curry instead. Reaching for it with the same sideways swing of his upper body he scooped up a carton of rice and spooned some into his mouth. 'So Sam and Jenna,' he resumed through a slow mouthful. 'Yeah, everyone could see it at the start, but it was no big deal, not then. He used to hang around her like a rash, helping with the chores, going to the supermarket, doing these fancy recipes with her, making her laugh. Real innocent stuff, right? Chet – he understood that. He had no problem with it. He was good to Sam, like a big brother, you know? But then . . .' Dave dumped the carton on the sofa and gave a troubled sigh. 'Chet went off to India and Jenna was seriously pissed off with him. None of us knew why. But she moped around for a couple of days in one seriously silent mood, and Sam was the only one managed to cheer her up. So then she starts to cry on his shoulder, she starts to whisper with him in corners, she starts to give him looks across the dinner table, she starts to touch his arm in passing. You get the picture? And we're all thinking this is not a good idea. He's too young, he won't be able to handle it. But when we try and say something, Jenna gets all holier than thou, says this is a pure and beautiful friendship and what are we saying here. Basically tells us to mind our own business. So we sit the scene out, we watch from the sidelines.'

Momentarily distracted by a clatter from the kitchen, Dave scratched the sparse stubble on his long chin. 'So next thing, Chet doesn't show,' he went on. 'He's due back but he doesn't appear. No message, no nothing. We weren't around for a while, me and Zoe. But the rest of the gang, they said Jenna went all sort of quiet and deadly, that if she let things go too far with Sam it was then that it happened.' Dave shook his head slowly. 'So Chet's a no-show and Sam's crazy with love, and Jenna – she's talking about leaving, about being finished with Chet, and Sam thinks this is the start of their life together. He's totally ecstatic. Totally over the moon.' Dave made a rueful face, he said almost to himself, 'Sort of awesome how much he loved her. When we got back, Zoe and me, we could see, like he was in real deep.'

A low whistle sounded from the kitchen and grew to a high-pitched fever before the girl removed the kettle from the gas. Was the girl Zoe? Joe hadn't seen her face and he wasn't sure he could remember what she looked like anyway.

Dave sighed, 'And then there was all the stuff with the weir.'

'Tell me about the weir.'

'Yeah, well, it's on the river, up near—'

'I've seen it. I've been there.'

'Right. So you know there's this sort of walkway along the top? Well, Chet he went and walked the parapet once.'

'Just decided? Out of the blue?'

'No, no. He was on a mission.'

For some reason this didn't surprise Joe in the slightest.

Dave elbowed his string-bean body up into a sitting position. 'We stopped off at the weir late one night on the way back from somewhere. Six of us. Maybe seven. It was midsummer's night, and warm, first warm night for ever and ever. We're just sitting there, talking, watching the water when there's this cry, like an animal in pain, from across the river. I said it was just a fox strutting its stuff, marking out its territory, whatever. But Jenna, she says no, this animal is in pain, I know it's in pain, and she won't hear any different. She gets all mystical about it and mournful and sad, so Chetwood says if it'll make her happy he'll go and take a look. There's a bit of a moon, but the other side is seriously dark, he doesn't have a hope in hell of finding anything, but he's doing it, right? He's crossing the river to make her happy. So he climbs over the gate and goes across by the path and he's gone a long time. We call out once or twice, but either he can't hear us over the water or he's too busy. In the meantime, the animal's bunked off or gone to heaven, because the cries have stopped. Half an hour, maybe longer, and suddenly we see Chet standing on the parapet in the middle of the weir, right over the water, and he walks along the parapet towards us, and we're all scared shitless, except for Jenna who's sort of sighing with the magic of it all and having no doubts at all about whether he'll make it, not a single one. So Chet walks the wall like it's something he does every day, and when he arrives he says it was a fox in a trap and he's set it free. I wasn't too convinced about that myself, and the others weren't either, except maybe for Sam. But Jenna – well, Chetwood's the all-time hero. He's set the animal free, he's done it all for her, and then he's walked on water. Well, a guy can't go too wrong with a record like that, can he? So then it becomes this big thing, the way Chet walked the wall, and every time we talk about it Jenna gets all misty-eyed about her hero. So . . . I guess at the end of the day, Sam wanted to be a hero too. He wanted to show Jenna he was the greatest. Difference was, he didn't make it.'

'But he went and tried it alone?'

'Seems so, yeah.'

'Hard to be a hero if there's no one there to see you do it.'

Dave gave a pensive nod. 'I guess.'

'Did he tell anyone he was going to attempt it?'

'Hey. You're asking me? At the inquest Jenna said he just disappeared from the house and she didn't know where he'd gone.'

'What was the inquest verdict?'

'It was . . .' He half-turned his head towards the kitchen door. 'What was it, babe?'

A pause then the girl's voice responded, 'Open verdict.'

'Yeah. An open verdict.'

'And what did everyone think about that?'

Dave lifted his coat-hanger shoulders. 'Nothing *to* think. We didn't know anything for sure.'

'Anyone unhappy about it?'

'Everyone was unhappy about the whole damn thing. But Sam was dead. That was the end of the story, right? Nothing was gonna bring him back.'

'Did anyone take it up with the police? Or the coroner?'

'You mean, complain?'

'Yeah.'

'I heard that the family made a few waves. But then they were never gonna be happy, right?'

'Anyone else who felt . . .' Joe made a gesture that was deliberately vague.

'There were things that hadn't been said?'

'Yeah.'

Dave was beginning to shake his head when a swish of silk heralded the girl again. She had a mug in one hand, and an elfin face which Joe recognised from his visit to the farm. She crossed the room without acknowledging either man.

Joe assumed she'd gone until her voice sounded from over his shoulder. 'The sister was seriously hacked off.' Joe spun round to look at her, but she'd already vanished.

'Oh yeah,' Dave exclaimed in a tone of enlightenment. He called after her, 'Yeah, you're right, babe.' Then to Joe: 'Yeah, Chet's sister, she was in a serious rage.'

For an instant, Joe couldn't make the leap, he kept matching the idea to the facts he'd been assembling so studiously in his head and stumbling at every turn. 'His *sister*?' There was no link, no logic. 'You mean . . .' And still he hesitated. 'You mean Kate?'

Dave pointed a slow finger of agreement. 'Yeah – Kate. She came up around the time of the inquest. She started throwing a few heavy ideas about. Like Jenna was to blame. Like Jenna wasn't saying all she knew. That kind of thing. She and Chet had a huge barney. At least that's what we heard. Zoe and me,

we sort of ducked out pretty quick, you know what I mean?
We didn't stick around.'

And still part of Joe was in revolt. 'You're saying Kate
knew Sam?'

Dave was examining the remains of his joint. He looked up
with his characteristic expression of benevolence. 'Oh yeah.'

'They were friends?'

'Sure they were friends. It was Kate who brought Sam up
to the farm. It was her who brought him for a weekend. Then
he came back another time on his own, and then he sort of
stayed on. Oh yeah, Kate brought him. That was how he came
to be there.'

Joe drove south through darkness and rain. At the point where
the motorway forked, where it was either London or the south-
west, he took the road to the south-west. He told himself the
decision could have gone either way, that it had been very
finely balanced indeed, but in his heart he knew there had been
no contest.

At first he drove too fast and too wildly, earning himself a
flash of headlights and an aggrieved horn-blast. Slowing down,
he listening to music, he tried to empty his mind, he resisted all
temptation to reconstruct the story, he concentrated instead on
the single basic fact: Kate had known Sam. Beyond that, he
made no judgements, no assumptions, nothing that might get
in the way.

As he came into the web of lanes near Coln Rogers and
prepared to get lost, his phone signalled the receipt of a
message, but he gave it no thought until he'd negotiated, with
a couple of hopelessly wrong turns and at least fifteen wasted
minutes, the last two miles to Weston Manor Farm. He finally
arrived at eight thirty. Several cars were parked on the rough
grass at the side of the stable block and there were more inside
the yard. The lights of another car had followed him up the
track and gone on towards the front of the house, which

looked jam-packed. Parking on the rough, Joe was half-way out of the car before he remembered the message and dropped back inside.

Bringing the message up on the screen, starting to read it, Joe realised immediately who must have sent it, yet disbelief made him scroll rapidly through to the end to check.

It was signed Sarah.

And before this: *Love you.*

He stared, he felt a rush of feeling. Then, just as rapidly, a stab of doubt. What did she mean? Was it a declaration? A quick sign-off? A wistful token towards what might have been? He dismissed the sign-off immediately: in messaging you didn't waste extraneous words on your friends; they got plain *luv* or *xxx*, or more often than not nothing at all. A nostalgic gesture then? A recognition that they'd had some good times together? But in that case surely she would have made it *loved*, past tense. In fact, been exceptionally careful to make it past tense. You didn't mess with the word love.

Which left a declaration. He hesitated to believe it; he was longing to believe it. He smiled in the darkness, he felt a squeeze of absurd happiness as he scrolled back to the beginning of the message. Here surely was confirmation, an offering of love if there ever was one, for at the risk of God only knew what, Sarah had found him the name and address of Sam Raynor's family.

Walking through the stable yard, the two small words kept ringing in his brain. *Love you.* By the time he reached the back of the house, they had lost any lingering capacity to torment him. Whether or not it was a declaration of intent, or a tribute to the past, she had said it, and somehow that was enough. Though even as he persuaded himself of this, he couldn't rid himself of the quietly electrifying conviction that the words had come straight from her heart.

A caterers' van was parked close to the back door. In the kitchen he found two uniformed staff working on platters of food, while a couple of waiters sped in and out of an adjoining scullery. From the body of the house came the babble of voices and the occasional shriek of laughter.

One of the waiters agreed to go and look for Kate. He was gone for no more than fifteen seconds before Kate swept in through the pass-door.

'Joe! What on earth – ?' Her look of surprise was rapidly overtaken by alarm. She clutched at his wrist. 'It's not Jamie, is it? Nothing awful's happened?'

'No.'

'The police haven't arrested him again?'

'No.'

She closed her eyes, she spread her hands against her chest in an extravagant gesture of relief, and cried, 'Thank God! Thank God!' Another sigh and she looked at Joe again. 'What are you doing here, Joe?'

'Sorry to interrupt your party.'

'It's not *my* party, it's Mummy's, for her birthday.'

Kate was wearing a strapless dress with a full knee-length skirt in a shade of baby-blue that matched her eyes and set off the golden brilliance of her bouncy girlish hair. She was wearing more eye-makeup than he'd seen on her before, and lipstick that appeared too strong for her full upturned mouth.

Joe said, 'I've come to talk about Sam.'

They were standing in the passage, close against the wall, to avoid the procession of trays going through into the body of the house. With a twitch of her lips and a swing of her skirt, Kate turned abruptly and led the way past her father's study to a door which opened into a small storage room, unheated, with a single overhead light and a wooden chair drawn up in front an industrial sewing-machine.

Kate took a couple of steps inside and, turning to face him, hugged her arms close against her chest as if to guard against the cold.

'So?' she demanded.

'Sam was a friend of yours.'

'Yes,' she declared defiantly, with a lift of her pretty head. 'He was a friend of mine.'

'You took him up to Pawsey Farm?'

'What's that got to do with anything? What's that got to do with Jamie and getting him help?'

Sensing that the strange undirected panic of their last meeting wasn't far away, Joe waited a moment before saying very calmly, 'It scems Jenna got some angry letters after Sam's death. Someone who thought she was responsible —'

'She *was* responsible!'

Joe bowed solemnly to this. 'Well, perhaps this person actually came and killed her.'

'That's ridiculous!'

'Well, somebody killed her, didn't they?'

Her eyelids fluttered in sudden agitation, she said bitterly, 'The worst thing I ever did in my whole life, taking Sam to the farm. The very worst. The single most stupid thing. In my whole life.'

Again, Joe gave it a moment before asking, 'Why didn't you tell me before?'

'What was the point? You were Jenna's friend. You were in love with her.' Before he could object, she insisted petulantly, 'That was what Jamie always said. That was what he always told me. I knew you'd never believe anything bad about Jenna, so I didn't bother to tell you.'

With some effort, Joe let this pass. He said in the same quiet unhurried tone, 'So you took Sam up for a weekend?'

'Worst luck.'

'And he stayed on?'

'He thought he'd arrived in heaven,' she cried scathingly.

Joe leant back against the doorframe and waited.

'He thought it was the answer to *everything*! He was desperate to get away from London, that was the trouble – he just *hated* London. He was longing to go somewhere beautiful and peaceful where he could paint and draw and see if he could make it as an artist. Poor booby, he couldn't *believe* his luck when she invited him to stay.'

'Jenna, you mean?'

Kate rolled her eyes. 'Of course *Jenna*! Oh, she pretended it was for *art*. She went on and on about the landscape and the wonderful light and how *marvellous* it would be for Sam's work – though it seemed to rain absolutely non-stop, so far as I could see – and how *wonderful* it would be to have an artist around the place, because they had nothing but musicians and writers there and an artist was just what they needed. She made it sound like some amazing artistic colony, like they were all on this great *project* together!' The eyes flashed expressively. 'But really, she just wanted to have someone around – that was all. She wanted someone to keep her from getting *bored*. Poor Sam – he'd always dreamed of working in a sort of artistic community. He couldn't see that they were just using him, that they just liked having him around.' She dropped her arms, she sighed mournfully, 'But then everyone loved having Sam around. *Everyone* adored him.'

'How did you meet him?'

'What?' she said distractedly. 'Oh, through friends.'

'What was his background?'

'That was the whole thing – he had no real family. He lost his parents in a crash when he was young. He was brought up by his grandparents. Church-going types. They didn't understand about his art at all. They kept telling him to go out and get a proper job.'

'You ever meet them?'

'Once. At the funeral.'

'And were they happy with the information they were given about his death?'

Kate scoffed, 'Absolutely not! The whole family were disgusted! There was an uncle and aunt who lived abroad somewhere. A married sister. They tried to get the police to reopen the investigation.'

'On what grounds?'

'Well, that no one had told the truth!' she declared as if this should have been obvious. 'They hired a lawyer. I think they did their own investigation – the uncle and aunt. Or maybe it was the married sister. They were definitely very unhappy.'

Joe had a picture of Sarah's text message, the address of the Raynors, but couldn't remember if there'd been a phone number.

'How long was Sam at Pawsey Farm?' he asked.

'Oh, ages. *Months.*'

It occurred to Joe that he must have been reasonably happy to have stayed so long, but he didn't say so.

'Oh, he *thought* he was happy,' Kate argued, as though reading his mind. 'He loved the whole *idea* of it so much, of being in this lovely supportive environment. But in the end it was *him* who did all the supporting! *Him* who tried to keep everyone happy!'

'You went and visited him?'

'Twice. It was all I could stand.' Whether from this thought or the cold, she gave a violent shiver.

Joe slipped off his padded jacket. 'Here.'

She took it with a cursory nod and slipped it round her shoulders. Her eyelids resumed their nervous fluttering. 'I hated it there! I hated the way Sam was always at Jenna's beck and call, always rushing around after her. Totally wasting his time. He was meant to be getting an exhibition together – he had this gallery interested and *everything* – but in all his time there he didn't paint a *single* picture. Not *one*! Just silly sketches and drawings he gave away for *nothing* to *anyone* who wanted them. He was completely – completely' – she grappled help-lessly for the word – '*gone.*'

Somewhere in the passage, china smashed on stone and a male voice cursed, while in the body of the house the babble of voices seemed to have shifted onto a higher note.

Kate pulled the chair clear of the sewing-machine and sat down, shoulders slumped, full skirt sticking out around her, like Coppelia.

'Then he was dead,' she said in a small wispy voice. 'I cried for a week, a *whole* week. I just couldn't believe it. He was such a lovely person, Sam. The *most* lovely tragic person in the world.'

'How did you hear about his death?'

'Jamie called me.

'What did he tell you?'

Kate looked down, she brushed something off her skirt with her fingertips. She replied sullenly, 'He said it was an accident. He said Sam'd fallen into the river.'

'He didn't say how?'

'Not then. Not till I went up there. Then he told me Sam had been trying something stupid on the weir and slipped and fell. But it didn't sound right to me. It didn't make any sense,' she argued, gaining momentum. 'Sam wasn't a daredevil type! He wasn't the sort to go off and do something stupid like that! And on his own? In the middle of the night?' She straightened her back, she flexed her shoulders, glanced up at Joe with an uncompromising gleam in her pretty blue eyes. 'So I started talking to the others. They told me about this stupid thing Jamie had done, walking on the weir, and how it had become a big joke, a sort of challenge, and how Sam had boasted about trying it – not *boasted*, he could never *boast* – but said he'd like to give it a try – something like that – and how Jenna had egged him on. But when I said, "So she dared him to do it?" they all went silent on me. They wouldn't – or couldn't – give me an answer. But even then it didn't sound right, Joe. It just wasn't *Sam* to go and do something like that.' Her voice tightened. 'I knew there had to be something else. I just knew. It took me a while to find out what it was. But I got there in the end.' She added with a spark of steel, 'I wasn't going to leave that place till I'd found out!'

She was distracted momentarily, and he found himself urging her forward. 'And?'

She brought herself back with an effort. 'What had happened was that Jenna had got Sam to fall in love with her. She told him it was all over between her and Jamie, that she wanted to be with him instead. All a lie! A complete lie! She had no intention of leaving Jamie. She was just playing one off against the other, trying to get Jamie to give her more attention. Disgusting! Utterly disgusting! She just wanted someone around to feed her vanity! To pander to her ego! Well, you can't do that with someone as lovely as Sam. You can't play around with someone who feels so *passionately*, who's so honest and straightforward and decent and . . . Well, she might as well have gone to the weir and pushed him over the edge herself!'

A woman's voice sounded in the passage. 'Kate? Anyone seen Kate?' Joe reached for the open door and closed it silently as the click of heels approached along the flagstones. 'Kate? Kate?'

For a breathless moment they were two conspirators; they held each other's gaze as the footsteps paused for what seemed a long while before clicking away down the passage.

Joe said in a hushed voice, 'So it was suicide?'

Kate dropped her eyes. When she spoke again, it was in a murmur. 'None of them would talk about it openly. No one was prepared to get up and tell the truth in public. But yes, that's what it was. He died of a broken heart.'

'Nothing was said at the inquest?'

'Oh, I had this terrible argument with Jamie about it! Just awful. I said I thought it was disgusting that the truth wasn't going to come out. I said it wasn't fair to the family, that however hard it was for them they deserved to know the truth.' She stopped abruptly, as if she'd said rather more than she'd intended.

'But he wasn't convinced?'

She grew distant, she pulled at the hem of her skirt, she wouldn't meet his eye. She stood up slowly and pushed the chair back into place in front of the sewing-machine. 'He persuaded me it wouldn't be a good idea,' she said at last.

'Because?'

With a slight shrug, an evasive glance, Kate came towards the door and waited for him to move aside.

But Joe wasn't ready to move. 'Because Jenna was having a nervous breakdown?'

She gave a dismissive snort. 'Oh, I didn't care about *that*! Even if it was true, which I didn't believe for a moment. No. Jamie persuaded me it would only do more harm than good, that it would be better to leave everything well alone. I should never have listened to him of course.' Catching Joe's unasked question, she said, 'Well, Jenna didn't deserve to get off! If you ask me, she should have been punished!'

Chapter Twelve

THE HOUSE was thirties stockbroker, in the style of Lutyens, with a tiled façade, a deep tiled roof, leaded windows, and several pairs of tall octagonal chimneys that showed no smoke. It lay behind a heavy screen of shrubs, beyond an ornate five-bar gate, at the end of a short curved drive. A dark house, it was made darker still by the surrounding trees which even in winter seemed to grow too close and too tall, reaching to the very edge of the mossy roof.

The garden had an air of mild but sustained neglect: the creepers around the porch looked broken and thin, there were dead plants and live nettles in the flowerbeds and a variety of weeds poking up through the worn gravel on the drive. The porch was recessed and dark, with a giant boot-scraper equipped with a tall handgrip, its moth-eaten bristles worn down to the wood. The door was heavy and Gothic, with a castle-sized knocker and bell-pull. Joe tried the bell and heard an answering tinkle deep in the house.

Nothing happened for a long time. He remembered too late that he was fifteen minutes early and elderly people liked to run their lives by the clock. He was about to turn away and wait in the car when a bolt was drawn slowly back, a lock turned, and the door opened a short way to reveal the bent figure of an old man.

'Mr Raynor?' Joe took a step forward and introduced himself.

Before he could offer his hand the old man had moved back to let him enter.

'Come in.'

The hall had a dark wood floor and dark wood furniture and a series of murky lithographs in black frames. A staircase with a dark carpet and dull metal stair-rods rose dimly towards the only source of light.

'Good of you to see me,' Joe said.

Mr Raynor turned stiffly away from the door and gave a formal nod. He was a gaunt man of eighty or more, with pale rheumy eyes overhung by drooping lids, thin white hair combed flat against his skull, and a face that hung in a series of folds as though it had in its time supported a much greater weight of flesh.

He was not hostile, but he seemed troubled. They had spoken on the phone the previous night at almost ten o'clock. If Mr Raynor had considered it rather late for a call he had been too polite to say so. Joe had explained briefly about Jenna's death and the many uncertainties surrounding it.

'I'm not sure we can help,' the feeble voice had responded.

'I heard that your family carried out its own investigation into Sam's death,' Joe had said. 'It would be extremely useful to know what you found.'

There had been a long pause. 'Perhaps you could call again in the morning.'

Joe had called at ten, and been invited for twelve thirty.

Mr Raynor said 'This way' and started diagonally across the hall. He walked with a marked roll as though one leg were a bit gammy, or possibly it was a hip, and carried one shoulder higher than the other as if to compensate for it. Breathing audibly, he opened a door to a living room.

'If you wouldn't mind waiting.'

'Of course – I'm early. I'm sorry.'

The old man gave another formal nod before turning away, only to swivel back, his whole body all at once, as if age or disease had fused his spine, and lift a clawed hand towards the room. 'Please make yourself at home.'

'Thank you.'

The door clicked, his shuffle faded, and the silence was absolute. It added to the room's museum feel, everything clean and polished but untouched by habitation. The room was dark and low, with a predominance of wood: wooden panelling and wooden beams and bulky antiques: a tallboy and two display cabinets with china plates on stands. There were paintings so dark they were barely distinguishable from the panelling. The sofa and chairs were fat and squat and covered in unmatched flower-patterned fabric in swirls of brown and cream and what might once have been yellow, with frilly skirts and puffy cushions. There were wall lamps and standard lamps, none of them lit, making the grey light from the window almost blinding. Beyond the leaded panes he glimpsed a rear garden with a lawn and borders overshadowed by trees.

There were no books and no magazines, the fireplace had no ash, the heating was low or non-existent, and he guessed the room was used just once a year, for Christmas. At first glance he thought there were no photographs either until going deeper into the room he saw beyond one of the display cabinets a side table with china ornaments and photographs in silver frames. His eye fixed immediately on a picture of a young man with golden hair. He held it aslant to catch the light. The shot had been taken in the shade on a sunny day. Sam – he assumed it was Sam – looked eighteen or nineteen. He was sitting sideways, head tilted slightly back, looking at the camera with an infectious smile. Joe heard Dave's words: *That smile was quite something. You couldn' help but smile right back.* Yet for Joe it was the eyes that told the story. Open, fresh, full of life. But also – he had to search for the word – innocent perhaps. Or vulnerable.

Another picture showed a family group, parents and two children of ten or eleven, boy and girl, but the boy wasn't Sam. He supposed the mother was the married sister Kate had mentioned, though quite whose sister he wasn't sure. A third picture showed another couple on their wedding day, the groom fair-haired and tall, the bride willowy and pretty, and he wondered if these were Sam's parents, the ones who had died.

He was just glancing towards the fourth photograph, a studio shot of an older sibling bending over a podgy baby, when the door sounded and an elderly woman came into the room.

Too much happened in the next instant to be contained in a single moment. Confusion locked his throat, he couldn't breathe, he couldn't speak, his brain seemed to stall, his mind to expand at terrible speed. He was there in the room, he was staring at the elderly woman; yet he was a world away, and still travelling. On one level he took in the fact that the elderly woman was distressed and was speaking to him urgently. On another, that this house was no more than fifteen minutes from Faversham, that deep in his mind this had sounded a chord which he had ignored or suppressed, that Sarah's name was Goddard, which meant nothing when anyone could have any name they chose, particularly when they'd been married. On another level, he was already turning back to the photograph, knowing what he had seen, knowing what he would see again, yet all of him in revolt: reason, logic, pride, heart, but most of all pride.

The instant held still as he looked down, reached for the photograph, held it in his hands.

Mrs Raynor's words began to sound in his brain. 'If you could leave now. We think it would be best.' Then again, in a trembling voice: 'Please – if you could leave now.'

His eyes still on the photograph, he heard himself say in a voice so strange it might have belonged to someone else, 'Is Sarah here?'

There was no answer and he looked up to see Mrs Raynor gazing at him in despair.

'If you could tell her I need to speak to her.'

Mrs Raynor's pale eyes dulled. She said in a tone of defeat, 'It'd be best if you left.'

'I'm sorry.'

Mrs Raynor dropped her head and went soundlessly from the room.

Joe had no idea how long it was before he heard Sarah's footsteps. Seconds. Less. He stayed where he was, by the side table, the photograph in his hand.

She came in, she saw the photograph. 'I'm sorry you had to find out this way.'

'Would there have been a better way?'

'I was going to meet you at the door. That was what I'd planned. But I hadn't finished explaining things to my grandparents. I couldn't leave them till I'd explained.'

He stared at her unforgivingly.

With a long slow breath, she closed the door and came towards him. She seemed pale but sure, and it was this that caused the fury to break in Joe.

He felt his hands tremble as he put the photograph back on the table. 'You set me up,' he accused. 'Or am I missing something rather more subtle here? You set me up to find Jenna.'

A slight hesitation before the grey-green eyes met Joe's gaze full on. 'Yes.'

'You couldn't find her on your own, so you used *me* to find her.'

Another hesitation. She opened her mouth as if to argue before thinking better of it. 'Yes,' she said simply.

'Call me slow, but I'd just like to get this absolutely straight in my head – the two of us didn't meet by chance?'

'No.'

'You came to that wine bar specially?'

'That ex-Merrow guy, the one who introduced us – he told me you'd probably be there.'

'What, you found out that I knew Jenna and you made a point of *happening* to meet me.'

'I knew you'd been to Pawsey Farm. I knew you'd grown up with her. I discovered you worked at Merrow.'

'You mean, you made it your business to find out?'

She couldn't or wouldn't answer.

He shook his head in utter disbelief. 'And that was all right, was it?' He heard the bitterness in his voice, and all his pain welled up in the revulsion he felt for it. 'You didn't have any problem with that?'

Her eyes drifted away, and this only fuelled his anger.

'So, everything – *everything* . . . You were just – it was all—' He stopped abruptly. Now that he understood the full extent of his own humiliation, his mind was free to move on. New realisations rolled up one after another and caught him like a succession of blows. His mind made jumps and connections in an unstoppable cascade of logic, until he came to the end of the chain and was brought up short by a single conclusion that was like running into a wall it was so startling. His anger subsided in a single lurch. He felt his stomach drop away, he felt a stab of nausea, he had the sensation of losing his balance.

Sarah said, 'Come and sit down, Joe, and I'll explain.'

But he couldn't move, he could only stare at her, he could only think the one appalling thought. He steeled himself to ask her straight out, he opened his mouth to speak, but guessing what was coming, or fearing it, she forestalled him with a hasty shake of her head. 'I'll explain.'

She went to the circle of puffy chairs and, stationing herself in front of one, waited for him to join her.

He chose a chair at an angle to hers, then changed his mind and moved to the sofa opposite. Sitting down, they faced each other once more. Sarah's face was a mask, one side drenched with cold light from the window, the other in shadow. Her features seemed both strange and achingly familiar to him. He could not take his eyes off her.

'There's one thing I'd like to say right at the outset,' she began in a voice that contained a strong element of rehearsal. 'You may not want to hear this, you may think it's – inappropriate – but I'd like to tell you all the same, if you don't mind.' She glanced away for an instant and when her eyes returned to his they were almost apologetic. 'Whatever else, my feelings for you weren't faked. In fact, quite the opposite. I felt more for you than I ever told you. And, yes, I'd planned a lot of things, but I hadn't planned on us becoming involved. I hadn't intended to feel so . . . strongly about you. But I did. The text message I sent you yesterday – I meant it. About the love.'

She took one quick look at him before rushing straight on, as if she didn't expect or deserve an answer. 'Not that it's worth anything now, of course. I realise that. But I just wanted to tell you. Right at the outset. So you'd know it wasn't all – false.' Again she hurried on. 'But otherwise, *yes* – I met you on purpose. *Yes* – I hoped you were in touch with Jennifer Chetwood or that you'd know someone who was. I'd tried everything else, you see. Absolutely everything. It was a last resort.'

In that instant Joe felt he hated her. 'You let me do all your dirty work.'

'I didn't mean it to be like that, Joe.'

He thought he had squared all the circles, that there were no gaps in the depressing chain of logic, yet a moment after she'd said this, another realisation struck him, and he felt a fresh stab of humiliation. 'The property, the stupid house,' he said painfully. 'You set it all up.'

'I thought it would encourage the family to try and look for her again—'

He stopped her with a sharp gesture, a rapid upward slice of his hand. A dozen questions swarmed into the front of his mind, but he couldn't voice them, the hurt kept getting in the way. Finally, he managed to say: 'You *knew* she owned the house?'

'I searched the Land Registry. Around Hereford, all the places I thought they might be hiding. I worked my way down England and Wales. Always in his name. Then one day I tried her name, I tried her home town—'

Mine too, he almost corrected her.

' – and there it was. I went to see the house. I realised it'd be very hard to sell. It had a terrible crack down the front. So I thought I'd put in an offer. I thought it might prompt the family to try and find her again.'

Hating the sarcasm in his voice but unable to suppress it, Joe said, 'Well, you must have been *delighted* with me. I must have been beyond your wildest dreams. Going to endless trouble. Taking out ads, finding postmarks. You must have been thrilled!'

Sarah was very still.

'And when I asked if it wasn't too much trouble to trace the number Jenna called from! My God! Yes, you must have been thrilled! You had it on a plate!'

He had been deflected earlier from the main question, but he wasn't prepared to be deflected again. He said in a voice that was deliberately calm, 'So you tracked her down and had her killed?'

Sarah looked as though she'd like to put this off again but, catching his expression, she said quietly, 'I didn't kill her, Joe.'

There was a silence like darkness.

'Well, someone did, for God's sake.'

'Oh, I wanted to kill her,' Sarah said. 'I think I meant to. But in the end I couldn't do it.'

The grass was ankle-high and sodden. As they walked, Joe's shoes turned black from the wet. They had crossed the lawn and passed through an archway into a side garden with a vegetable patch gone to seed at one end, an unkempt hard tennis court at the other, and a brick path across the middle. At the far side, almost hidden in a tangled hedge, was a gate which they forced open to reach a field with woods in the distance.

Sarah had wanted air. She had got to her feet abruptly with something close to panic or maybe claustrophobia, and from surprise and perhaps his own need for space Joe had agreed to go for a walk. Now he wondered if it was air she'd wanted or an outlet for the sharp tension that had so suddenly appeared in her, like a bolt of fear, because she strode out with restless energy, sometimes forging so far ahead that she had to wait while Joe, walking at an altogether steadier rate, caught up. As she walked, she talked to him over her shoulder in a tone of urgent absorption.

'Before anything else, you need to understand about Sam,' she began. 'About the sort of person he was. About the past. When our parents were killed, we came to live here with Granny and Grandpa. Our uncle and aunt lived in Malaysia then. There was no one else to take care of us. I managed all right – I've always managed. But I was older – twelve – and I had clear memories of Mummy, of the way she was and how much she loved us, and that kept me going. But Sam – he was only six. He couldn't understand what had happened. He couldn't understand where Mummy and Daddy had gone, why everything had changed so drastically, why he wasn't loved to pieces any more. Don't get me wrong, Granny wasn't cruel, but it was a shock to her having young children around again. Having her routine upset, having things in a mess, noise – all the usual things with kids. She was very strict with us, very impatient, she kept telling us off, sending us to our rooms. Sometimes she flipped her lid, and then there'd be a scene. She'd start saying we were wicked, bad. Me – well, it didn't bother me, I always gave as good as I got, an argument for everything. But Sam – he couldn't take it, not when he was so young, not when he'd been so completely loved by Mummy and Daddy. It cut him like a knife. He couldn't understand why the world was suddenly a dark and treacherous place. Why he was suddenly meant to be bad and wicked. It damaged him – he sort of closed down, withdrew. I decided then that I'd take care of him. That I'd look after him in the way Mummy would have looked after him. As close as I could anyway. That I'd defend him, just like she would have defended him. That I'd always be there for him.' She paused, she half-glanced at Joe. 'And that's what I did.'

They had reached the corner of the field. Following the perimeter path, they turned along the side of a low hedgerow. The sky was an indeterminate grey, the air damp and still, and their breath emerged in wisps of vapour.

'They tried to send me away to school,' Sarah said, 'but I wouldn't go. I insisted on going to the local school instead, though it was forty minutes away on the bus and pretty poor academically. There was a big argument. I think they didn't want a nasty teenager around the house – they were rather frightened of me and my tongue. Anyway, I won. And that was the turning point. From then on, I sort of took over Sam's life. I looked after his school work, his projects, I read him his stories at night. I organised it so he got to see other kids and went on trips, and had a bit of normality.'

The picture that came to Joe evoked very little normality for Sarah.

'Those arguments with Granny and Grandpa, I suppose they got me hooked on the law,' she threw in as an aside. 'Planning my case, choosing my tactics, covering every possible angle. Don't get me wrong, I grew to love them as I got older, just as they grew to love us. They mellowed a lot, particularly Granny. But at the end of the day I always felt it was just Sam and me against the world. And that it would stay that way till Sam found a safe haven of his own, till he found work, love, stability.'

She'd settled into something approaching a normal pace, and now they walked abreast. In profile, her face had never seemed more grave or more lovely. 'But his teens were difficult. I was away at university, I couldn't be around all the time. He didn't settle well at school. He was bullied, he fell behind academically. All he wanted to do was his art, but he got so little time and so little encouragement that he got frustrated, he started to drift, he began to mix with a bad crowd. I worried that he'd be drawn into drugs, the whole scene. So I persuaded Granny and Grandpa that he should go to art school straight away, without doing his A levels. That was another fight – you were dead without qualifications – but they saw sense in the end. They let Sam do a foundation course, and he got a place at Chelsea a year later. Best of all, some friends of Mummy and Daddy's who lived in Fulham gave him a room. He loved it there – a home, you see. A family. But of course they couldn't have him for ever. Meantime, I'd gone and committed matrimony. An act of pure insanity which I tried to salvage for at least a year too long. So instead of there being this second home for Sam, there was just a big messy mistake falling apart at the seams. More ground shifting under his feet.'

Stopping, she cried fiercely, 'I've made Sam sound like a lost soul, haven't I? Like some awful drag. But that's completely wrong. He wasn't like that at all. He was wonderfully alive, wonderfully gifted, deeply special. The most generous, funny, loving person you could imagine.'

She was waiting for some sign that Joe had understood, so he nodded.

Satisfied, she went on, 'It was just that there was this gap in his life, a gap he could never fill. To lose your parents – people think they can guess what it's like, but they have no idea. Sam wanted the sort of love that no one could snatch away from him, he wanted an anchor.' She reached out and gripped Joe's arm. 'You understand what I'm saying? You realise how easy it was for Jenna to destroy him?'

Joe gazed back at her without speaking.

Sarah exhaled abruptly as if she'd been holding her breath. Dropping her hand from his arm, she began to walk on, but more slowly now, as though the strange nervous energy was finally spent. 'He couldn't stop talking about the farm, how beautiful the place was, the amazing band of people there, how much he liked everybody. He'd never seemed happier. I was thrilled. It sounded just perfect for him. He said he was painting, he said he was doing some good work. Looking back, I suppose I should have realised it all sounded too good to be true. But I only had his calls to go by, his voice, and he seemed so happy.'

She was lost in thought for a while, and it was all Joe could do not to urge her on. They completed the circuit of the field and went back through the reluctant gate. In the kitchen garden, Sarah led the way to the far end of the derelict vegetable patch where they sat on a bench set diagonally across the turn of the path. The wood was encrusted with the silvery patina of damp and age.

Resuming the story, Sarah stared straight ahead. As the afternoon wore on, Joe realised she was looking at him rarely, if at all, as though having made her most damaging admissions face to face she was now anxious to distance herself from him.

'I didn't realise anything was wrong till Sam started saying strange things about Jenna,' she said. 'Oh, he'd talked about her before, of course he had. In fact a huge amount. All the things they were doing, what fun they had. But I thought she was much older, ten, fifteen years, a sort of mother-hen figure. It wasn't till Sam said how beautiful she was, how amazing, that I realised she was a rather different sort of animal. But so long as she was in a relationship, so long as she was with her partner – well, what was the problem?'

In front of them, rows of canes supporting the withered remains of runner beans rose like skeletal teepees out of the tall grass. From somewhere at their base came a furtive animal rustling.

'We always spoke at lunchtime, Sam and me,' Sarah continued. 'One day he was bursting with excitement, but he wouldn't tell me what it was about, which was really strange – normally he told me everything, *everything* – and I remember sitting in the office, feeling uneasy, not quite knowing what I was uneasy about, but absolutely sure something wasn't right. Two or three days later, he came out with it. He was in love. More than that, this was the love of his life, this was his spirit-companion, his soul-mate, for ever and ever, the greatest thing that had ever happened, he never imagined it was possible to feel this way. And so on and so on. He was wild with joy, too wild. When I realised who he'd fallen for, I tried to get him to slow down, to talk it through in an atmosphere of calm. But he was beyond all that. He was . . . *gone*. It was a terrible time, the next two weeks – the sense of things running out of control. When I phoned, he wasn't always there, I couldn't be sure of what was happening. And when we did talk, he was full of how they were going to set up home together, how they were going to live in a cottage up in the hills, how they were going to be happy for ever and ever. I asked what they were going to live on, but of course he didn't want to think about that. In fact he laughed. He never worried about money. He'd worked for a few months in a delicatessen, he'd find something else till he got his exhibition together.'

Sarah's expression tautened, her voice as well. 'Then one day I got Jenna on the phone. I said how amazing it was that she and Sam were together, or something like that, and there was this definite pause, I mean a pause that gave the whole game away. She said something sort of patronising, like what a lovely person Sam was, and how wonderful it was to have him there. And I knew immediately she was stringing him along, she was making a fool of him. I asked her then if the relationship was serious on her part, but she skirted round that one, she wouldn't give me a straight answer, and I was horrified, *terrified*, because I knew Sam had gone completely overboard for this woman, that he trusted and adored her, that it'd be disaster if things went wrong. I tried to explain to her, I tried to spell it out, the awful danger, but she went cold on me, basically said there was nothing to discuss. I tried to argue with her, I tried to make her understand that she had this absolutely huge responsibility, that she must be extremely careful what she did and said to Sam. But she put the phone down on me. I couldn't believe it. She just put it down! The absolute b—' She corrected this to: 'Cow.'

'She denied any relationship with Sam?'

Sarah shot him a frown as if he'd understood nothing at all. 'She was denying everything. *Everything*.' She took a steadying breath. 'So . . . I tried to talk to Sam, I tried to make him realise, but he just laughed, he said it was all okay, not to worry so much. It was the first time in his life he hadn't listened to me, the first time he hadn't trusted my judgement. I wanted to go up there and see him straight away, but I had a ton of work to do. I couldn't get away till early Saturday – three days later.' Sarah faltered. 'Then on the Friday night—' She turned her head away, it was a moment before she managed to speak, and then in a hoarse whisper. 'There was a message from Sam. He said . . . he said he loved me and he was sorry. I knew immediately. His voice – it was so absolutely empty. I knew he was already dead.'

She drew a terse breath. 'I told the police everything about Jenna, but they didn't want to know. To them Sam was just another statistic, a depressive who'd killed himself. They weren't interested in responsibility. The inquest was the same. The coroner listened but took no notice. I knew then that I wasn't going to get any recourse from the law, and oddly enough it was a kind of freedom, knowing it was going to be left to me, knowing I had no choice. Oh, I never had the slightest doubt about it,' she argued suddenly, as if he'd challenged her on the point. 'Not the slightest. It was nothing less than manslaughter, you see. Why should she be allowed to continue her life as if nothing had happened? Why should she be allowed to get away with it? I wanted her to acknowledge her guilt, I wanted her to suffer, I wanted her to pay.'

'You wrote the anonymous letters?'

'Yes,' she agreed bluntly. 'Two of them.'

'You threatened her?'

'By any other name – yes. I said she'd never be safe, I said she'd be tracked down wherever she went, I said she'd be made to pay. For a while I thought that it would be enough – knowing she'd got the letters, knowing they'd be on her mind the whole time, knowing she'd always be looking over her shoulder. But it wasn't enough, nothing could be enough. She had killed Sam, she had killed someone unbelievably special, for no good reason than her own repulsive ego. I decided I was going to confront her. Well, no, it was more than that – I was going to make her confess, on paper, so it'd be there for everyone to see.' At this, Sarah pitched forward and clutched the edge of her seat, her knuckles white, as though the accumulated memories were threatening to unbalance her.

Joe said, 'Once you got the address of the phone box Jenna called me from, how did you track her down?'

Sarah straightened up again and sank slowly back against the seat. 'Oh, I went up there armed with a photograph. I copied it from one of yours, I'm afraid. I snooped around your flat.' She shrugged. 'There was nothing I wouldn't do, you see. I loved Sam more than my life. I loved him as if he were my own child.'

A fresh rustling sounded deep in the grass, and Joe watched a blackbird emerge onto the path and run over to a greenhouse, which was so full of bolting plants that it looked like a crowded tube train, all the backs pressed against the doors.

He said, 'You found someone who recognised her?'

'In Llandrindod Wells. The garage where she bought her petrol. They told me she lived somewhere up Nant Garth valley.'

'And you found her?'

Sarah nodded. 'I watched for her in the valley and followed her up to the log cabin. I went there again the next weekend, and the next, trying to work out how to get her alone. They had this routine. Chetwood took the dog for a walk in the morning while Jenna took the pony for a ride. It was the only time when she was alone, but it wasn't ideal. But then this one weekend I realised Chetwood wasn't around. His car was gone, and it was Jenna who took the dog out first thing. So when she went to take the pony for a ride I simply waited in the cabin.'

She seemed in no hurry to continue, so Joe said quite roughly, 'Go on.'

Emerging slowly from her thoughts, she murmured, 'Yes

... So ... I'd prepared it all in my mind, every possible scenario. Anger, denial, arrogance. I'd imagined every possible reaction except the one she produced. Total silence. That was what got to me! She just sat there like this bloody nun, looking holy and not saying a word. Well, I'd had quite enough of defendants claiming their right to bloody silence. I totally lost it. After all those years I wasn't going to put up with that sort of rubbish! I was totally incensed. So I tied her up *tight* – and I mean *tight*. I wanted to hurt her! I did hurt her! I was *glad* to be hurting her. I was so angry I could have killed her!'

'And you almost did.'

Sarah gave an involuntary shudder. 'Yes!'

'You almost strangled her.'

'I have no memory of actually putting my hands round her throat. None at all. All those defendants who tell you they don't remember half killing someone, that they had a sort of blackout – well, they're absolutely right. It's rage that does it. The first thing I knew I was squeezing her throat as hard as I could and her face was bright red, her eyes were – horrible. I stopped immediately. I stopped as soon as I realised what I was doing.'

Joe sat forward, the better to watch her face.

Sarah was rushing on now, as if to get the story over and done with. 'But I told her that if she didn't start talking I really would do it, I really would kill her. She said she wouldn't blame me. That's the first thing she said after – well, after she'd got over all the coughing and spluttering. "I wouldn't blame you." She told me it had been on her conscience all those years, that she bitterly regretted what she'd done, how it never left her, not for a single moment, how she'd loved Sam, how she would give up her life a dozen times over if it would bring him back, how she'd thought of killing herself hundreds of times. All this stuff. Well! At first I thought she was having me on. I thought she was just trying to talk her way out of it. But I've seen too many people in the witness box over the years, I've seen too many people lying through their teeth. If she was lying, she was the best I'd ever seen. Not that I let her off the hook,' she added sharply. 'No – I made her spell it out for me. Chapter and verse.'

'What happened with Sam.'

'Everything.' She fluttered her hand in a gesture of impatience, as if she didn't have much time for this part of the tale. 'According to her, she thought Chetwood had left her, and it drove her a bit mad.' Sarah flashed her eyes derisively. 'Well, we could all say that, couldn't we? That we all get a bit mad from time to time. She fell in love with Sam on the rebound, she said. Well! Not a term I would have used – *love*. Anyway – then Chetwood came back, and he and Jenna had this huge night-long discussion, and Sam—' Her voice broke abruptly, she sucked in her cheeks. 'Sam waited through the night, thinking Jenna was finishing with Chetwood, believing he and Jenna were going to be together for ever, never doubting . . . Eventually, Jenna went and told him that she was going back to Chetwood, that she'd loved him all along. At which point Sam announced that he couldn't live without her, and went out to the car. According to Jenna, she would have gone after him' – Sarah turned her pale gaze on Joe – 'but Chetwood talked her out of it. That was her story – that Chetwood persuaded her to let Sam go, persuaded her that Sam would calm down by the morning.'

Now she was facing him, Joe noticed that her nose had gone white at the tip, and her cheeks were transparent with cold. Even as he gazed at her, she shivered slightly. He stood up and offered her a hand. 'And you let Jenna go.'

'She started going on about God – what else could I do?' Avoiding his hand, Sarah got to her feet. 'Damnation and judgement and all that stuff. I realised there was nothing I could do to her that she hadn't already done to herself.'

They began to walk. Joe said, 'You had no idea what she was planning when you left?'

'None. She was upset, but no more than she deserved to be. At first I was glad she'd killed herself. Now . . . well, you could say I recognise the benefits of forgiveness, even if I can't bring myself to practise it.'

They passed under the arch onto the damp lawn. Confronted by the dark house, Sarah seemed to hesitate. 'The CID in Wales,' she said in a brittle voice, 'did they seem fairly bright to you?'

'They did, as a matter of fact.'

'In that case I won't bother to call them.'

'To say what?'

She gave a caustic laugh. 'Why, to give myself up, Joe. To turn myself in.'

He stopped and caught her arm. 'For what?'

'Oh, GBH or attempted murder. I can't imagine it'll be much less.'

'But . . . do you have to?'

'I don't think I have much choice. They'll have traced everything back to me by now. They really can't fail to.'

He groaned. 'The bloody passport.'

'And other things, Joe. Plenty of other things. I didn't exactly cover my tracks.'

'So what'll happen?'

'Oh, it'll be a custodial sentence of some sort.'

'My God, Sarah. *My God.*'

She would have turned away, but he held her back with a hand on her shoulder. She would not meet his eyes.

'At least let me come with you. Make sure you're okay.'

She almost smiled as she shook her head. 'But thanks anyway. I have no regrets, Joe. And if I do' – she stole a quick glance at him – 'then I'll learn to live with them.' She gave a shudder as if from the cold and, swinging away, walked rapidly towards the house.